T0283105

# THANATIUM HEROS:

# SHARDS
## OF FATE

Edward Loom

# SHARDS
## OF FATE

**Addison & Highsmith**

# Addison & Highsmith Publishers

Las Vegas ◊ Chicago ◊ Palm Beach

Published in the United States of America by
Histria Books
7181 N. Hualapai Way, Ste. 130-86
Las Vegas, NV 89166 USA
HistriaBooks.com

Addison & Highsmith is an imprint of Histria Books. Titles published under the imprints of Histria Books are distributed worldwide.

Library of Congress Control Number: 2023948276

ISBN 978-1-59211-385-9 (hardcover)
ISBN 978-1-59211-406-1 (eBook)

# CHAPTER I

# ICE TAINTED BY LOSS

At the far corners of the known cosmos lies a white planet, enshrouded in a perpetual blanket of snow and violent blizzards, covering the plains below its skies. It was a chilling, dense, and too harsh environment for any life-form to develop — a dead world, posing no interest to anyone. And yet, on its frigid plains, warded against the cold touch of death, a lone being stood near an icy pillar. A slim blue-eyed woman, her long brown hair containing several silvery strands swept to the side of her shoulder, she remained silent and unmoving. Donned in a dark blue robe akin to those worn by the sorcerers on Earth, she was known on her homeworld as Wizera, the Silver Sorceress. She had come to this secluded place to pay respects to her deceased husband. Through the use of her powers, she had formed a tombstone of ice many years ago. One that marked an empty grave, for not even ash remained from Thieron, her husband's body after he made the ultimate sacrifice to save her and their son. She stood there, eyes closed, thinking of better times... Thinking of him. A rebellious tear managed to escape her stubborn grasp. She wiped it away, and upon opening her eyes, gazed at the place that reminded her of how much she had lost that day. Yet, were it not for her husband's courage and selflessness, it would've all been for naught, and they wouldn't be alive today. Amidst the chilling, howling winds, the sorceress's voice moaned a sorrowful serenade.

"Hey, it's been a while. I...," she began to slowly murmur while holding the tear-shaped pendant that hung over her chest with both of her hands, "don't know how much time has passed since my last visit, but back home, it has been yet another year without you. I know that I should've visited more often, but... it is still hard to... see this place. To relive the moment when we last saw each other and be reminded that I'll never see that beautiful smile you used to carry." She ceased her mournful speech a second time, granting herself some time to restore the tone in her voice. "Thaidren has grown so much since then. I can hardly believe how fast time seems to pass." As she continued speaking, her sadness was somewhat balanced out by the love and happiness brought by the thought of their son. "He is seven years old now, and Nez'rin has already begun teaching him about the world. He will accomplish great things like you did before him." She shot another glance at the block of ice placed in his memory. "But it's already late now, and I should take my leave. Maybe next time, I'll bring him along, so you can see each other…" She waved her hand and chanted a few words of power to open up a gateway through space that led back to Earth. *I hope that you somehow heard all that. May you be at peace wherever you are, my love. We… I… miss you.* She ambled toward the portal without looking back as she passed through it, heading back to her homeworld.

Upon arriving back on Earth, the first sensation came in the form of warm sunlight touching Wizera's face. The gentle breeze of the wind that traveled between the trees complimented the birds' harmonious chirps, along with the rippling of a small river flowing downhill. She had no more need for the water symbols drawn on her right arm, which served as a protective runic inscribing against the cold. The sorceress waved her hand toward the river, borrowing its waters to wash away the symbols on her skin. With that out of the way, she continued to walk for a few minutes before reaching a two-floor mansion. A place for her to call "home," where Thaidren had been raised his entire life. A place shrouded within a peaceful forest that lay in the vicinity of a prosperous capital known as Tiosa. While approaching it, the sorceress could see her son from afar. He was in the middle of his training session, engaged in swordfight with his Uncle Thraik. The dwarf had been left with an injured shoulder from the same fight that took away the child's father, yet he was still more than capable of teaching the little cub a thing or two about the art of combat. For a few moments, she relished the moment from afar, not wishing to perturb their enjoyable session. A faint simper washed away some of the sadness caused by the loss of Thieron.

"Keep yer stance up, lad. Today I don' care about how ye attack, but how ye defend yerself. So just relax yer shoulders while staying upwards, and parry me as best as ye can."

"If I can block you ten times, can I skip my magic lesson today?" asked the child in a hopeful tone.

"Ye need dem lessons too, lad, and I ain't tellin' dat sack o' bones ta let ye skip his class."

"But I don't wanna… I like to train with you. All that Nez'rin does is talk. He keeps promising me that he'll teach me magic but never does!"

His innocent honesty managed to stir a prideful grin on the dwarf's face while also bringing him a sentiment of joy over the thought that the boy preferred him more than the lich. "If ye have time ta complain, ye have time ta block better."

At a distance, Wizera decided to stay out of their sight for a little while longer. She was content to observe and enjoy the thought that, despite their past hardship, they managed to end up here. In a peaceful place, veiled from the prying eyes of whoever might seek Thaidren's ill-being. However, the scars of the past left her unable or unwilling to let her guard down entirely. Not after all her previous experiences. Not after everything that transpired before his birth, and even more so, considering what she knew regarding her child's fate. Still, she was trying her best to keep that part of herself hidden away from the others. Perhaps it was her motherly instinct that wouldn't allow her to relax, she would often tell herself. It did not matter in the end. For now, she just smiled as she watched her son training. The following moment, an echoing voice that resonated from behind her shook off the sorceress's sense of serenity:

"Back so soon?" asked Nez'rin, who recently returned from a short journey through the woods.

"Yes." Wizera looked back at him. She tilted her head down as some of her grief came back to haunt her. "Visiting his grave is painful, even after all these years."

"I can imagine," the lich answered as his voice shifted to a more grieving tone. He remained silent for a few moments before changing the subject. "I have gathered the items you requested. What am I to do with them?"

"Just leave them in my study chamber. Thank you, Nez. I'll be sure to make good use of them."

The lich bowed his head before leaving to store the items. Once finished, his focus shifted toward preparing his tomes of arcane knowledge for his lesson with the young master. For a reason unknown to him at the time, during that particular day, he seemed distracted.

*So eager to use magic at such a young age. Unfortunately, it is just not the right time yet. It almost reminds me of my days as an early scholar.* The thought seemed to bother the undead sorcerer. He enjoyed teaching Thaidren about the various forms of energy and their applications. If he could, he would've liked to teach him some spells from day one. Unfortunately, the boy was too young to be able to channel his soon-to-be-awakened potential. For now, he could only converse with him about magic rather than teaching it.

Nevertheless, he found himself digressing too much, so he dismissed any thoughts regarding the matter. He went outside and waved at the dwarf, signaling him to end his training session with the boy. It was his turn to contribute to his teachings. The lich was well aware that the boy did not enjoy the mere act of conversing about magic without any actual practical lessons. In light of this realization, a thought came to him. *Perhaps it is time for a different method.*

"Today we are going to keep our lesson outside," he stated. The child smiled, an encouragement for Nez'rin to press on. "Do you recall the history of Earth I told you about in our previous lessons?"

The boy nodded. "When the angels and demons fought?"

"Precisely, young master." The lich waved his hand and chanted briefly, creating a small projection of the Earth. Scattered across it, countless dots, like fireflies, moved throughout the surface of the planet. Some of them radiated in a bright yellow nuance while emanating a faint trace of heat as well. Others were as crimson as the fresh color of blood, exuding a much more ominous aura. Each dot was an individual representation of angelic and demonic battalions that once roamed the planes of Earth. "It was a time in which our world was enveloped in conflict and despair," continued the lich as Thaidren gazed upon the interactive projection. "The battles between the angels and demons were ravaging the lands, with casualties on both sides and countless collateral human deaths."

The boy felt compelled to interrupt his teacher. "Were you alive back then?"

"No, I was not," responded the lich. "My mortal life began a few decades after their conflict on Earth had ceased. However, that is a story for another time. As I was saying…"

From that day on, Nez'rin realized that this was a more suitable method for him to catch the attention of someone as young as Thaidren. *Children love stories*, thought the lich. With that in mind, he had a few opportunities to show him small displays of magic as well. Even if they consisted of trivial, minimalistic projections. *He is a fast learner, like his father before him.* The thought brought some peace to his mind.

Days passed and the young prince trained in the art of combat while studying the teachings of the arcane in tandem. He would have to be prepared and become as resourceful and knowledgeable as possible before he could venture into the world.

The coming weeks passed like days, with Wizera traveling to the city every now and then to get supplies or help the people of the kingdom in her stature as a mage. She was not to neglect her son, though. She still spent most of her free time with him, playing and teaching him her own perspective on magic.

With the end of summer closing in, during one night with a clear sky and a full moon, Thaidren and the rest of his family were sleeping inside the mansion. The boy had his bedroom located next to Wizera's, on the upper floor. Outside, Nez'rin, who had no need for sleep, devoted his night time to studying and improving his techniques. "One can always improve themselves," as he would always remind his young master.

Inside Thaidren's bedroom, he was experiencing an unusually restless night's sleep. A horrendous nightmare refused to offer him peace as he struggled to dismiss the images that swirled through his mind. It felt slightly different than a simple construct of his imagination. It felt lucid, real even, as his consciousness dove deeper within the dark ocean of his subconscious. He found himself on a desolate, icy land, covered by a blanket of dense snow. An enormous blizzard obscured his vision to the point where he could barely see his own hands. From time to time, the snowstorm's density would fade away, creating small windows from which he could briefly see images unfamiliar to him. These images were hazy and imprecise, yet they were distinguishable enough to paint a scene. He saw his mother running through snowy plains while holding him to her chest in one vision. Behind her, monstrous shadows were chasing them. At the same time, several other silhouettes seemed to fight in an attempt to keep them at bay. Two of the figures, in particular, seemed most prominent. One gave him a feeling of familiarity and comfort. Having one eye glowing in bright blue, Thaidren felt a sense of safety when looking at it. The other one, however, seemed ill-intended. Its eyes glowed in an eerie dark purple while holding something akin to a giant scythe in its hands.

He saw many images of this kind. Some of them seemed filtered in a way that he would be able to comprehend them. Others seemed incomplete. The next thing he saw was the blue-eyed figure vanishing, along with all the monsters haunting his dreams. In a shockwave that seemingly struck him as well, only he and his mother remained, crying in the snow. He woke up, screaming. Even though his nightmare ended with the shadowy figures disappearing, he could not help but feel terrified. This dream seemed so real and, at the same time, incredibly vague to him. In his mind, it lasted days, but only a few hours had truly passed. Alarmed by Thaidren's cries, Wizera entered the room, ready to attack and destroy whatever was causing the child to scream.

"Thaidren!" she shouted as she entered, her hands glowing and fused with magic. The boy turned his head toward the floor, displaying a sense of shame while quietly weeping.

The sorceress sighed, then smiled at her child, realizing no threat was present in the room. Her glowing hands turned back to normal as she took a seat near him. "It's all right, it's all right. It was just a bad dream." She grabbed her son's cold hand, which was as frigid as the chilled room. A portion of the sheet next to

Thaidren's hand had frozen solid. She stood silent for a few seconds, giving her time to understand what had happened. This was the first time that Thaidren's magical powers had manifested themselves.

"Incredible," she whispered. *He has an affinity for water. It must've manifested subconsciously this time, but still... To be able to freeze objects already...*

Thaidren felt scared and happy at the same time after seeing what he had done. He always thought of what it would be like to have his own magical powers and learn how to master them. However, to see it unfolding with his eyes made him realize that it was more significant than he could've imagined.

"Go back to sleep. We'll discuss this tomorrow," said Wizera as she kissed her son on the forehead. She changed the partially frozen sheet, then covered him with a blanket. She left the bedroom door slightly open before going back to her bedroom. A couple of hours later, Wizera woke Thaidren early. She made him breakfast and led him outside after finishing their meal.

"Where are we going?" the boy asked curiously.

Wizera simpered. "It's a surprise. You'll see."

They went into the woods while the still-rising sun illuminated the trees, forming countless rays of warming light that brought a sentiment of serenity and peace. After a ten-minute walk, Wizera and Thaidren arrived at their destination. He gazed at the sight of an ancient monument, covered in vegetation. Near it, several other structures, including a giant fountain, stood as a testament to whoever or whatever beings had built them.

"What do you think?" asked the sorceress.

Thaidren had never seen anything like them in his life. Truth be told, he rarely had a chance to get away from home. Except for a few trips to the nearby city, he'd never traveled anywhere else. He walked his hand across one of the sculpted surfaces. The architecture and scribing on it filled his heart with a sentiment of awe. "It's beautiful," he said, captivated by the splendor of a lost, unknown civilization.

"Glad you like it," Wizera answered, "because this is a very special place for me. I've wanted to bring you here for a long time."

"Did someone live here once?"

"To be honest, dear, I am not sure. I found these ruins a few years before you were born." She paused for a moment, sadness washing over her face. "With your father…"

The boy was surprised to hear his mother speak of his father so freely. It was unusual for her. Despite Thaidren's young age, he had raised the question of his father's absence a few times in the past. Whenever he would, though, she and anyone else would avoid the subject.

"Yes, with your father. I know that I haven't talked to you about him very much, but… maybe it's time I do…"

That day marked the first time that Wizera told Thaidren about his father and how he sacrificed himself for their sake. Over the coming years, she would add further details to the story, as the boy could not grasp the extent of it the first time around.

***

Three years had passed, with Thaidren reaching the age of ten. His magical powers began to consciously manifest, although they were still in an early stage. Under normal circumstances, even a gifted child would have his affinity toward magic revealed around twelve. However, given Thaidren's intensive training regime and heritage, it was not all that surprising to see his powers were developing faster than expected.

Aside from Nez'rin's lessons and Thraik's swordsmanship sessions, he would constantly visit the ruins where Wizera had taken him three years ago to train there as well. Over the first two months, he learned how to freeze small objects, having gained a better understanding of the nature of his abilities. However, unlike the Silver Sorceress, Thaidren's powers seemed more restricted. *His calling is to the element of water; there's no doubt about that,* thought his mother. *But I think he is limited to ice only. So far, he doesn't seem to be able to manipulate water in liquid or vapor form. Maybe it's too early to tell.*

Meanwhile, at the mansion, Nez'rin kept arguing with Thraik about the boy's future. "He needs ta get out into da world, maybe visit da city. We can't have 'im isolated here forever."

"It is not our decision. Lady Wizera is trying her best to figure it out herself. Give her time."

The frown on the dwarf's face didn't hide the disgust he felt for thinking the same way Nez'rin did. "I kno', I kno'... But da boy will have ta face da world one day."

Nez'rin briefly lost his interest in the discussion as he felt a presence closing in on the house. It wasn't ominous or ill-intended, yet somehow felt dangerous to him.

"I couldn't agree more," they both heard from behind them as a familiar silhouette approached them.

***

Back at the ruins, where Thaidren was practicing his elemental magic under Wizera's supervision, it was about time for them to head back home. With the sun now on the verge of settling down, it began leaving behind a pallet of orange rays of light that engulfed the dilapidated structures and the surrounding forest in its retreat. Such a mesmerizing sight compelled both Wizera and her son to sit a while longer and enjoy the peaceful scene for a few moments. Nevertheless, it was getting late, so they started to amble toward home. Upon returning, the sorceress felt a distinctive yet familiar magical aura. She smiled as they approached the house, suspecting who would be waiting for them there. A knight in golden armor, massive in size and yet with a most gentle smile on his face, greeted them upon arrival. A large two-handed hammer lay sheathed on his back, yet the sight of it did not stir Thaidren any feeling of hostility. On the contrary, something about this warrior figure gave the boy a sensation of safety. From that moment on, the knight would provide an idealistic image in Thaidren's mind about what he would like to become after reaching adulthood. Or rather, how he would want to see himself at the very least. Despite his warmth, upon approaching, Thaidren felt somewhat intimidated by his presence, making him hide behind Wizera as she caressed his shining silver hair.

"It's been a while," Wizera said to the golden-armored warrior.

"More than you'd think," he replied. "Yet I see that time has been kinder to you than to me, Wiz. You haven't aged a day since we last saw each other, twelve years ago." His attention shifted toward Thaidren, still hiding behind his mother. "And who is this sturdy little man?" He bent down on one knee to look at the boy.

Wizera made the introductions. "Thaidren, this is Attern, an old" — she paused briefly — "friend... of mine and your father's. Attern, this is Thaidren."

"I see. So, you're the brave man of the house. I doubt anyone would have the courage to face you." He patted the boy on the head, alleviating some of his sentiment of coercion.

It made Thaidren feel like he was in the presence of a hero. He let go of Wizera and went to Thraik. There was a slight difference in height between them, yet Thaidren waved his hand as a gesture for him to lower his head.

"Is he a knight?" he whispered with a hint of excitement.

The dwarf laughed. "Aye, lad. He is a paladin, and like yer ma said, an ol' friend."

*A paladin...* An esteemed order of warriors that operate under the teachings of the Holy Church, most of them practitioners of the element of light and under the servitude of the angelic power under the same name. Everybody knew about them, and Thaidren was no stranger to their reputation either. "He won't take Nez'rin away from us, will he?" he continued to whisper.

Thraik was surprised that at such a young age, he managed to put two and two together and conclude that a paladin and a lich wouldn't normally get along well. Be that as it may, they were an exception. Attern had fought many times alongside Thieron and Nez'rin. Learning, in time, not to blindly trust The Light's teachings that claim all undead to be evil in nature. He was a more open-minded individual than most paladins in that sense.

"No lad, he ain' takin this hoary bastard" — he paused for a brief moment before turning his head a bit and whispering the rest of his sentence — "I ain' dat lucky."

The lich had known for a long time that Thraik wasn't exactly an affectionate kind of dwarf, if such a thing even existed in the first place. That was his way of trying to pretend he didn't care. He figured the best way to cope with him was to merely see past his foul mouth. Or ignore him. Nevertheless, considering the lack of skin and flesh on his skeletal appearance, Nez'rin was difficult to read through body language.

"Lady Wizera, can the boy and I be excused for the time being?" Nez'rin asked. "We are due to start our daily lesson."

"Of course. If there's anything else, we'll be here," she answered.

Feeling that Attern and Wizera wished to have a private conversation, the dwarf walked over to the mansion's forge. "I should go too. I have some weapons ta sharpen and prepare for me lesson with the lad tamorrow."

"I'll catch up with you afterward, Thraik," replied Attern.

"Of course ya will. Ya've owed me a drink for twelve years. With da added interest for it takin' so damn long."

Attern added a subtle smile. There was once a time when he, Thraik, and Thieron were inseparable. They fought through fire and brimstone together, forging stories the likes of which a bard would kill to turn a profit with. He was always the oldest brother, the one taking upon himself the responsibility to take care of the others. Unfortunately, not all those nostalgic memories were happy. As Attern's smile turned to an expression that only emanated grief and sadness, he set his eyes on Wizera's before turning his gaze to the ground.

"Let us head a bit further away from the house," he said.

The sorceress nodded while heading to a trunk a few meters away that fell many winters ago. It made for an excellent natural bench as they both sat down with their backs toward the house. Wizera wanted to start the conversation, but Attern interrupted her by holding up his hand. It took him a moment to find the right words to express the thoughts etched into his mind.

"Wiz… when I heard about what happened ten years ago, I was so ashamed of myself that I couldn't find the strength to even attend the funeral." His tone fell nothing short but being full of regret. "I couldn't be there for you and Thieron, and there are no words that can express how sorry I am for that." He paused mid-speech with his hands folded together, looking toward the ground, then back at Wizera. "I… keep asking myself if he would still be alive had I been present back then. I am not asking for forgiveness from you nor from the others. Yet, I hope that somehow you will understand why I couldn't be there."

Wizera looked at him and placed her hand over his shoulder plate as she closed in on him. "Dear cousin, we've known each other since we were little. I never blamed you for what happened, and neither did anyone else. If you're feeling guilty for not being there, just imagine what Thieron would say to you if he knew. He would've probably thrown a punch at you just because you'd think of him as a person who would blame you. What's in the past stays there, and for better or worse, we are alive and well. I am alive. Thraik is alive. Thaidren is alive, and no one knows of our current whereabouts. And I'm… We're doing our best to prepare him for when the world can wait for him no longer."

"Well, regarding that matter, I might be able to help him. Since last we met, I was granted the position of commander over the Cathedral of The Light near Leor. Most of the disciples that train there aspire to learn the teachings and lifestyle of the paladins. However, we accept anyone who wants to fight the forces of evil, not just those who wish to embrace The Light and serve the congregation. Your son will be safe there, and he will have access to knowledge and training that you are unable to provide him."

The sorceress did not answer him immediately. She took her time to consider all the aspects of this surprising offer. *The cathedral would indeed make a good place for Thaidren to grow in strength and hone his powers.* Yet, she was not fond of the idea of leaving him in the care of others. Even if it was her cousin, Thaidren's uncle. *How long will he be gone? How will that make him feel? Is it indeed his best option?* Those were some of the many questions that surged through her mind. It seemed difficult to make such a decision, but after talking it through with Attern, she reached a verdict. "I think it would be a good idea."

"Very well then. If it's settled, I'll go talk to Thraik and explain the situation to him too. We'll depart tomorrow afternoon. That should be enough time for the boy to pack his belongings."

"I will go and talk to Nez'rin."

"Let me handle Nez'rin," said Attern. "You should be the one to talk to your son. And do not worry about his safety; I give you my word, I will take care of him as if he were my own child."

His reassuring words brought a smile to her face. "I have no doubt you will."

"One more thing. I noticed something when you introduced us to each other."

"What is it?"

"Do you wish for me to refrain from telling him that we're related? Is it of any concern to you if he finds out?"

The sorceress realized as well that she did not mention that Attern was Thaidren's uncle. Initially, it came as mere unspoken information. However, now that Attern posed the question firsthand, she was unsure of how to answer.

"To be honest, I don't know. I fear it may turn into a double-edged sword for both of you."

Attern shook his head while rubbing his beard, devoid of any pigmentation except for the mustache that still carried fading traces of dark brown. "I see. Don't worry then. I will not tell him anything until you decide the time is right for him to know."

The sorceress nodded. "Thank you."

What remained of that evening passed at a seemingly accelerated rate for the mother who was about to send her son away from his home. It was not an easy-to-make decision but, in spite of her hesitation, she was aware it would prove more beneficial for Thaidren in the long run. Paladins often received job requests addressed to the *Congregation of Paladins*, meaning that Thaidren would most likely travel throughout the vast lands of Iroga in the upcoming years. That being said, the sorceress tried to dismiss any negative scenarios about the consequences of his travels. She trusted Attern to keep an eye on her son and protect him. *I will focus on that aspect,* she thought.

The next day, Attern had tended to the two horses that would transport their carriage back to the cathedral. He checked the saddles and the steeds as Wizera brought Thaidren to them, holding him by the hand.

"All right, we are ready to depart," stated Attern while looking at the young boy. "You ready?

"Yes," he answered.

The caravan carried some supplies that needed to be delivered to the cathedral. There was enough space in the back of the carriage for Thaidren to sit. As he gazed at the house where he lived all of his life getting smaller, he waved at his mother and the others. They waved back at him, knowing that today marked his first step toward the long journey that would be his life.

A few hours into the voyage, the caravan passed by the city of Tiosa. It was the only place that Thaidren had ever visited up until then. The perspective of expanding his borders and visiting new towns gave him a sense of happiness. Yet, at the same time, it bore a frightening feeling. Attern would throw a look at him from time to time, reassuring him there was nothing to worry about.

"I'm sure you'll enjoy yourself at the cathedral. There are a lot of other students there for you to play and practice with."

The idea sounded alluring. He did not have the chance to interact with other children before. He smiled at the paladin before gazing around at the empty planes that surrounded them, anxious for them to reach their destination.

"Is there a city near it?" he asked.

"Of course. The cathedral is located about half an hour by horse from Leor."

Thaidren did not recognize the name. "Leor?"

"It is a city, larger than Tiosa, with a multitude of things and places to explore. We go there often, so don't worry, you'll have plenty of chances to visit it." The paladin paused. "As a matter of fact, I remembered that we will have to stop there on the way. Some of the goods in the back are for a local business there."

As a few more hours passed, with the sun starting to settle, there was still no sign of a city.

"How much more do we have?"

"We'll arrive there in an hour or two. Perhaps less if the road is smooth and the horses have enough strength left in them."

Thaidren turned to the back of the wagon. He leaned between a basket of fruit and a heavy barrel before falling asleep. Attern continued to keep watch as they drove toward the city.

After the long journey with a stop in Leor, Thaidren could finally get a glimpse from afar of the Cathedral of The Light. He was unable to distinguish in detail how far or how big the structure was, but at this point, he was content with the fact that he could see it.

Attern smiled at the young boy's excitement. "I'm taking it you like what you see," he said with a chuckle.

Thaidren's heart was beating rapidly. He could not wait to meet the other paladins, hear their glorious stories, and be trained by them. It made him forget the sadness of leaving home.

"When we arrive, I'll most probably have some matters to attend to. I will take you to your bedroom, and someone from the cathedral will come to give you a tour tomorrow. Sound good?"

"Yes," answered the boy.

"You will be sharing the room with two boys your age, one of them is my son," continued the paladin. "He is my pride and joy. I'm certain you'll both get along well."

Thaidren was happy at the prospect of having a future friend and roommate. He and Attern went up a large circular set of stairs within the cathedral's main tower before stopping near its top. The paladin then pointed toward one of the four doors that stood before them.

"This is it," he said. "Go inside and meet up with the other kids. I'll see you tomorrow."

As he left, Thaidren timidly entered the chamber. Inside, two boys were playing with wooden sculptures that depicted warriors and sorcerers. Upon noticing him, they stopped and looked at him.

"Hi, I'm Thaidren," he introduced himself.

"Hey," answered one of them, "I'm Aramant. You must be the new guy." The other one remained silent. "He's Epton; he can't speak."

Inside the room, there were two sets of bunk beds. Thaidren looked at all of them for signs of which ones might be vacant for him to use.

Aramant pointed toward one of them. "You can have the upper left bed. No one is using that one."

Thaidren threw his small bag near the bed and climbed up. It was a comfortable one; he would sleep well here. And with the imminent nighttime knocking at their door, plus the tiredness of the trip, he fell asleep in less than an hour.

The following day, Thaidren awoke refreshed and anxious to see the rest of his new home. He got out of bed and glanced outside the window. From his room, he had a nice view of the courtyard and the city in the distance. Knowing that someone would come to give him a tour soon, he started to get dressed. To his surprise, though, he noticed that his boots had disappeared. He opened the door leading outside the room only to stumble upon one of them, with a note inside: Find the other one. From within the tower's staircase, the loud footsteps of an adult could be heard approaching. A man, wearing an assortment of plate armor over which a fine threaded tabard complimented its style, similar to that of Attern, reached their floor. He seemed frailer and thinner than an average fighter.

"Ah, young Thaidren, I see you are awake already," he said. "I am Master Baav. I was assigned as one of your teachers and as your guide toda — " He stopped midsentence, noticing the boy was barefoot and holding one boot. He rolled his eyes as if he knew exactly what happened. "But first, we'll need to get you a new pair of boots, it seems. Don't worry. Young Aramant has quite a reputation around here; you'll get used to it…"

*He did this?* The thought stirred a sense of disappointment in him. Aramant didn't seem like a bad person. Nevertheless, it would appear that his stay at the cathedral might not be as event-free as he thought.

# CHAPTER II

# NINE YEARS AFTER HE LEFT

*Thaidren is nineteen years old now.* The thought seemed unreal to Wizera. *I wish I could see him on his birthday, but alas, I have more pressing matters to attend to.* Over the passing years, the sorceress managed to visit him several times. The last time being two winters ago, on his seventeenth birthday. He was pleasantly surprised to see her. As was she to hear the praising words of all his tutors and Attern himself. Despite the kind words about his development, she also received some not-so-good news regarding his relationship with Aramant. The two of them had come to despise each other, often competing over anything they could and causing trouble in the aftermath.

However, Attern had faith and assured her that they were just messing around. "In their case, this kind of rivalry can prove to be a motivating factor for them to become better," he said. What he did not want to divulge to Wizera was that their interactions had indeed proven to be a handful at times, with both of them only listening to reason when Attern intervened directly. It was of no importance to him, though. The sorceress seemed happy to know her son was doing fine overall.

During the past two years or so, based on numerous rumors and unsupported pieces of intel that the Council of Mages had received, Wizera was assigned by the institution to verify their veracity and report any findings she may find on the matter.

As for the Council of Mages itself, the institution had also undergone severe changes, both good and bad, over the last few decades. Back in the days of old, there had been tens of thousands of sorcerers across the world. Today, their numbers lay in the hundreds, maybe a bit more. The Council of Mages still has influence and receives tremendous respect from other institutions and many, if not all, kingdoms across Iroga. Still, it has seen better days, with the mortality rate annually increasing faster than that of new apprentices showing up at the gates of Cologan to study the applications of magic and earn the title of sorcerer. It would stand to reason that at some point in history, another magical-oriented institution might rise and attempt to overthrow the existing one. Such events had happened in the past, having depended on the newly formed organization's intentions and goals. Some of them were integrated into the Council of Mages, while others were deemed unfit for society and dissolved. However, in the event of rare, extreme cases, they ended up eliminated through force.

At the council's request, Wizera would often end up traveling in search of anything that could prove the existence of a new, mysterious cult. Her latest intel led to a remote town known as Ghefi. At first impression, it seemed like a warm and peaceful village. Nevertheless, as she knew all too well from past experience, appearances could be deceiving.

***

Thaidren had already had his fair share of missions in the name of The Light. However, young apprentices were allowed to go on the more trivial assignments, albeit supervised and assisted by a veteran paladin. Depending on the task itself, one to four apprentices would be allocated in a senior's care. So far, Thaidren's supervisor, known by her title as one of The Five Lanterns, was Nebrina. Her position represented the most esteemed students of their generation, those that, through hard work and exquisite results, had been granted certain privileges by Attern himself. As for their current status, they both had returned from their last assignment. As they entered the cathedral's sacred grounds, Thaidren noticed Aramant leaning on one of the entrance's walls.

"Messed up another one, eh?" he asked in a mocking tone.

Thaidren began to amble toward him with his fist clenched.

Nebrina grabbed him by the shoulder plate, forcing him to stop. "Stand down, both of you!" Her tone made it clear that she would beat some sense into both of them if needed.

Aramant stepped up and walked past Thaidren. He unclenched his fist, then waited for a few seconds before whispering, "Jerk..."

Nebrina slapped Thaidren on the back of his head. "I told you to cut it off. Do NOT let him get in your head. We are all brothers and sisters under the guidance of the Holy Church. We protect and respect each other as we serve The Light."

"I'm not so sure he would raise a shield to defend me," Thaidren replied.

"But would you do it for him?" Nebrina asked.

The comeback made him hesitant to return an answer. Although, deep down, Thaidren knew — or at least, wanted to believe — that if Aramant's life were to be in peril, he would defend him. Probably. Hopefully, he would never have to find out. He and Aramant did undergo several missions together in the past, but out of concern that they would constantly be distracted by one another and at each other's throats, Attern had avoided putting them on the same team. On top of that, Aramant was also known to have a rough reputation. Not because of his skills or combat prowess, but because of his personality. He was the proud son of the Highlord of the Cathedral of The Light. With his father's name carrying heavy influence, it filled Aramant's head with pride and arrogance as a consequence. His childhood friend, Epton, had remained by his side since day one. He was probably the only one who had gotten used to him. As for their appointed handler, Illia, another member of The Five Lanterns, was frequently worried while pointing out to Attern that his son may one day suffer the repercussions of his attitude.

The Highlord was well aware of it but remained unsure of what needed to be done. He was not the kind of man to believe that beating up your child solved anything. Yet scolding him only seemed to affect him for a few hours, maybe days at best. *His arrogance is a product of his youth. He will learn to be humble... in time...* he would often attempt to reassure himself with the thought. However, he felt conflicted by the prospect that perhaps he should consider a more direct approach. Later on that day, near sundown, Attern requested Aramant to present himself in his chambers. The boy answered the call and entered the Highlord's room, saluting him out of respect.

"Father, I understand you have requested my presence."

Attern sat at his desk, reading through one of the many documents piled on it. He removed his reading glasses and turned his gaze to Aramant.

"I have received the last mission's report from your supervisor," he said with a deep, disappointed tone.

Aramant remained silent for a few seconds before finding his words, "I can explain — "

The sound of Attern's fist pounding the desk interrupted him. Despite his violent gesture, he spoke quietly. "Explain what? You had a simple assignment: go to the Foreton harbor and negotiate the price for our new shipment of parchments and equipment for the recruits."

"But that's what I — "

Attern's fist hit the desk harder the second time, and a few scrolls dropped onto the floor. "Instead, you offered an unreasonably low price to the merchants for their services, and without coming to any sort of compromise with them. And what did that lead to?"

He kept his eyes on the recently abused desk, "Well…"

"Well? Tell me, son. What did your actions lead to?"

"The merchants refused to sell us the equipme — "

"Oh, and there's more. Because of your stubbornness and disrespectful attitude toward them, they are reluctant to do business with us ever again." Attern sighed as he rubbed his forehead. He lifted himself out of the chair, walked to the door, and as he passed by his son, the Highlord signaled the prodigal son to follow him. "Come with me. There is something I wish for you to see."

***

In the village of Ghefi, Wizera was searching for clues that might indicate activity or existence of the alleged new cult. As far as the townsfolk were concerned, there was nothing out of the ordinary. Or at least, so they claimed. Nevertheless, the sorceress did not rely much on their apparent sincerity, given that she was a stranger in their eyes. As the sun started to settle, she decided to call it a day and get back to the inn. Instead of resorting to a simple teleportation spell, she chose to enjoy a relaxing stroll. Along the road, she gazed to her left and right, at the fields primarily used for farming, filled with lines of either corn or wheat. It depicted a serene image that helped her relax and put some order to her thoughts. *I wonder what Thaidren is doing now,* she would often ask herself. *Maybe when this is over, I'll be able to visit him. Maybe even spend some more time at the cathedral.* She smiled at the prospect.

Suddenly, her attention focused to her left. The sorceress saw a dense cloud of black smoke, which appeared to be coming from one of the houses off in the distance. Wizera assumed the worst and rushed toward the source of the smoke and fumes. Upon getting closer, she noticed that a fire engulfed one of the farms, from the crops to the barn, including the house. She could hear screams coming from inside, but she was unable to see anyone in the dense smoke. The sorceress summoned her elemental energies by mimicking a powerful rain cloud that poured its waters over the fields on fire. It did not take long before the flames were extinguished.

With the inside of the house and barn still gripped by the charring flames, Wizera manipulated the gathered water into a stream that looked like a giant living serpent. She pointed it toward the house, then, with a signal from her hand, doused the remaining fire. With that taken care of, she searched for survivors. A man and a child stood on the dining room floor. They appeared to have suffered only minor burns. Wizera could not disperse the smoke and fumes using her magic but assisted the man and child to get outside safely. Once they were outside, the man pointed to the house.

"My wife! She's still inside the h — "

Before he had the chance to finish, the walls collapsed. The damage inflicted by the flames proved to have been too great, and the house turned in on itself. The man collapsed to his knees and covered his face. His child was in shock, standing still, staring at the burning remains of what she once called home. Wizera turned her gaze to the ground. A sentiment of guilt rose within her heart. She didn't see the woman through all that smoke, and because of that, a child had lost her mother. Soon, the nearby neighbors came to see what had happened.

"How did this happen?" asked one of them.

The man stood up and hugged his daughter. She was still in shock and did not react except for a few tears that trickled down her cheeks.

Wizera took two vials from her bag. She poured their contents on the burns of the farmer and his daughter.

"Here," Wizera said to the farmer, "continue to apply it on the wounds until the substance is completely absorbed by the skin." The man nodded. She wanted to ask him what had happened, but that could wait for later. Instead, she waited for the smoke to disperse and walked over to the remains of the house to take a closer look. A sense of horror surrounded the sorceress as she discovered the dead woman. Her corpse lay close to where she'd found the man and their child, burned, with her arm stretched out, trying to reach out to them. *She was right near me. I was but an arm's length away from her, and I didn't see her.* The harsh realization intensified her already profound sense of guilt.

She forced the thought away to focus on the task at hand and continued to search for the source of the fire. While passing through the burned rubble, she sensed an odd smell, one similar to that of sulfur. Not long after that, she found shattered fragments of minerals that proved to have small amounts of sulfur in their composition. On top of that, she sensed something else coming from the minerals: a weak yet undeniable trace of elemental magic. *Something about these rocks seems unnatural. They appear as if they were infused with magic.* If the sorceress's assumptions were correct, it would mean that this may not have been an accident. She took a shard of the unknown mineral and returned to the inn. There was nothing more to do at the burnt house for now.

The next day, after having a meal at the tavern, Wizera began analyzing the mineral fragment she'd taken from the burned farmhouse. Because of the sulfur's composition, there was a risk that the minerals could be toxic, flammable, or both. *Despite that, sulfur does not ignite on its own. There must have been some condition or factor that triggered it.* Another thing that raised concern for the sorceress was the pitch-blackness of the shard itself. Initially, she thought it was because of the charring flames that had engulfed it. Yet, after cleaning and removing any impurities from it using her water magic, the color remained unchanged. *This is without question a sulfurous crystal that has been infused with elemental magic artificially. But what type?* She had some ideas, but none of them offered her a sense of comfort. Whatever the case, this shard was created with malicious intent. *But why bother burning up a peasant's farm with a complex magical crystal? It doesn't make any sense. A torch would've had the same results with less effort.* A muffled knock on her door interrupted her thoughts.

"Excuse me, miss?" a voice asked from the other side.

The sorceress opened the door to find the farmer she had saved the other day. Judging by the slumped shoulders and weariness on his face, it was obvious he was still worn out by the recent events.

"You're the Silver Sorceress, yes? You were at the fire the other day."

Wizera responded with a nod. "How are you? Is your child all right?"

"Well…" The man paused briefly while clearing his throat and taking a deep breath. "She cried all night over her mother. She just went to sleep before I came here."

"I am sorry to hear that," Wizera replied. "Is there anything I can do to help?"

"To be honest, I was hoping that we could talk."

The sorceress nodded a second time. "I'm listening."

The man looked at the alchemy table where the dark crystal stood. "That strange rock… I think it was what started the fire."

Wizera was well aware of that. Yet, she was curious to know the reason why the farmer believed so as well. "Do you know what that rock is? Or where it came from? Where did you get it?"

"To be frank, m' lady, my daughter found it laying in our fields a few days ago. She thought she had found a precious stone and brought it home. It felt uncomfortable to have it in the house, but I thought it was just my imagination."

Wizera did not want to reveal all she discovered regarding the stone. "I see. Do you have any idea where it came from? Or if there is someone around here who might know?"

"The only thing I know is that there is a local story about a cursed mine filled with monsters and creatures of nightmare. It's located at the bottom of a mountain, west of here, near the hills leading to the old town."

"Old town?" asked the sorceress.

"Yes, m' lady. The old town is where most of our parents used to live. It was burned to the ground during the War of The Spider, when the local chaos and civil wars began. Don't know what else to tell you."

By the time the farmer finished speaking, the Silver Sorceress had already formed a hypothesis. "And you think it originates from the mine?"

"I don't know… Maybe."

"I see. Well, thank you for the information. I'll see what I can do." She turned back to her alchemy table and picked up the book that was lying next to the stone. She could still sense the farmer's presence behind her.

"M'lady, if you can spare just one more moment?"

She turned around. "Of course. Is there something else?"

"Thank you for saving my daughter and me. We are in your debt."

Her gaze turned toward the floor. "You have nothing to thank me for. No debt at all. I could've saved your wife as well."

The man closed in on her. "What happened was not your fault, m' lady. My daughter and I are still alive because of you." He quietly stepped back and closed the door behind him as he left.

Wizera felt a moment of relief passing through her, reducing her troubled feelings. She was aware of what he said to her, yet, in a perfect world, she would've saved his wife too. *I'd better start preparing for the journey ahead. Tomorrow I'm going to investigate that mine. I just hope it isn't what I think it is.*

The day before her departure, after analyzing the shard more thoroughly, the sorceress discovered that it could have been used as a conduit for interspatial travel.

Perhaps even a portal key, or some form of spatial anchor. As soon as she finished her breakfast, she went to pay for the room before going upstairs to pack her things. A cloudy day waited for her outside. A storm seemed imminent. As she left the building, right next to the inn's entrance stood the farmer's daughter. Wizera was surprised to see her again. She looked pale, and her eyes had dark circles around them, no doubt due to a lack of sleep.

The sorceress greeted her with a smile. "Where is your father?" she asked, looking around.

The girl appeared to have come alone. There was no one in sight. Wizera noticed that she was holding a straw hat in both of her tiny hands. The girl raised it toward her.

"You want me to have this?" the sorceress asked.

Accompanied by a firm nod, the girl answered, "You saved Daddy."

For a brief moment, this innocent display of gratitude melted Wizera's heart. She smiled at the girl and gently took the straw hat from her hands. "Thank you. I will treasure it dearly."

"It will help against the rain," the girl answered.

The Silver Sorceress put the hat on and patted the girl's head before departing. On her way to the old town, she passed by the burned house once again. It stood as a cruel reminder that there were few happy endings in the world. She avoided staring at the rubble for too long. *The mine might hold the answers to what is happening*, and refocused her thoughts on that prospect. Still, at this point, she was skeptical as to whether a new cult existed, or if they would've had anything to do with this town. She continued to walk along the path, leaving the village of Ghefi behind.

The road was more of a path and without any paving. On the left, one could see the plain fields on which the farmers raised their crops. On the right side, one could see the hills and the archipelago behind them. That was where the Silver Sorceress had to go. It was safer to take the road leading there than to roam directly through the woods. Even if it meant to prolong her trip by a few hours or so. As for her ability as a mage to teleport, that was not an option to be taken lightly.

Certain conditions had to be met for a mage to bend the laws of space safely. One of them, in particular, was the reason why she would not dare to use it. The requirement of a strong visual memory of the place, is to see it directly when casting the spell. An alternative consisted of having left a magical rune to act as an anchor for her to teleport to. Yet the latter implied for it to not have been her first time to visit the location.

She did not mind walking, though. It helped her clear her thoughts and reminisce about better times. Times when Thaidren was little. Times when Thieron was still alive. Despite her past life being filled with danger, that did not seem to matter when thinking that she was close to the people she loved. They fought, laughed, and cried together. By the time she got herself out of her reverie, she had reached a crossroads. The sign that was supposed to point out where each road led seemed to have been broken for a long time. It did not matter to the sorceress, given that she possessed a map of the region. She was already entering a path on which not many had traveled.

After several hours of following the pathway, Wizera stumbled upon a disturbing omen. The soil near the road seemed soaked with blood. It appeared old, and it wouldn't have been surprising that it might have come from a wild animal. However, it still meant that these roads were rarely frequented by humans, so wild animals were not afraid to use them.

*I still have a good number of hours before sunset*, the Silver Sorceress thought. Yet, because of the surrounding trees' density and tallness, the sun's light was mostly cut off. It gave the illusion that it was sunset already. The trees also looked ominous and sickly, raising Wizera's concerns about what may await her in the old, ruined town. She pressed forward, to the end of the road. After several hours, the Silver Sorceress had reached her destination. The buildings, or, to be more precise, what had remained of them, still held the charred pigmentation from the past flames. It was surprising that most of them were still standing after so many years. A stench of death and decay coated the air. Except for some necrophagous beasts, no wildlife would want to tread near such a place. However, it would make a more suitable settlement for… darker entities.

The Silver Sorceress gazed around. *The mine should be nearby, at the western border of the town.* As she passed through the ruined city, Wizera kept an eye open for magical runes and signs of necromancy. Those who dwelled with such corruptive forces would have a place like this heavily warded against uninvited guests. All around her was quiet. Sinisterly quiet. No birds chirping, no howls, not even the sound of the wind blowing. Only Wizera's footsteps perturbed the surrounding silence. Once she reached the western border, she immediately found the entrance that led to the mine. It seemed as decrepit and deserted as the burned city residing next to it. Amidst the abandoned ruins, something unusual caught her eye. Namely, chunks of massive minerals rose from the ground and engulfed the mine's entrance. They seemed precious and had a faint green glow. *If those minerals were valuable, why would the miners not take them?* She took a few precautious steps back and drew out a translucent crystal from her bag. By shoving it into the ground, she conjured up a magical circle with runes all around her. After chanting a few words of power with her eyes closed, a wall of thin ice formed around the sorceress, engulfing the circle's outline. Within a few moments, the ice wall shattered and crumbled to the ground, turning into water. It then began surging into a strong torrent that entered the mine.

A spell of this caliber filled two purposes. One of them was to cleanse and disperse any magical runes that it encountered. The other was to act as a means to detect any form of profaned magic, being particularly effective at detecting necromantic or demonic signatures. If the waters returned to Wizera tainted, it would mean that someone or something befouled by such energies resided within the mine. The sorceress hoped that it would return crystal clear despite the surrounding's ominous feeling. No sound came from the mine as she waited for a verdict. No echoes of drowning animals or struggling human beings, meaning that the mine was devoid of any souls. As the waters returned to Wizera, they appeared to be clean, just as they were when they entered. It was a good sign. Or at least, it marked the absence of a bad one. The rocky formations that surrounded the mine's entrance had begun to glow after being exposed to the Silver Sorceress's spell, revealing their purpose. It turned out they were conduit crystals that could absorb vast quantities of magic and turn it into a form of natural light. In simple terms, they were nothing more than a fancy magical lantern. The miners must have left them here to act as a light source. Assuming they had a magic user who could activate them. She took a smaller shard from the lot and stepped inside the mine. She found several crystals inside as well, all glowing from the magical torrent that washed over them moments ago.

The structural integrity of the mine seemed stable. Nevertheless, Wizera knew about the risks of old tunnels that could collapse without a moment's notice. She forced away her concerns and focused on the potential findings she might come across inside such a place. As she delved deeper into the mine, she eventually reached its end. This last section of the mine offered her two conclusions. The mine had been abandoned, yet it was once used by people who dabbled into the forbidden arts of necromancy. Her cleansing waters may not have found any wards, but she suspected that whoever used this place had removed them before leaving to cover his or her tracks. Opposite the tunnel that led to the chamber was an alchemy table. Near it, washed onto the ground, was a large book with a thick wooden-decorated cover, resembling a magic practician's tome. Unfortunately, the spell that Wizera used previously washed it away and deteriorated the pages within. Whatever the contents of the book, they were now indecipherable.

After putting her thoughts in order, there was still one aspect that did not add up. *Why would someone leave a necromancy book behind if they wanted to cover their tracks? It could be that the book was a trap set for whoever was bold or stupid enough to investigate this place. The cleansing spell must've removed the curse. No, it couldn't have been from that.* Even though the pages were worn out and water-damaged, some of the inscribing may still be comprehensible. While scrutinizing its contents, Wizera stopped in shock at a drawing on one particular page. *No, it can't be... It almost looks like... Urostmarn. I need to restore the scribblings on this tome to be sure.*

She kept the book and began chanting an interspatial spell that would take her back home. There was nothing more that she could do here. It was time to call it a day and get as far away as possible from this ancient, foul place. Despite her curiosity and desire to uncover the book's secrets, she could not help but fall prey to a powerful sentiment of dread at the thought of finding out what profane mysteries its pages may hold within its lines.

***

Meanwhile, at the Cathedral of The Light, the sunset, and the cold night were near, meaning that most of the instructors and recruits were inside. Aramant was curious and slightly worried as to what his father wanted to show him. They passed the main entrance and continued around to the side of the cathedral. Behind it stood a plain parch of land, surrounded by hills on all sides. This place, however, was seldom visited and did not serve any training purpose. A grated gateway with two torches on each side marked the entrance to this secluded back section of the cathedral. Attern took a torch and opened the squeaking metal gate. He invited Aramant with a gesture to pass through the gate before him.

"Do you know what this place is, son?" Attern asked with a saddened expression.

Aramant responded in a quiet, unsettled tone. "It's the cathedral's graveyard."

"Indeed. This is the place where I, and probably you too, will be buried."

Attern looked him in the eye, then pointed toward a massive pillar placed in the center area. It resembled a gigantic gravestone, taller than a medium-sized tree.

"And do you know what that is?" Attern asked.

Aramant grew up at the cathedral. He had explored its outskirts so much that he could traverse it blindfolded. This place, however, was one of the few areas that he would not visit lightly. Ever since he was a boy, this massive monument had engraved on its side a series of names. Throughout his growing up, more and more names would occasionally be carved here during burial ceremonies. He knew exactly what this monument represented. Still, he indulged his father by hearing him out.

"I call it The Dim Pillar. It doesn't have an official name, but I consider this one to be befitting." He chuckled for a split second before his face turned mournful. Aramant stood there, slightly confused, without saying a word, but listening to his father's words. "It is a testament to all of our brothers and sisters who fought the forces of evil and perished. However, their names being engraved here also means that their bodies were never recovered." He paused, trying to find the right words. "Some of my best friends' names are here. Alas, there are seven of them to whom I owe my life and also to whom I've wronged. The mistakes of my youthful self cost them their lives." He turned against the pillar and grabbed Aramant with his arms on both shoulders. "Listen, son, there will come a time, a moment, or even several, in the life of a man where your actions and decisions will forever define who you are and what kind of person you will become. There are people here who are confident your attitude will cost you dearly, and to some degree, I am concerned that might end up being the case as well. I cannot change you, nor do I want to imply that the way you are now is wrong. But when those moments catch up to you, please do not let your pride cloud your judgment. Choose for yourself and try to make the best decision possible. There are plenty of people, creatures — especially demons — that will stop at nothing to make you suffer by exploiting your flaws."

Aramant's forehead wrinkled with a frown. "So, you brought me here to scold me and tell me that I have an attitude problem?"

"Aramant, that is not what I — "

"You know what? Fine, I'll be an obedient dog… just like you and the others wish me to be." He pulled from his father's grasp and strode away. Attern called him out when he reached the cemetery gate. Despite his fury, he complied with the old man's request and stopped.

"One of the names on this stone is your mother's…," murmured Attern, as if he would've hoped for his son not to hear him.

He turned back, unable to hide the shock from what he heard. "What?" he asked as he approached his father with a shaking hand. "You never, ever, talk about her, and now you suddenly drop this on me? What do you mean her name is there? Was she a paladin? How did she die? Is she one of the persons that died because of you?"

The last question stirred Attern's anger. "There are things that you do not understand, boy."

"Then explain them to me!"

"Now is not the right time for this!"

"Then when is it going to be? Or better yet, why did you bring it up in the first place?" He strode back and forward, unable to filter his words with care anymore. A clenching fist swiped through the air, opening up the final line of his anger. "Do I have to wait another twenty years or so for you to mention my mother again?! Will there ever be a 'right time'?"

The old paladin unclenched his fist, his tone turning back to its initial, mournful state. "No, and I promise you that we will talk about this. But right now, you are not well. Your mind is tainted with rage. Go inside the cathedral and calm your nerves. I will join you soon in a few minutes."

For a split second, the thought of throwing a punch at his father crossed Aramant's mind. Nevertheless, he was not that kind of person, nor did he believe that he would land the punch unless Attern allowed it. He felt his blood boiling but took in a deep breath and decided it was not worth it. "Don't bother yourself with it. It's not hard to see how you can disappoint your family. I guess I get that from you."

The next day, Attern decided to personally go to Foreton harbor and make amends for the wrongdoings caused by his son. It offered an opportunity for him to leave the cathedral for a while. One of the burdens of being in charge of everything is that he could rarely leave. Being able to do so occasionally proved to be a welcomed, relieving experience, despite the nature of his trip still being in the cathedral's interests. Attern was not the kind of paladin who would take an escort or even an assistant. He mounted on his steed and traveled to the city alone. The trip would take about an hour, giving him some free time to relax and clear out his thoughts. Or so he hoped. His mind was still preoccupied by the dispute he had with Aramant last night. His son's choice of words in particular raised questions about how he had raised his son.

*Maybe I could've done this another way. I guess you could have gotten that from me after all.* Still, Aramant was of no help with regard to the situation. Since a few years back, they seemed to rarely reach a common ground. *It felt easier to communicate when he was younger. Is he just still in his rebellious phase? Or is it something more? Did I fail him as a father?* These thoughts would not give him peace. Nevertheless, he looked around, trying to dismiss the fog of doubt that stirred the unrest in his head.

He could see hundreds of meters in the distance, over the fields basked by the sun's warm rays. Before he realized it, he had already reached his destination. He left his steed at the stable and decided to walk by foot through the city. Unlike Leor, which was closer to the Cathedral of The Light, Foreton had an opening to the sea, making it ideal for trading over vast distances across the ocean. Still, being a city of fishermen and sailors meant it was accompanied by a strong and very specific odor as well, one that Attern was neither used to nor fond of. He made his way to the port where he knew the sailors to whom his son spoke could be found. As soon as he got there, it occurred to him that the port was suspiciously barren, with close to no people anywhere in sight. He would've imagined the place to be far more active and populated. He reached out to the sailors' barracks and knocked at the door and received no answer.

"Ye won't find anyone there now, mate," a voice said from behind.

Attern turned to face the man. "Do you know the sailors?"

"Aye," he answered. "I used to sail with those blaggers up until a few years ago. When the sea became a far too dangerous place for an old man like meself." The old sailor displayed a sad tone in his voice.

"I'm sorry to hear that. Do you have any idea when they will return?"

The man remained silent for a few moments. His gaze shifted toward Attern's decorated armor and vestments. "Well, you didn't come at a good time. This time of year, all sailors be on the sea. T'is the busy season, turnin' this excuse of a port into a ghost town. But you're in luck today, for I am still one of 'em at heart and soul, so I take care of some of their businesses on the shore. Here, let's talk inside." He pulled a key chain from his left pocket and unlocked the door. As he guided Attern inside, the old man ambled toward a large wooden desk filled with documents and a hefty register in the middle of it. He opened the log somewhere in the middle, where the last entries in it had been made.

"So, what business do ya have here?" he asked.

"I came to apologize for the behavior of one of my subordinates who came here to do business in the name of the cathedral."

The old man pulled off his glasses and stared at Attern. "I see... I remember the boy. Young, arrogant, and with a bitter tongue."

Attern looked at the ground while covering his eyes with his hand, then he rubbed his forehead. "That would be him... yes."

"I gotta tell you, that kid is something. He pissed off the captain up to the point where I thought he would shoot him." He paused and chuckled briefly. "Don't worry about it, the captain will get over it. Just listen to an old man's advice, and next time send someone else to do the talking. I pity the poor soul who fathered him."

At that point, Attern did not care about the man's last comment. He was pleasantly surprised that things were not as bad as he'd imagined. "So, I take it everything is fine then? Can we count on your men to do business with us in the future?"

The old sailor raised an eyebrow as he began to notice the resemblance between the brat and the seemingly shameful paladin standing in front of him. "They aren't my men, but aye, ye can count on it. The extra payment washed away the frown on the cap's face."

"Wait," Attern said, "what extra payment?"

"Yesterday, another of yer order showed his face at the harbor, a few hours after the boy left, right before the crew was about to set sail. He offered the cap'n a fat bag o' gold, saying that it's from your lot as an apology. Wasn't it?"

Attern's confusion began to turn into concern. "No. No paladin from the Cathedral of The Light was sent here yesterday to give away a bag of coins."

"Well, then ye boys have a benefactor. Between you and me, lad, I'd say ye take it as a gift and don' mention it to yer superiors."

"A-hem... Thank you. I must be going now. Take care of yourself, old man."

"Will do, and you of that boy." The old man received no response from Attern, yet his silence was proof enough for him that his suspicion was correct. "He seemed like a handful."

*You have no idea...* The Highlord took off with his task completed. Upon leaving the harbor, Attern decided to spend the night at a local inn and depart the following day. A sign with a sculpted whale and the words "The Drunken Whale" caught his attention. He entered the pub and ordered a tankard of mead before taking a seat at one of the free tables. The place was mostly empty due to the busy season being over, making it a quiet place for one to clear his mind. Yet, Attern could not help but think of the recent events. Thoughts about both his son and the mysterious benefactor at the harbor would not let him enjoy a peaceful drink. His attention was not focused on the outside world. That is until he noticed someone taking a seat at his table.

"How fortunate to finally meet you, Highlord Attern Igtruth," the stranger said.

Attern did not recognize the stranger, nor did he feel that he was well-intended. Compared to him, he seemed young, about the same age as Aramant or so. He wore a shroud over his head, with plated armor, complimented by a dark tabard. It resembled the paladin gear style, except this attire was dyed black, giving it a more ominous aesthetic.

"Do we know each other, boy?" he asked while taking a sip from his tankard, masking his suspicions.

"Don't be so modest, Highlord. Many people know who you are. But to answer your question, no, we have not had the pleasure of meeting each other up until now."

"Then may I ask you your name? If you don't mind, that is."

The uninvited guest smirked. "I appreciate your interest, yet my name is irrelevant. I only wish to speak to you about something."

Attern was starting to slowly lose his patience. "I am listening," he answered, slowly moving his arm toward the hammer on his back.

"Easy now; no need to be concerned," the man replied. "That's no way to treat someone who yesterday spent a large amount of money to clear out your subordinate's mess."

Attern's hand fell back down on the table. "You are the mysterious benefactor who paid the sailors? Why?"

"A prime motive would be that it seemed a good conversation starter, don't you think?"

"Enough is enough. What is it that you want to discuss with me, boy? No more chitchat."

"Very well. I see I've put your patience to the test already. Since you are a man interested only in business, I'll get right to the point. I represent an organization."

"An organization? Who do you speak for?"

"That is also irrelevant. What you need to know is that we are aware that you have someone rather exceptional at your little church."

Attern abruptly got on his feet and grabbed his hammer. Before he could strike, though, the man interrupted him by putting his palm over his shoulder. He pulled Attern's head closer to his and whispered, "It may be best for you to sit down, Highlord. It's late, this pub seems nice, and I have the means to kill everyone here, including you. How about we just sit back down and continue our discussion in a civil manner?" He then pointed at the barkeep. The bartender had a dark circle above his head. With Attern observing it, as the barman moved, so did the circle. Shadow manipulation. Seemingly of a high level of mastery. The old paladin took a moment to look down to his side, only to observe small spikes made of shadow on the ground near him. "See? Just sit down, and let's not cause a ruckus."

For the time being, Attern found himself with no other choice but to comply. As he sat down, the shadowy manifestations faded away. This was no ordinary magic practitioner. The element of shadow was known to be among the most volatile and difficult to master. Yet, an experienced user could manipulate the shape of shadows as he pleased, being theoretically limited only by his imagination. Attern found himself in a dire situation now. The words that previously came out of the man's mouth disturbed him greatly. *There's an entire organization that knows about Thaidren?! This is not good! Not good at all! I have to get out of here and reach Wiz. The cathedral is no longer safe.*

"If you're done daydreaming, I would like to continue," said the acolyte. "As I was saying, we know of your precious little protégé. And I am sure you did a great job at teaching him how to fight and play paladin all day long."

*What do they want with him? How did they find out about him? Do they have spies in the cathedral?* Attern was in shock. He could only listen to what this representative had to say. *Maybe he'll reveal something.*

"But it is time that we take care of him from now on. So, I've come to you peacefully, to talk about making a peaceful arrangement to surrender the boy to us. You do not have to answer right now, but before you make any kind of decision, let me just inform you, Highlord, that there isn't a single place in existence where Thaidren won't be found by us."

*He said his name. It is him that they're talking about!* Every cell in Attern's body wanted to unsheathe Viz'Hock, his prized holy artifact, from his back and pound the man's skull into the ground. Alas, he was not in a position to do so. He had to survive this. To go back to the cathedral and talk to someone. Anyone. And to warn Wizera afterward.

"You have two days to consider our offer. After that, if you decide against it or do not provide a concrete answer, we will resort to force. Keep in mind that we could have taken him anytime he was on a mission, and you would never have found out what happened to him. Now, don't try anything stupid, and let us depart without incident." The man politely saluted the old paladin and got up from the table, heading slowly toward the inn's exit.

Immediately after he left, Attern stormed out in search of him.

Unfortunately, there was no trace of the dark acolyte anymore. He had vanished, without leaving any clue of his whereabouts, or whoever he represented. A clear sky with a full moon glowing in the darkness of the night marked the terrifying encounter. Without losing any more precious time, Attern rushed over to the stables, violently knocking at the house of the stable master to take his steed back. Once that was done, he left the city and rode back to the cathedral as fast as possible. His trusted steed galloped swiftly like the howling winds that accompanied the misty darkness around him, with only the moon shedding some of its dim light upon his path. The old paladin's aging lungs were starting to feel the imminent pressure of a panic attack. *I have to get there! I have to warn them! By The Light, I hope I won't get there too late.* For a few moments, those were the only thoughts that flooded Attern's mind. Apart from Thaidren, he had other concerns to consider. The Cathedral of The Light being assaulted... This had not happened during his time as its commander. A direct act of threatening it would mean that whoever these people were, they had the boldness to make the Congregation of Paladins their enemy. A foolish thing to do, given the congregation's global influence.

*Unless...* There may have been something even more disturbing about this organization. It could be borne from within the congregation itself. That would put Attern into an even more precarious position. He would not know whom to speak to about all of this. *Calm down. You have no proof of anything of the sort yet. It may be a bluff,* he thought. Still, there was no room for him to take that chance. He forced away any further thoughts and focused on getting back home to defend his students. His friends. His family.

After what seemed like an endless night's journey, the Highlord could see the peak of the cathedral's highest tower from a distance. The adrenaline surged through him when he reached the cathedral and barged into the main hall on his way toward the living quarters. A moment of lucidity caught up to him, making him stop mid-hall. He could not exhibit his dismayed state to the other staff members or the students who might see him. He could not start a panic in the middle of the night. Right now, the best person to talk to was master Baav, whom he left in charge of the cathedral in his absence. He was a trusted and well-respected advisor of the Highlord; they had known each other for decades and had forged an ironclad trust between each other. As soon as the old paladin found him, despite his attempt to maintain a calm posture, Baav immediately concluded that something was amiss.

"Highlord? Is there something wrong?" he asked with his hands clasped behind his back.

Attern grabbed him by the chest plate armor with one hand and his shoulder with the other, looked into his eyes and drew in a heavy breath as he pulled him closer.

"We are in danger… My office…"

Baav studied his friend's behavior. He rarely saw him in such a distressed state. He subtly nodded once toward him and whispered, "Let's go to my office instead. It's closer."

Attern nodded. They both turned to the corridor that led to Baav's office, then closed the door behind them. While Attern took a seat, Baav drew a circular symbol using a chalk piece on the inside of the door. The rune would conceal the sound of their voices. He then offered his superior a glass of water, so it would help him clear his throat.

"Well then, Highlord, what is happening? Try to relax and tell me everything."

Within a few moments, Attern began feeling better. He told his advisor everything that had happened since his departure. "There seems to be a rogue organization that knows about Thaidren, about where he is and WHO he is." Baav's eyes widened as Attern continued speaking. "They approached me to negotiate a peaceful way for us to hand him over."

"That's absurd," Baav replied. "Did they threaten you? It would mean threatening the entire congregation."

"That may be part of the problem. I do not have any proof of this now, but I think that this organization may have ties to the congregation. If so, then perhaps it even has spies infiltrated deep within our ranks."

Baav moved his head closer to Attern's. "You ought to be cautious with such claims, Highlord," he whispered.

"I am, old friend. You've known me long enough to know that I would never speak my mind about such things lightly. The acolyte that I met seemed well-versed in the art of shadow manipulation. He had the upper hand to kill me at any point. On top of that, he had the means to pose as a paladin. He had sensitive intel about us, and he wore a version of our standard paladin attire, only dyed black."

Baav remained speechless for a few moments. He opened his mouth, but no words came out. Before he had a chance to speak his mind, Attern continued.

"We need to prepare for an imminent attack. The acolyte said that they will strike in two days if they get a decline from us, or no answer at all. I will send word to some of the higher rankings of the congregation, but I am afraid that if I'm right, some of them will end up in the wrong hands, alerting this new, domestic enemy."

Baav waited for his superior to finish before reaching for the empty glass that he held in his hand. "Highlord, I'd advise caution before sending any report to anyone who is in a higher position than yourself. It's still too early to know who to trust and who not to."

"You're right, but I don't see any other options. They will attack in less than forty-eight hours. We need to take some form of — " Suddenly, Attern's head felt heavy. His vision started to blur as he fell from his chair and lay nauseated and weakened. His senses were slowly leaving him, as he realized what had happened. "Baav, yo — " Before he'd finished his sentence, Attern fell unconscious.

"Forgive me, old friend... We'll talk about this when you wake up."

# CHAPTER III
# LAND OF THE BLESSED
# AND THE CURSED

Between the threat of an imminent attack at the Cathedral of The Light and the fate that befell Attern at the hands of Baav, across the Brun Sea, on a small continent known as the Old Earth lay Wizera's next destination. Housing mostly ancient, monstrous beasts and strange phenomena with strong ties to the world's primordial energies, few people dared to tread these forsaken lands. It had been here where the Silver Sorceress came in her youth to hone her skills and attain a better understanding of the nature of her powers. Now, after many years, Wizera returned to these forgotten places in search of an old friend; one who might help her with the restoration and deciphering of the ominous-looking tome that she found in the mines, drenched with the stench of necromantic magic.

There were no ships that sailed to the forbidden lands. Anyone wanting to come here would have to do so via spatial magic or have their own private vessel. As Wizera set foot on these ancient lands, old memories started to resurface. The scenery around her was exactly as she had remembered. Wild, brimming with raw and untamed magic, yet decaying and unattended. Books almost as old as the history of mankind stated that this continent, once referred to as Ghangaan — Land of the blessed and the cursed — represented the origin spot of mankind. Where humanity flourished for the first time and where it almost met its end. Where the forces of light and fire fought tirelessly until their banishment from the world of man came to pass. The only time man fought here in more recent history was when people set foot on its harsh lands during the War of the Spider, as the demonic brood queen had originated from this place. Remnants of that awful war and the Eternal Conflict alike could still be found lurking on its planes.

The person that Wizera sought carried the name Haara, an earth sorceress and a once invaluable companion of hers during the war. When the conflict ended, the two of them exchanged trinkets that carried their magical signature so that they could find each other in times of need. Nevertheless, this form of magic did not do all the work. It was able to point the Silver Sorceress to a location close to her friend, and help her track her energy signature. It would serve her as a compass that forever pointed toward Haara.

As Wizera traversed the ancient forest, with trees that dwarfed the mightiest and oldest of the rest of the world, she kept her eyes open for signs of manipulated magical energy. Every element or form of magical power in the world would possess a specific signature, especially those that were associated with living beings, or that were used by them. In this particular case, the traces of magic that she had detected from Haara were weak.

Soon, the sound of violent trampling from afar interrupted her thoughts. She canceled the tracking spell and hid behind a natural mound of earth, waiting calmly as the sound got louder. The crashing of collapsing trees betrayed the imminent approach of whatever creature was responsible for their uprooting. It came closer and closer until it eventually stopped a few meters from her. The sorceress remained silent and attempted to peek over the mound. There was a creature indeed, unlike any other that she had ever seen. With a body resembling a giant ape, yet covered in scales and with a reptilian, crocodile-looking head; it depicted the subject of a dozen nightmares. *A mutated species, most certainly,* thought the Silver Sorceress, *resulted from the abnormal conditions of these lands.*

The creature seemed alarmed. It sniffed the ground, then looked in every direction, searching for something. Or someone. *It may be attracted to magical sources,* she thought. Fortunately for her, should her assumption be correct, the vast amounts of magical energies that resided in the soil would make it all the more difficult for the creature to find her. However, she was still too close to it and Wizera was forced to make a decision. To silently wait and hope for the creature to leave, or to face it. In the event of the latter, her main problem would be if it was the only creature that got lured in by her spell. If it was, then she would have no surprises and could theoretically defeat it with ease. However, there was never a certainty in any battle scenario, and she knew that all too well.

In a moment of carelessness, Wizera stepped on a pile of dried leaves. The creature was immediately drawn by the noise and let out a mighty roar as it turned its attention toward her. At this stage, there was no point in hiding anymore. The sorceress showed herself, raised a hand above her head, and started chanting. Three ice lances the size of small trees formed above the Silver Sorceress while her eyes glowed in the mesmerizing nuance of the blue seas. She pointed at the beast and sent one of them to test the creature's resilience. It struck close to its shoulder, making it derail from its intended track and fall to the ground before it had a chance to reach its target. Wizera then aimed the second one at one of the creature's legs, making it scream in agony as the spear reached its mark. Upon observing the previous shots' effects, she dismissed the last one, figuring it proved unnecessary.

It wasn't in her character to kill a creature doing what was only natural for it. She preferred to merely prevent it from attacking again. With the threat taken care of, the sorceress could now resume her search. As she turned to get back on her trail, Wizera heard the creature roar again, along with the sound of shattering ice coming from behind it. The creature had gotten back on its feet and leaped toward the Silver Sorceress in a frenzy. It slapped her with the back of its hand, throwing her several meters. Luckily for her, she managed to conjure a thin ice wall to block most of the impact. Alas, the reverberating bursts of pain on her side told the sorceress that she may have had one or two broken ribs. Fueled by a surge of adrenaline, she struggled to her feet, took an agonizing deep breath, and chanted again.

Upon seeing her lips moving, the beast jumped at her, aiming to finish its prey quickly this time. The sorceress had no time to chant a spell that would stop something that big in time. She had no means to evade the attack either. She closed her eyes, succumbed deep in her thoughts. There had to be something she could do, yet the fear of death brought on reflections that clouded her judgment. This was not to be her end. It couldn't be. *Not here. Not like this. Not without seeing Thaidren one last time.*

"NO!" she shouted from the bottom of her throat as she opened her eyes. The beast lay frozen solid and entangled in a multitude of vines. Subconsciously, she resorted to a dangerous move that no magic practitioner should take on lightly. A reckless gesture of bursting out all of one's elemental energy at once. In Wizera's case, it resulted in freezing everything near her. The first thought upon seeing this was how displeased her old master would be if he were to see this. However, better displeased than mournful at her funeral.

*But what of the vines?* They were not frozen, meaning that they appeared after the creature and its surroundings were affected. Their presence betrayed a deliberate act of earth manipulation. From her right side, the sorceress saw a silhouette, one whose voice she remembered well.

"It's not like you to panic like that, Wiz. You must've gone soft over the years."

The friendly mocking in Haara's voice filled Wizera's heart with relief. Yet, she found herself unable to answer back. Her energy burst had taken a toll on the Silver Sorceress, draining her stamina. Her vision blurred and she swayed. The sorceress fell to her knees.

Haara approached her and reached into her bag, drawing a couple of aromatic roots from it.

"Hey, hey, stay with me. Here, smell this."

A powerful, herbal smell woke her enough to regain her vision.

The Silver Sorceress slowly got back on her feet, with Haara helping her to maintain her balance. "It's been a while, old frie — " She coughed up blood and licked the taint of it from her lips.

"Shh, don't speak. There'll be plenty of time for that. Come with me."

After several minutes of walking, Haara and Wizera ended up in a dense forest section. It was so abundant that the trees and vegetation almost completely blocked the sunlight, creating the illusion of a premature sunset. It would be troublesome for most creatures to roam around here but it was not an issue for Haara. The earthen sorceress waved her hand and chanted a few words in front of a giant oak.

The multitude of vines that entangled it began to move and reveal a hidden entrance inside the tree. It had served as a home for her for many years.

Inside the tree sat an alchemy table, along with several other peculiar pieces of equipment, spread across the room. Haara placed Wizera on the floor which was covered by a green carpet of moss. She then reached to her alchemy table and grabbed a vial with a liquid in it.

"Here, drink this," she said to Wizera as she held her head up.

The Silver Sorceress continued to cough violently. However, she started to feel better after ingesting the substance, confident she was in capable hands. Haara was one of the best earth sorceresses she had known, her techniques had developed to support and heal allies rather than develop as combat skills. She rested her eyes for a few moments, letting go of all concern.

Later that day, the Silver Sorceress woke refreshed. The after effects of unleashing all her magical energy at once had subsided, and she was back to almost full strength. Upon waking, she found herself on a wooden bed instead of the floor. *I must've fallen asleep; I wonder how long I slept.*

Haara was standing silently next to Wizera, examining her with a relieved expression. "You sure were lucky that I found you when I did."

The Silver Sorceress nodded. "Yeah… How long was I asleep?"

"Almost two days. But considering what you did, it should've been more than that. You're a piece of work; I'll give you that."

*Two days…* That was more than Wizera would've wanted. She was not in a position to waste time. And that was even before the recent events. *Finding Haara was a must to restore the bo —*

"The book," Wizera gasped. "Where is it?"

"Relax," Haara answered swiftly as she pointed at the round table. "I guessed, that apart from wanting to see me, you came seeking my help as well. So, when I saw that beaten-up tome, I figured you wanted me to restore the ink and paper on it." Haara paused and stared into Wizera's eyes without uttering a word. Her look was one of concern. "Now, do you mind telling me why you carry a necromancy book with you? What have you gotten yourself into this time?"

It took a while for the Silver Sorceress to fill in the blanks for Haara. She explained in detail what had happened to her over the past few weeks, with the earthen sorceress's expression revealing a profound sentiment of distress as she listened. After pondering the subject some more, and after taking a closer look at the manuscript, she offered Wizera definitive proof that it was indeed a necromancy book. *Perhaps Nez'rin would be best suited for unlocking its mysteries once its restoration is complete.*

"Wiz," Haara said, "there is something you should know. This is not an ordinary necromancy book, but rather a manuscript. It was written by someone more versed in the art of toying with death than an average necromancer. You should treat this with utmost care."

Wizera smiled at Haara's concern. "Don't worry; I will."

"After all, you have a son to return to when all of this is done."

The sorceress lowered her head in confusion. "How did you…"

"The earth speaks to me, old friend. And besides, I know that the world ain't undone yet, so I put two and two together."

A figment of memory passed through the Silver Sorceress's mind, stirring a sense of mourning within her. She lowered her head yet again, looking at the floor. It didn't take long for Haara to realize she had struck a nerve.

"I'm sorry, Wiz, I shouldn't have…"

"You have nothing to apologize for," she replied laconically.

"He is with the earth now. He is at peace."

"Yeah…" *If only I could believe so.* She wiped the tears of the past and dismissed the thought, for the present was more important. "You know, I could use a hand in all this mess."

Haara gave it some thought for a moment. She did not want to leave this place, where she had learned to live without the burdens and persecutions of society. Yet, she owed her life to Wizera many times over, and their friendship meant a lot to her. The earthen sorceress nodded and waved her hand at one of the interior walls of the house. After chanting a few words, the wall opened, and a gateway formed. "You're going to be the end of me one day. Lead the way."

Wizera smiled at the prospect of once again having a traveling companion. After so many bad experiences in her life, there were times when her perspective on the world was painted in bleak colors. She would often forget that she was not alone, that she had friends, not just family. "For old times' sake," she answered with a smile. They both entered the portal to report their findings to the Council of Mages.

# CHAPTER IV
# THE CHAINS OF LEGACY

Underneath the chambers of the Cathedral of The Light lay a series of underground tunnels. Used in the past as a maze that led to secret exits, including one near the nearby city, it was at the center of these ancient tunnels that Attern had awakened. With his vision still blurry and uncertain how much time had passed, he recalled the last moment in his memory: a betrayal. One that he would have never suspected, making it sting all the more when it happened. His advisor, his friend. Someone for whom mere hours ago he would've sacrificed almost anything for his sake. *Why? Why would he do this?* he thought. The absence of an answer was slowly eating away at him, yet he had more pressing concerns at the moment.

He looked around and saw himself chained by the wrists to a monument inside a circular room. Having recognized the architecture, he knew where he was. However, that posed little relief to him. He was deep underground, in a labyrinth that stretched across the cathedral grounds and much of the surrounding land. Help would not come here for him; he had to escape on his own. Every exit of the circular chamber was illuminated by torches, marking an increased frequency in their use by Baav and possibly whoever else he was working with. At this point, the old paladin was certain that his backstabbing advisor was not alone in this endeavor.

Isolated, surrounded by glimmers of light from the torches, and with his armor stripped from him, Attern's first thought was to check out the chains that bound him. They were ordinary chains: no enchantment, no magical seal, nothing. *Did Baav do that on purpose? Did he leave me with a chance to escape? Or did he belittle me so much so that he thinks magic isn't necessary?* It mattered not for now. After a few attempts to pull out the chains from their pivots, Attern concluded he had to resort to something else. He may have been a formidable warrior, but his strength was still within human levels at the end of the day. He panted and groaned as he made several more attempts to break free. Frustration was quickly building within him with each failure. He stopped and wondered what else he could do. He was not one to give up like that. Nor one who would accept to die in a place like this. From within the labyrinth, he began hearing noises — multiple footsteps, followed by the voice of the one who stabbed him in the back.

"I see you are as sturdy and obstinate as ever."

Attern licked his dry lips. His voice was guttural and heavy. "Baav… what did you do…?"

"At this point, I doubt you'd be able to believe in my words anymore, Highlord, but I meant it when I said that I was sorry for having to do this."

Judging by his lips and equally dry throat, Attern figured he must've spent at least a few hours without water. "What do you want with Thaidren?"

Baav let out a surprised look on his face. "So, you figured out that much. Well, I'm afraid the rest will have to remain a mystery to you. Once I am done wiping out the cathedral and claiming the prize, I will deal with you."

"Not… not if I kill you first," answered Attern with a groan.

"Kill me?" Baav asked, trying not to laugh. "You can't even speak properly, let alone free yourself or kill me." He slowly approached Attern's ear and whispered, "The Light has abandoned us, brother. You, in particular, more than others."

Attern did not have the opportunity to reply to his former friend. As Baav took a few steps back from him, dozens of footsteps could be heard from every tunnel of the maze. *Soldiers? Does he have his own army?* A more shocking discovery came when Attern saw what that army consisted of. *By all that is holy.* It was far worse than he ever expected. Out of all humans, Baav, an alleged servant of The Light, allied himself with fanatics who delved into the most blasphemous form of magic known to mankind: necromancy. The soldiers were walking corpses, reanimated, twisted puppets that should have been left alone, sealed in their graves. An undead army that would not feel pain nor stop until they had fulfilled the bidding of their master. Among them, several masked individuals marched as well. As they passed by Attern, one of them stopped and removed his hooded mask.

"How intimidating you looked when we first met at that inn," he said with a disappointed tone. "Truthfully speaking, I find myself mildly disappointed to see you like this." It was the same dark acolyte to whom Attern spoke back in Foreton. Despite the apparent discontentment in the acolyte's voice, his face had a satisfied grin on it. "How the mighty have fallen. But don't worry, we will take care of everything, Highlord." He pointed at another acolyte who was holding something wrapped up in a leather rug. It approached Baav, bent down on his knees, and unfolded what had been hidden from the eyes of the men and the prisoner.

"You have received permission to use it as you see fit," he said to the advisor. "For now."

Attern began to pant uncontrollably as he attempted to let loose a threatening shout. He struggled to break free yet again but fell to the floor exhausted.

"I know, I know," Baav said. "It was yours for a long time, but now I have been deemed worthy of using it."

The acolyte was holding Viz'Hock, Attern's longtime weapon before it was captured. A renounced and powerful artifact, strongly tied to the angelic powers whom the paladins serve.

"You... you don't understand... Baav" Attern desperately stuttered, as if trying to warn him.

Throwing an indignant look at him, Baav listened to the old paladin's words.

"You know all too well that the hammer cannot be wielded by everyone. You know that it doesn't hold just The Light in it."

Baav paused briefly before smirking. "I don't need The Light within hammer. No, no, no; I intend to use its TRUE power." He lifted the hammer and immediately felt a surge of energy rush through his body. Yet, it was not the blessed embrace of The Light that enveloped him. In a matter of moments, the hammer started to change shape. Like a lizard shedding its skin, the blunt end of the weapon fell off, with the remaining tip and the hilt beginning to sharpen as the artifact turned into a blazing crimson sword. The grip's end changed into a demonic-shaped skull, and even Baav's body started to change. His muscles began to grow, bursting out through his armor. The gloves he wore melted in a sudden burst of flames and revealed a pair of demonic hands with sharp claws.

He fell on his knees, with one hand gripping the weapon as he tried to keep his balance. Baav's shoulder-length hair grew even more and gained a pitch-black pigmentation. A pair of small horns emerged from his forehead, his skin turned red, and fiery, glowing veins appeared throughout his body. Even his eyes were no longer those of a human. They turned reptilian, red, glowing with bloodlust: demonic. Baav turned into the very creature that paladins had sworn to fight against. As soon as the pain ceased, he got back on his feet and let loose a beastly roar at Attern.

"This power… I can't believe we were so blindly ignorant. That we fought against it. That you refused it. I never thought of you to be a fool, until now," Baav cackled.

"That "power" will consume you," Attern answered.

"How would you know? You've denied it all your life." Having realized he was becoming angry and potentially unstable, Baav restrained himself, clearing his throat. "It matters not. It is time we take the boy." He gazed at Attern with a smug look. "And bolster the ranks of our undying army."

The undead slowly marched on through three of the corridors that led to exits near the cathedral. Attern continued to struggle in vain as he watched them move on, ignoring him. At least they had not killed him. He could still seize an opportunity to escape and help the others. Luckily, the cathedral was not short on skilled paladins that could face this threat. *But what about the students? And we're talking about a small army, after all. Most people here have fought small to medium groups of enemies at best. They are not ready for an open battlefield of this scale.* He had to do something, anything. Hoping he may have loosened up his bounds, Attern attempted to break free once more. But the chains wouldn't budge. He prayed for the blessing of The Light.

Light in heavens from above,

I call upon your blessed touch

Turn me into your vessel,

of might and strength

To seek out the darkness,

and drown it in your rays

To sever the head of the snake,

and set aflame its tail

By all that is light and holy,

grant me the power to vanquish evil,

For now, and forevermore

I am your tool; I am your servant.

Alas, nothing happened. Attern received no strength from the heavens. No answer. No help. He was alone here, where even The Light could not reach him. He would usually have supplies of magical items for this kind of situation, but all of his belongings and armor were taken from him when he was imprisoned. The monument he was bound to was somewhat similar to what he called The Dim Pillar. However, it had a completely different purpose. The labyrinth he was in could easily get a person lost in it for days, even with several exits at hand. This monument was a marking point, the center of the maze, but it was more than that.

On it, there was also an inscription. Carved long ago by someone not even remembered in these times, it held the words: Even in the darkest shadow, you can still find The Light. Do not despair and press on. It was a reminder to never give up. Attern had read these words before. He knew what was at stake here. It did not matter for him if his body would crumble. He would give his last breath for a chance to save the people at the cathedral. His friends, his family, he couldn't live with himself, knowing that they died because he gave up on breaking a pair of ordinary chains. His brothers, his sisters, his sons, and daughters. His sons… They all depended on him. The old paladin stood up yet again and repeatedly tried to pull off the chain pins from the ground and the monument. After several tries, his foot slipped and got grazed in a sharp small stone. A superficial cut, yet it added further hindrance in using that leg.

Suddenly, Attern stopped. He glanced at his foot and the blood dripping from it. A flash of memory brought a subtle smile to his face. He remembered a secret that an old paladin taught him long ago, back when Attern was about the same age as Thaidren and Aramant. The words of that precious memory echoed through his mind.

*If you find yourself in a situation where The Light can't help you, and you have little to no options, there is still something you can do. As paladins, we became akin to The Light's embrace, and even though we cannot store it in our bodies, we can absorb it from almost any source. But be warned that it is a dangerous technique to use, and it will leave a mark on you. Quite literally. You will need to draw a specific symbol on your body using your own blood. After that, you will be able to harness light estranged from the heavens for a short time.*

*I never thought it would ever come to using this,* Attern thought. *May The Light grant me strength.* He bit his thumb and drew a magical rune on his chest. As soon as he was done, the sign started to burn, as if it had been freshly branded using heated metal. A couple of moments later, Attern could feel his physical strength returning, exceeding that of his normal state. He was absorbing energy from the light generated by the torches. He stood up and grabbed the chain pins holding his arms with his hands. He then pulled as hard as he could, shouting as loud as his breath would allow him. The pivots began to move as he continued to absorb energy from the torches until the chains finally broke loose. He rested for a brief moment before doing the same with his leg chains. Now he had to preserve his remaining power and get out of the maze. He grabbed a torch and walked down one of the tunnels. *I'm coming, everyone. Please be well until I arrive.*

\*\*\*

Above the tunnels, near the Cathedral of The Light, Thaidren was enjoying a quiet evening by himself. He found a unique, private spot atop a hill nearby from where he could see both the cathedral and the closest clock tower. It offered a peaceful view, one that, in times of thought, helped him ease his mind. He leaned on one of the larger trees on the hill and watched the sunset. However, that spot was neither a secret nor exclusive to him.

"When I couldn't find you anywhere, I figured you'd be here," he heard from behind.

Thaidren was not bothered by Nebrina's presence. Although he wasn't sure why his handler came here. "If you want, have a seat and enjoy the view."

Nebrina, one of The Five Lanterns, leaned her arm on the same tree near Thaidren.

He did not look her in the eye, yet he felt her gaze on him.

"We still can't find him," she said after a few seconds of silence.

"I am not worried. Maybe he went off on business again," he said in an attempt to sound indifferent.

Nebrina, on the other hand, did not share the same alleged apathy. "The Highlord wouldn't do that without saying a word to anyone. Plus, I doubt he would leave again so soon after his return. He rarely leaves to begin with."

"You worry too much, Master. The church can survive for a day or two without him."

"Cathedral. Not 'church.' You know the difference all too well," Nebrina snarled.

"Yeah," Thaidren smirked, "one word annoys you, the other doesn't."

"Watch your tongue, disciple. Don't forget your place." She sighed, then softened her tone. "I'm sorry. It's just that I find it strange for the Highlord to be missing like this."

"Have you spoken to every — " Thaidren stopped mid-sentence.

Nebrina followed his gaze and found herself speechless as well.

They both saw a dark mass in the distance heading toward the cathedral.

Nebrina snapped out of her shocked state first. "Heavens protect us, is that an...?"

Thaidren turned to her. "GO. Sound the alarm and prepare everyone. I'll catch up with you."

There was no time for further chatter. Nebrina could not afford to wait for someone fully donned in heavy plating like Thaidren. Wielding a short sword and a dagger, combined with her choice of thinner, lighter armor, she rushed down the hill, hoping that maybe someone else at the cathedral might have seen them. The Lantern yelled as loud as her voice would let her. "Sound the alarm! We are under attack!"

Thaidren grabbed his swords and followed her. *What the hell is happening here? Why would anyone attack this place?* However, their priority now was to gather intel on who the enemy was and what their weaknesses were. Only after that would there be room for their motives. Yet, it seemed strange for anyone to show interest in a place like this, other than those who wanted to train here, of course. He had to gather the men. In the absence of Attern, he figured that The Five Lanterns would have to assume command.

Nearing the cathedral, Nebrina arrived to warn the people of the imminent threat. The alarm bells rang throughout the entire area, alerting everyone to ready themselves for combat.

Illia and Aramant were the first to talk to her. "What's happening?" they both asked at the same time.

Nebrina panted for a few moments before managing to catch her breath. "There's... an army. They're heading toward us."

"Wait a minute. Are you sure they are hostile?" Illia asked.

"Trust me, they did not seem friendly. There is something ominous about the army. I can feel it, but I am not sure what it is yet."

Illia nodded and turned her gaze upon Aramant. "Gather everyone and organize them into battalions. Then find the rest of the Lanterns."

"Not every Lantern is here now. From what I know, Kelsi and Vermizi are both away, each on their own mission," Aramant said.

"Dammit. Just find Issin and explain the situation to him!"

Aramant left to fulfill his order. The two Lanterns looked at each other, each expecting the other to come up with something.

"The Highlord is missing, and so are two of our best paladins. I doubt this is all a coincidence," said Nebrina.

"Do you think that they're...?"

"There's no time to assume now. We must concentrate on repelling the invaders."

Illia smiled. "Hmph, it's been a long time since we fought side by side, Master."

She responded in kind. "Yeah... it has been."

Most of the paladins at the cathedral were still confused as to what was happening. As Aramant left in search of Issin, he guided the men to the main road, where Illia and Nebrina were standing. In the meantime, Thaidren had arrived back from the hill and was doing the same. On his way to the main road, he ran past the graveyard. It was then that he stopped for a moment, in shock. From the crypts of the cemetery, undead soldiers began to rise. Their aim seemed to revolve around getting inside the cathedral and the living quarters. At the graveyard's entrance, Issin and several paladins were desperately trying to hold them back. Yet, they were constantly pushed further and further back. Thaidren decided the best course of action was to join them while hoping that Nebrina and Illia would manage to find reinforcements from elsewhere.

"What in the bright sky is happening here?" Issin asked.

"There's an army marching toward the main road. Nebrina should already be there by now," Thaidren answered.

"And what about this blasphemy? Who — What — are we fighting?"

"Your guess is as good as mine."

"Well then, whoever this unknown enemy is, he, she, or they are toying with the dead. A feat that not many people can do with ease."

It was the first time for Thaidren, and many others, to see an actual undead, let alone a small army of them. They knew that such abominations could be summoned into the world. Still, to experience it firsthand was something no book, lesson, or other teaching sessions could prepare one for. The stench of the rotting flesh, the sinew hanging and falling off their brittle bones, the empty eye sockets, and the blackness within them. People were hesitant to fight such creatures, to say the least. Nevertheless, they had to. Among those fighting at the graveyard was Epton, Aramant's childhood friend. Upon seeing him, Thaidren grabbed the mute paladin by the shoulder.

"Go and find Aramant," he said. "Get him here along with as many people as you can."

He nodded and ran off. The other warriors on the main road were probably unaware that they were also about to be ambushed from behind. But at least they were not fighting the undead. Or so Thaidren thought.

Back at the main road, the army got close enough for Nebrina and the others to understand what they were going to face: a legion of undead soldiers, dark acolytes, and worst of all, a demonic behemoth among their midst. Towering any human or undead there, it would stand to reason that he was the one in charge. Capturing him may prove helpful in the long run, yet it posed no priority unless they found out he was the mastermind behind the attack. Nebrina and Illia charged forward, followed by several battalions of paladins, each of them ready to defend their home and loved ones.

"Chaaaaargeee!" Illia shouted.

The demon pointed forward with the tip of his sword as the undead started to rush ahead. Snapping their jaws and screaming beyond the sounds akin to the living world. The two armies clashed. Everywhere, maces, swords, and axes met one another in battle, some shattering and some bringing their wielders victory. The stench of the dead had been quickly accompanied by the smell of fresh blood spilled on the battleground. Baav, with his new demonic powers, would send dozens of his former companions into oblivion with a mere swing of his sword. He would set them ablaze, then reabsorb the fires so that the corpses could be raised as new soldiers in his army.

Nebrina and Illia were fighting back-to-back, crushing as many undead soldiers as twenty capable paladins could. Nebrina waved her hand over her dagger, then her short sword as they began to glow with the brilliance of The Light. She continued to slash through the ranks of the undead, yet it felt as futile as scooping out water from a lake using a pierced bucket.

In the distance, Baav noticed her presence and started to move toward her and Illia. They were two of The Five Lanterns, after all. It would be better for him to take care of them first, to tip the scale of the battle in his favor even more. However, his newly-gained, superior body granted him more strength and magical power at the cost of more sluggish movement. He pursued without haste, relishing the thought of what he would do upon reaching them.

At the graveyard, the situation had rapidly escalated from bad to worse. The vast number of undead soldiers that came out from the crypts were flooding the area. Thaidren and the rest were repeatedly pushed back, with no chance to repel them faster than others would take their place.

Issin was already beginning to feel the strain of fighting too long. "We're getting nowhere. If this goes on for much longer, they will reach the graveyard exit, and they'll be able to move freely."

"They've already started." Thaidren pointed at parts of the graveyard's surrounding fence-walls. Many of the risen had already climbed or jumped to the other side. Things would soon get out of hand for the warriors of The Light.

"We HAVE TO close the way out. Even if we have to destroy the crypts themselves. Thaidren, buy me some time."

Thaidren nodded as he ordered the men. "Everyone! Form a circle around Master Issin. Defend him at all costs."

Issin grabbed him by the shoulder. "After I'm done, you'll have a few moments to seal the entrances." There were five crypts in total, and Issin knew that Thaidren was the best person present to destroy them. *By using his ice magic, he should be able to block the entrances, maybe even collapse the crypts' interior on the undead.* With that thought, the oldest of The Five Lanterns let go of Thaidren and focused on his task. He kneeled, closed his eyes, turned his head to the sky, and started to pray.

"Hold them off," Thaidren yelled in an attempt to inspire the other paladins. "We can do this." Between the clashing of weapons and the screams of both the dead and the living, it was hard to say who could hear him. As for the young warrior himself, he was cutting through the ranks of the enemy like a scythe over a field of grains. So far, he had not tapped into his elemental powers. It was necessary to preserve them until the time was right; for when the crypts would become accessible. He felt rushed by a temptation to unleash his magic but dismissed the thought.

Seconds passed on as if they were minutes. It did not take long before Issin stood up and raised his hand, pointing at the sky, his eyes still closed. From the darkened skies, a surge of radiating light came forth to surround him. It went straight into the earth, creating a shockwave of pure light that dissipated the remains of the undead, cleansing the foul magic that moved their brittle bones and turning them back into what they should be: corpses. Although many of them were outside the range of the attack, the shockwave cleared enough of their ranks to give the paladins a chance. Thaidren rushed as fast as he could to the two closest crypts and froze the entries off. The crackling of ice and the bony shrieks of the undead trapped inside painted a horrific image of death and chaos around him. He turned his attention toward the remaining three, stacked up in a line, and reached out to them. While having to deal with the newly-surfaced soldiers, he briefly sensed something. Between the clanking of metal and the inhuman sounds of the undead, he faintly heard something reminiscent of a human's voice. A presence, not too deep inside the fourth crypt, panting and screaming. *There's someone in there*, he thought. *But how? No. It cannot be...* Even though logic dictated otherwise, Thaidren decided to run past the third crypt and go straight to the fourth. Issin saw him as he slowly recovered after channeling the powers of The Light.

"What are you doing, boy?" he screamed at him in vain. They were too far apart, too much noise between them.

Thaidren reached the fourth crypt and ran inside, going through the undead army, tackling them, breaking their bones, and throwing them down the passage's stairs. Within the deep passageways below, he saw a flicker of roving light, similar to a firefly. Upon taking a closer look, he realized it was none other than Attern, still absorbing light energy from his torch while fighting off the undead. The image petrified the young warrior for a split second as his mind struggled to accept the reality before his eyes. A paladin, in his late years, with no weapon or armor, trapped underground and slaughtering unnatural monstrosities, all by himself. He quickly let out a mighty war cry before rushing to Attern's aid.

"Attern," he shouted with a sense of both relief and surprise.

"Thaidren. Thank The Light!"

"No time… We have to get out of here. Can you run?"

The old paladin was exhausted from fighting the undead and in a terrible state. "I'll try," he answered.

Outside, Issin received reinforcements from Aramant, whom Epton had found minutes ago. With their help, they managed to hold off the undead march but barely. They still couldn't advance to the crypts to seal them off. Not to mention the already defeated soldiers had formed piles of bone and rotten flesh that blocked their way.

"Nebrina and Illia are at the main gate. They need our help as well," Aramant said to Issin.

"Right now, I'm more concerned that WE need some extra help," replied The Lantern. At the same time, he was convinced that Thaidren had perished inside the fourth crypt. *He couldn't have survived fighting so many of them. Damn, he was the best-suited man to take them down*, he thought. He could not wait any longer, simply holding off the horde of abominations was not an option. Somehow, they had to start advancing. "Ok, men," he shouted, "I'm going to give you ten seconds to build up your courage and take a deep breath, after which we are somehow going to march forward and bury the bastards!" The countdown was as much for his men as it was for himself. "I want you all to give one hundred and ten percent, and may The Light protect us all." Aramant started praying, and his sword glowed with light. Some of the more experienced paladins followed his actions.

"Onwaaaarddddd!" Aramant let out a battle cry before pressing on, slashing one undead after the other, Issin right behind him. Despite being shaken up by the surge of energy he unleashed earlier, The Lantern still kept up with Aramant. They continued to do their best to advance, but even with two of the crypts sealed off, it was challenging to progress more than a few steps at a time. With the brink of exhaustion steadily closing in, taking a break to even catch their breath meant slowing down their already sluggish advancement, a predicament in which Issin was aware that the men could not keep up with for long. But there was no turning back now. Either they sealed the tombs off, or they would die trying. While pressing on, Issin tripped and fell to the ground. He continued to fight even then as he slashed the feet of some of the undead soldiers near him.

Aramant rushed to his superior's side and offered him his hand. Yet, in doing so, he exposed himself by letting his guard down. One of the skeletal soldiers managed to land a blow with its sword on Aramant's shoulder. His armor blocked most of the attack, leaving him with only a superficial cut.

The group had nearly reached the third crypt entrance. Issin's gaze shifted toward one of the heavy-armored paladins in the group. He wielded a two-handed mace that could easily break the brittle bones of the undead in a single swing. He rushed toward him and signaled to switch weapons, lending him his sword and shield and taking the hammer. His goal lay one step farther, and as soon as he reached the crypt, he swung the hammer as hard as his strength would allow him, destroying a segment of the lower structure of the burial catacomb. Other hammer-wielding paladins followed suit, under the hope that their brothers in arms would be able to defend them.

Their efforts were rewarded as the third crypt fell apart, the undead coming out of it being buried beneath its rubble. *Only two more to go now*, thought The Lantern as he took a couple of seconds to catch his breath. Alas, Issin's squadron could not advance anymore. Wherever he looked, he saw each of his fellow paladins outnumbered and overwhelmed. One by one, they fell to the ground, lifeless and drenched in blood.

Aramant's movements became slower, less coordinated, as did his reflexes and focus; a consequence of the long battle. At this point, panic started taking root in his mind. His survival instincts compelled him to run away, but it was not in his character to do so.

*Don't think, don't think... Don't THINK!* he thought as he continued to fight on. He swung his weapon, hitting a dozen undead and shattering their bones only to gaze at the hundreds of others that would take their place. He was struck again, this time near his wrist. He dropped his weapon, and in a short burst of fear, he took a step away from it, leaving himself unarmed. *This is it,* he thought. *It's over. We're going to die.*

His moment of discouragement was interrupted by the image of Issin rushing to his aid. After clearing the undead surrounding the young paladin, he threw a hard punch at him.

"Snap out of it, boy!" he shouted as if he seemed ready to kill him himself. "You can give up when you die. Not a moment sooner!"

His words reached the young paladin, redirecting his fear for a brief moment and bringing him back to his senses. After that, he felt a strong sentiment of relief to have someone like Issin leading him. He quickly grabbed two shields, discarded by their nearby fallen friends, then placed himself back-to-back with Issin, constantly rotating in the swirl of undead that surrounded them. Where Aramant would focus on the defense, Issin would concentrate on landing the improperly-said killing blows. Having no other choice at this point, they started stepping back from the remaining crypts.

"What are we going to do?" asked the young paladin.

Issin remained silent. On the one hand, he was too preoccupied with fighting. On the other, he did not know how to answer. "I don't know yet, but we'll have to find another way to get there. Fast."

The only place they could retreat to was the graveyard entrance. It would be a tighter, easier-to-defend spot. That is, assuming the enemy wouldn't climb up the graveyard walls again. The remaining paladins attempted to regroup at their location, in a small formation. For better or worse, at least now they were coordinated once more.

As the fight pressed on, aid seemed to have come in the form of arrows shot by some of the less combat-suited disciples from the cathedral tower. Circumstances dictated that anyone capable of lending a helping hand would do so, despite their status. Inside its walls, the medical staff were preoccupied with treating the critically injured that were brought back. After that, they would have time to help the ones outside.

*Arrows, shot from the top tower.* Issin's thoughts turned to an idea. He knew that inside the cathedral, in the basement, sat canisters of flammable oil.

"We need fire," he yelled at the people in the tower, hoping they would hear him. "We need fire," he shouted several times over to make sure his words were heard. Aramant and the rest called along with him. If they could incinerate the graveyard or at least a part of it, they might turn the situation in their favor. One of the archers above nodded and ran back inside.

"Bring the oil canisters from the basement! ALL of them!" he commanded.

Outside, Issin and the others were desperately trying to hold off the undead at the gates until their newfound plan could be set into motion.

"Hold them off, men. Just a few minutes." Glancing to the side for a moment, Issin noticed that his fears were coming true. Several dozen undead soldiers had climbed the graveyard walls and stormed the outside without resistance. He signaled to some of the paladins to go and hold them off by any means necessary. With the number of troops under his command slowly decreasing, he soon realized that only he, Aramant, and a handful of others were left to defend the gate.

"They're too many," he heard one of the paladins yelling from a distance. The screams of the wounded and those still able to fight echoed across the cathedral grounds. Shortly after, the sounds of agitated horses housed at the stables could be heard. Understandably so, as it was the closest structure to the graveyard not blocked by a gate. The undead that had managed to get outside had ended up driven to the stables by the squeals and screeches of the horses. Aramant remained silent. He was terrified himself, but at this point, he realized he could only fight back for as long as possible.

"Do not leave my side, boy," Issin said to him. "I want to look Attern in the eyes with pride as I tell him how we both survived, so stay with me, and don't you dare lose your focus." Issin was just a few years younger than Attern, yet their history together could fill at least one book. There were countless instances in which they had fought side-by-side, like brothers in arms, similar to how he was fighting alongside Aramant now. Despite the dire situation they were in, the atmosphere stirred a subtle feeling of nostalgia within him. He would not let the son of his friend die here. And he would prefer to emerge from this alive too.

Aramant nodded at him and let out a war cry as they continued to hold the gate. Considering the number of enemies that had gone past the walls, it quickly became a back-to-back situation again. Within a few moments of their reaching exhaustion, a voice from the cathedral's bell tower yelled:

"Incoming!"

What followed was the sound of shattering ceramics on the graveyard grounds, soaking the earth and undead in flammable oil.

Issin let out a battle cry and shouted alongside Aramant. "Fireeee!"

On the other side of the graveyard, Thaidren was trying his best to defend Attern as they made their way back outside. Exhausted and without a decent weapon, the Highlord could barely fight back anymore. The only element in their favor was that Thaidren managed to freeze and collapse the tunnel behind them, leaving only one more crypt from which undead soldiers came. Nevertheless, more enemy forces were heading toward them, blocking the exit. At the same time, the majority of the undead continued their assault on the cathedral. At this point, Thaidren had depleted a considerable amount of his magical energy. If he were to use more, he might risk exhausting his physical stamina as well.

"Come on, just a bit more," he said to Attern as they slowly pressed on.

The beaten Highlord could only pant and nod at him while trying to be as little of a burden as possible. He still had some time left from the light-absorbing symbol on his body, yet its borrowed power was leaving him with each passing moment.

As they climbed the final steps outside the crypt, Thaidren felt a surge of adrenaline. He made use of his heavy armor plating again by tackling the corpses that stood at the exit. Before he could exit to clear a path for Attern, the sound of oil canisters breaking made him pause. With a glance upwards, he quickly understood what had happened so far and what the others planned. As soon as he saw the archers at the tower windows, aiming at the ground with fire arrows, he rushed back inside the crypt.

The ground caught fire, scorching the corpses of the defeated and preventing the remaining undead from exiting the last crypt. Unfortunately, it prevented Thaidren and Attern from getting outside as well.

*Dammit*, thought the young warrior. *We have to get outside the graveyard somehow.*

Attern lay a few steps behind his protege. Seeing Thaidren backing up, he figured that something outside was not right. He then saw him getting closer as the clear view outside the crypt's exit was blocked by a dense layer of burning smoke.

"They burned the graveyard grounds," Thaidren said while helping Attern climb closer to the exit.

Attern's eyes quickly opened. "Did... did they use oil?" he struggled to ask.

"Yes, they threw canisters from atop the bell tower."

The beaten-up face that resided on the Highlord showed a brief, subtle smile. "We need to get out!"

"What? We cannot get past that fire," Thaidren said. "And even if we do, the smoke is going to — "

"Thaidren..." Attern waved his hand, pointing toward the exit, "have faith."

*Has he gone mad?* It was the first time that Thaidren asked himself such a thing regarding Attern. He dismissed the idea quickly. He had known him for so long. He began seeing him as a fatherly figure a long time ago. He may not trust the fiery embrace outside, but he did trust the old paladin with his life. Without any more hesitation, Thaidren signaled Attern to grab him with his hand on his shoulder and they started moving toward the exit.

The smoke was too dense for them to see or breathe properly. Attern started struggling from Thaidren's grasp, trying to drop to the ground. At first, he was afraid that he felt his lungs burning from the inside and couldn't handle the pain. The thought of returning to the crypt did cross his mind. However, no sooner than Thaidren had time to react, the Highlord touched a spot of burning oil. He groaned for a moment, then, before Thaidren's eyes, the fire started to change its color to a bright yellow. The old paladin was sanctifying the ground and the flames covering it, turning it into a holy fire. He also used the painted symbol's ability to draw out the flames' energy, healing some of his lesser injuries and regaining some of his strength back. He panted briefly as he stood back up and put his hand back on Thaidren's shoulder.

"Let's get out of here," he said. "The fire will not harm us now."

Trusting, yet hesitant, Thaidren pressed on with Attern through the smoke and scorched ground. Covering their faces as best as they could to avoid inhaling the smoke, Attern stumbled across one of the two-handed maces of the fallen paladins. He tossed the rusty weapons he had picked up from the undead and took a firm grip on it. At his side, Thaidren was still feeling unease. The flames did not harm him, just as Attern said, but the heat and the smoke were still a real threat. In an attempt to find himself a waypoint of a sort, he reached with his arm to the closest wall. He soon realized that it was one of the last of the crypt's inner walls, from which undead soldiers still poured out before meeting their end at the hands of the infused fire.

With the flames being holy in nature, as soon as any of the dead soldiers touched them, they would be instantly turned back to their natural state. The crypt's exit was already halfway blocked by the pile of bones gathered from the mindless undead that attempted to get out. Yet Thaidren and Attern could not leave it unattended, for when the fire would cease, the abominations would resume their march. He pointed at Attern's mace and signaled him to give it to him. Similar to how Issin broke the lower structure of one crypt, so did Thaidren with a few swings. Now all the burial tombs had been sealed, and the undead were buried underneath the graveyard's scorched grounds. However, there were still some remnants of the army that needed to be taken care of.

As soon as they got out, Thaidren rushed with Attern toward the cathedral.

"Help," he shouted. "The Highlord is wounded and in dire need of medical assistance."

Upon reaching the cemetery exit, Aramant spotted Thaidren carrying his father. His desire to go to them was stopped by Issin's hand, which grabbed his arm.

"He's going to be fine. We still need to focus on the task at hand. It's not over yet."

A fiery explosion in the distance made it clear that this was no place for Aramant to argue. He let out a subtle nod and rallied the men as they began preparing to head toward the main road to assist Nebrina and Illia.

Several members of the medical staff took Attern and placed him on one of the tables in the dining hall, which served as an emergency, improvised infirmary. One of them looked toward Thaidren and nodded.

"Go," she said, "we'll take care of him for now. You're needed outside."

Before leaving, Thaidren took a quick look at the medical ward. He wanted to see how many injured were there and who they were. He could not spot Nebrina or Illia. That could only mean that they were still fighting or... *No,* he did not want to think of the alternative.

The young warrior walked back outside, culling off the remaining few undead soldiers who had gotten out of the graveyard before it had been incinerated. Shortly after, he spotted Issin and Aramant, and some other fellow paladins doing the same.

Issin felt relieved that he was wrong about Thaidren's demise. "Glad to see you in one piece, son," he said, smiling.

Thaidren shared his sentiment, yet the time to celebrate was still a long way off. The battle was far from over.

"The crypts are all sealed."

"So I've noticed," replied Issin. "But back to more pressing matters, Nebrina and Illia are holding their forces at the main road. Most of our troops are there."

*So, their main force was not the one at the graveyard?* Thaidren felt discouraged to hear that. They had already gone through what seemed like enough to last a lifetime, let alone what awaited them next.

"Where did they get so many bodies? Even the ones from the graveyard aren't enough to justify their numbers," Thaidren said.

"There must be something else. Maybe the crypts connect to somewhere else," replied Issin.

"It's either that or…" Aramant paused mid-sentence, shocked at the thought, "or they slaughtered a nearby city."

*The Foreton Harbor in Leor…* It became clear to everyone that some of the enemy forces were not long-ago mere citizens of the port. Their population was in the thousands. The opening to the sea would have also allowed the enemy to bring their undead forces by ship. A gruesome perspective, to say the least, yet there were many people in this world capable of such horrors.

"Enough," Issin said abruptly. "We need to go to the main road and support our fellow paladins. We can chitchat later."

Thaidren put his hand on Issin's shoulder. "You should go to the medical ward."

Issin pulled away from his arm. "As long as I have breath in my lungs, I will continue to fight these monstrosities. Besides, I want to have a "conversation" with the one leading them."

Seeing he had no way of convincing The Lantern to back down, Thaidren's attention shifted to Aramant.

"I… found Attern," he said.

"I saw you dragging him inside the cathedral. How is he? Is he safe?"

"For now, he needs to rest. The medical ward is taking care of him. I don't know how or what he was doing there, but he was underground, near the exit of the fourth crypt."

Issin was beginning to understand. *So that's why he ignored the third one and rushed to the fourth.* He looked at Aramant, knowing he would probably want to go see him. He shook his head in dissent. "Be at his side when he wakes, victorious and alive."

Aramant did not answer. He looked at Issin, then at Thaidren. After a brief moment, he clenched his fist and tightened the grip on his weapon.

Issin looked at both Aramant and Thaidren with concern. He knew all too well that they could not stand each other. Yet he hoped that when the situation demanded it, they would be able to cast aside their quarrels and fight alongside one another. He took a short moment of reprise and sighed before turning in the direction of the outer road.

"Unfortunately, the undead have massacred most of the horses at the stables. We were only able to save a few of them by cutting them loose. They fled long ago." He paused for a moment. "We will reach our brothers and sisters on foot. Anyone have a problem with that?"

Thaidren, Aramant, and the few remaining paladins shook their heads.

"Good. Now, let's go, men. Let's show them what it means to mess with servants of The Light."

# CHAPTER V
# FADING CANDLES

As Thaidren, Issin, Aramant, and the remaining squadron of paladins that defeated the graveyard assault forces were heading toward the main battlefield, the situation there seemed unfavorable for the warriors of The Light. Even without Baav's constant decimation of the lower-ranked troops, there were still acolytes using the element of shadow as a means to kill from a distance. In the meantime, the undead army served as a shield for them. The destruction they inflicted was merely an added bonus. Inside the chaotic amalgam of clashing weapons and the elements of shadow and light trying to overcome one another, Nebrina and Illia ended up separated. With Nebrina noticing Baav in her proximity, the two of them were now advancing toward each other. Nebrina, however, was not alone. She was surrounded by a squadron of spear-wielding paladins, all of them wearing heavy-plated armor. They were also equipped with massive greatshields that could protect them to some extent from the brutal swings of the demonic commander.

The squadron aligned their shields into a triangular formation, slowly advancing in a coordinated and steady manner. None of them had been injured nor died so far because of that. With their shields surrounding them, they created a barricade that the undead soldiers could not break. Aside from them, there were other, similar formations scattered across the battlefield.

"Maintain the formation!" It was something that they would hear frequently. They had to compensate for their lack of numbers with sheer discipline and efficiency. Although the greatshields provided them with heavy protection, they also impeded their vision. For now, the trade-off was worth it.

From the grounds closer to the cathedral, bolts of pure light were shot by the most advanced clerics to repel some of the undead masses. It was also a means to strike the shadow acolytes from afar. The biggest problem that the paladins had at the time consisted of the time of day, namely nighttime. It bolstered the abilities of those who used shadow while diminishing the powers of The Light as well. Unless sunrise was near, the circumstances were unfavorable to the paladins.

At this point, Nebrina was too focused on Baav to worry about the squadrons. *Illia should be able to manage without me,* she thought. *I need to cut off the head of the snake. Perhaps that'll put an end to this bloodshed.*

With only a few steps separating Baav from Nebrina, a confrontation between the two of them was inevitable. The traitorous advisor leaped right through his own troops, eager to speed up the battle's progress. With a single blow from above, aimed toward her, he cracked half of the shields that her comrades rapidly placed between Nebrina and the blade engulfed by flames. The strike had mostly frightened her as she ended up with just a few superficial, small burns and a minor scratch from dodging the attack.

Baav quickly raised his sword. This time he thrust it into the ground, creating a flaming explosion that scorched anyone within a few meters. Nebrina and a couple of the remaining soldiers managed to hide behind the last remaining greatshields. The shields would probably resist one or two more attacks at best before turning into melted metal. Their struggle for survival was compelling Baav to grin. He was pleased to see how his display of power terrified his enemies from the bottom of their souls. It was intoxicatingly good. He wanted more. He did not want it to end this fast. *No…* he would revel in this for as long as possible before seeking out his next victims. He waved his colossal hand, signaling the undead and acolytes alike to avoid the charred area. It was his arena now, his playground.

Nebrina was furious that the demonic entity would think so low of them. At the same time, she was relieved the undead army wouldn't bother her anymore. The other two remaining soldiers near her were chaotically turning around and around like trapped rats desperate to escape.

"We're going to die," one of them screamed.

Without a moment's notice, Baav grabbed the soldier and put some distance between himself, Nebrina, and the other soldier. What followed was a pure display of how estranged he had become from being human. He quickly tore apart the armor of the paladin, starting with his helmet. As he struggled in vain to break away from the demon's grasp, Baav proceeded to feast upon his flesh while still alive. Starting with his ears, followed by small bites of his face, his cheeks, to one of his shoulders. Some parts he devoured like a savage animal. Others, he ripped off while reveling in his victim's painful screams.

Nebrina and the other paladin turned pale. They could not move a single muscle from the shock. In the distance, Illia saw what was happening, but it almost came at the cost of her life as fear paralyzed her. She figured that Nebrina must've been there, but she had no means nor time to help her. *May The Light protect you, sister. May it protect us all.*

While the grotesque feast upon one of her fellow brothers-in-arms continued, Nebrina finally came to her senses. She tried vigorously to slow down and stabilize her breathing. Yet, she was unable to stop herself from gasping. The Lantern turned her attention toward the last remaining soldier from her squadron. He stood beside her, unable to utter a word or move. She took off his helmet and slapped him.

"Hey… HEY!" she shouted. "It's going to be all right. Get yourself together!"

The soldier turned his horrified gaze from Baav, yet he was still in shock. His tongue would twist and articulate sounds but couldn't form words. He could only babble without making himself understood.

"Hey, soldier!" Nebrina continued. "What's your name? Tell me your name."

Finally, he stopped shaking and replied. "A… A… Altimor."

"Listen to me, Altimor," she whispered, "we don't have much time until he comes for us. I want you to calm down and STAY alive. I will end this demon's life. I give you my word, all right? So, hold on a little longer, please."

Altimor managed to force a nod despite his constant shaking.

As they raised their weapons back up, the screams of the partly-devoured paladin suddenly stopped. His torment was finally over. Baav, on the other hand, having his toy used up, once again set his eyes on Nebrina and Altimor. He let out a frightening roar and rushed toward them while still dragging the corpse he had consumed, intent on using it as a throwable hunk of meat. He ignited the mutilated body and hurled it toward them. They both dodged it, each in a different direction. Now there was some distance between Nebrina and Altimor. At this point, she had little to no time to analyze the situation and develop a strategy. *If he goes after him, I have to take the opportunity to at least try to disarm him if not go for the kill. But if he goes after me...* She was not reconciled with the idea of using her frightened brother in arms as a means of distraction. Nevertheless, she did not know what she would do if Baav decided to attack her first. It would be the most logical strategy, considering that she was more emotionally stable.

With the hungering demon a few steps away, it became clear to Nebrina that her assumption was correct. Baav was heading right toward her. And in her case, it did not seem like he was going for the play-with-your-prey move, case in which her only option was to try to successfully dodge his attack.

As he closed in on her, Nebrina felt a sense of time-slowing around her. She also felt incredibly calm, and at peace, in a manner she could not fully comprehend. *Is this how the last moments in someone's life feel?* She closed her eyes while dodging, convinced that she would get trampled by the demon's charge. She closed her eyes in anticipation while images flashed into her mind, showing her memories of better times. Memories with friends, with family. With the order of light, her family. Other instances when she thought she was done for, countless battles that she never wanted to have to fight in the first place. In an ideal life, she would have liked to live in a world where they wouldn't be forced to fight for food, territory, or survival. *Yet in the end, it was nice to dream of a world like that,* she thought. *I wish I could've said my farewells to them at least...*

Her thoughts did not last long, as Nebrina snapped out of her trance and opened her eyes. What she saw made her come back to Earth. Baav changed course and was leaning toward his right side. His right shoulder seemed to have burn marks. *But the only thing that can burn a demon's body is the power of the heavens.* The powers of The Light.

While in her trance, Baav had been shot from afar by several clerics who combined their beams of light to achieve a more powerful version of the spell. Upon taking a direct hit, he quickly lost balance and collapsed near the phased-out Lantern, almost letting go of his sword. It marked the perfect opportunity to strike. Nebrina gathered her strength and ran toward him while enchanting her sword with holy magic. She would not take any chances, aiming directly for the demon's throat. It was laughably unthinkable that a few seconds ago, she was at peace with the idea of her demise, only to witness a total turnaround of the tables of war, now unveiled before her eyes.

Illia managed to arrive with a second squadron of paladins from the opposite side of the scorched earth ring. As they approached Baav's collapsed body, she noticed the advisor clenching his fist and tightened his grip on the blade. With a swift move, he rotated his body and stretched his arm toward Nebrina. It ended up piercing her abdomen and setting her ablaze.

Nebrina fell to the ground. Filled with adrenaline, and without fully realizing the severity of her injury, she somehow managed to roll on the ground in a desperate attempt to extinguish the flames. Before she had the chance to finish, though, Baav got back on his feet and raised his fiery weapon in the air, readying it for another strike.

Illia witnessed this nightmarish scene from too far away to be of any help. "Nebrina!" she yelled to warn her. Unfortunately, there was too much noise surrounding them, and, within the next few seconds, the giant flaming sword descended upon Nebrina, instantly ending her life as it stirred the flames that engulfed her body even more. All that remained afterward was her charred, mutilated corpse.

An instant later, another concentrated beam of light hit Baav on the left side of his face. A direct impact that threw him off-balance yet again. His left eye was rendered useless, and the painful burn made him drop to his knees once again.

On the other side, Illia almost fell on her knees as well, but she shook it off with her immediate desire to enact revenge. She pointed to her men, and with a loose war cry, they began charging forward to finish what Nebrina started. All the speared paladins maintained the initial formation, dropping down their greatshields to add more running speed to their charge. Between ten and fifteen spears were now pointed at Baav, with the intent to put an end to his bloodlust.

The time for toying around was long overdue. Baav let out a fierce roar and waved his mighty weapon as soon as the squadron got within range. Some of them got hit and ended up being torn in half. Others managed to dodge the attack, including Illia. What followed was a swift, brutal tail sweep that knocked back those who survived the initial attack.

*He's trying to put some distance between us. He's starting to play defensively*, Illia thought. She approached him with caution this time, ready to avoid his attacks.

Baav readied his weapon to strike yet again but was interrupted as he tried to dodge another beam of concentrated light. He would not let himself be struck by the cleric's projectiles again. Some of the dark acolytes went into the arena to help their commander. In retaliation, the ever-crazed fiend swung his weapon at them, killing them instantly as punishment for their disobedience.

"I said to continue marching," he shouted with a threatening tone.

*Killing off his own soldiers... Monstrous tyrant...* While Illia gathered her thoughts, a hand from behind touched her on the shoulder. Her instinct was to swing the sword around and strike blindly. As she dismissed the impulse mid-air, she realized she had made the right call. Aramant, Thaidren, Issin, and a few other paladins arrived on the battlefield, bringing their support and reigniting the flames of hope in the hearts of the few remaining survivors. Their reinforcements laid eyes on Illia as she got back on her feet, ready to resume her fight with the monster ahead of them.

Thaidren gazed toward the group. There was no sight of Nebrina, only mutilated, scorched bodies on the ground. He assumed the worst: one such body was hers, lying as a lifeless carcass on the ground. A brief moment of blind rage compelled him to rush over to Baav and repay him for his display of bloodshed ten times over. Issin grabbed him and pointed out there was no need for that. All the while, the demon was running toward them already. He aimed to break their formation and massacre them in the chaos one by one. However, he had lost blood as well, making him slower and less focused. He was now posing as nothing short of a wounded, angry beast.

The majority of the group managed to get out of Baav's way. Thaidren, however, moved only slightly to his left side. The side where he could reach with his sword the easiest. Issin attempted to grab him, to pull him back, but did not reach him in time. The young warrior placed his palms on the ground and enveloped the surrounding ground with a thin layer of ice. The affected area was insignificant, yet it proved enough to make Baav aware of what he wanted to achieve. He slowed down and ended up between two separate groups of soldiers.

*He would have used his ice magic more if he aimed to make him lose balance and fall. No, he wanted to make him think that was his plan, in order to slow the demon down. To surround him and inevitably kill him, Issin realized. Clever, but it would still be hard to achieve.*

Within the first moment of the demon being surrounded, Aramant had struck the first blow, severing part of Baav's lizard tail and stirring him into a frenzy of anger and pain.

"Now," shouted Illia.

As all the remaining fighters proceeded to attack, they would make sure to make it count, even at the cost of their last, dying breath.

Aramant managed to strike one of the beast's legs. Two squadrons of paladins impaled his other leg while Illia scored a direct hit in his back. In the meantime, Thaidren charged at him, double-stabbing the monster in the chest and throwing him on his back while letting loose a war cry that pierced the skies above.

It was done. Baav fell to the ground and lost his grip on the flaming sword. His last corporeal sensations came in the form of his body reverting back to its natural, human form. Or at least partially. He felt the demonic energy fading, leaving his soul with nothing left but the inevitable journey to the great unknown abyss of his demise. His empty husk lay on the ground, lifeless and mutilated from both his transformation and his battle wounds.

The shocking realization of whom they had fought made everyone forget for a moment that the battle was not over. One of the spear-wielding soldiers was instantly impaled by a projectile made from the acolyte's darkness energy. It brought everyone back to their senses. They continued to fight the hordes of undead and the acolytes scattered amongst them.

# CHAPTER VI
# UNHALLOWED GROUNDS

In the distance, atop one of the hills that had a perfect view of the Cathedral of The Light, stood two silhouettes. One of them wore the attire of the acolytes, only more decorated. The other, older one seemed more akin to a sorcerer, judging by his choice of clothes and the dark, ominous-looking staff that he wielded. They were not interfering with the battle that transpired below. They merely observed from afar, in silence. Moments after they witnessed the fall of the demonized Baav, the shrouded mage began to speak.

"Seems our initiate failed us." He paused briefly. "A pity."

The decorated acolyte seemed still focused on the scenery before him. "The "face" may have fallen, but the "mind" and "limbs" are still working."

"The "limbs" are being severed as we speak," replied the mage.

"Should we consider intervening?"

A pronounced sneer covered the mage's face. "There is no need for us to expose ourselves more than we already have. We are more than prepared for minor setbacks like this." He pointed toward the battlefield. "Can you feel it?"

The acolyte seemed confused. "Feel what?"

"The overflow of death energy surrounding the place," the mage explained as he sniggered. "Hours ago, this was a sacred place. The holy grounds of the agents of The Light." He paused briefly to enjoy the moment while straightening his back. "And now, look at it. Defiled, decrepit, and tarnished. The Light has abandoned this place and left room for death's enveloping miasma. We may have failed to complete our mission, but we managed to deal a heavy blow to our enemies nonetheless."

"You sound a bit too pleased, considering that we did lose."

The mage turned his head over with a dismaying gaze at the acolyte. "Youth… The lack of vision… The desire to rush things…" His voice took a more saddened tone. "So much power. So many possibilities in the hands of those who won't appreciate them properly — "

"Nor profit from them?" the acolyte interrupted him, with his words bringing back the mage's grin.

"There may still be some hope for you left, boy."

"So, what follows now?"

"There is nothing more for us to do here. We're leaving." The shrouded figure waved his aged, frail hand and chanted a few words of power before opening a portal. "Come."

The acolyte was hesitant, maybe even a bit rebellious at the decision of his master. "Just like that? We're leaving?"

"Bigger picture," the mage answered before entering the portal, with the acolyte following suit shortly before throwing one last look at the battlefield, thinking of how different the outcome could have been. *Next time…*

***

Even after Baav's fall at the hands of Thaidren and the others, there was still a significant part of the remaining undead army that had to be dealt with. Most of the acolytes ran away, while those who survived but could not escape, killed themselves to avoid being taken as hostages and interrogated. From the road that led to Leor and through the Cathedral of The Light, the entire field was soaked in the blood of the paladins and acolytes who fell. The field was full of corpses, decorated with the bones and rotting sinew of the undead army. It was, as the mysterious figure who observed the entire battle said, that what was once a holy ground was now unhallowed, tainted, and dead. The remaining survivors looked around in silence, hoping to see one angle, one scene, anything that would not depict such a dreadful image.

Thaidren sheathed his weapons and gazed at the blood-soaked soil beneath his feet. Along with Aramant and Illia, they closed in to where Baav's mutilated cadaver lay. Issin was but a few steps further back. They looked at the fallen advisor for a few moments without saying anything.

The medical staff and the remaining personnel from within the cathedral interrupted the silence covering the battlefield. They rushed outward, horrified at the sight that lay before them as they desperately tried to distract themselves by aiding as many of the injured as possible.

"Well," said Thaidren as he looked at Issin, "you've had your conversation with their leader."

Issin was, like everyone else there, under too much distress to answer immediately. "I don't understand."

Among all of them, Illia was probably the one most affected by what had happened. Baav had always represented a fatherly figure to her. A flash of a distant memory came to her mind, distancing her from the present. It took The Lantern to a time when she was just a starving orphan who lived on the streets. One of her earliest memories was being caught trying to sneak into one of the food supply caravans for the cathedral people. Attern was not in charge of the place during that time, and the previous Highlord was not as warm-hearted as him. He had wanted to lock Illia in the dungeon and let her rot there for a few days or so, all for the sake of teaching her a lesson, as he put it. That's when Baav stood up for her and assumed full responsibility for her actions. He never forced Illia to stay at the cathedral, yet he welcomed her with open arms. In time she became respected, loved, and admired by the people from whom she attempted to steal food in the past. She never forgot the kindness that Baav showed her then and every day since.

Seeing him like this... It angered and confused her. Most of all, it made her want to cry. She saw the man she considered a father, killing one of her best friends, tens of others, and had even attempted to kill her — the one she'd always hoped he'd consider an illegitimate daughter — in cold blood. She fought against him when she had been confident that she would only ever have to fight for him. She wanted to say something but started to vomit from the shock. Issin patted her on the back as she leaned toward the ground. Then, he took her by surprise with a hug, a thing that he would never have done under normal circumstances. Not like he didn't care about her or the others, but rather that he believed more in tough love and discipline. After a few moments, Illia came to show her true feelings, tears washing over her cheeks and ultimately soaking the ground with grief and pain.

Aramant stood silent. It was not because he could not say anything; rather, he did not think there was anything worth saying. He felt betrayed as well. All those years, he considered Baav like a member of his family, an uncle who could provide wisdom and clarity to his thoughts whenever he or his father would…

"Father," he gasped. "I need to see him."

Thaidren hurried after him, leaving Issin and Illia behind.

As they approached the cathedral's open main gates, a sense of dread overwhelmed Aramant, making him stop for a second. *What if he's…?* he cut himself mid-thought. *No, no. He's all right. He HAS to be. He just has…* After taking a deep breath, the young paladin resumed walking toward the cathedral. Thaidren followed in his footsteps while maintaining a short distance between them. He figured it was better that way.

Right before entering the cathedral, Aramant ran into the head of the medical staff. A capable healer and a renowned priestess, Hamalia, waited for him at the entrance as she gently signaled the young paladin to stop. He did so right next to her, noticing that she avoided making eye contact.

"Hama…" he said.

She took Aramant's palms in her own, still fixated on the wooden floor. She murmured something, a short prayer that Aramant did not recognize. Only after did she dare meet his sight. Her lips were shaking, unable to speak without stuttering.

"I… I c-couldn't… I'm sor — "

Before she had the chance to finish, Aramant struggled from her hold and rushed inside the cathedral. All around, he could see his fellow brethren, mutilated by the battle that had taken place. Some of them had engulfed the halls with their agonized screams, while others appeared disturbingly silent. He made his way through to the far end of the main corridor that led to the dining hall. Inside, among other soldiers whose corpses were placed on the tables, lay the body of Attern.

Aramant was frozen to the spot. He started to shiver as if experiencing the coldest touch of winter. No words could come out of his mouth, no breath from his lungs, not even a blink from his eyes. Thaidren arrived a few moments later. His initial reaction was not that different than Aramant's, but he shook it off, knowing that whatever he felt paled in comparison to what the young paladin was feeling. After all, how could he know how it felt? He never had the chance to experience such trauma. For a brief moment, Thaidren almost felt relieved that he had not. However, Attern was still a fatherly figure for him, and seeing him like this was something that could not be described in words.

Aramant closed in slowly, gazing at his father's face. Behind him, Thaidren stood still. Hamalia entered the hall, but Thaidren held his hand up, signaling for her to stay where she was. All the while, Aramant began to talk softly, his words within reach of the others.

"Why are you looking like this, father?" he murmured at first, then his voice rose progressively louder and angrier. "You look so beaten up. I never would've imagined. What is this? Why are you looking like this? How could you allow yourself to lose? HOW?! You're supposed to be the damn Highlord!" His voice softened and shifted to a more saddened tone. "You're supposed to watch over us… You're supposed to be a model to us…" His voice became angrier once more. "You're supposed to protect us." He clenched his fist and hit the table, near Attern's head, repeatedly.

Thaidren could not stay behind any longer. He grabbed Aramant and tried to push him back from Attern. Under normal circumstances, Aramant would have responded violently toward him. Yet, this time, while he could not ignore Thaidren's grip, he chose to strengthen his own on Attern's body. The young paladin began shedding tears. It was unclear to him whether he was angry, sad, or both. Eventually, Thaidren managed to pull him away. The instant he did so,

Aramant grabbed him and squeezed the young warrior so tight it made him feel like passing out. Having assumed the worst, Thaidren managed to land a few punches on Aramant's back and shoulder, with only one hand free from his grasp.

Thaidren was so caught up in Aramant's violent grip that he hadn't even noticed the young paladin was not hitting, pushing, or trying to make him lose balance; rather, he was hugging him. Truth be told, it was unlikely that Aramant himself was aware of who he was holding in the first place. His mournful weeps drowned out those of the injured for what felt like hours. The battle at the cathedral grounds may have come to an end, and the paladins emerged as the victors, yet it did not feel like it.

Over the following couple of days, news about the attack at the Cathedral of The Light had spread like the rippling effect of a rock thrown into a lake. The remaining paladins requested aid from the neighboring settlements, both for the cathedral's residents and to help form search parties for Leor's potential survivors. Except for Hamalia and her medical staff, who were tending the wounded, the rest of the surviving members helped with the preparations for the funerals that would come.

Epton, Aramant's friend, was one of the many who were counted among the severe losses suffered that day. This news only strengthened the hollowness in the young paladin's heart. He continued to help anyone in need, but he had not uttered a word since his father's demise. He felt unsure of himself, could barely sleep, eat, or drink, and would often seek to distance and isolate himself from the others.

"He just seems… lost," said Thaidren.

"He's been through a lot," said Illia as they observed him from afar. "He more than the others." She patted Thaidren on the shoulder before throwing a sympathetic smile toward him. "Give it time."

Everyone around them was trying to cast aside the horrors that had transpired, even if only for a moment. Still, the vision of the cathedral standing as a beacon of hope for paladins all around the country now seemed like a distant memory. The outside, as well as its halls, were still painted with the blood of the fallen. The old graveyard was incinerated and decrepit. The Dim Pillar had survived, however, but it did not bring any form of consolation. After all, many names would soon be added to it.

It was decided that there would be two ceremonies: one for all the fallen paladins and one for the Highlord. The circumstances put Issin in a position where he was chosen to take on the mantle of leadership, at least for the time being. Despite him being reluctant to bear so many responsibilities, he was more than capable of handling them. However, he was not confident regarding one aspect of his leadership: inspiring and mending the hearts of those who followed him. He was never good at pep talks or speeches of any kind. Instead, he focused on the more palpable tasks that needed to be handled right away. One such task was to incinerate the graveyard once again, as it was now piled with corpses of both the undead army and their fallen paladin companions. *We will cremate most of the bodies,* Issin thought. *May The Light have mercy on us and let the fire cleanse their souls.* His focus shifted toward the living now. He realized that he had not heard from or seen Thaidren in the last hour. The thought turned his mind to the memory of a conversation he had had with Nebrina in the past. She said that whenever Thaidren wanted to be alone, there was a lovely spot, as she would put it, atop the hills from which he could see the entire cathedral. *Should I go check on him?* It did not take long for him to decide.

Atop the hills, away from the stench of the rotting corpses, Thaidren arrived at his favorite spot in the hope of clearing his mind, reminiscing, contemplating, and clearing the storm in his head. He had maintained a calm stature up until this point, seeing that Aramant's reaction was more than enough for everyone. However, once he found himself alone, he realized that the chaos in his head was just the beginning. His awareness of the real world was soon replaced with memories of Attern, along with the emotions they carried. From the days when Thaidren was but a child that arrived at the cathedral as near as only a few days ago, before this nightmare started. He could not hold his tears anymore, succumbing to an overwhelming stream of sadness and guilt. Suppose he would've heard Attern sooner; perhaps he could've done more for him when they escaped the graveyard. The thought would not give him rest. Amongst his volatile cocktail of emotions, in a brief moment of rage, the young warrior shouted and hit the tree with his fist, leaving a mark on its bark. He looked toward the ground at his falling tears, realizing he was being watched.

"A-hem… if it's a bad time, I can come back later," said Issin.

Thaidren did not answer, but he did sign with his hand that he didn't mind his presence. He leaned on the tree, as he had countless times in the past. Issin approached him. Before he started speaking, The Lantern gazed out at the view.

"Nebrina, may The Light rest her soul, once told me that this is something of a special place to you."

*Nebrina…* another name that belonged to the dead now. Thaidren grew up with her, trained with, and was trained by her. He viewed her as an older sister who would take care of him whenever he needed her, that she would want to teach him to be independent and strong.

"You know, we used to argue and tease each other about everything." He paused briefly as a fond memory traversed his mind. "Remember Eidri?"

There was no chance for Issin to forget that name. A few years back, Eidri was his apprentice and an exceptionally good one, to say the least. A part of him was happy that she hadn't been here now. After Issin had finished training her to become a paladin, she was reallocated directly to the main headquarters of the Congregation of Paladins. An impressive feat that made him and the other members of the cathedral proud of her. Yet, this was not the reason why Thaidren mentioned her.

"Of course I do. If I remember correctly, you had a soft spot for her and made a fool out of yourself."

They both began to chuckle. Even Thaidren, over time, became fond of the embarrassing memories he had of her.

"Yeah… she was my first crush" — His saddened face started to slowly show signs of a subtle smile — "and Nebrina knew about it."

Issin continued to laugh. "Boy, I think she knew about it before you did."

"Probably. Anyway, she wouldn't stop teasing me about it. Always telling me to go and tell her how I feel and stuff like that."

"And why didn't you?"

"I don't know. I guess I was timid, maybe a bit intimidated. She was admired by everyone at the church, and surely I wasn't the only one who liked her that way. Besides, she was older than me. In her eyes, I probably looked like a child."

"She is only three years older than you, you dense brat," Issin added with a sigh.

"Well, at that time, it seemed like a huge difference. At any rate, I remember how one day she came to me and asked if I wanted to spend some time with her."

"Boy, everyone remembers that moment."

"Yeah…"

"Because for some reason, your dumb self decided to panic and make a run for it before even letting the poor girl ask you out properly. You embarrassed yourself so badly that day, people still talked about it years after."

Thaidren simpered. "Not to mention the smacking Nebrina gave me after hearing it herself."

"She did not smack you because of that." He paused for a second. "Well, not for that alone."

"But for what else?" Thaidren asked.

"Because she wanted you to be happy, and seeing you sabotaging yourself pissed her off. I mean, you were trained to face demons and all kinds of monstrosities in battle. And, with that in mind, you ran… from a girl…"

"I wa — "

Issin interrupted him once again. "Not to mention that she was the one who told Eidri how you felt."

Thaidren was not expecting to hear this, yet he felt like he needed to. "She did what?"

"Well, after telling you God knows how many times to go and do it yourself, I figure she had enough of you and went to her in your stead."

"I should've guessed. She always helped me out. Even if it was by force."

"And look at you now, boy," he said. "You've outgrown the scaredy-cat that you were and became a man. A reliable one. One to whom I would entrust my life and safety. Just like Attern and so many others would."

The fact that Issin wouldn't usually say such things out loud made it all the more significant. Yet, the unease in Thaidren's heart could not be fully tempered by words alone.

"Yeah... Attern did that. Look where it brought him..."

Issin's face suddenly turned red with fury. "That's what you got from what I said, boy? By all that is holy, maybe I praised you too much earlier. Attern chose to trust you, and you should be honored by that."

"I am, bu —"

Issin's yelling silenced Thaidren's attempt at a response. "And the fact he died does NOT mean, in ANY way, that it's your fault. You stood there, with him, and fought side by side as best as you could. While many of our ranks were trembling in their boots at the sight of the undead, you plunged straight into their den, based on a hunch that someone was trapped there. God knows how many of those abominations he fought alone, in the dark, before you got to him. Hamalia checked him while trying to save his life and felt the same way as you afterward. I told her the same thing I'm telling you now. Neither of you is at fault for his death, and you'd better accept it. Stop loading yourselves with pointless guilt about it." His raging tone subsided, and changed to a saddened one. "His wounds... were severe, far before you found him. It was a miracle he survived for that long, to begin with." He patted Thaidren's shoulder. "You're a good man, Thaidren. But please, don't let yourself get consumed because of that kindness. I hate that about people like you." He paused briefly and took a deep breath. "That fool, Aramant's old man, he had the same defect as you."

Thaidren nodded. He would try to live up to what he had been told that day. Their gaze then turned to the view from atop the hill once more as they stood silent and enjoyed a precious moment of serenity.

"I'll be going now," said Issin. "I still have a lot of work to do. Keeping the fort up and all that. You take your time, but I don't want to see or hear about you being bone-idle for too long either."

Thaidren shook his head, with Issin having one last thing to say before leaving him with his thoughts.

"And, Thaidren."

"Yes?"

"You may not believe it, but I think you are most fit to go talk with Aramant. Try to bring him back to his senses, would you?"

Thaidren was not fond of the idea, yet understood Issin's point. "I'll try," he answered with a subtle hint of hesitancy.

"Good. If you need anything, you know where to find me."

At the Cathedral of The Light, near the scorched cemetery, Aramant and other paladins were clearing the grounds. All around the young paladin, his fellow companions were murmuring about the battle. Many of these whispers were about the passing of the Highlord. One way or another, all of their conversations led to one question: what would they do after they honored the dead?

Under normal circumstances, Aramant's prideful personality would trample their whispers with raging screams. He would tell them to shut up and be strong instead of behaving like a bunch of confused, sad children. Yet, he stood silent, without even a glance at them. He was too lost in his own thoughts of what had happened. He kept replaying them inside his mind a thousand times, trying to analyze what went wrong, desperately seeking a way to see how things could have gone better. *When did he leave the cathedral? What was he doing in the crypts? How many of the undead did he have to fight to get back to the surface?* Those were just a few of the multitude of questions that troubled him. What was even worse, though, was that between these questions lay one undeniable fact that he wished to avoid thinking the most.

Suddenly, a voice came from behind. "Why are you staying so far away from the rest?" He recognized Illia's concerned tone. He looked around him before answering her.

"No reason," he said softly.

"Aramant," Illia sighed, "after so many years, you think you can hide from me?" He grunted as a sign of being slightly annoyed by the question. However, for his master to see this meant it was a somewhat normal sign.

"Did you come here to cheer me up?" he asked with an almost mocking tone.

"Normally I would've," she quickly answered, "but since Issin can't be in more than one place at a time, he gave me some responsibilities to attend to."

The following line marked one of the very few times when Aramant proved disrespectful and indifferent toward Illia. "Then, what do you want?"

Her first instinct was to make him eat those words. But given the circumstances, she took a deep breath and swallowed her pride. "I want you to take a break from this and go wait at the main road for a shipment of supplies that is due to come."

"A shipment of supplies? I thought those were for the survivor search parties near the town."

"Most of them are, but we need something to keep us going as well. The city closest to Leor has sent this shipment for us."

Without giving much thought to it, Aramant shook his head in acceptance and agreed to go. As he reached the rendezvous point, the young paladin had begun to feel exhausted. It was past mid-afternoon, and the sun was already preparing for its calming descent. Aramant felt envious of the medallion glowing in the sky, thinking such a blazing titan to be unaffected by the petty emotions bestowed on mankind. He leaned on a nearby tree, gazing at the horizon. At this point, time seemed irrelevant. It did not matter if there would be seconds, minutes, or hours between now and when the shipment arrived. He sat there, lost in thought. The scar left by his father's passing was still too fresh, not to mention the other people in his life whom he cared for who ended up with the same fate.

Since the day of the battle, Aramant hadn't put on his paladin armor. It felt suffocating to even look at it. Delving too much into his thoughts would end with his hands shaking uncontrollably and with his heart feeling as if it was being torn apart. Perhaps he was merely imagining these sensations. Perhaps the trauma had shifted from a mental one to one of the physical realm. It mattered not. He just wanted these torments gone.

*Where is that damn shipment?* he wondered as his patience grew thin. From the cathedral's direction, he heard the sound of footsteps closing in on him. Aramant turned around to see the person whose presence he would usually despise the most. He threw a somewhat indifferent look at Thaidren, still wearing his armor as if he were prepared for a second fight with the enemies of The Light. The thought stirred a brief moment of disgust within him, but it soon passed. For the time being, he didn't care if it was him or anyone else. The young paladin figured that maybe he was sent to help him carry the supplies back to the cathedral, or to supervise him. His string of thoughts was abruptly silenced when his dark-gray-haired rival spoke.

"Nothing yet?" he asked.

Aramant stood silent for a moment. He dismissed the annoyance brought by the question before answering. "Not yet." He shifted his view back toward the road.

Thaidren looked down at Aramant. It was unclear for him as to what to say or how to react. Even without the recent events, they did not communicate much, or at least not in a peaceful way. He reached his hand toward the young paladin, in a benevolent offer to help him get on his feet. To his surprise, Aramant took it before Thaidren briefly turned his head toward the cathedral.

"It's still there," Aramant added.

Thaidren's tone shifted to one of grief. "From here, it looks almost normal."

"You mean not defiled and wrecked?"

"I mean like home. Where you and I grew and learned so many things. Where we would return after assignments and be glad to see our rooms and beds."

"Where we would enjoy hot meals, prepared with care at the dining hall below," Aramant added with a brief half-smile.

"Where we would have good friends and company waiting on us…" the young warrior paused for a moment, "and you."

Aramant didn't take it to heart that time. Moreover, it looked like he showed signs of amusement on his face. "Fair enough."

Thaidren simpered. "So, you can smile after all."

"Part of being human, I suppose."

"I suppose…" *It's been a while since I saw him smile.* Although they were never on the best of terms, Thaidren felt at ease. From his perspective, Aramant was the one who had suffered the most, the one who lost the most. And, unexpectedly so, that moment marked a rare occasion for them to speak freely and without conflict in their eyes toward one another. Consequently, one question echoed within Thaidren's mind.

"Aramant?"

"What?"

"Why are we like this?"

Aramant felt mild confusion and some annoyance upon hearing the young warrior's question. He focused more on his sentiment of curiosity. "What do you mean 'like this'?" he asked.

"Why have we been like this with each other for so long? I mean, I know when it started, but I never got the chance to ask you why?"

Aramant's temper escalated. "And what? You figured this would be a good time for that?"

"I don't know… but with all that's happened, I thought that maybe we should at least try to fulfill Attern's wish to get alon — "

A heavy fist lunged toward his head. Thaidren fell on his back only to see Aramant's raging face as he tried to get back up.

"You want to respect his wishes NOW?" he asked with fury burning in his eyes. "To honor him by trying to patch things up with me? Very well then, 'friend', let's shake hands and become blood brothers from now on. Say, you want to go have a drink and forget our troubles ...? Guess what, it ain't that easy, you naïve idiot."

"I was trying to…"

Another punch came toward him, one that Thaidren intercepted by placing his hands over his head. A sudden urge to return the blow rushed through him, yet he chose to ignore it.

"To what?" shouted Aramant. "To make me remember how much he favored *you*? The "good son," who couldn't do wrong while I stood like a pain in his back? You have NO right, and NO idea what it's like to be his son because you never WERE." He panted uncontrollably for a few seconds. "You… never were…," he stated as the fury in his voice quenched, only to rise back again.

Upon hearing this, Thaidren's instinct to return several strikes at him reignited. Yet, once again, he somehow managed to deny the urge.

"I was not trying to make you feel that wa — "

Aramant charged at him with his bare fists yet again. However, before reaching his target, the young paladin felt himself being grabbed from behind and partly turned around, after which *he* ended up with a punch to the face. One that made him lose balance and fall. As he rose his head to face the uninvited assailant, Issin's words pierced his ears.

"Get up!" he hollered.

The young paladin complied, only to meet a second blow from the substitute leader. He got up again with an itch to strike back, but he quickly cast the idea aside. He would not steep so low as to hit one of his superiors, no matter how he felt.

"It's consuming with you two," Issin puffed, shaking his head in disappointment afterward. "Like trying to talk to two dense, brick walls… He came here to try and help you and bury the hatchet once and for all, not to torment you."

"Bury the hatchet…," he mumbled as his voice turned to a more mocking tone. "Like we're burying Father now?"

Issin raised his hand to hit Aramant, yet restrained himself in the end. "You think you're the only one who feels like that here, boy? Look around, goddammit! We are less than a quarter of the people we used to be. Fathers, husbands, even brats like you and Thaidren have died at the hands of those blasphemous monsters. And me… Well, I'm the unlucky bastard who has to publicly explain to all their loved ones why we were unprepared for such an event." He paused briefly, with his lips starting to shake. "I have to look each of their loved ones, women and children mostly, in the eyes and tell them that. Honestly, I would've preferred to perish in the slaughter-fest instead."

Aramant stood silent under a pressuring sentiment of guilt. Alas, he could not help but feel furious about Thaidren whenever he'd think of his father.

"Go find Illia," Issin turned to Thaidren. "She'll give you something to work." As the young warrior left, and with Aramant's nerves calming down, Issin had refocused on him. "As for you, come with me."

"But what about the shipment?"

Issin turned to him with a threatening face, then made one swift hand gesture to signal Aramant to follow.

"Fine, fine," retorted Aramant with half-raised hands. "Sorry for earlier."

"I'm not the person to whom you need to apologize," Issin mumbled. "And there is no shipment. It was my idea to try and bring the two of you to a quiet place and settle your issues. A fool's wishful thinking…"

Soon after they left the main road, Aramant and Issin ended up at the cathedral's vault. It sat in a more remote zone, which under normal circumstances would be guarded at all times from both the inside and out.

"Why are we here?"

Issin searched his pockets and pulled out an old key that he used to unlock one of the vault's doors. Once inside, Aramant realized the cellar was empty, devoid of any artifacts or valuables.

"I don't understand," he said in a confused tone.

Issin remained silent while checking the giant stone bricks of the wall facing the entrance. After a few moments of searching, he removed one of them and took out a long piece of old cloth that clearly concealed something within its fabric.

Upon unwrapping its content, Aramant's confusion rapidly turned into concern. "What is *this* thing doing here? What do you want to do with it?" A short-lived moment of paranoia overwhelmed his thoughts as a flash of Baav's betrayal compelled the young paladin into assuming the worst.

"Settle down," Issin said, while slowly stepping away from the item. "Hear me out first; it's not what you think."

Aramant had never been given any reason to mistrust Issin in the past. Yet, the same could be said in regard to Baav as well. He took a deep breath and hesitantly nodded while still in shock as he laid eyes on what was in the cellar with them: the very flaming sword that the aforementioned traitor carried — the one responsible for his demonic powers. After taking a second deep breath, the young paladin managed to find his words. "I'm listening…"

# CHAPTER VII
# A FINE COVER,
# HOUSING ROTTEN PAGES

Knowing of the hollowing of the once sacred grounds and with the image of the enemy leader's weapon in sight, Aramant could not help but feel paranoid. Issin had drawn him to a remote location, where if they were to fight, they would be neither interrupted nor heard by anyone. Yet, he refused to let himself believe that his role model, teacher, and one of the few people in the world whom he could call a friend would be another traitor, waiting to seize an opportunity as well. The young paladin agreed to listen to what Issin had to say. Him wanting them to have a conversation meant that, at the very least, there would be a point he'd want to address. *But what kind of message?* Perhaps a more diplomatic approach than his deceased ally had taken. *As if that could be possible after everything.*

Aramant was determined that the second he could be sure Issin was not on his side, he would lunge at him without holding back. A part of him was desperately hoping that would not be the case. Another wished to just charge in already and be done with it. He was aware, however, of the massive disadvantage he was in at the moment. With all things considered, he was unarmed and not even wearing any form of protection. Yet, if the situation would demand, he would have nothing to lose and would take his chances.

"Are you listening, boy?" Issin asked. "You seem lost in your thoughts."

"Yeah, sorry about that," Aramant replied. "Can you start over?"

"Well, I wouldn't blame you if your mind started spinning now that you've seen this. I would probably do the same. Let me begin by saying that I'm not another traitor, as was that bastard, Baav. I merely was the one who picked up his blade and brought it here. I'm not the only soul who knows it is here, but I am the only one who has the key to the vault room."

"Why did you take it? Have you thought it could've reignited and burned you up? Or worse…"

"I was cautious, boy," Issin responded with a subtle mocking tone. "This ain't my first day of duty. And I couldn't leave the sword there and risk it being picked up by someone else."

*Fair point*, Aramant thought. *But why go through all the trouble of hiding it? Why not destroy the weapon? Let it be shattered back into oblivion, from where it came.*

Issin continued to speak as though he heard Aramant's thoughts. "And I can't destroy it either. Or, to be more specific, there are several good reasons not to."

After hearing this, Aramant experienced a short moment of unsettlement. *What reasons? Does he intend to use it? If such is the case, it can't end well.* His line of thought was interrupted as Issin resumed his explanation.

"You are mature enough to realize that even we, as paladins, both individually and as an organization, have our fair share of secrets." He exhaled and threw a disappointed look at the extinguished blade. It was rusted and dull. "This artifact is one such secret."

Aramant was experiencing a swirl of emotions, shifting from calmness to a sentiment of persisting dread. "What do you mean?"

"Maybe you've noticed it, maybe you didn't, but haven't you wondered why Attern was not carrying his weapon when we found him?"

"Of course I did," he answered, "but he was also stripped of his armor and was wearing chains around his wrists."

"Fair enough. I suppose in this context it wouldn't seem surprising he was unarmed. Still, his hammer, you know all too well that it is a special relic of The Light." Aramant had some follow-up questions regarding this, but for the moment, he chose to remain silent and let Issin talk. "It is a weapon of many stories. Having been passed down from one wielder to another, this particular weapon has been known to possess a form of… sentience, let's call it. But you know that already. It chooses its wielder." He glanced further at the demonic artifact and pointed his hand at it. "And now, it lies here. In its true, original form."

Aramant understood what Issin was hinting at, but he couldn't make peace with the idea. He had to be sure there was no place for interpretation. "What are you saying?" he asked with a sense of dread.

Issin sighed. "I'm saying what you're thinking already, boy. This is Viz'Hock. Your father's hammer."

Aramant's bewilderment prevented him from speaking at first. He could not understand how such a thing could be possible. What he had in front of him was a sword, not a hammer. On top of that, this weapon was of demonic origin, reeking of the stench of the Burning Underworld. His father's hammer was a symbol of light. A holy relic that would bring peace and warmth into the hearts of those it would protect. He looked at Issin, then back at the blade several times. His master gave him a moment to gather his thoughts before resuming.

"Viz'Hock is a demonic weapon at its core. As you've seen with Baav, it can easily bring out the worst in one's heart. Physically, mentally, and spiritually alike. Yet, in cases such as your father, he had the pure heart and spiritual strength to suppress its malevolent nature and turn it into a beacon of hope. Instead of unleashing its demonic influence, it ended up purified by the soul of its wielder. It's a two-case scenario: either the weapon corrupts the user, or the wielder manages to cleanse it. Baav was not chosen by the weapon. In Baav's case, I suspect he had been tainted by a lust for power many years before. When he took your father's weapon, whatever darkness he had piled up deep inside him came out and revealed its true colors."

Their discussion continued for a while longer, with Aramant processing the information given little by little. He asked Issin question after question, yet he could not provide answers to all of them. With all the new knowledge in his mind, Aramant could only ask himself one thing: *What now?* Unable to answer it himself, he resorted to asking it out loud.

"So, what does that mean now?" he asked Issin. "What am I to do with this?"

"Wait a second, boy. There is still one thing that I haven't mentioned. I was not there when you were born; however, in your father's story, he claims that the hammer started to glow as soon as you took your first breath in this world."

Aramant remembered well that story. His father had told it to him as well in the past. He had always hinted that Aramant would be the next wielder of Viz'Hock. The thought made him happy when he was little, but knowing what he knew now, the prospect ceased to bring any joy. His conviction that he was able to purify the hammer had diminished. Even more so recently. And now, learning that there was a chance that the weapon could bring out the worst and consume him, he was even more reluctant to try taming it.

"I…," whispered the young paladin with a distressed tone, "I can't."

Issin did not try to enforce it. His initial thought was that it might've helped him regain his ambition, but perhaps it had the opposite effect. Either way, there was no turning back now. *When or if he will be ready to accept this legacy is up to him.*

"I understand," The Lantern replied softly as he covered the sword up before placing it in the safe, then covering the secret vault with the stone brick. From one of the small bags attached to his armor, he pulled out another key, which he then placed in Aramant's hand. "Take this." He closed the young paladin's fist. "It opens the bottom drawer of your father's desk, up in the Highlord's chamber. I dared not open it myself, but from what I do remember, there should be something in there for you." He paused briefly as he turned his head one last time at the Viz'Hock's hiding spot. "You don't have to change your mind, but if you ever do, you know of this place, and I'll leave the spare key with you."

As they left the vault, Issin began to walk back to the cathedral. Aramant stayed behind for a time, next to the vault's entrance. He raised his hand and looked upon his clenched fist, while he thought about what Issin told him. The key was given to him for a reason. His father wanted him to have it. It may be related to the weapon, or it may not. Either way, he knew what it opened, and after contemplating for a few moments what he should do next, a sense of curiosity trumped his doubts. He made up his mind that he would see what lay in that drawer.

***

Meanwhile, at the Cathedral of The Light, preparations for the ceremonies were almost done. From all across the country, tens, maybe hundreds of family members, loved ones, and friends of the deceased began to arrive. They were announced of the upcoming ceremony via pilgrims and messengers hired by the Congregation of Paladins. There was even a rumor claiming that some higher-ups from the congregation might show up to display their support and help however they could. As for burials, there wouldn't be many. The ceremony would consist of an homage to those who fought until their last breath, followed by the engraving of their names on The Dim Pillar. Lastly, it would end with the burying of the few members whose bodies remained intact. The rest had already been incinerated to dissipate the stench and cleanse the land by fire.

The majority of the cathedral's surviving members had completed their tasks and were now waiting for the events to start. Thaidren and Illia stood at the cathedral's entrance, greeting the mournful crowd that lay before them. They both knew that there were no words nor means for them to alleviate the suffering. Yet, they maintained their composed state throughout the welcoming. After a while, they saw Issin sneaking past everyone and entering the cathedral through a secondary entrance. Given that he was the Highlord's substitute during these times, the duty to hold a speech for the departed and to supervise the entire event would fall on his shoulders. Thus, it was not the time for him to meet with the families and friends of the deceased.

The cathedral hadn't been this full of people in a long time. Not since its glory days, when it would account for almost a thousand paladin apprentices and hundreds of staff members. It had not seen such days during Attern's leadership, not because he couldn't handle such a feat but because of the expanding influence of the Congregation of Paladins, which led to more and more training facilities opening across the country and the rest of the world.

As Thaidren was welcoming the guests, he spotted a familiar face near the cathedral's entrance approaching him. He leaned down as he saluted his Uncle Thraik, with a broad smile. Years had passed since the two of them saw eye to eye, with Thaidren now being almost double the size of the bearded warrior. For a split second, the joy of seeing him again made the mournful fog vanish from within the young warrior's heart.

"I'll be damned, lad. 'T has been too long."

"It's good to see you too, Thraik," replied Thaidren.

The dwarf waved his hand, signaling Thaidren to come closer to him. He gave him a warm hug and a pat on his armored shoulders before whispering in his ear. "We need ta discuss somethin'. In private."

Thaidren suspected he knew what the subject would be. He nodded and turned to Illia. "Can you handle them alone for a bit?" Then pointed at Thraik. "We have to talk about something."

Illia looked down at Thraik, then back at him. "Is this the dwarf uncle you mentioned?

"At yer service, madam," said Thraik as he bowed his head.

Illia smiled at him, having felt the urge to playfully tease the dwarf. "Heard a lot of stories about you. You seem to know your way with the sword."

Thraik shook his head. "Eh, more so with an axe than a blade, but aye, you wouldn't want me as yer enemy."

Illia giggled at the dwarf's statement. "Neither would you want me."

Thraik turned his gaze at Thaidren. "I like this one."

"Go on ahead then," Illia told Thaidren. "I'll handle the crowd."

"Thank you. It won't take long."

While walking away from the cathedral's main entrance, Thraik turned his gaze one more time toward Illia. "Quite some gal ye be havin' here. Should've come more often."

Thaidren chose to quickly dismiss any mental image of his uncle flirting with Aramant's master. He was not in the mood for such subjects. Furthermore, he was curious about what Thraik had to say. And the reason behind his secrecy.

"So, what did you want to discuss?"

"Look, lad, t'is about yer mother."

Upon hearing this, Thaidren couldn't help but interrupt him. "Is she all right?"

"Aye, aye, she be fine. That's not wha' I meant. She wanted ta tell ya that she's sorry for not bein' here. She has some things ta deal with."

*What could she possibly have to deal with for her to not be here?*

"Poor lass is even blamin' herself for not being her' ta help when things went south." He exhaled once and resumed his speech. "I kno' that maybe this is not a good time for this, but she asked me to take ya with me back home after we attend the sermons."

Thaidren found himself surprised to hear this, yet upon reflecting on the idea for a moment, he understood why his mother would want that. Still, to abandon the cathedral so soon after its darkest hour seemed cold. There would be many other things that needed to be done even after the ceremonies ended. It would feel wrong to leave the people here on their own.

"And another thing, lad," said the dwarf. "Yer mother asked me ta talk to that lad ye always get in trouble with. Said she wants him to come with us too."

*Aramant? I don't understand,* Thaidren thought as he frowned. *What does he have to do with all this?*

# CHAPTER VIII

# ATTERN IGTRUTH

Inside the cathedral's upper levels, Aramant's footsteps echoed through the building as he headed toward his father's office. Its location lay at the top level of the cathedral's tower, representing his rank and strong connection with The Light. A circular staircase, that ended at a sturdy door awaited his arrival. It was one of the few times in his life that Aramant saw the door closed. It had been locked up as a sign of respect for the former Highlord and to prevent documents from being stolen. Baav's betrayal had left a deep wound in the hearts of everyone at the cathedral, as well as a layer of paranoia. Fortunately for Aramant, he was one of the few people who held one of the four keys that would open the Highlord's office. After unlocking the door and entering the room, a brief sense of nostalgia embraced him. The office was untouched, exactly as Attern had left it: impeccably clean, organized, and with a sense of welcoming warmth. The young paladin looked all around the office as if he had just entered for the first time. His mind flew to distant memories of his early childhood when he would come here to spend time with his father. Attern would often hold him in his lap and flood his son's mind with stories from either his past or stories from other renowned paladins. Often ending them by stating that this desk and office would one day be his.

From time to time, he would even express his happiness at the thought of Aramant taking his place one day, sharing stories with his future children. *Those were better times.* It was simpler when he was young. When they were young. *If he were in his prime when this assault happened, Baav and his undead army would've been quickly dusted away. No,* he knew that was untrue. It may have been better, and it may have ended up with fewer casualties, but in the end, the result would've been the same. *He would've sacrificed himself anyway.* The thought stirred Aramant to clench his fist. Yet, it was not entirely out of anger. It was hard to make peace with such an internal dilemma. He shook his head briefly and focused on the reason he came here.

The desk that Attern used to sign different documents regarding the cathedral's administrative issues had not had time to gather dust. The young paladin inspected it from both sides without taking a seat in the chair. It still felt wrong for him to do so. Like it did not belong to him. However, he finally dismissed the sentiment and sat down. He did not bother to check the first drawer nor the second. Those were never locked, and he had peeked inside them in the past. They were mostly filled with older, less significant documents. He reached for the bottom drawer and unlocked it. Apart from the drawer itself, which seemed older and less used than the other two, its contents seemed rather disappointing at first. It had an envelope with the Highlord's stamp on it and what seemed like an old, medium-sized book.

Aramant picked up the envelope, ignoring the book for the time being. At that moment, even the simple act of opening it made his thoughts spiral uncontrollably. Nevertheless, he forced away the storm raging in his mind and focused on reading the letter inside. It was addressed directly to him.

*My son, since the days you were but a child, I felt in you the same void that resided within me — one birthed by the parting of your mother. I know that over the years, I have been reluctant to tell you more about this extraordinary woman, that without the slightest of efforts, managed to steal my heart. I want you to understand that because of the love I had and still have for her, it was excruciating to even mention her name. I realize it may be unfair, and I hope that by the time you'll read this, I'll have overcome enough of the grief I carry to be able to tell you about her. Alas, in the event that it won't happen, I want to apologize to you.*

*Right now, for you to read this letter means one of two things: either you somehow managed to take it from the drawer before its time, a case in which I'll demand both an explanation and you put the letter straight back where you found it, without reading it any further; or that I am no longer among the living. If the latter is correct, then there are some things that I wish to pass on through these words.*

*I think about my death often. This letter itself is a result of those thoughts. One of the most important things that I need to tell you is about Viz'Hock, my hammer. It is a well-guarded secret that this artifact has a rather darker origin than the Congregation of Paladins would allow the world to find out. Nevertheless, the least I can tell you is that its origins are demonic in nature. From what I understood, it has been turned into a holy weapon through some historically lost means. But be warned, my son, for its original form will never be cleansed entirely, and it may try in time to corrupt you. It has tried to do so with me as well. Always be careful about this weapon, yet trust that it can be used as a beacon of hope in the hands of the worthy. I have no doubt that you will always hold back its darkness and that your heart will never be swallowed by it.*

*As for the book that I pass on with this letter, it is a prized heirloom passed down from one generation to another. It is a half bestiary, half journal, containing the tales and discoveries of all those who possessed it. I only ask that you take it and add to it your own story, and when the time comes, pass it on to your children.*

Aramant paused briefly. He turned to look at the book, then back at the letter. A part of him did not want to continue reading. It saddened him to be reading the last message from his father. Still, he drew a deep breath and continued reading what remained of it.

*I cannot imagine what you might be feeling while reading this, but I am asking you to stay strong. The Light has guided me in life, and it is The Light that will offer me comfort in death. With that being said, there is another secret that I should have told you a long time ago. Yet, I think that the best way to do so is to have you hear it through someone else's words. Seek out the Silver Sorceress, Thaidren's mother, Wizera. She can be trusted, as can he. I pray that one day, you two will get past your differences and realize you have more in common than you think.*

*I will forever be in your heart, Aramant. And I will always stand by your side. I should've said it more often, but you have no idea how proud I am of you. I always was. Just as much as I was happy when your mother blessed me with you. Be good, my son. May The Light guide your path, always.*

*Attern Igtruth*

Aramant dropped the letter on the floor and covered his eyes with one hand. He clenched his teeth briefly and wiped away a tear of loss and regret. *I don't know what to do.*

His moment of sorrow was interrupted by the sound of the cathedral's beckoning bell. The ceremonies were about to commence. He thought about taking the book and letter with him but chose to let them stay in the drawer a while longer instead. Before he left, he took one last glance at the book. Curiosity compelled him to turn it over and read the title: *The Index of Existence.*

# CHAPTER IX

# DEPARTURE

Inside the cathedral's halls, Issin discussed the ceremony with Illia and the other staff members. Due to a larger-than-expected number of attendants, it could not be held inside as was initially planned. It would instead take place outside, with Issin speaking on behalf of the Congregation of Paladins at the cathedral's entrance. He was not fond of the idea of him being the one to look at all those people, knowing that it had been part of his duty to protect their loved ones and failed. While lost in his thoughts, he felt a gentle pat from Illia on his shoulder.

"Nervous?" she asked with a soothing voice.

Issin nodded. "How could I not be? I'm about to bury my head in shame."

"Don't think of it that way," Illia said. "This is not about shame or guilt. What happened, happened, and we did our best to protect ourselves and everyone else."

"Tell that to the parents, their brothers and sisters, their lovers."

"You worry too much. Don't think that you speak on behalf of the congregation. Don't think of this as an official event. Just speak from your heart and be sincere. Both to yourself and them. Everybody at the cathedral could always count on two people."

"Do not mention Attern's name along with that traitor Baav!"

"You've assumed wrong. I was going to say Attern and you. You two were always busy with something yet never refused to help any of the students. Or staff members. You were the ones we could count on. And the fact that you don't consider yourself to be that only strengthens our collective belief that you are. You taught at least half of the people who ever entered these halls about the path of The Light, if not all of them. About what it means to be a paladin. Our values, our morals, our pride and sense of responsibility, they were all taught by you." She let go of his shoulder and unsheathed his sword. "You don't need this here. You'll go there unarmed; you will honor their memory and make us proud."

Issin briefly closed his eyes and nodded, unable to hide the alleviation Illia's words brought him. "When did you become so wise?"

"I don't know, but I had a good, patient teacher."

They both shared a laugh. Issin still felt unprepared to face the crowd, yet, he was now determined to proceed regardless.

Outside, the people waited for the ceremony to start. The myriad of voices scattered in front of the cathedral was indistinguishable given the number of people attending. After the last count, 227 people had been victims of the attack. Each of them had at least one person attending the ceremony honoring their memory. Most of the paladins remained on the side, while the civilians were closer to the central area. Thraik and Thaidren stood in the back of the crowd, waiting.

"I can't see a thing. Has it started yet?" asked the dwarf.

Thaidren shook his head. "Not yet."

"So, about what we discussed earlier…"

"We'll have time for that later."

There was no sign of Aramant. Thaidren turned his gaze to the crowd, then at the line of paladins. *Where is he? He should be here.* The young warrior felt compelled to go and search for him, yet before he could turn around to pursue his urge, the main gate had opened widely. Issin, along with Illia and several other staff members, briefly marched in a V formation, with Issin in the middle. The main entrance's acoustics allowed anyone who would speak from there to be heard from across most of the cathedral's grounds. Upon seeing them, everyone turned silent. It was time for Issin to start his speech. He gazed at the vast mass of people before him and took a deep breath, putting his thoughts in order.

"Dear guests. We have gathered here today for reasons more sorrowful than any of us would have wanted." He paused for a moment, sighed, reminding himself of what he would say next, then continued. "This cathedral, once a symbol of prosperity for the newer generations and for anyone with the desire in their heart to purge evil from the world… has been raided. The fact that we stand here today is a testament to our victory. Yet, in the hearts of many, myself included, it doesn't feel anywhere close to a triumph. I look around, and I see grieving parents, wives, husbands, friends, children, to whom I can only say what you know already. We were supposed to assure the safety of the students who would come here, and we failed. We failed — "

Thaidren turned to the right and saw Aramant joining the ceremony in the back of the crowd. The young paladin stood there, gazing at Issin, seemingly enthralled by his words.

An armored figure approached the young paladin. It was the representative from the Congregation of Paladins' headquarters: High Inquisitor Robnethen. It was the first time that Aramant had seen him. Other than that, he and Thaidren knew only the stories and rumors about him. In a sense, he was much like Attern, having fought alongside him in the past. Although, unlike the Highlord, Robnethen was leading the division of the Blood Crusaders. An elite paladin task force, whose members were allowed to tap into and use the element of blood as well as The Light. As far as the rumors went, they were far more violent in battle than traditional paladins, granting them respect and a sense of fear at the same time.

Aramant paid no heed to Robnethen's presence. Perhaps he did not care. Thaidren, however, kept a close eye on them while listening to Issin's speech.

"I failed. And I can't apologize because I know that there are no words nor actions that the congregation or I can use to mend your souls. Those responsible for this horrible event have met their judgment, yet they deserved far worse. As paladins, we strive for peace, and we teach our disciples to aspire for the same. But one of the first lessons that we teach here is that to preserve peace, you must be willing to fight for it. There is a bitter irony that comes with that." He paused for a moment. "For those of you who still have your loved ones standing as paladins, I understand if you resent the idea of letting them stay here any longer, and I agree with you. Which is why, in the name of the Congregation of Paladins, I hereby dismantle the Cathedral of The Light. It will not be used as a training ground for paladin aspirants anymore. The Light has forsaken this land. And so, we must move on to new horizons."

In the background, upon hearing these words, Robnethen prepared to unsheathe his sword and lunge at Issin. *Sacrilege* was the only word etched into his mind as his rage exploded. Thaidren saw that and was ready to move on him. However, before Robnethen had the chance to advance any further, he felt Aramant's grip on his wrist. Though without armor and unarmed, the look on the golden-haired paladin sent a clear message. He would not tolerate this kind of behavior from him. Robnethen grinned and let go of the hilt slowly.

Having observed what had happened, Thaidren moved closer to them. There was no need for him to intervene — for now — yet he preferred to be cautious.

"I will ask of you all to turn your attention to the graveyard to your left. The crystalline structure that you see there is one of our oldest monuments. Our former Highlord — may The Light guide his steps in the afterlife — called it The Dim Pillar. On it, the names of our dearest companions are etched. Those whose bodies could not be retrieved and buried, and many others. Before you all arrived, a total of two hundred and twenty-seven names were added to it. Most of them were not even past their twentieth year. If I could, I would trade my life to save even one of those kids. It is not the elders who should come back from the battle alive. The young ones should."

Issin continued on, having commemorated every single soul that gave their life that day. He spoke fondly of many, yet he did not refrain from their flaws as well. He spoke his heart precisely as Illia had told him and the people appreciated that.

With the engraving of the new names on The Dim Pillar, the monument would remain untouched after that day. The cathedral and all its surroundings would be abandoned and removed from the congregation's structures. Such a decision should've been made by the high council of paladins, not Issin. He knew he would answer for making this decision in their name. It was not in his power to decide the fate of the cathedral, yet he did so. He would most likely be put on trial, and depending on the final verdict, some form of punishment was to be expected. However, the congregation was not merciless, and Issin had always been a loyal and exemplary servant of The Light. Unfortunately, Robnethen did not share these thoughts. Aramant may have stopped him from causing a scene during the commemoration of the fallen, but that is not to say he had been subdued. As soon as the Highlord's funeral ended, he would not hold back any longer.

Around half the number of civilians who attended the ceremony had started to leave. Some openly blamed Attern's leadership for the disaster that took place. Others chose not to think of it that way and remained behind to pay their respects to the last beacon of light that guided these once-sacred grounds. No matter the public opinion, in the eyes of every person who ever walked these halls, Attern was an embodiment of what it meant to be a paladin.

Unlike with the previous sermon, Issin wouldn't be the only one to monumentalize Attern as a person. Each of the cathedral's higher-ups joined in with their homage to the Highlord. All but two persons: Thaidren and Aramant. One of them did not know what to say about his parent. The wound was still too fresh. As for the other, he was scared of the thought that all his sorrow might burst out at once if he were to commemorate him out loud. Thaidren was still holding in all the emotions brought by Attern's death, unable and unwilling to confront them. *Not here, not yet, and not in front of all these people.*

The last part of the ceremony consisted of the cremation of Attern's body. He was brought on a stretcher, wearing his decorated, dress armor. Carried by Issin, Illia, Thaidren, and Aramant, they placed him on a woodpile. They watched as Hamalia ambled toward them with a lit torch. Aramant stepped in front of her.

"Are you certain?" she asked.

He nodded once and took the torch from her hand. Before setting his father's body ablaze, he took one last glance at him. For the first time, he realized how gray Attern's hair had become over the years. It was the first time he saw him as what he had mockingly called him for years: an old man. However, the thought did not bring him sorrow as he would've expected. Strangely, it made him smile. *Rest in peace, Father. You wait for me in the world of the dead. When my time comes, I'll have a lot of stories to share with you.* He briefly closed his eyes and lit the pyre.

"Until then, may The Light guide your spirit to peace."

To his left, Thaidren stood silent. His thoughts were not that different from Aramant's. Before he had a chance to place his hand on his shoulder, Illia did so instead. She did not say anything to him. She merely stood beside him. Behind them, Issin took a few steps back only to meet Robnethen's unwelcoming glare.

"Quite a commemoration you held there, Issin," he said with a subtle, derisive tone. "It is always unfortunate when one of our own departs this world. Even more so when the said someone is of such a high ranking."

Issin was aware that Robnethen did not stop him from exchanging a few words in Attern's memory. He was not a man known for his sympathy or manners.

"What do you want, Robnethen?" he asked with an indignant tone.

Compared to Issin, Robnethen was a goliath. He closed in on The Lantern and looked down at him. "Feeling arrogant today, are we?" he asked with a sinister grin.

"You're one to talk. I know it's hard for you to understand human emotions, but in case you haven't noticed, we've just ended the funerals for over two hundred people. You'll excuse me if my voice doesn't sound so full of mirth."

Robnethen's grin did not fade. If anything, it grew more disturbing. He was practically holding his hand on his sword's scabbard.

"So, what do you want?" Issin asked again.

Robnethen closed in on him even more, forcing him to take a step back. "Well, if you would be so kind as to answer one question," he muttered slowly. "I was wondering, who gave you permission to announce that the cathedral will be abandoned by the congregation?"

From further away, Thaidren's voice interrupted them. "Hey, what's happening over here?" His eyes fixed on Robnethen.

Aramant also turned his head toward them. He was ready to step in at a moment's notice.

"Nobody," Issin answered Robnethen's question. "You know the rules. In the event of an appointed commander's death, a temporary substitute will be chosen.

And a commander can request the congregation's intervention with decisions of high importance."

"Indeed, a temporary substitute, NOT an appointed commander," continued Robnethen. "Even more so, you admitted that even if you were, you should've requested permission from the congregation, NOT take such decisions on your own. Every peasant that attended here today now knows this place will be abandoned. The news is already cast into the air, making us look like fools if we announce that it was false. How, I ask you, do you plan to fix this, substitute commander?"

"I don't," Issin responded firmly.

Robnethen unsheathed his sword and raised it above his head, preparing to strike. "How dare y — "

A shout from his side interrupted him. "Hey, baldy, what in The Light's name do you think you're doing?!" Illia stepped in, with Aramant close behind her. They both had their weapons unsheathed, ready for battle.

Seeing himself outnumbered, the Crimson Inquisitor, as he was known to some, had seemingly calmed down. He slowly placed his sword back in its shield-attached sheath and turned his attention to Issin once again.

"There, there, now, you can call your puppies off, old man."

Thaidren, the only one close in terms of height to Robnethen, slowly approached him.

"This "puppy" already has fangs."

"How adorable," he answered with a skeptical, mocking grin.

"Enough!" Issin shouted. "Both of you! Robnethen, I know I acted outside the congregation's interests, and I plan on going to the main headquarters myself to face their judgment. For once, stop being such a bloodthirsty sociopath, and listen until the end. Spilled blood is the reason why we ended up here, and we've already had enough of it." With one hand, he pushed Thaidren away from him and signaled Aramant and Illia to stay put with the other. "And you two, you stay out of this. He's enough of a loose cannon without being pushed into a corner."

Robnethen turned around and walked away without saying another word. For the time being, his priorities lie elsewhere.

"What was all that about?" asked Illia.

"Nothing of importance," responded Issin. "Rabid dogs like him simply don't know any better."

Thaidren felt conflicted. Robnethen may not be from around here, but he was a member of the congregation just like them at the end of the day. *He should stand as an ally, not a new enemy.*

"Well, with that gorilla out of the way, I still have some things I must attend to," said Issin. "I'll see you all a bit later."

Thaidren turned to him as he was about to take his leave and grabbed The Lantern's arm to stop him. "So, the cathedral not being used by the congregation anymore is not official?"

Issin chose his words carefully before answering. "It has become so. And I'll assume full responsibility for it. Worst case scenario, I'll be demoted, but I don't care about rank nor prestige. Not anymore."

"I am more concerned about people like him," Thaidren responded. "He seems bent on making you pay."

"Hmph. You worried about me, boy?"

"A bit, yes."

The thought put a smile on the old man's face. "Well, don't. Worry about yourself. This is not the first rabid animal that showed me its teeth. Won't be the last."

"So, what happens next?"

"What happens is that everyone has to make a decision."

"What do you mean?" asked the young warrior.

"With the cathedral being relieved of its function, it's up to everyone to figure out what they want to do next. In a few days, I will depart for the main headquarters of the congregation. I'll answer for my actions and bring with me anyone who wants to continue on the path of The Light. They will most probably be reassigned to other stations around the country, maybe even outside of it." He threw a look at Aramant, then refocused on Thaidren. "Will you come with me, boy? If I could make you and Aramant stay in the same space for five minutes without killing each other, I'd be lucky to have such companionship."

Before Thaidren answered, he remembered his discussion with Thraik. He said that he would meet the dwarf at his old spot, along with Nez'rin. Initially, Thraik wanted to speak with Aramant before the funeral. Thaidren convinced him to do so afterward and assured him he would bring Aramant along to do so.

"I wish I could, but I have some matters of my own to attend to."

"Fine. I'll settle with the little lion if he agrees." The nickname brought a swirl of memories to Issin. It was what Attern used to call Aramant when he was little. He'd always say that it came from his mother before her passing. A bright blond-haired child was considered in the culture of men to be blessed by the heavens. Even more so for paladins, who worshiped and served The Light.

"Before he gives you an answer, I have something to discuss with him as well." He turned around. "Come to think of it, Aramant was here a moment ago."

"Said he had somewhere to go," answered Illia. "He seemed a bit secretive if you ask me, but I didn't pay much attention to that."

"I guess I'll go search for him then."

"You do that," Issin said. His gaze then shifted toward Illia. "You go on as well. Unless there's an emergency, I want to enjoy a moment of peace and quiet. It's been a long day."

***

Aramant headed back to his father's office to pick up the letter and book. Now that the burial ceremony was over, his resolve seemed a bit clearer than before. He decided to heed his father's words and go speak with the Silver Sorceress. Perhaps she held some answers to his questions. As he was about to leave, he took one last glance at the office. Like his father once told him: there may come a time when he would venture into the world for good. He would come to experience great adventures, meet new people, and when all his tales would be done, he'd return to his home to tell them to his future children. The last part of that dream did not seem plausible anymore.

He left the door wide open and proceeded downstairs. Upon exiting the cathedral, he immediately saw Robnethen waiting near the main exit.

"Waiting for someone?" Aramant asked with a subtle hint of aggression.

An opportunistic grin covered the crusader's face. "Glad you asked, son of Igtruth. Yes, I am waiting for someone."

"Wouldn't want to be the unlucky bastard," Aramant answered as he was about to walk past him. Before having a chance to distance himself, he found himself in Robnethen's grip.

"About that, little one, you just so happen to be the 'unlucky bastard.'"

Aramant found himself confused and slightly worried. He would've expected him to wait for Issin or even Thaidren after what happened earlier. *But me? What does he want with me?*

"I think we got off on the wrong foot earlier," the humongous crusader said smoothly. "You see, the congregation sent me here, specifically, at my request."

At this point, Aramant didn't care about his intentions. "Congratulations," he said as he again attempted to walk past him. Robnethen's grip grew stronger, preventing him from struggling his way out of it.

"There's no need to be so hasty. Aren't you a bit curious as to why I did that? You should listen to what your superiors have to say."

"I usually listen only to those whom I respect. But since you seem so determined to enlighten me with your motives, it seems I don't have a choice but to hear you out."

"Atta boy," he answered while loosening his grip on the young paladin.

"I don't suppose you came here personally to pay your respects to the fallen or my father."

"I can pay my respects and have additional motives."

"Right… You sure have a peculiar way of showing it; by threatening Issin."

Robnethen chose to ignore the bitterness in Aramant's tone. "Issin is but an old man, long-retired from the front lines. He acts tough around his little squires, but his fangs have long dulled. He is a great teacher from what I've been hearing, yet that is what he is now: a teacher. You, on the other hand, are not even in your prime yet. And in spite of that, I've heard many good things about you. You're young, competitive, and full of energy and strength. The only thing you lack is experience. Real experience."

"Competitive? I find it hard to believe that's a quality befitting of a paladin."

"You're not wrong, most people would agree on that. Still, I consider myself more open-minded. Under the right training and with proper discipline, it can serve as one of your greatest strengths."

"You're trying to make a point out of this?"

"My point is pretty obvious. Issin declared this place non-redeemable. Nobody can continue their lives here. That includes you. I came here with an offer that I made to your father a few years back as well. Join my elite crusader division, Aramant Igtruth. People like me, like you, are what makes us strong together."

The young paladin clenched his teeth in anger. "I am nothing like you."

"Deny it all you want, but looking at you, I see a young variant of myself. Within my ranks, you'll be able to deliver justice in its purest form and purge the true horrors in our world. Don the symbol of the blood crusaders and join me in our glorious pursuit of peace."

"Your pursuit is not glorious. It is tainted with blood. My resolve is to help people in need while being guided by the path of The Light. Yours is to exploit The Light's judgment to smite its enemies by any means necessary. You don't think nor care about the consequences or the innocents that may end up as casualties. I've heard about your order, and, boldly speaking, I'm disgusted the congregation allows your existence. You're a bunch of bloodthirsty hounds who hide behind the congregation's ideals to satisfy your desire for conflict. I will not 'join' your so-called "cause." Not now, not EVER."

Robnethen's smirk turned to a frown. With a swift move of his right hand, he grabbed Aramant by the neck and raised him in the air. Unarmed and without any armor, the difference in size between them seemed even more pronounced. The young paladin struggled to escape his grasp, but to no avail.

"Perhaps I was wrong. We are not so much alike as I would've thought. You inherited your father's weakness. His arrogance. You pretend to be better than my division and me because you've always stood on the "bright" side of the spectrum. You yourselves hide behind the concepts of "morality" and "protecting the innocents." Furthermore, you ignore that WE take care of the matters you don't want to stain your hands with. The Light is not always soothing and pleasantly warm, whelp. Sometimes, it needs to leave a mark through burning."

He threw Aramant on the ground without much effort. He wanted to make it clear that in his eyes, he was an insect, one that Robnethen could squash at any moment. "Pathetic. Like your ol — " The Crimson Inquisitor saw an armored fist out of the corner of his eye, closing in on him. He attempted to protect himself with his left arm, but wasn't fast enough. The fist pummeled him in the face, making Robnethen lose balance and fall to the ground. He groaned in pain from his seemingly dislocated jaw.

As soon as Aramant managed to catch his breath, Thaidren raised his hand to him, helping the young paladin get back up.

"Find Issin. Tell him the rabid dog still barks and is thinking about biting." While the young paladin appreciated his help, he didn't want to leave him alone with that brute. Before he could answer him, Thaidren took him by the shoulder and shook him back to his senses as he yelled, "NOW! You can't fight as you are now."

Robnethen was too focused on the pain to pay attention to Thaidren. He rose to his feet and grabbed his own jaw.

This would be the first time that Thaidren would witness the healing capabilities of blood magic. The sound of Robnethen's crackling jaw being forcefully reattached sent goosebumps down his spine.

The Crimson Inquisitor's gaze quickly turned toward his assaulter as he spat blood on the ground. "The "puppy" with the fangs," he smirked. "I'll give you that; you've got guts."

"You're about to find out," Thaidren answered as he imbued his weapons with frost energy, making them leave frostbite marks on whatever wounds they would cause.

Robnethen felt the air around him get slightly colder. With one look, he analyzed the enemy he was so eager to punish for his misbehavior. His stance, weapons of choice, reach, taking into account every aspect that a veteran fighter would. There would be no interruptions this time. The High Inquisitor unsheathed his sword from his shield and charged at the young warrior.

Thaidren was aware of the odds not being in his favor. Strength and combat expertise would not win this fight for him. He had to be smart, and as a result, a potential resolve came in the form of a simple idea. As Robnethen rushed toward him, he froze the ground in his path, then moved away. Considering the size and weight of a goliath covered in heavy-plated armor, he did not have the means to stop quickly nor control his balance on a slippery surface. He fell a second time as Thaidren put distance between them. His armored boots were specially designed with spikes on the sole, allowing him to avoid slipping on the ice.

Robnethen was now determined to go as far as possible to kill the insolent brat that angered him. He jumped to his feet and tried to regain his balance.

Thaidren now had a massive advantage in controlling the battle. Yet it wasn't the first time Robnethen had to deal with frigid opponents. He needed to adapt to the environment. These kinds of tricks, as he would see them, would hardly work a second time.

*A paladin, running to seek help.* A sour taste formed in Aramant's mouth. He could not listen to Thaidren's order. Considering his fight with Robnethen was taking place near the cathedral's main entrance, he figured that someone had to eventually hear the clash between him and Thaidren and intervene. Having thought of this, he decided to head further away, to the vault. It had been ages since the vault had held any magical artifacts within its walls. That is until recently when Issin hid Viz'Hock in one of the secret compartments. The young paladin unlocked the corresponding vault room and removed the artifact from its hiding spot. Upon unwrapping it from the piece of cloth, the dark-omened sword started to glow bright red.

After everything that happened, the young paladin was hesitant to touch Viz'Hock. He didn't understand how it worked, how it would reshape itself back into the hammer that he was accustomed to seeing. There was also the risk that it would corrupt him, just as it had Baav. He did not feel worthy of getting a hold of it and cleansing its corruption, yet he had no time to suffer from cold feet. For the first time, he was concerned for Thaidren's safety. His sight turned toward his hand. It was shaking just as much as it had since the battle with the undead army. He closed his eyes, took a deep breath, and without overthinking it, took the sword in his hands. The young paladin felt his palm burning with a violent surge of power passing into his body. It bore a sensation unlike anything he had ever experienced before.

In the vicinity of the cathedral's main entrance, Thaidren was struggling to withstand Robnethen's fury. He may have landed the first punch, but now he was beginning to worry that he would end up receiving the final blow. The High Inquisitor wanted to pound Thaidren into the ground. In contrast, the young warrior was desperately trying to think of a way to immobilize him. The thought of fighting one of the elite warriors of The Light was understandably frightening to him. Even more so when it came to fighting their leader. He concluded that his best option would be to stall for time until Aramant came back with reinforcements or until someone inside the cathedral heard their rumble. The problem with the latter was that the front entrance resided on the opposite side of the living quarters. The halls had a strong acoustic resonance, but there wasn't any guarantee that it would be enough.

Robnethen was relentlessly swinging his longsword and spiked shield at Thaidren, making the thought of just freezing him alive sound more and more tempting to him. Yet, both Wizera and Attern explained to him in the past that such a feat required great finesse and mastery over ice magic. Mastery that he did not possess enough to guarantee the safety of the frozen target. Upon reminding himself of that, he dismissed the thought, with another one taking its place. *Maybe if I freeze his weapons, they'll shatter into bits after a few hits.* The idea did not sound bad, yet to execute it, he would have to engage Robnethen in close combat. The risks involved amplified his state of anxiety, but for the moment, he saw it as his best option besides waiting for help. He could not wait and hoped for help to come forever.

The young warrior rushed directly toward Robnethen, giving the impression he was mindlessly charging to deliver a strike that they both knew would never work. Robnethen saw through his bluff, but he played along. As soon as Thaidren got close, the blood crusader threw his sword in the air. The young warrior was caught off guard by his gesture. *Is he surrendering? I don't understand.* What he did not grasp fast enough was that his gaze turned toward the thrown sword above, giving Robnethen a clear opening on him. He seized the opportunity with his spiked shield, slamming Thaidren with it and throwing him to the ground, making him drop his weapons. But Robnethen did not stop there; an instant afterward, he threw himself with his shield head-on toward Thaidren. The young warrior rolled while on the ground to avoid being crushed and impaled by the spikes. He got back on his feet first, then froze the ground again to slow down his opponent.

At this point, Thaidren was bare-handed, against a spiked shield three-quarters as tall as he was. He made a tremendous mistake taking such high risks against an experienced enemy. Before he could gather his thoughts, he saw a second display of blood magic from his adversary. He felt awed and disgusted at the same time, as he witnessed Robnethen gathering the spilled blood on the ground from his previously broken jaw to create a crystalized blood sword. *That was his backup plan.* Unlike Thaidren, his risk of losing his weapon had been calculated, and he corrected it with a simple act of blood manipulation. With a splattered swing at the ground, he shattered enough ice from beneath him to move unhinged. It seemed he was also able to alter the sword's velocity, turning it from liquid to crystal at will.

Robnethen swung his weapon toward Thaidren, dispersing it as he transformed it back into normal blood. Its strike resembled that of a whip, with the exception that he recrystallized the blood droplets as soon as they got close to his target. Thaidren ended up with a grazed face, with some of the fragments managing to hit him between his armor parts as well. He had only suffered superficial cuts, but this was not about causing physical damage. Robnethen wanted to intimidate him, and it was working.

From afar, in a brief moment of respite, the young warrior saw Aramant rushing toward them. Thaidren positioned himself to make sure his enemy wouldn't see the young paladin coming. Fortunately, the blood crusader was already boiling with rage, his vision tunneled toward his prey. Thaidren was surprised to observe the young paladin carrying in his hands the recently restored holy hammer of his deceased father. As he charged toward his unsuspecting target, a loud voice came from one of the cathedral tower's windows.

"Robnethen! Cease this madness at once!"

The High Inquisitor paused from his battle stance for a moment. "You don't give orders to me, old man."

A beam of light energy was cast at him, forcing Robnethen to block it with his spiked shield as he turned toward the cathedral's entrance, from where the blast had come.

"Yes, he does. Stand down, or the next shot won't be so gentle," added Illia as her weapon was still glowing in the radiance of The Light.

Aramant kept his distance. There was no need to throw himself into a battle without armor anymore.

Illia looked at Thaidren as she approached. "Are you hurt?" she asked with a concerned tone.

"I'll be fine. He just grazed me."

"You DARE oppose me? I represent the highest authority of the congregation here. I will brand you all as traitorous filth!" yelled Robnethen at Issin. He took a closer look at the tower. Almost every window in it had at least one cleric or paladin ready to fire at him with rays of light, or bowmen holding their aim ready.

"Your justifications are personal. You are not subjective, making your authority here null. And you raised your sword against one of MY disciples. I won't tolerate that even if it wasn't personal. Now, I will say this only once, Robnethen: give up the fight and leave. You are not welcome here anymore."

Robnethen dismissed his blood weapon, then picked up his real sword from the ground and sheathed it in its hilt. "One transgression after another. I will make sure the congregation is informed of this." He turned toward Thaidren and glared at him. "Next time I see you, pup, one of us will die." The young warrior eyeballed him.

With Robnethen heading toward the stables to depart, and his domestic dispute out of the picture, Thaidren could finally persuade Aramant to come and talk with Thraik. A realization came to his mind, making him lose himself in thought. If Issin and Illia hadn't intervened, he would've jumped into a fight without any kind of protection to save him. *Of all people ... Perhaps deep down, Aramant can be a good person*, he thought. The prospect was refreshing and welcomed in his mind.

"Hey," he heard Aramant's voice from his side, "you still in one piece?"

At this point, the two of them still didn't know how to talk to each other. "I've fought worse," said the young warrior, with a hint of doubt.

"Good," replied Aramant, "good." His attention shifted to his right hand, which was no longer shaking.

From the cathedral's tower, Issin looked out over them, focusing his gaze on Aramant. *You've gotten your courage back, boy*, he thought with a smile. *This time, hold onto it. I have a feeling The Light has just begun to reveal your path.*

The young paladin turned to Illia and the cathedral's entrance. "I'll go change into some armor. It's been a while, and, come to think of it, I've been feeling small from not wearing any."

Illia giggled. "At last, you're back to normal. I'm glad."

"Maybe not fully, but better than yesterday," said Aramant. He walked past her and headed toward his room. It seemed like ages since he had been there even though it had only been a day. For the second time since the cathedral was assaulted, he felt tired.

"Wait," he heard from behind him, "there is something I want to ask you," called Thaidren.

Normally he wouldn't even care to listen to what he'd have to say, yet after everything, he turned around and answered back. "Yes?"

"My uncle, the dwarf you saw me speaking to, Thraik, wants to talk with you. Would you meet up with him?"

"Your uncle... the... dwarf?" he asked, confused.

"I don't need to share the same blood to consider him family. But never mind that, what do you say?"

"Fine. Any idea why or what he wants to discuss?"

Thaidren suspected he knew the answer, yet he chose not to share his speculation with the young paladin. "I don't know."

"Fine, but meet me here in an hour. I want to take a short nap after all this mess."

*Fair enough,* thought the young warrior. He could use that time to rest as well.

Away from the cathedral's grounds, atop the hill where Thaidren had his secret spot, Nez'rin and Thraik were waiting. The dwarf was not fond of having to sit with him. *Where in da blazes are those numbskulls?*

***

Aramant saw Illia sitting in a chair at the table in his room, watching him in silence. He got up, rubbing one eye with his hand. "What are you doing here?"

"I came to wake you up," she replied.

"Then why did you take a seat?"

His master let out a brief chuckle. "You seemed peaceful when I entered. I told myself to allow you a few more minutes of rest."

"Well, thanks I guess." He cracked his neck and exhaled. "Feels like I've slept for days."

"Just for about an hour. Time to meet up with Thaidren. He's waiting downstairs, in the yard."

*Has it already been an hour?* Aramant thought. *I should've asked for more time.* He had given himself a few extra minutes to rouse completely. "I'll be down in a minute."

Illia nodded and closed the door behind her as she left. The young paladin got up, looked through his room, and began packing the things he considered to be essential in his travel bag. He took the Index as well. It had a supporting cover that allowed it to be mounted on the belt or one's back. With a final glance around his room, his focus turned to Viz'Hock. He grabbed the weapon and studied it briefly. The thought that it now belonged to him still seemed unreal. Yet, he felt relieved that he had not been corrupted by its dark nature, as Baav had. He sheathed the hammer on his back and went downstairs.

Thaidren's secluded spot was about ten minutes away on foot. Thraik greeted them both upon their arrival. He and Aramant had exchanged a few words in the past, yet they were still unfamiliar with one another.

"Glad ta see me boy convinced ye ta come," said the dwarf with a smile.

The young paladin turned his head toward Thaidren for a moment, then back at him. "He said you had something important to discuss with me. After giving me a hand, I figured I owe him to at least hear you out."

The dwarf shook his head in confusion. "Givin' ya a hand? Something happened?"

"Nothing relevant anymore," replied Aramant. "So, what do you want to talk about?"

"Firstly, I want ta offer ya my sincere condolences. I've known yer pa since we were 'bout the same age as you two. He was a good lad. Ye seem to get that from him." His focus shifted to the paladin's weapon for a moment. A fleeting smile showed on the dwarf's face. "Ya know, he used ta wear dat hammer of yers the same way." After noticing his apparent saddened reaction to his words, the dwarf cleared his throat and changed the subject. "But back ta da reason I called ye here for." He pointed toward Thaidren as he began to explain. "This lad' mother asked me to convince ye ta come with us. She is sorry she couldn't attend the ceremony herself, but she got hung up with some important witchy stuff. I wouldn't know how to explain it ta ya any better than dis."

Aramant was skeptical of this being a coincidence. He asked the dwarf what he was thinking to make sure he wasn't misunderstanding. "Thaidren's mother? Wizera, the Silver Sorceress?"

"Aye, lad, she wants ta — "

"Fine, consider myself convinced," Aramant interrupted.

"Well," said Thraik, still showing signs of bewilderment, "that was easy. Ya boys pack up yer stuff, and we'll be on our way in an hour or so."

"Actually," said Aramant, "I've already packed my belongings. I am ready now if you are."

Thraik turned toward Thaidren. "Lad, ye need some time ta pack?"

"Well, I suspected you came here to bring me home since I spoke to Issin about the cathedral's fate, so I packed my things as well."

The figure next to the dwarf stood silent up until this point. The lich Nez'rin, disguised to look like an old sorcerer, carefully examined the exchange of words between Thraik and Aramant. He pulled his hands out of his long sleeves and fixed his gaze on the dwarf. "Since the master and his companion are ready, shall I teleport us home?" The disguise shrouded his true nature until even the sound of his voice ended up replaced by one more akin to a human. It stirred an eerie sentiment in the young warrior, having known his authentic one.

*Master? Companion? He's acting as a servant*, thought Aramant. *Is Thaidren of noble heritage or something?*

"No, ya dam' sack of — " The dwarf stopped mid-sentence, having realized that the young paladin didn't know what Nez'rin truly was. He suspected it wouldn't be a good time to drop more surprises on him at that point. "No. We're gonna travel on foot. Take yer damn teleport elsewhere."

With him disguised as a human, it became bizarre for Thaidren, especially for Thraik, to see the lich having facial expressions. Nez'rin raised an eyebrow and looked down at the dwarf with disappointment. "Very well," he said, "I will go and inform Lady Wizera of your wishes." He raised one arm above his head, chanted a few words, and as soon as he let his arm descend back, he vanished into thin air.

"That was weird," said the dwarf without realizing he did so out loud.

"What?" asked Aramant.

"A-hem… nothing. He, in general, is a weird lad. Aight, nevermind 'im, let's get a move on then."

Thaidren and Aramant looked at each other. For once, their thoughts seemingly reached a common ground. *Maybe we should've gone with him.*

# CHAPTER X

# SHACKLES AND STONES

The cathedral's image was getting more obscure with the passing distance, making Aramant and Thaidren feel nostalgic. They had left their home in the past when tasked with different missions in the name of the Congregation of Paladins. Given the nature and difficulty of some assignments, they would sometimes think that their latest departure would end up being their last in a worst-case scenario. In a sense, they were relieved that the last time had nothing to do with what they imagined. From a self-preservation perspective, that should've been enough. Yet, this was their home, which now lay abandoned and forsaken from the protection of The Light. Aramant had made peace with the sentiment, mostly. Thaidren, on the other hand, had not. He knew that the initial reason behind his training in the ways of the holy path wasn't to end up as a paladin. For a time, though, he wouldn't have dismissed the idea, seeing as their moral code and ideals were similar enough to his. Recent events had changed this. His faith in The Light may have never been as strong as it was compared to his fellow paladins, but he believed that it would protect the people and the cathedral's grounds. He was proven wrong, and ended up angry because of it. *Why didn't it do more? How could it simply forsake us in our hour of need?* Those were a few of the multitude of questions that lingered in his mind. All the while, Thraik's voice in the background managed to interrupt his line of thoughts.

"And that's how yers truly had left a giant with one eye. Bastard may now as well go and drink with the other one-eyed giants. They should be havin' a different name altogether," said the dwarf, laughing.

Some of the dwarf's stories were pleasant to hear, others sounded exaggerated. Both Thaidren and Aramant were hoping to zone out during most of them. Yet, the dwarf's loud voice proved hard to ignore time after time.

"Ye boys didn' like that one?" he asked upon receiving no reaction from them.

While his last tale proved somewhat better than the previous four, it was still far from being good. Aramant would picture a scenario in which he told Thraik to shut up, or one where he would cut off his own ears. The young paladin remained silent for the time being, hoping that Thaidren would respectfully tell him to quiet down. His faith regarding that was gravely misplaced. Thaidren did not utter a word. Same as Aramant, he remained silent.

The dwarf sighed. "With boys like ye, I would've fallen asleep if I weren't movin'."

***

At Wizera's mansion, the old lich had recently arrived from the cathedral's grounds. The Silver Sorceress sensed his presence, but paid him no mind. She was too engaged in her work. After going with Haara to the Council of Mages, things got a little tense. The reason behind this was Haara, or rather her presence. In the council's eyes, she was branded as a rogue mage who didn't abide by the institution's will. She was not welcomed there anymore. Yet, after talking through with the institution's leading figures, the Silver Sorceress managed to convince them to set aside their animosity in favor of achieving a common goal, or at least, to bear with it. As for the necromantic book, Wizera decided to keep it a secret from them until it could be restored and translated. Haara was to contribute the most to this matter. In order to establish a stronger connection with the earth, she created an underground room with her powers, a few meters away from the house. There, the earthen sorceress would use her magic to undo the damage suffered by the book's pages while carefully restoring the ink etched on them. Nez'rin offered to help with deciphering the finished product once it was done.

Wizera began regretting her decision to show the council the mysterious shard. She was tasked to conduct research on it and to find out as much as she could. It felt for her as if she was on a tight schedule. So far, she hadn't uncovered much since her return home. The shard had lost most of its energy source, but there were still traces of it that could be studied and identified. With one hand covering her forehead, she took a seat on a nearby chair and exhaled. From behind her, the lich's skeletal fingers beating on the door could be heard before he entered the room.

"You seem troubled, m'lady."

The Silver Sorceress kept rubbing her forehead as she spoke. "Yeah. This object or whatever it is. It's driving me crazy."

"If you allow me to speak frankly, perhaps you should consider taking a break. Or, at the very least, accept my assistance?"

Before she had a chance to answer, in a moment of clarity, Wizera realized that Nez'rin's return meant that the others must've done so as well. "Never mind that," she said with an impatient tone. "Where are they?"

"The dwarf insisted they would come here on their own."

"What?"

"He halfway-called me a 'sack of bones,' became aware that it wouldn't have been a good time to reveal that to the young master's companion, then instructed me to take my teleport elsewhere while they come here on foot. He does not like to travel through magical means," continued the lich.

"But still... Thraik." She exhaled loudly to express her irritation before deciding to move on with her research while waiting for them. In truth, she could've teleported at them without necessarily knowing exactly where they were had she given Thraik a magical trinket to serve as an anchor point. However, she did not think that he'd need to have one. "Thank you, Nez. That'll be all."

Wizera turned back to the research table, with the lich standing silently, without leaving the room. Compelled by an unspecific human reflex, he cleared his empty throat. The sorceress turned back to him.

"Is everything all right?" she asked with gentleness and compassion.

The necromancer cleared his throat once again. "If I may speak openly..."

"Of course you can," she replied. "There's no need for you to ask permission for such things. You should know that by now."

"During all the years that you visited the young master, you never mentioned how much he resembles Master Thieron."

Wizera's eyes narrowed, followed by a saddened and contemplating expression. "Yeah, he does. I guess I never stopped to think about that or maybe I didn't want to. He's grown to look just like him. He even has the same gentle look in his eyes."

"Except for his hair color," said the lich in an attempt to cheer her up. "He resembles you in that regard."

She smiled briefly. "You mean my strands of hair color? He's fully silver, unlike me."

"I am sorry if my words have caused you pain."

"No, no, that's not wha — "

The lich raised his hand to his chest, signaling Wizera that there was no need for her to explain herself. "I will give you some privacy. Should you need me, I will be close by."

"Nez?" asked the Silver Sorceress before he had the chance to leave the room. He turned back at her, waiting. "Thank you." The lich nodded and closed the door behind him.

***

The sunset was nigh, marking the time for Thaidren, Aramant, and Thraik to set up camp for the upcoming night. They had been on the road for half a day already. As soon as the campfire was set and lit, they each unpacked their food supplies.

Aramant had packed only a handful of provisions, mainly consisting of vegetables and some meat that could be mixed into a stew. Thaidren's pack carried similar supplies, along with a large pot for meals. As for the dwarf, his bag was filled with one thing: alcohol. After the commemoration ceremonies, Thraik had asked Issin if he could take some of the numerous bottles and small kegs that lay in the cathedral's stashes. It would've been a pity to let them go to waste, after all. He did not wait for the boys to prepare their dinner before starting to drink. They paid him no mind.

For a time, everything around them remained silent, with each of them lost in their own thoughts. The crackling fire and boiling water inside the pot were the only sounds that disturbed the stillness. As soon as the food was ready, Aramant and Thaidren began to eat. Thaidren then pointed to a bowl for the dwarf.

"I'm good, lad," he said. "I got all dat I need her'," he continued as he looked at a half-empty bottle, smiling.

Thaidren raised an eyebrow in disagreement. Yet, he did not express his thoughts out loud. He figured that it wouldn't change Thraik's mind and only worsen his mood.

The young paladin moved further away from the other two. He was partially lost in his thoughts while, at the same time, trying to not let himself feel overwhelmed by them. A constant wonder of what he would find when they'd reach their destination perturbed him. He asked himself whether Wizera could offer him closure regarding his father or not. In an attempt to distract himself from the subject, he looked at the dwarf and pointed at the bowl Thaidren had offered him before.

"Your 'lad' cooks pretty well. It'd be a shame to let it get cold."

Thraik looked back at Aramant. "Fine; pass me da stew, lad." They sat down and enjoyed their meal. Thaidren finished first before dishing himself another serving. *Who would've thought,* he wondered? To sit alongside Aramant in the wilderness and enjoy a meal without being at each other's throats. If someone would've told him that a few months back, he wouldn't have believed it. The same could be said for Aramant. He would've been infuriated by the idea. After everything that happened, they seemed to have buried the hatchet, or at least reached a point of tolerance with one another.

"Ah, 't was a fine brew that ye paladins had holdin' up at yer church," said Thraik as he emptied a total of three-quarters of one bottle of ale.

*How much can one dwarf drink?* The question baffled both Thaidren and Aramant.

"A quiet night like dis and sittin' around a bonfire calls for a story, wouldn't ya agree? Anyway, 't was about thirty-five year — "

The violent sound of an explosion interrupted the dwarf. Its shockwave put out their campfire and engulfed the surroundings in darkness. Thaidren and Aramant quickly rose and took hold of their weapons, with the dwarf slow to react. Given his age, plus the alcohol in his system, it was of no surprise.

"It came from that way," shouted the young paladin.

Thaidren rushed in the direction from where it had come from, followed by Aramant. Upon venturing further into the woods, they stumbled across three armed men wearing leather armor, usually more suited for hunting due to their lightweight and lack of noise produced when moving. Unfortunately, the garments could also be associated with those worn by common bandits. Thaidren and Aramant assumed the worst.

"Hold yer horses and keep yer heads down," whispered Thraik.

The alleged bandits seemed to roam around with a predefined purpose. Most likely they were searching for something. *Something or someone,* thought Aramant. Either way, they hadn't yet spotted him and the others.

One of the men kept grunting something indistinguishable. He signaled the other two to follow him.

The group followed them. It proved difficult for both Thaidren and Aramant to sneak quietly in their armor. To compensate for the clanking of their moving plates, they maintained a larger gap between them and their targets of interest.

After a few minutes of shadowing them, it became clear what they were searching for. Down on the ground, small puddles of blood formed a crimson trail in the grass, leading to whatever lost soul had left them. To the surprise of both Thaidren's party and the bandit group, the mysterious target made its presence known by throwing a stone toward one of the bandit's head. It struck true, causing him to fall unconscious to the ground, dropping his torch in the process. One of the remaining bandits rushed toward the torch, extinguishing it before it had a chance to turn the grass into a blanket of flame. The other ran in the direction from where the stone had come. Their target emerged from one of the tall bushes and slashed him on the shoulder. The bandit reacted with a counterblow, pounding his ambusher to the ground.

From a safe distance, Thaidren, Aramant, and Thraik realized the bandits were fighting a woman, an unusual-looking one, similar to a human, yet there were differences indicating she was something else. Apart from being taller than an ordinary person, her ears were longer and pointy while partially covered by her dark, almost black, purple hair. Her skin was gray, and her eyes radiated in a bright yellow. Seemingly malnourished, her waistcloth, the only piece of clothing she wore, was tattered and dirty. The slash attack that ended on the bandit's shoulder was clearly intended to strike his neck. *She must've missed due to her condition,* thought the young paladin.

"We should help her," he whispered to Thaidren.

"Agre — "

Before the young warrior could finish, Thraik jumped from his hiding spot with his axe in hand. He threw it toward the first bandit, hitting him straight in the chest as the dwarf let loose a fierce battle cry. "Accursed bandits! Ye have da nerve ta chase down a poor woman like dat? I'll give ye somethin' ta remember!"

Thaidren and Aramant followed in his steps, aiming to surround the other assailant. The last remaining bandit attempted to run away seeing his companions' defeat. He found himself held by the foot by the woman, somehow still conscious after the suffered blow. Thraik jumped on the bandit's back, followed by a punch from Thaidren. As his fist hit the mark, the bandit fell without ending up unconscious. Aramant aimed his hammer at him, ready to strike in the event he attempted to get back on his feet.

"Give up. It's over."

Thraik opened his bag and tossed a roll of rope toward Aramant. "Here, lad. Use this ta tie up da bastard."

"Why do you carry rope with you?" asked Thaidren.

"Why wouldn't I?" He pointed back at the bandit. "Ya never know."

At this point, Aramant stepped away from the bandit and offered a hand to the mysterious woman. She proved hesitant to answer his gesture at first, but after a brief moment, she accepted his aid. Upon getting up, Aramant noticed that what he and the rest thought to be the woman's top piece of cloth was actually a mass of solidified mud that covered her chest. The young paladin swung his arm backward, grabbed his cloak, and tore it from his armor. He offered it to her to cover herself with it.

"Th... Thank you," she murmured.

Both Aramant and Thaidren wanted answers. Yet, they believed that the girl needed some medical care and probably a hot meal before being ready to answer any question. Thraik, on the other hand, did not feel the same way.

"Who're ye, lass?" he asked as soft as a dwarf's guttural voice could be. "Wha' happened ta ye?"

Thaidren raised his hand to signal Thraik to cease the questioning for now. "No need for this yet. You look exhausted. And famished. We have a camp close by. Let's go there, get you something to eat, then we can talk if you feel like it. What do you say?"

With a shaky nod from the woman, the group escorted her toward their camp, with Aramant helping her walk. A while later, the woman began to slowly show signs of recovery. After receiving the bare medical attention that the three party members knew and finishing her second portion of stew, she seemed a bit embarrassed for eating almost half of the remaining pot herself.

Thraik searched his bag and took out one of his two spare shirts. It was partially drenched and reeked of alcohol. Still, it was better than nothing. It barely fit a girl her size, but at least she could use it as a top for the time being. She seemed grateful for his gesture but was still holding the cloak that Aramant had so chivalrously ripped from his back.

"What's your name?" asked the young paladin.

She cleared her throat. Using her voice still caused her pain, yet she did her best to sound coherent. After a few coughs, she answered. "Elarin."

Thaidren looked at her as she struggled to talk. He boiled some water in a bowl and mixed in some herbs he knew had healing properties. It wasn't as effective as a healing spell, but at least it would help her throat for the time being. He handed the bowl to Aramant, and he passed it on to her. *Smells terrible, but it'll do her good.*

Elarin held her nose with each sip. After a few struggles to not regurgitate both the stew and the dreadful medicine that challenged her stomach, she found it easier to talk.

"I know it tastes bad," said the young warrior, "but it's meant to help you."

She cleared her throat a second time, with her voice sounding less guttural and painful this time. "It did." Her fatigued eyes offered a thankful glance to each of them.

Despite the fact she was still weak and in need of rest, everyone wanted to know more. "Can you tell us what happened? Who were those men, and what did they want from you?"

*And what are ye?* Thraik held himself back from asking this question for the time being. He was more concerned about other things. Judging by the girl's bruised wrists, she must've been chained up recently. There was no doubt in his mind the word "slave" would pop up if or when she was to elaborate on her story. Naturally, it would've angered him to the core, but knowing that her pursuers were dealt with made room for his empathy toward her.

The dwarf kept one eye aimed at their silent prisoner. They searched him for hidden weapons, then tied the bandit, with his hands behind his back, around the trunk of a medium-sized tree. At first glance, he wouldn't seem more than a common thug, yet Thraik suspected otherwise. After throwing a disgusted look at him, his focus shifted back to Elarin as she started to slowly fill everyone in with her tale.

"In my native tongue, we call ourselves Lu'Derai. I think your people know us as moon elves. Through some circumstances that I prefer not to say, for now, I ended up here, in your world. As soon as I arrived, I was — ambushed — I think." She paused for another moment as she rubbed the back of her head. "I was left unconscious, and by the time I woke up, I was already chained and forced to mine some strange minerals in a series of caverns not too far away from here."

*Our world?* Aramant was confused by her choice of words. While Thaidren and Thraik were more educated with regard to the concept of otherworldly travel, he was a stranger to this notion. Up to this point in his life, he barely had visited the entire country, let alone this world as a whole. *Are there other worlds?* He'd never asked himself that in the past. He had no need of such knowledge before. And now, his first encounter both conceptually and physically came in the form of this alien being, standing next to him. He was not scared. Instead, he was intrigued by the possibilities that this new information could offer. *What other worlds lie there? Are they like ours?* The answer to these questions would have to wait. For now, the focus was on Elarin's tale. And the alleged slave operation in the nearby mines.

"How long have you been imprisoned there?" asked the young paladin.

"I am not sure. Most of the time was spent inside the caves. The only source of light came from torches placed in the tunnels, making it difficult to tell. It could have been weeks, maybe more."

Thaidren clenched his fist. The thought of any person being treated like nothing more than a tool made him sick. *Robbing them of their freedom; of their time.*

"Are there others that escaped with you?"

"No… Many of us sought to escape, yet only I managed to evade their search parties. And that was thanks to you. Others were captured and are most probably back in chains by now." A swift shiver swept down her spine, and she paused. "Or worse…"

Thaidren closed in on Elarin. He bent toward her as he sat down. "It may be too much of me to ask, but can you show us where these mines are?" There was a certain vengeful look in his eyes, yet Elarin did not perceive it as being meant for her.

She shook her head. "I'm afraid these woods are confusing for me. And with all the time spent underground, it seems to have dulled my sense of direction. I would not know how to get back there even if I wanted to." The elf tightened her grip on the cloak with both hands as she squatted. "I wish to get as far away from that place as possible."

After their series of questions, the group had enough information to paint the gruesome image of slave camps and human trafficking. There was, however, one last question that they were reluctant to ask. Ultimately, Aramant took a deep breath and stepped up.

"Your clothes," he whispered hesitantly, "did they... do anything to you?"

"No," she responded after a short moment of silence, "but other slaves... there... were... incidents. Sometimes more than once a day." She touched her chest through the cloak. "We covered ourselves with dust and, if we got lucky, mud... to make us look less appealing to our oversee — "

"I've heard enough!" shouted Thraik.

*That makes two of us.* Thaidren stood and wrapped his arms around his chest.

The dwarf rose and walked toward the prisoner.

The bandit raised his shrouded head enough to see Thraik's legs advancing toward him. His body shook, but he remained silent.

"Well, lad, time ta spill yer beans."

Threats from a dwarf didn't seem to scare the bandit into submission. He stared at Elarin, with an ominous grin.

"Where's da slave camp?" Thraik asked, with a threatening stare in his dark green eyes.

Seeing Thraik's interrogation had led to no avail, Thaidren decided to step in. Once again, the prisoner remained silent, yet his face betrayed a subtle hint of fright. After all, the second interrogator was bigger than a regular human, even more so than most of the slaves he was used to. All of that was further amplified by his armor, enhancing Thaidren's height and bulkiness even more. Yet, judging by the same attire that denoted his status, the bandit figured paladins the likes of him would not lower themselves to such primitive methods as torture or violence.

He was wrong. Without warning, Thaidren unsheathed his sword and plunged it into one of the bandit's feet.

Upon seeing that, Elarin's initial reaction was that of shock. She was not expecting one of her saviors to do such a thing.

Aramant was just as shocked as the elf. In all the years he and Thaidren shared the same home, he didn't recall ever seeing him be cruel. Granted, the person to whom he revealed that side was a degenerate with no compassion for someone else's life.

The bandit's agonizing screams echoed in the camp's silence. As he panted uncontrollably from the pain, Thaidren grabbed him by the chest armor and lifted him upward, forcing the prisoner into a standing position that only added more pain to his injured leg. With the bandit's hands still tied around the tree, his leathery sleeves ended up grazed by the trunk.

"I am going to say this only once," Thaidren whispered in a threatening tone. "I'll give you one chance, and one only, to start talking about the slave camp. I want you to tell me everything. How many are you, where is the camp located, how many slaves are there, what do you plan to do with whatever mineral you're excavating, ALL of it. I want to know all there is to know about every aspect of this despicable operation, or else…"

He stopped for a moment. With his other hand, Thaidren grabbed the sword that pierced the bandit's foot and twisted it. He used a small portion of his energy to freeze the tip of the blade, making the twist even more excruciating. Once again, the bandit screamed in pain.

Aramant and the dwarf threw each other a surprised and worried look. Nevertheless, they did not intervene.

These displays of fury revealed to Thraik something: he was just like his father used to be. *A noble, caring, and gentle soul, yet press da wrong buttons, and he'll turn into a monster that can compete with da devils of da underworld in terms of cruelty.*

Thaidren abruptly let go of the bandit. He fell back on his bottom and grazed his hands on the bark of the tree. Before he had a chance to start talking, the young warrior turned around and moved away from him.

At this point, the bandit's stare shifted from fear to confusion. *What was the purpose of all that if he simply walked away?* He then saw his fierce interrogator close in on Aramant and grab him by the shoulder.

"Play along," Thaidren whispered.

They both turned with a menacing stare at the bandit and started to slowly advance on him. Aramant pulled the hammer from his back while Thaidren was holding his other sword, imbuing it with ice magic as he closed in. The bandit was faced with the image of two hulking warriors closing in on him with the intent of squeezing out all the information he had. And at least one of them proved prone to use whatever means necessary. Thaidren focused his gaze on the bandit's stabbed foot.

"That foot, it will end up being your good one."

Aramant remained silent at first. As soon as they closed in, the young paladin raised his hammer into the air and aimed at the bandit's other leg. "One swing, then it's your arm's turn."

After hearing this, the bandit immediately succumbed and caved in. "All right! All right!" he shouted as he kept panting. Thaidren grabbed the bandit by the chest armor once again, raising him back to his feet.

"Speak! Or I'm letting the quiet one have his way with you before I rip your teeth out myself," he said.

"Th… The camp is south of here. It's a cave known on most maps as Berriva Mine. It was abandoned a few years ago when people thought there were no more minerals to be extracted from there."

The young warrior was far more concerned about the encampment's present rather than its past. "How many?"

"Around fifty men."

"How many slaves?"

"A bit over a hundred," said the bandit, avoiding eye contact with Aramant.

"What are you after?"

The bandit was hesitant to answer the question. He struggled and shook his head in denial. "P… please… no more."

Thaidren's hands immediately started to emanate a chilling mist, and the bandit's armor plates whitened in freezing glass. The leather hardened, and its upper layers started to peel off. The chains and other metallic parts of the armor began to crack, ready to shatter at a moment's notice. The same infectious effect had slowly spread to the rest of the bandit's body, reaching out to his skin, making him shiver as he was clearly trying to prevent his jaws from clicking together.

"Pass me the hammer," said Thaidren while reaching one hand toward Aramant. He was well aware that the hammer's selective nature would not react well to someone other than its chosen wielder. However, the bandit did not know this, and Aramant, while proving himself intimidating, did not offer the same vibe as Thaidren. "You've outlived your usefulness."

The bandit gazed deeply into his interrogator's eyes. There was no mercy, no remorse, no warmth in them. For a split second, he thought he saw his eyes turning into a brighter shade of blue as if they flickered once. "WAIT!" he shouted before erupting into a violent cough. He barely managed to snap out of it in time, before Thaidren's icy grip reached his body. "I don't know, I swear. We… we were hired. T… to dig up those mines for some strange crystals. Our boss… he knows more about it, but we were provided with a very hefty sum of gold as well as the slaves themselves in exchange for not asking any questions. I don't know anything else; I swear it. No names, nor anything else. I don't even know what our contractor looks like. I… I beg of you, have mercy."

Thaidren let go of the bandit, after which he removed the blade rooted in his foot.

Behind him, Thraik was already checking their map of the surrounding area. "Berriva Mine, hmm." He dragged his finger over the map. "Aha, found it. T'is south of her', lads. Like da bastard said."

"Good," replied Thaidren and Aramant in unison.

Judging by their response, Thraik figured that the boys wanted to enact justice on the bandits as soon as possible. However, he was aware that the odds were not in their favor and needed to hold their reins in check.

"Whoa, whoa, whoa, whoa, lads!" he shouted.

"Listen to your dwarf," added the bandit. "You can't go there alone and not end up dead."

Thraik walked toward the bandit and punched him in the face. His groans of pain irritated him. "Blast. I was hopin' I would knock da bastard senseless in one go." He hit him a second time and a third time after that. As soon as he had knocked him out cold, Thraik reassembled his thoughts back together and continued.

"Hate ta say it, though, but da bandit's right. We can't just get into a camp full o' armed men with nothin' but our muscles flexed. We need a plan. And reinforcements."

"Well, we don't have any," replied Thaidren, "and every minute we hesitate is another minute of suffering for the prisoners."

Thraik's voice softened. "Lad, trust me, I understand how ye'r feelin'. But ya got ta understand as well. We can't fight fifty armed misfits alone. At best, we'll probably take down around half of them before they overwhelm us."

"We can't abandon them either," intervened Aramant.

"Nobody's abandonin' anyone. Listen. Da first thing we'll do at sunrise is ta go to da nearest village and see if we can get any help from there, all right?"

While both Aramant and Thaidren wanted to rush to the mines and free the captives as soon as possible, they knew Thraik had a solid argument. Such an endeavor would require a greater deal than sheer force and strength alone. The thought made them feel powerless. It appalled them both as they refused to accept the situation.

"I agree," said Elarin with a saddened tone while gazing at Thraik. "As much as I wish to free the other slaves, we lack the means to do so right now. We should rest for now. By tomorrow morning, I should be well enough to offer some assistance in fighting them. I want to see all of them pay for what they did."

Hearing her opinion, and thinking it through made the two of them agree with the dwarf's idea. It seemed like the only feasible option.

"Now then, the night is still young, lads. Since we got a bandit camp ta worry about now, we need ta sleep in turns. Any volunteers for da first shift?"

"I'll stay up," said Thaidren.

"I'll be the next in line," continued Aramant.

"Fine. I'll wake you when it's your turn."

With everything settled, Thraik, Aramant, and Elarin went to sleep. Thaidren found himself a warm seat on a trunk they used as a bench near the campfire. His morality was still itching at the prospect of having to wait. *Curses,* he thought as he sighed softly.

# Chapter XI

# Den of the Crocodile

About an hour or so afterward, and past midnight, Aramant woke up by himself. At first, he was still lethargic and not fully aware of his surroundings. He soon realized that Thaidren was nowhere to be found. *Please tell me he went a bit farther away to take a piss or something...* He never thought he would hope for such a thing. *Should I wake Thraik and Elarin?* He looked all around him, waiting a few more minutes before letting himself jump to any assumptions. *Damn idiot,* he thought as he swiftly yet silently began to head south, where the slave camp resided. Not long after that, he spotted the young warrior standing crouched near a bush, scouting the camp. He whispered so that he wouldn't startle him.

"What in the name of all that's holy are you doing here?"

"What're you doing here?" he whispered back.

"Don't play stupid," the young paladin replied angrily. "I came here because I knew this is where you had gone to."

Thaidren turned back toward the camp. He had already scouted a good portion of it before Aramant interrupted him. He wanted to personally check if the intel provided by the bandit they captured was to be trusted. So far, it seemed like he wasn't lying. Assuming there would be no slave masters inside the mines during the night, he could approximate their numbers in the fifties. Some of them seemed carefree, while some were regularly patrolling around the camp.

"We have to get out of here," whispered Aramant.

"Wait. Maybe there's a way for us to get rid of them without endangering the slaves."

Aramant's voice almost changed from being silent to a fully-fledged yell. "Are you insane? We CAN'T fight them all."

"We may not need to."

The young paladin had seemingly quenched his alarmed state, even if slightly so. Thaidren's words baffled him, yet they stirred an itch of curiosity. "What do you mean?"

"If we can find a way to lure some of them outside the camp, one by one, we can take them down."

"And how exactly do you plan on doing that?"

That was an answer Thaidren did not possess yet. He continued to scour around and thought about what might set such a strategy into motion. Luckily for him, the bandits did not seem well organized. Some of them were either asleep or half drunk. Out of the fifty men there, only about thirty or so seemed able to fight at a moment's notice.

"That's it," Thaidren said.

"What is?"

"We need to start a fire. They'll figure that something is wrong, but they will send some men to extinguish it. We can take advantage of the confusion, the fire itself, and their reduced numbers."

*This sounds so crazy that somehow it might end up working.* If they are not to be seen, or rather be mistaken for other bandits at a distance, they could take down some of the men in the camp. *Worst case scenario, the fire will be put out quickly, and we'll end up taking down fewer men than we wanted, but they would still be scattered and away from the camp.* Aramant did not give Thaidren an answer immediately. There were still a lot of risks involved and even more what-ifs. Yet they were already there, and he resented the idea of prolonging the slaves' torment as much as Thaidren. The young paladin's final answer came in the form of a firm nod.

The young warrior smiled. They were on the same page once more. "Good. Let's do it then. We'll both go and ignite several spots in the woods. We'll meet up in the middle. Hopefully, the fires will have enough time to grow and expand to a chaotic state."

"But what if they get out of control too much?" asked the young paladin.

"If worse comes to pass, I can stop the flames with my ice magic. Don't worry about that."

Aramant would usually be more prone to trust only himself. However, there was a certain confidence in Thaidren's eyes. One that inspired him to believe as well. "Who would've thought we'd end up working together like this."

"We'll have time to congratulate ourselves after we get out of this alive and save everyone," he replied.

***

Inside the bandit camp, the atmosphere was calm and carefree for the slave masters. The bandits in charge of patrolling and surveilling the surrounding area had not found anything suspicious to report or worth raising the alarm. Near the cave entrance, a watchtower and other smaller wooden structures were built to house the leader of the bandits, a notorious outlaw, infamous for undergoing medium- to large-scale projects for private contractors. A man wanted for misdeeds that covered accusations from simple robbery to multiple murder charges. With time, he received the nickname "The Crocodile" due to his relentless business approach. He's had similar contracts in the past, yet this was a bit more peculiar given the extreme secrecy imposed by his latest employer. He did not care about such things, however. *All that mattered was for the coin to keep flowing.*

At first glance, he did not seem much of a threat: a tiny, skinny man with bad teeth donned in black-tinted light leather armor. His base of operation, where he would spend most of his time, housed a heavy crossbow, as it consisted of his usual weapon of choice. Above him, the wooden watchtower harbored two bandits that interchanged shifts with other pairs every few hours or so, constantly vigilant of the camp's surrounding area. Its placement within the forest resembled the geographic formation of a large crater, meaning that intruders would have a higher vantage point at scouting unless they were to be seen by the men in the watchtower. A few meters away from the other side of the cave's entrance lay several cages that could easily house around twenty people each. Most of them were full of beaten-up prisoners. With rags that barely covered anything on their frail bodies, bruises all over them, and malnourished to the point where it seemed a miracle they were still able to stand, it was only a matter of time before they would succumb to the everlasting embrace of death. Most of them lost both the energy and the ability to hope for salvation a long time ago.

While gazing upon the distant dark fields, the bandit scouts saw several flickers of light emerging from the woods. One by one, lighting in a pattern that almost seemed as if they were surrounding the camp, more and more such lights emerged. After a moment, the scouts realized what was happening.

"Fire! Fireeeee!" shouted one of them.

The Crocodile turned his attention to the blazing horizon. He immediately dispatched some of his men to wake up every subordinate, then sent half of them into the woods armed with buckets of water and whatever else they could use to extinguish the fires. Inside the cages, the slaves could only watch as chaos flourished around them.

With the flame blanket's rapid expansion, it made the leader of the bandits suspicious. Apart from wondering what caused them, he assumed there had to be something more flammable than mere wood and a bunch of fallen leaves for them to spread with such haste. He decided to dispatch a few extra men to put the fires out as quickly as possible. After a brief pause and some thought, he remembered something. Some of the more elevated classes of warriors or survivalists knew how to create what was commonly known as a wall of flame, a technique that consisted of setting ablaze a portion of land in a straight line to form a natural barrier against the spreading of another fire. *It could also be used to surround a camp and to stir up panic.* Unfortunately for him, it was too late for many of his lackeys, as Thaidren and Aramant were already reaping the fruits of their strategy.

*** 

Back at the camp where Thaidren and Aramant left Elarin and Thraik alone, the dwarf woke up from the sound of crackling wood, accompanied by a wave of heat that seemed too intense to originate from their campfire alone.

"Wha... wha' in da..." He rubbed his nose, then looked around, still sleepy. In a moment of clarity, the dwarf realized that the boys were missing. "SON OF A...!" he shouted as he fully woke up. He turned all around, searching for any sign of the fools whom he would smack when he found them. A blanket of blazing light and smoke covered the sky to the south. *Not good, not good, not good. Blast those numbskulls... If ya dare die on me watch, I'll make sure ta bring ya back from the dead just ta send ya there meself.* He turned his attention toward Elarin for a moment. "Aye, missy. Wake up!" he shouted as he shook her from a deep slumber. Normally, the elf would respond with a more violent reflex, but she was too exhausted to do so at that moment.

"What happened?" she asked as she gazed at the same horizon that stirred panic in Thraik's heart.

"I'm gonna kill em, that's what's gonna happen. But first, we got ta save em," he said. He ran toward his belongings and took his axe in hand before rushing in the blazing light's direction. It didn't take long for Elarin to understand what was going on. She was still weak and not in a proper condition to fight. Still, she grabbed her peculiar, decorated dagger and followed in the dwarf's footsteps without hesitation. She wanted to both make sure her saviors were all right and enact vengeance upon her captors.

At the slave mine's outer fields, Thaidren and Aramant were reducing the forces of the slave masters, dividing and conquering them one bandit at a time. Some of them organized in groups of two to five men. Those would prove a bit more challenging to handle, but not impossible. Furthermore, none of the bandits used magic against them. Perhaps they simply lacked the training, knowledge, or discipline to control it. Or perhaps they were missing the simplest of affinities toward the mystic arts. Either way, it worked out in Thaidren and Aramant's favor.

Inside the camp, The Crocodile became restless. With his crossbow in his hands, he left the camp's perimeter and hid in the woods. He came by a large old tree and hid behind it, with the entire camp visible from that vantage point. Should any attackers try to enter his territory, he would have a clear shot to take them down. However, there was also the matter of him being mindful of his back as well. After all, the entire camp was surrounded by flames. He knew neither how many enemies were out there nor from what direction would they emerge. By using dirt and fallen leaves, he covered himself as best as he could. Now it was only a matter of standing still and being patient.

Aramant had moved a bit farther from the fires to deal with a small group of bandits. It was the first time he had fought since claiming his new artifact. Viz'Hock proved a formidable weapon in his hands, strengthening his blows ten times over what he could've normally accomplished. Despite its sheer size, it felt lighter than the one-handed sword he was accustomed to. Nevertheless, with each strike, he could hear the sound of his enemy's bones crackling and breaking as if they were made of thin glass. It felt good and intoxicating at the same time. The sensation of such power surged through him. He was aware the feeling came as a manifestation of the weapon's corruptive nature trying to seduce him toward a darker version of himself. It made him constantly vigilant, thus denying Viz'Hock the satisfaction of his succumbing to its power.

On his side of the chaos, Thaidren was preoccupied with the bandits while maintaining control over the flames. So far, the young warrior kept count of how many enemies he took out. However, because he could not know precisely how many assailants Aramant dismissed, he could only guess their remaining numbers. Assuming Aramant took down at least as many opponents as he did, his rough estimation revolved around a total of twenty remaining enemy forces. After finishing off the last small group in his vicinity, he decided it was time to head toward the camp and free the prisoners.

The Crocodile continued to survey the camp. No sign of any of his men could be seen, yet he could hear their screams across the area. Sweat dripped from his forehead, and his lips felt dry as he moved his tongue over them. The heavy crossbow would allow him to shoot a bolt from about thirty, maybe forty meters away at best. He wouldn't be able to reach the opposite side of the camp, but his bolts could go as far as the entrance of the mine and the slave cages nearby. Suddenly, his patience had seemingly paid off. A few meters to his left, he saw one unknown character emerging from the woods and entering his camp. A colossal man wearing shiny decorated armor and with one longsword in each hand. He seemed cautious, looking all around him in search of other enemies. *Not yet*, the bandit leader thought. If he were to increase his chances of killing this interloper with one shot, he'd have to wait for him to loosen up his guard. Furthermore, considering the heavy armor plating that enveloped him, he would have to strike someplace between the plates to be sure the bolt would bury deep within his flesh.

From Thaidren's perspective, things seemed suspiciously calm. Upon entering the camp, there was not a soul to be found except for the slaves in the cages. They couldn't have just been left behind. After all, they were the workforce of the entire operation. He couldn't believe the prospect of him and Aramant wiping out all of the enemies nor that the remaining ones had fled. The young warrior searched for any sign that could either confirm his paranoia or quell it. It was quiet. Too quiet for Thaidren to let his guard down.

From a few meters away, the slaves had spotted their alleged savior and started to desperately call out for his aid. He approached them only to realize that their cries for help were, in fact, warnings directed at him. A small blade made contact with one of the plates from his arm without piercing it. The sound startled Thaidren, making him turn toward the direction it was thrown. Behind him, he saw about ten bandits slowly distancing themselves from one another in order to surround him. Soon after that, upon hearing several footsteps echoing from the mine entrance, he saw another group of six men emerging from the cave. He was surrounded and outnumbered. Some of them carried either throwing knives or bows and arrows, while the rest were equipped to engage him in close combat. Even with the protection of his armor, he would still have to be cautious.

Meanwhile, Aramant finished dealing with the remaining bandits on his side and was heading back toward the camp. He would have to leave the flames unchecked, as he had no means to extinguish them. *Once Thaidren would be done on his side, he'd come here to put them out,* he thought. His hammer's corruptive nature seems to have subsided as well, granting him a moment of partial relief. Aramant could not help but wonder if it would act the same every time he'd fight. He forced away the concern for the time being.

While on his way to the camp, Aramant stopped at the sight of Thaidren being surrounded. On top of that, to the young paladin's right side lay the bandits' leader, taking cover behind a giant tree and aiming his crossbow. The Crocodile waited to take advantage of the opportunity that his men gave him when they ambushed Thaidren. The problem was that he was constantly moving as he defended himself. Should the bandit leader fire and miss his first shot, he would lose the element of surprise. Aramant could not reach Thaidren in time to help, but he could cut off the head of the snake. *He will have to deal with the rest by himself.*

Thaidren's movements became more erratic, more sluggish. His constant struggle and the previous fights took their toll on him. At this point, the physical exhaustion would influence his control over his powers, making them harder to control. *If I were to use them now, I'd risk injuring the nearby captives as well.* He resorted to strengthening his weapons with ice magic. *Enhancing magic won't pose a problem.* Slowly but steadily, the number of his attackers diminished, yet not at a pace he would've been comfortable with.

After wiping the sweat from his forehead, The Crocodile was ready to take down Thaidren. With both his hands steadily holding onto the crossbow, he took his aim at the frost magic user. As he was about to press the trigger, he saw something off to his side: the alarming image of Aramant charging toward him with his hammer, ready to strike. He abruptly turned his aim toward him and shot the crossbow bolt, mostly out of reflex. It hit and pierced Aramant's right shoulder with most of the impact absorbed by his armor.

The young paladin lost balance in the process, but swung his hammer before tripping and falling to the ground. The bandit leader dodged the swing of the hammer and immediately drew out another bolt to reload his weapon. His aim was true the second time, yet it struck a thicker plate of Aramant's chest armor, rendering the shot ineffective. He would not be given a third chance. With a furious swing from Viz'Hock, Aramant struck The Crocodile, leaving him unconscious. He quickly turned his attention back to Thaidren, only to see him overwhelmed, slowly being driven to the front of the mine entrance.

With most of his stamina depleted, Thaidren began to lose his confidence along with the ability to deal with the remaining enemies. He briefly made eye contact with the prisoners inside their cages. Their despair, their dread, most of all, their fear would've been evident to the most oblivious of beings. Among the many scattered faces within the boxes that held them, the younger ones' faces caught his attention the most. They were experiencing the very same sentiments that their older kin were, but they had room in their hearts for something else: hope. It may have been the first time they saw someone fighting for their rescue. Someone willing to help them, to free their humble souls from both their literal and metaphorical shackles. He couldn't forgive himself if he were to shatter that hope.

Thaidren could not think of any other solution to his current plight. He turned to the bandits that emerged from the mine and rushed toward them. He tackled one enemy and ran past the other ones as he entered the mine. He was well aware that in doing so, he'd trapped himself inside, but at the same time, the young warrior cleared himself from being surrounded anymore. If he were to put some space between himself and the slave cages, he could unleash his icy powers and deal with his attackers with more ease. Upon delving deeper into the mines, Thaidren ended up stuck between his pursuers and a dead-end with a wall entirely encased in some strange glowing yellow-nuanced crystals. He had no time to wonder about their purpose. The one thing that mattered was he could unleash his powers here. The time to hold them back was long overdue.

Outside, Aramant was heading toward the entrance of the mine. When Thaidren entered it willingly, the young paladin shouted at him not to do so. Unfortunately, he was too far from him to make himself heard. *Dammit... that idiot trapped himself in there. What is he thinking?* Before he had a chance to follow him, the angry shouts of Thraik startled him.

"Aramant, ya damn fool. Where's da other numbskull?"

The young paladin pointed at the mine entrance as he answered. "He's inside. I'll go after him. You free the prisoners."

After a brief sigh, seeing as there was no time to waste, the dwarf nodded and signaled Elarin to help him free the prisoners. He then proceeded back into the woods to make sure that there weren't any bandits that could surprise them.

*I'm on my way, ice-brain,* thought Aramant as he delved deeper into the mine. *Don't make me regret agreeing with your plan.*

At the edge of the camp, The Crocodile woke up groaning in pain. The last hit he received left him with a couple of broken ribs and incapable of standing up. *Blasted paladin... I'll have your head on a spike.* He looked around and saw Elarin in the distance, freeing the other slaves from their cages. She was easy to recognize. *The elf... Did she bring the warriors here?* The thought infuriated him. Enough so that he managed to push through his agonizing pain to stretch out his arm and grab the crossbow once more. Right now, he only cared to make someone pay for his recent misfortunes. How he would correct them was a matter for a later time. He rolled on his abdomen and targeted her, with his hands still trembling from the pain. Before he had the chance to aim properly, he found himself at the sharp end of a small axe tossed at him. It struck him in one of his shoulders, making him press the trigger and launching the bolt aimlessly.

"Don' even think about it, lad," he heard from his side. The image of a dwarf smiling at his defeated expression caught his attention. The following and last memory of that night came in the form of a punch thrown at his face that knocked him unconscious. It marked the end of the businessman and his operation.

In the meantime, with Aramant searching for Thaidren inside the cave, a powerful sound, reminiscent of an explosion, made him stop briefly. *Oh no...* He hastened his pace. After reaching his destination, his theory was proven: a section of the mine had collapsed. He saw Thaidren grunting and struggling to free one of his legs that had ended up beneath the rubble and debris. The young paladin felt both relieved and furious to see him like that.

"What in the name of The Light did you do?" he asked while giving him a hand.

Thaidren slowly stood up, still dizzy from the collapse and grunting from the pain. "I… I'm not sure. I was fighting the bandits, then a shockwave hit me from the back."

*A shockwave?* Thaidren's choice of words stirred confusion in Aramant's head. "You mean somebody attacked you from behind?"

Thaidren steadied his breathing and cleared his throat. "Not possible; there was a dead-end behind me, filled with crystals."

"Crystals? What crystals?"

"Most probably the ones the slaves were mining. I don't see them anymore. They're all underneath the rubble now."

Aramant patted Thaidren on the shoulder and helped him walk toward the exit. "Doesn't matter anymore. Let's get out of here." As soon as they were outside, covered in dust, with the young warrior still limping, the dwarf scolded them in such a manner that rivaled with the times when Attern did so.

"Ye damn fools. What were ya thinkin'? To march by yerselves against a small army of no-gooders. You couldn't just wait ta get ta a nearby village ta get some help?" He pointed at Elarin. "Or at least ta leave the poor lass there to rest instead of dragging her back here."

A quiet yet decisive voice came from Elarin. "I wanted to free the prisoners as well. That is not their faul — "

"Don' interrupt me while I'm scoldin' these two, missy," he said with a stern tone. "Dat wasn't da point."

Aramant and Thaidren kept their mouths shut. They would not dare to defend themselves against Thraik in the given circumstances. Thaidren, at least, knew all too well that you couldn't come to terms with an angry dwarf. You had to let him cool off.

Thraik shifted his attention to Thaidren. "If something were ta happen with ye while I was takin' a nap, it would've broken yer mother's heart." His gaze shifted to the ground for a moment. "And mine. Not ta mention she would've had my head on an icy spike afterward." His look then turned back at Aramant. The young paladin felt as if their roles were swapped in terms of height, one of the few times when he truly felt small.

"And ye, lad? I may not know ye as well as this other numbskull but yer father often described ya as the less reckless one. How in the blazes did he convince ye 't was a good idea ta take such risks? I swear by me beard that I'll — "

A small, frail hand grabbed Thraik by his leather armor. It belonged to one of the enslaved children that had been locked in the cages. Weakened and malnourished, the child couldn't have been more than ten, maybe thirteen years old. With another trembling hand, she pointed at them, and with a guttural, hoarse throat, she struggled to speak.

"M... Mo... Mommy. Sh... She went to... s... sleep."

From within the slave mass, a man who seemed somewhat less weakened than most others approached the dwarf. He pointed with his hand to the cages as well.

"Her mother, she felt relieved when she saw you and your warriors laying waste to our former masters. I saw her closing her eyes before the silver-haired one entered the mine. She hasn't opened 'em since." He cleared his throat and allowed himself to rest a moment to think before continuing. "As you can see, they didn't care whether we died or not. Nor did they ever bother to pay respects to the dead and give them a proper burial. We had no choice but to gather the bodies into a corner. Some, who fell prey to insanity from starvation, went on to eat their rotting flesh. Needless to say, they did not last long either."

"Who're ye, lad? Ye seem a wee bit better than da rest of em."

"Name's Oron, master dwarf. I was among the last batch delivered here before your arrival."

"How long ago was that?" asked Thaidren.

"You have to understand, young warrior. This treatment makes you lose the ability to tell time. If I'd have to take a guess, I'd say I've been here for a week or two." He looked at the girl and raised his arm, pointing at her. She let go of the dwarf and grabbed Oron's hand with hers. "She and her mother, they were here for much longer... These thugs... their cruelty knew no bounds. Lacking even the slightest shred of compassion. We were no more than tools in their eyes. Tools that can and would be easily replaced. It didn't matter for them how many of us died. They would simply acquire replacements."

"But from who?" asked Thraik. "Who could have da means ta provide dat?"

"To be honest," said Oron, "I'm not interested in finding out. I'm glad at the mere thought of being set free, and I think most of us feel the same."

"There's a small town not too far away," said Aramant. "You should all gather up. Pack your things if you have any. We'll escort you there just to be safe."

"You have our gratitude, heroes. Thank you for giving us our freedom back."

Thaidren remained silent. He slowly moved away from the mass of people and closed in on the bandit leader's quarters. He gazed at the pile of bodies left behind in the cages. It was a disgusting sight. The thought of people, humans just like him, being able to inflict such cruelty… He took off his helmet and ran his hand through his silver hair before dropping it down with his fist clenched. Such events were consuming him from an emotional perspective. In an attempt to distract himself from that, he reached out to inspect The Crocodile's belongings. Nothing there proved to be of interest, yet close to his quarters lay several containers filled with coal and the same crystals that he'd seen inside the cave. They were all shattered into small pieces that could easily fit in one's pocket. He grabbed a few and placed them in his bag. *Maybe Mother can figure out what these are.* A moment after that, the young warrior found himself startled by the realization of Elarin standing close to him. *I couldn't hear her at all.* Her attention seemed drawn to a medium-sized jewelry box from which she took out a silver necklace with a multicolored, glowing stone, etched in the middle.

"They may have been bandits, but I don't think it's time to take their loot," said Thaidren.

The elf's gaze turned toward him as she squeezed the necklace in her hand. "This piece belongs to me. Along with the dagger, they are the only two memories of my world."

Thaidren turned his gaze downward, betraying his sentiment of apology. "I'm sorry. It was wrong of me to jump to conclusions."

"Your logic was understandable. I do not harbor animosity for such things." She unclenched her fist and put the necklace on with a seemingly nostalgic smile. "This… was a gift from my elder brother. He said it would be something to hold onto when I would suffer from homesickness." She chuckled briefly as she looked up to the sky. "He would also say that no matter how many stars are between us, this pendant would always help me find my way back home. To him."

Thaidren remained silent. He nodded at Elarin, then left her to be alone with her thoughts.

From the crowd of slaves, many of them, if not all, expressed their gratitude to Elarin for her part in their escape. If she hadn't risked her life to escape and go search for help, they'd still be in chains and at the mercy of their former masters. From a physical perspective, she felt much better than the rest. After all, she'd had the chance to eat a proper meal and rest.

"It is finally over," she said as she let out a deep breath.

"Darn," said the dwarf while hitting his forehead with his hand, "I almost forgot somethin'." He made his way out of the crowd and headed toward the giant tree where the bandit leader had hidden. Seeing he was still there and unconscious, the dwarf dragged him back into the camp. "Is dis bastard the one they be talkin' about?" he asked. "He seemed a wit or so smarter than the other goons."

The slaves were glad to see The Crocodile in such a state. Yet, their mirth paled in comparison to their sentiment of anger. If not all, most of them wanted to enact revenge on him, and Elarin was no different. She tightened her grip on her dagger and started to slowly close in on him in a seemingly hypnotic trance. The slaves let her pass, clearing a path for her. At that point, Thaidren was still further away from the crowd, while Aramant was deeply surrounded by the people they had saved and couldn't see what was happening.

An imposing shout from the dwarf managed to snap Elarin out of her trance. "Enough!" He was studying both Elarin and the rest of the slaves' reactions. If they would prove to be genuinely thirsty for the blood of their enemy, he had no real means to stand in their way. Since they perceived Elarin as their representative figure, he made eye contact with the elf as he placed himself between her and the master of the slave trade.

"I don' blame ya for thinkin' da way ye do now. A younger version of meself would've even helped ya in a heartbeat. But a wise man once taught me dat such impulses have consequences. Strike him down now, and ye may find some peace, but it won't last, lass. Sometimes, ti's better ta just leave bastards like him alive. Let them suffer in dis world a bit more before good ol' Death saves him from da wrath of da living."

The elf's hand began to shake. The urge to kill The Crocodile was still fresh and held a firm grip on her. Despite that, the dwarf's words did reach her, diminishing the vengeful storm in her soul. Having attained a more transparent state of mind, a curiosity emerged.

"But can you guarantee that he will suffer for what he has done?" she asked. "That he will not end up escaping the hand of justice to spread his cruelty once more? Killing him may be an easier solution for both him and us. It will also prove most effective. How can you claim otherwise?"

"For starters, if ye kill da bastard in cold blood now, before ye realize it, ye'll be no different than him. If there's a better way ta end dis than a simple kill, as ye put it, then ye should seek it and use it."

Elarin's hand stopped trembling. With a hesitant gesture, she sheathed her dagger. Her frustration, their frustration, had not been erased. However, she channeled her negative emotions toward the thought of her former master rotting in a cellar. It turned progressively more tempting as she kept thinking about it. "I do not completely agree with what you said, but I understand your words, dwarf. And this is your world, after all. I will abide by your judgment."

Thaidren, Aramant, and Thraik looked around. From the original one hundred or so slaves forced to dig into these caves, around sixty lived long enough to taste freedom again. In a more literal manner, none of them had tasted anything in days. Hunger was a screaming plague that plighted all of them. The mine was a few hours away from the nearest town. Under the circumstances, the grim prospect that some of them might not last that long shrouded their minds. They had no time to stop and rest. The path ahead would be a difficult one for most of them. Elarin was aware of that as well. She felt guilty for having the chance to eat something before them as she looked around and took a deep breath.

The elf turned to the rising sun, marking a new beginning that she and many other slaves thought they were never going to get. About an hour later, the group of warriors, as well as Elarin and the former slaves, had almost reached the nearby town. Once they could see it from afar, their uncoordinated march began to slow its pace as the former slaves became aware of their fatigue. Combined with starvation and who knew what possible diseases they might have caught, some chose to stop next to some trees near the road and catch their breath. Elarin saw them and feared that they might collapse and give in to an eternal sleep.

"We will go on ahead and bring food, water and medicine here," she said to a small group of people who couldn't find the strength to walk any farther. They nodded and watched as she and the others continued on their path. Aramant closed in on her and put his hand on her back.

"They're going to be all right," he said. "Thanks to you, they'll soon remember what it's like to have their bellies full."

Elarin let a subtle smile form on her lips. "Your words are kind, and your actions even more so. Still, it is not me they should be thankful to."

"Yes, it is. If it weren't for you, they'd still be in their cages, waiting to be sent back into the mines to die of exhaustion, serving masters who only saw them as soulless tools. You were brave enough to escape while everyone around you reeked of helplessness and despair. And after that, you didn't just run to save your life alone. You found us and asked for our help. You were concerned about their lives when you needn't be. If it weren't for you, we'd have been yet another group of travelers passing by without having a clue what was going on. It is you who started this chain of events that freed them. Don't underestimate the importance of that."

Aramant's words broadened the elf's smile even more. It was the first time he had seen her that way; happy. It made him glad.

Behind them, at a short distance, Thaidren was guarding the back of the crowd. He passed by the same group to whom Elarin had spoken a moment ago.

"Are you all right?" he asked.

"We'll manage," answered one of them, "but I doubt we can walk any farther. The tall woman told us that she'll come back with food and medicine from the town."

Thaidren's sight turned to the front of the group for a moment, then back to the end of the line. The town was close by. Enough so for him to make up his mind. "Then allow me to stay with you until they return."

Shortly after, Thraik passed by them. The young warrior signaled him to keep moving. After a long night and all the fighting, Thaidren too, felt the need for a good night's rest. That would have to wait for the time being, though. Among the small group he stayed behind with, there was a child who burned with a fever, sweating and shaking uncontrollably. Thaidren closed in on him and put his hand on his forehead. He channeled a small amount of his magic into cooling off his hand and lowering his temperature. It proved a more arduous task for him than it initially seemed. Over the years, Thaidren had struggled with a problem that he desperately tried to hide from others. His magic was... unstable, meaning he couldn't properly control the frigid nature of his energy. It marked one of the main reasons why, up to this point, he resorted to imbuing his weapons with power and freezing objects by touching them only. Other actions required finesse in the art of magic manipulation that he did not possess. And right now, the simple act of keeping a constant temperature to help the child resting next to him proved challenging. Using too little of his power would diminish its effects to almost nothing. Using too much of it would turn him into a meat popsicle. He forced away those dreadful scenarios as he focused on his control. He may not have had the means to cure the boy, but he could stall his fever until Elarin and Aramant came back with help.

"Please tell me that he's going to be all right," said a female slave near them. "My little brother, he's all the family I have left. Please, don't let him perish."

Thaidren's face betrayed his uncertainty. "I promise I'll do my best until my friends come back with some medicine."

Another half an hour or so later, Thaidren slowly began to feel the fatigue of constantly depleting his magical energy. He was not used to this kind of strain for so long. The boy had stopped trembling some time ago. He assumed that must've been a good sign. Glancing in the town's direction, he saw two distant silhouettes running toward him. He recognized the short one in a heartbeat, and breathed a sigh of relief at the sight of Aramant and Thraik.

"Hurry up," Thaidren shouted as soon as he thought they would be close enough to hear him. "There's a child with a fever here. He needs medical care."

Aramant and Thraik picked up the pace. They both carried huge backpacks, filled with fresh fruit, vegetables, and herbs. The local alchemist had even provided them with a few helpful potions.

"Show me da boy, lad!" said the dwarf as he unpacked what he thought might help with haste. In the meantime, Aramant distributed the food to the rest of the group. The joy in their eyes was evident, yet their attention was still focused on the afflicted boy.

"Please save him," begged the older sister, as a tear trickled down her cheek.

Thraik's hastened movements were interrupted abruptly. He reached into one of his pockets and took out a small mirror before placing it next to the boy's nose.

"He… He's not breathin' anymore, lass, I'm sorry."

A moment of silence fell over the area, followed by the mourning cries of the older sister. Thaidren gently picked up the boy and placed him in her arms. She fell into him sobbing as she held his lifeless body.

Before the coming of the next sunset, Thaidren and the others returned to the town. They were greeted by the locals who offered shelter, food, and medical aid to the victims. Following the young child's death, Thaidren learned that a few of the slaves who did reach the town had also died. He was told that they were too weak to have survived. In all the years he'd spent in missions carried in the name of the Congregation of Paladins and The Light, death and all its negative aspects had come in many forms. However, this time, it was too much of a succession of events. He was not sure he had completely moved on from the assault at the cathedral, let alone everything else. It felt too much, too fast.

The dwarf figured out his inner conflict and patted him on the hand. "It's gonna be all right, lad."

Thaidren sighed. "Let's find Aramant and be on our way. We can't do anything else for these people." He heard someone from behind, clearing her throat.

"A-hem, if I may," said Elarin, "I could not help but overhear what you said. I wanted to thank you once again for everything you did for us. You gave these people something they never would have thought to get back." She paused briefly. "Myself included."

"Not to all of them," mumbled Thaidren as he looked down.

"Perhaps. But a wise man recently told me not to underestimate the importance of my role. You should do the same. I am sure this is not the first time you have been faced with the harsh reality that not everybody can be saved, but do not let that cloud your vision." She closed in on him and pointed at a group of ex-slaves. "Focus on the things right in front of you. They are here, alive, well-fed, and most importantly, with hope in their eyes. When I was with them in the mines, I had never seen any of them like that. Without you, this might not have happened. Without you, I might not be here right now, thanking you."

"I didn't do it for the gratitude."

"You have it nonetheless. Take it as a reminder to not treat yourself so harshly."

Thaidren raised his head back up and looked at her, still with the same sad expression on his face. "I'll try."

"Well then," said Thraik, "let's find Aramant and get a move on."

"What will you do now?" Thaidren asked Elarin.

Elarin's eyes betrayed uncertainty. "Before I was captured, I ventured across many worlds."

"Were you looking for somethin' in particular, lass?"

"Not exactly; it was more akin to a journey without a set destination. But after this enslavement chapter of my life, I feel like maybe taking a break from that. Reason for which I was wondering if you would accept me as your companion for the time being."

"I doubt anyone has any objections, but are you sure about that?" asked Thaidren.

"I am. You people are the first group of humans that seem noble at heart since I came here." Before Elarin had a chance to continue her speech, she saw Aramant approaching them.

"I don't think we can do anything else here," said the young paladin. "We should be on our way now."

"We were talking about the same thing," answered Elarin.

"Oh, will you be joining us?"

She nodded. "Yes, I am. If it is fine with all of you."

"Forgive me; I didn't want to sound like that. It was just something that I wasn't expecting. We'd be glad to have you around."

From afar, Thraik's grating, loud voice interrupted their discussion.

"Are ye lovebirds done throwin' rainbows and honey at each other, or do ye want me ta ask the local inn for a room for ye?" Both the elf and young paladin stared at him with a hint of affront. The dwarf looked at Thaidren. "Tough crowd with these two." He received no response from him either. "Bah, forget 'bout it; let's just head home before ye kids kill me with yer stares."

The three-man party, with their newly joined moon elf, resumed their journey to Thaidren's home.

# CHAPTER XII

# LAYERS OF THE WORLD

Wizera's concentration was put to the test. The Silver Sorceress found herself unable to focus on her work anymore. A particular thought would not let her rest. *It has been four days already. They should've arrived here yesterday.* As she struggled to repel the distress in her mind, behind her, the chamber door opened with a most unpleasant crackling sound.

"Can't work either?" asked Haara. After days of doing her own research regarding the necromancy manuscript, she had crawled out of the new underground study chamber that she had created near the house. "Can't blame you with the added worries that haunt your thoughts."

Wizera sighed briefly. "I'm not worried."

"Old friend, you're way past worried. You have a visible aura of nervousness surrounding you."

"Hmph, maybe you're right," simpered Wizera as she was reminded of Haara's straightforwardness and way of speaking her mind. The Silver Sorceress moved away from her desk and turned toward her. "What about you? You said you can't work either?"

"Yeah… whatever fate brought this thing into our hands, it's one of a kind, that much I can tell you."

The Silver Sorceress felt intrigued upon hearing this. "How come?"

"This tome is… I'm not sure I can explain it accurately, but it feels… ancient…"

"The majority of them tend to be," replied Wizera.

The earthen sorceress rubbed her nose, expressing her irritation at the comment. "You don't understand. I mean really, really ancient. I'm not talking tens, hundreds, or thousands of years old. I'm talking about hundreds of thousands, maybe even dating the era of infinite conflict on Earth. If that's the case, I'm shocked that it isn't a mere pile of dust. It makes it very hard to restore it completely. So far, I've managed to salvage some bits out of it, but nothing significant."

The deep tone of Nez'rin's voice filled the room before Wizera had a chance to react to what Haara said. "If I may speak up my mind, that should be impossible. Even the most efficient preserving techniques shouldn't be able to prolong a tome's integrity for such a vast amount of time. At least not those of earthly origin."

"Nez, you took a look at the tome already. Do you think it is from another world?"

"I doubt it. From the restored bits, I can tell the dialect is representative of early mankind. However, there are still people who know how to scribe it, even to this day. I assumed that it was written in this language as a means to be difficult to translate, not that it belonged to that era."

"And now, do you think the same?"

"Judging by what Lady Haara unraveled and with my added experience, I now believe she may be right. Yet, I have never seen the likes of a tome resist through time in such a manner. Either a very powerful individual, possibly an immortal, or a group of mages skilled in arcane arts could accomplish such a feat."

Wizera stood silent for a few moments as she unraveled some of the threads in the web of questions in her mind. Within those threads, there remained one question that she was hesitant to even ask. Still, there was a certain itch that compelled her to seek the answer.

"What about the blade? It was one of the few distinguishable marks on the book when I found it."

"It's hard to tell without the full context," said Nez'rin. "But from personal experience, a representation of Urostmarn in any scripture evokes a bad sign."

Between the lack of focus on her work and the dread of the others' discoveries, Wizera's objective shifted toward getting outside to get some fresh air. It felt like it had been days since she locked herself in her study chamber. Once outside, the gentle touch of the sun on her face was comforting, giving her a moment of serenity that she deeply needed. The Silver Sorceress tended to do these sorts of things from time to time; focusing on the tasks at hand so much that she'd end up with tunnel vision. It was difficult for her to snap out of such a trance.

From afar, on the naturally formed road that ended at their mansion, Wizera laid eyes on four silhouettes closing in.

"They're here," said Haara. "See? You worried for nothing."

A brief moment of panic overtook Wizera. "Nez'rin!"

"Already taken care of it, my lady," answered the lich as he shifted into his human disguise.

"I thought you said there would be three of them?" Haara asked.

The Silver Sorceress was as intrigued as her friend. "I thought so as well."

With the group's arrival, the warmest greeting came between Thaidren and Wizera. Despite him towering over her, she wrapped him in her arms as if she'd never want to ever let go. Thraik politely bowed to the two sorceresses and threw a vulgar frown toward his not-so-favorite sack of bones. As for Elarin and Aramant, they remained somewhat distant. Haara quickly observed that and went over to greet them. She focused more on Elarin, noticing her choice of clothes and the fact that she was not of this world.

"A moon elf," she said bluntly. "I have studied your race a bit through books and manuscripts, but to see one of your kind in person is something else, I must admit."

Elarin bowed in a manner unusual from a human perspective but perhaps something common for her kin. "It is a pleasure to meet you. My name is Elarin."

Judging by the size of the shirt she wore, along with the reeking smell of booze, the earthen sorceress figured it must've belonged to the dwarf. "How did you end up here? And what happened to your clothes?"

"It is a long — "

"Now, now, you don't look all that good," Haara said. "I'm an earth healer. Let's get inside and take care of you. We can talk there about the rest."

Elarin was pleasantly surprised. After all, she's been through, the elf ended up skeptical of the denizens of this world's ability to show kindness. Thaidren and his group marked the first step in changing that view. Even more so, now that she had seemingly found more people with kind hearts such as them. In the meantime, Aramant had finally laid eyes on the person who could have the answers to all of his questions. He hadn't given the matter much thought since they left. With all the commotion that happened at the bandit camp, he had cast such thoughts aside. Yet, here he was now, unable to delay his personal curiosity anymore. Wizera had taken notice of him as well. After all, she was also interested in exchanging words with him.

"Aramant, it's good to meet you in person. Allow me to offer my deepest apologies for not being able to attend Attern's funeral."

*Funeral.* The word echoed within Aramant's mind as if he imagined himself being on the verge of regressing to the traumatic meltdown he had suffered a few weeks ago. Furthermore, he felt the influence of the blade within his hammer, savoring his pain, feeding on it. Even though he wasn't holding Viz'Hock in his hands at the moment, it could tap into those sentiments out of mere proximity. He bowed his head toward the sorceress as he tried to dissolve the artifact's meal.

Wizera briefly looked at Thaidren and Thraik. "Could you excuse us for a moment? There is something I wish to discuss with Aramant in private."

Thaidren's confusion was evident, yet he had suspected that Aramant had come here to talk with her from the beginning. As for the subject itself, that was still open to question.

The dwarf patted him on the arm and signaled the young warrior to follow him. "Come lad, let's get to da forge. Yer armor is holdin' up like shit after everything it's been through. Let's give em' some space while I repair it." He turned to Aramant. "When ye're finished, come to da forge too. Yer armor is as shitty as his." As they moved on to the forge, Nez'rin followed them.

Aramant felt anxious and hesitant at the same time, and the Silver Sorceress sensed it.

"Relax," she said with a soothing tone. "If you'll follow me, there's a place where we can speak uninterrupted."

They walked for a while before reaching the same ruins Thaidren used to enjoy visiting when he was little. Shortly after their arrival, Wizera drew out a small crystal from her bag. She chanted a few words and used her water magic to place it over a runic circle inscribed on the ground.

"There," she said, "now we can talk."

"What's with the ritual?"

"It's an arcane cloaking field that isolates all sounds inside an invisible barrier."

"Why such drastic measures? There's no one around."

"Because I don't want to risk this discussion reaching someone else's ears. For the time being, at least."

"By someone else, you mean your son?"

"By someone else, I mean anyone. Including him."

The young paladin searched inside his bag and took out the letter from his father. "Then I suppose it's a good thing I haven't shown this to him."

Wizera reached out and took the letter. Upon reading it, she handed it back to him and took a deep breath. "You could've, but I'm guessing you didn't want to either."

"We're not the best of friends, as my father may have told you in the past, and I needed to understand what was going on before considering revealing this to him."

"What do you mean exactly?"

"I mean, what was your relationship with my father? He told me that you're the only person I can truly trust. Why is that?"

"Well, you see — "

"Were you together or something?"

"No. You've got it all wrong," answered Wizera, as a sly smile crept over her mouth.

Aramant's temper was stirred. "Then WHY?"

The smile on the sorceress's face faded, leaving room for something that could be interpreted as mournfulness. She took a deep breath before granting herself the courage to reveal the truth to him. "He told you that because if anything were to happen to him, he would entrust his cousin with your care."

For a short moment, Aramant thought he had misheard. Yet, the words of the Silver Sorceress gave him no reason to doubt their sincerity. His temper subsided as he found himself stunned and unable to utter a word in return.

Wizera backed away a few steps, unsure how he would react.

A moment later, Aramant closed in on her and grasped her within his arms, hugging her like a lost part of his family.

"Then you are my ...?"

She hugged him back and nodded, tears slipping from her eyes. "Yes, and you're my nephew."

It felt too long since Aramant had a reason to shed tears of joy. The fog that shrouded and disheartened him slowly began to wear thin. It would not vanish entirely, yet it made for a good start. There were still some unanswered questions left, with a couple more sure to emerge from the upcoming answers.

"So Thaidren and I are ...?"

"Yes," answered Wizera.

"Does he know?"

Wizera seemed hesitant to answer. She moved her hand through her long hair while speaking. "He doesn't. Neither of you were supposed to know."

The young paladin's voice changed to a more heated tone. "What do you mean by that? Why weren't any of us supposed to know? I just found out that I have you and him to count as family. What's wrong with knowing that? Why would it be wrong for him to know that?" He heaved a big breath. As he struggled to breathe normally, Aramant understood he was once again experiencing Viz'Hock's grip over his unstable emotional state. For him, it started to feel like this famous holy artifact was more of a burden than a blessing. Upon realizing that, he steadied his breathing. His focus shifted back. "I don't understand all this secrecy. You kept it hidden from him while my father kept it from both of us. Why would you do that?"

"Your father kept it a secret because I asked him to. If you want to blame someone, it should be me. But please, give me a chance to explain. It's not like I did not want you two to know without having a good reason."

Aramant went silent. He crossed his arms, skeptical that anything the Silver Sorceress would tell him would make him feel better about her hiding his family from him. He shook his head and waited for her to start talking. "I'm listening."

"The first thing you have to understand is why I asked your father not to tell either you or my son of this. It's all related to Thaidren. He is… special."

"What do you mean by that?"

"I mean that his very nature and destiny alike were written in stone before he was born. A fate that many fear and want to prevent from happening. I will start from the beginning as it was told to me by my husband many years ago."

*Thaidren's father… that's someone I've almost never heard being spoken of,* thought Aramant. *Not even by my father.* He took a few steps back and sat down on a broken column of the old ruins. From there, he granted Wizera his full attention.

# CHAPTER XIII

# BEFORE THE STORM

At the forge, located a few meters away from the house's garden, Thraik had begun repairing Thaidren's armor. Having worn it for so long now, it felt strange for him to be back in regular clothing.

"What's on yer mind, lad?" the dwarf asked as he tempered the sturdy pieces of armor plate with his hammer.

Thaidren sighed. "I wonder what are they talking about?"

"Which one? Da elf and da earth sorceress? Or ye ma with yer friend?"

"My mom and — "

"I know, lad. 'T was a rhetorical question. Ye're bein' too tense. Won't hurt ye to try replacin' dat frown of yers with a smile every now and then."

"I'm merely curious, that's all." He rubbed his chin. "And Aramant's not a friend. We couldn't be further away."

The dwarf's steady hands continued to bash and bend the metallic parts of Thaidren's armor. He took one eye off the forge and looked at him before letting loose an amused snarl. "Dat is not what I've seen so far."

"Trust me, we've been at each other's throats since we were little."

Thraik burst out laughing. He left the tempered pieces of armor in water to cool and turned toward him. "Lad, dat's exactly how brotherhood is born. Less than a couple of days ago, ye entered a massive bandit camp and smacked the heads of half a hundred of em. Ye were dimwits ta try, and ye still are. But ye wouldn't have come out of dat alive if ye didn't 'ave each other's back."

"We merely had a good plan," Thaidren said.

"Under yer circumstances, lad, da only good plan would've been ta listen ta me and get reinforcements. Two versus fifty men? Dat wasn't a good plan. 'T was dumb as the mortar firemen in da old dwarven empire. They did not know much; they just knew how ta shoot. Dat's why they were put there ta begin with." Thaidren's frown deepened. "Fine. Maybe that was an exaggeration, but my point is dat ye boys take care of each other on the battlefield. And so far on our journey, I haven't seen ye two argue, or as ye put it 'be at each other's throat.' The lad even complimented yer cooking if I remember right."

*Come to think of it, he did do that,* Thaidren thought. *It was a bit out of character.*

"Listen to da wisdom of an old dwarf: ye'll be best pals before ya even realize it. Ye're already on dat path. Yer pa and Attern were da same once."

Upon hearing this, Thaidren's curiosity was piqued. "I thought you didn't like to talk about my father."

The dwarf took a deep breath. "T's not like I don' like ta talk about 'im, lad. 'Tis just dat it's painful ta do it." He took a brief pause and cleared his throat. "But ye're no longer a child, and ye deserve ta know stuff about yer pa."

Hearing Thraik utter such words turned Thaidren's frown into the smile the dwarf was hoping to see. "How did they meet?"

He shook his head and settled himself into the chair near the forge like a grandfather eager to tell stories. "They met around da same age ye and his son are now. 'T was in da late years of da War of The Spider. Durin' dat time, many paladins and mages were dispatched all over da continent ta support and protect each region. Yer pa was one of da people with da initiative to strike down da Spider Queen herself. It took him a while ta convince the leaders of various kingdoms, not ta mention da paladins and mages, ta unite under one banner and set sail to da Old Earth and end da war. Attern was one of da first ta support 'im. Well, after they resolved their personal issues, dat is."

"What personal issues could they have had?"

"For starters, it is through Attern dat yer ma and pa met. In their early days, Attern was very protective of her. He was scared that yer pa was too reckless and unfit for her."

"Did he have feelings for her as well?" asked Thaidren.

"Nah, he just didn't like Thieron at first, and when he saw dem together, he turned his disapproval of 'im toward their relationship."

Thaidren remained silent at first, assimilating all the information in Thraik's story. "How did they end up as friends then?"

"They ended up as brothers, lad. As they got ta know each other better, and especially after fightin' back-ta-back, they realized they were more alike than they thought."

"Sounds like some fairytale with heroes of legend."

"T'is. 'Xcept t'is no fairytale. I swear it on me good eye. I was there. Saw 'em grow in power and each other's eyes. Those were da good times." He raised an imaginary jug of beer into the air. "May their legend last a thousand years."

Inside Thaidren's mind resided mirth and a feeling of disappointment at the same time. "Yeah... I would've chosen the person over the legend, though."

"Lad," said the dwarf with a saddened, guilty tone, "it wasn't his fault. He had no choice."

"I know," Thaidren murmured. "I know..."

Suddenly, several dozen hooded acolytes had teleported over the house and garden. They wore white, shrouded robes with a crest that Thaidren and Thraik did not recognize. Without any warning, they began casting offensive spells. From fireballs to floating ice lances, everyone at the mansion woke up in a storm of attacks that they were unprepared for. Thaidren and Thraik managed to dodge the attacks and hid behind the giant furnace behind the forge. However, neither of them was wearing any armor. They could not afford to get hit.

"Wha' in da name of Kamorah[1] is happenin'?" shouted Thraik.

"I don't think they care to explain," Thaidren replied.

---

[1] Kamorah: one of the five deities worshipped by the dwarven race, Kamorah stands as the embodiment of Wisdom and Intuition in their culture.

Near one of the furnace corners lay an old, rusty firearm. Thraik stretched out to grab it, along with the small bag of gunpowder and round bullets. Thaidren, on the other hand, was completely unarmed. He had left his swords near the entrance to the house. The dwarf loaded the firearm and aimed at one of the mages, hitting him in the chest.

"Only around twenty more ta go, lad," he shouted as he punched the air. The problem was, he didn't have enough ammo to shoot all of them. Still, he only needed to hold their ground and protect Thaidren until Wizera and the rest could join the fight. *I pity da fools who're tryin' ta face Wiz here.*

From within the house, Haara and Elarin heard the ruckus outside. Elarin put her finger to her lips, signaling Haara to stay silent. She unsheathed her dagger and climbed through the back window. Before she had the chance to ambush one or two mages from behind, others had teleported in, surrounding her in the process. One of them came dangerously close to her. Dangerously close to him. With a smooth swing of her arm, the elf slashed his throat, then proceeded to dispose of the rest of them one by one while dodging their attacks. A human being would not have been able to avoid so many projectiles, yet, the physical structure of the Lu'Derai, combined with Elarin's choice of light armor, allowed her to easily avoid her enemies' spells. Her initial estimation of enemies revolved around fifty, maybe more. With her intervention, their numbers would now account for less than that.

Haara could only watch from the top floor window of the house as Thaidren and Thraik hid behind the furnace. Unfortunately for her, she had no means of helping them. Most earthen magic demanded the user to have direct physical contact with the earth itself. And her offensive skills were not her strong suit, to begin with. From another window, she could hear Elarin fighting the second group of sorcerers. She quietly moved through the house, heading toward the stairs and back to the main floor.

# CHAPTER XIV
# SILVER TORRENTS

Aramant was in shock. Whenever he thought nothing more could surprise him, as Wizera told him more and more of Thaidren's true nature, he found himself proved wrong. It wasn't just a matter of the information itself, but the magnitude of it as well. He had no doubt of the truth in his aunt's words. Yet, it proved difficult to digest everything at once. On top of discovering his newfound relatives, it seemed like his ears would soon start to burst out steam. He had no time to put all this into place before more knowledge would be thrown over it. His mind had yet to sort out what he was being told. *Incredible* was the only word that echoed through, ricocheting in every corner of his mind.

With the realization of the young paladin's overwhelmed state, Wizera stopped speaking. "Are you all right?"

Aramant shook his head. "Yeah, I guess. It's just a lot to process."

His reaction brought a sympathetic smile to Wizera's face. "Trust me; it's perfectly normal the way you're reacting right now. I know all too well how it feels to hear it for the first time."

Amidst the swirling thoughts that the young paladin was experiencing, his focus shifted to a particular one. "Having me knowing this now, do you still want to keep it a secret from him?"

"I am not going to ask you not to tell him," replied the Silver Sorceress with a slightly guilty look. "I already made that mistake with your father."

"Yet, I think you'd prefer I wouldn't, right?"

"I will only tell you this: him knowing will only burden him more. He will feel responsible for your well-being, and he might one day disregard his own safety for your own."

Her words amused him. "He's already done that." After the chuckle faded from his face, his tone turned back to his usual self. "Look, uhm... Wizera. Wiz? Aunt? Aunt Wiz...?"

His babbling made her giggle. "Just call me whatever you want, Aramant."

He rubbed his neck. "Right. Look, I can't promise you I won't tell him. If it were me, I'd want to know. And if the roles were reversed, I think that he'd tell me as well."

A couple of small black smoke patches rose from the house's direction, visible from the clear area on top of the hill. It made Aramant stop speaking. Wizera saw them as well and canceled the sound-concealing rune. Their time for chitchat seemed to have been cut short.

"Can you teleport us back?" asked Aramant.

Wizera was hesitant. "If someone is attacking, we risk teleporting into the middle of the battlefield."

The young paladin got a head start as he charged downhill toward the mansion. "Fine, run then."

The Silver Sorceress looked at the sky. Within a moment's notice, her eyes started to glow with the color of clear blue water. *This is the place me and my husband built for Thaidren. It's our home. His home. No one will harm my son or anyone else while I'm here.* As her lips parted, ancient words spewed forth in a torrent. While harnessing the powers of the elements, the bright clouds over the region turned pitch black, with the thundering roar of an upcoming storm accompanying them. In an instant, rain poured down in sheets, starting with a singular droplet that rallied its innumerable siblings that would descend from the heavens. From atop the hill, several giant runes revealed themselves across the mansion in a circular pattern. Wizera had two decades to secure her territory. Any attempt to jeopardize her home's safety would bring severe consequences to the perpetrators. As soon as her channeling of the spell became self-sustained, she followed in Aramant's footsteps.

***

At the mansion, Thraik reveled in laughter as he derided the surrounding mages.

"Ye fools, now y'ave done it. Da lady of da house is pissed. If I were you, rather than end up facin' her, I'd let meself get shot by m — " He paused for a second, having realized what happened. "Son of a..." It was Thraik who could not deliver his end of the threat. His firearm had become a liability. With the gunpowder ending up soaked with water, Thaidren and the dwarf now found themselves disarmed in the face of the enemy. "Can't ya freeze something ta use as a weapon or somethin', lad?" he shouted.

Thaidren's first thought was to freeze the rifle's stock and use it as an improvised mace. He stretched his hand, signaling the dwarf to hand it to him.

Thraik shook his head after an obfuscated and shocked stare at him. "Not me gun for cryin' out loud. Somethin' else."

Unfortunately, nothing else was close or usable as a weapon. Despite that, the enthusiasm in Thraik's eyes was unquenched. Unlike the dwarf, though, Thaidren was skeptical if this was a good time for such an attitude. Their situation seemed dire, at the very least. Wizera hadn't shown up yet, only a sudden storm that, at first glance, gave them more trouble than benefit. *How can he be so sure it was her,* he thought. Furthermore, even though the fire mages were rendered powerless, it didn't mean they were out of the woods.

The same rationale crossed Elarin's mind as she continued to slash through their numbers. If she had known the fire mages would end up becoming harmless, she'd have focused her efforts on the other elemental practitioners first. She was now faced with the dilemma of treading the ground more carefully to avoid making a potentially fatal slip. Her tactic shifted to a more defensive state, slowly working her way back to the mansion, hoping to lure the mages into a confined space. When she was within a few steps of the house, a welcomed aid in the form of shadowy tendrils appeared.

It was Nez'rin's magic. While still in disguise, the lich refrained from using his necromantic powers. Instead, he synergized his mastery over water and the element of darkness, creating tentacle-like limbs that constricted their opponents.

"Thank you," said the elf.

The sorcerer bowed his head. He then turned his gaze upon the captured acolytes, and with a swift clench of his fist, he commanded the tendrils to suffocate them. All but one whom he intentionally made sure would end up unconscious and nothing more, thus keeping him for a later interrogation. "Come, it is not over yet."

In the meantime, near the now extinguished furnace, right next to Thraik and Thaidren, two small oak trees emerged. The young warrior saw Haara signaling him from the corner of the house. She had managed to sneak through the prying eyes of their enemies when the storm started. With her hands touching the ground, she shaped the two small trees to resemble bows using her earthen magic. A vine-made string knotted to their ends bowed the strip.

The dwarf stood by one bow and shouted toward Haara. "Can ya make some arrows too, lass?" *They should be the easiest to make*, he thought. In a matter of seconds, a multitude of sharp, straight twigs emerged from the ground, giving them enough ammo to shoot every mage three times over. To add a bit more kick to his shots, Thaidren froze the improvised arrows' tips.

One of the attackers saw Haara hiding on the side of the house and pursued her. Thaidren shot two arrows at the mage, yet his aim fell short. As the mage was preparing to use a serpent-shaped water mass to enter Haara's lungs and drown her on the spot, he found himself suffering from an excruciating stabbing sensation in his back. As he fell, Haara, Thaidren, and Thraik saw Elarin's dagger embedded in his back. She continued to fight the other nearby mages barehanded, using a form of combat art unknown to them. Taking them down one by one, she gave Thaidren and the others the means to slowly turn the situation back in their favor.

Nez'rin was standing behind the elf, casting either bolts or spear-shaped masses of dark water at the mages. Shortly after their appearance, Wizera and Aramant joined in to finish off the remaining enemy. After discussing with his aunt and filling his mind with so many overwhelming pieces of information, the young paladin wanted to let himself process all of it through some good quality *combat practice*, as he would think of it. Ultimately, his chance at detracting himself was intercepted by Wizera's desire to show the invaders the error of their ways.

Within a few moments, she drew power from the entirety of the place, filled with the water from her runic inscribing over the land. No other water mage would be able to tap this font of power without her will. She was in control here. It was her space to rule over. With a few chanting words of power, accompanied by a gracious display of wavering hands, she entombed every single remaining acolyte within a floating water bubble, filling their lungs with it until their souls were washed away from the realm of the living. It was a cruel act to witness, yet she considered it to be necessary. *In this world, you won't survive long with kindness and mercy.* She learned such life lessons the hard way in the past and was not willing to risk making the same mistakes twice. Among the empty vessels of the drowned, she nullified one of the bubbles prematurely, leaving one of the mages alive yet unconscious. She waved her hand at him and extracted the water inside his lungs before falling to her knees as the glow in her eyes slowly faded away.

"Mother!" shouted Thaidren.

The magically-induced rain had stopped. The runes across the area became dormant once more. Wizera was coughing and began to pant while the rest approached her. She covered the hand on which she spat a few drops of blood, then rubbed it against the soaked ground. Haara saw her gesture but remained quiet for the time being.

"Are you all right?" asked Thaidren.

She raised her hand toward him, signaling to give her a moment to catch her breath. "I'll be fine. I used a bit too much power, that's all."

Beneath the overwhelming sentiment of concern over his mother's well-being, Thaidren and the rest were impressed by her feat. Usually, mages had a level of elemental capability about the same as those that had attacked their home. Ordinarily, they did not possess more combat power than a regular warrior or a paladin. Wizera marked an exception to the rule, her last display of power stood as a testament to that. While the rest of the group fought a rough number of about twenty or so mages with difficulty, she had been able to single-handedly take care of the remaining ones at once. Be that as it may, the fact that it all happened on her territory had played a major factor. She wouldn't be able to harness such power anywhere else, at any time, without vigorous preparation.

Aramant and Thaidren helped the Silver Sorceress get back on her feet. She was dizzy, and her vision was blurry. From behind them, the cold, echoing voice of Nez'rin resounded.

"I don't know who the invaders were, but we have to assume the worst. More may be on their way, preparing to strike a second time when they realize the first wave fell. I managed to capture one of them for interrogation, my lady."

As the disguised lich brought in the prisoner, Wizera's focus turned to the second one that she had almost drowned.

"We don't need a second prisoner. Take care of him, please," she told Thaidren with an authoritarian tone, making it sound to him more like an order than a request.

*What?* This came as an unexpected shock to the young warrior. His mother had just asked him to murder a defenseless person. The mage may have been hostile, yet Thaidren had not been sent to the Cathedral of The Light to follow the moral code of the paladins only to ignore it. To say he was hesitant was an understatement. He did not blame his mother for asking him, yet it felt immoral to comply with such a request. In terms of cold, logical thinking, she was not wrong. He was an enemy. They usually didn't have a change of heart when you showed them mercy. He slowly walked to the front door, where his swords lay. He picked up one and returned, his hand giving in a subtle shake that betrayed his state of uncertainty. *I'll do it fast and painless*, he thought. *A clean death that won't disgrace Attern's teachings.* As he passed by Aramant, the young paladin grabbed him by the shoulder, giving him a compassionate look. He was willing to do it in Thaidren's stead. Before he had the chance to do so, Elarin took out her dagger and plunged it into the mage's skull. Just as Thaidren had intended to do himself, fast and painless.

Upon seeing this, Wizera's expression softened, having realized what she had asked of her son. "Forgive me if it sounded cruel, but he was an enemy. We don't even know why these people want us dead. They did it to themselves the moment they came here with ill intentions." She paused briefly and pulled her son close to her, hugging him. "I'm sorry for asking you this, but I'm not sorry for the action that needed to be done. I hope you can understand."

"Don't worry about it," whispered Thaidren. "Just don't push yourself like that."

"Trust me, son, I've been through things far worse than this," answered the Silver Sorceress with a gentle smile on her face. She turned back at Nez'rin while holding the remaining prisoner. "Get him in Haara's study chamber."

"I'll go help tie him up," said Aramant.

"Yer not goin' anywhere, mister," said Thraik. "There's no place for ye or Thaidren there. Besides, yer comin' ta get yer armor fixed. I almost finished the last one before da attack." He then pointed at Thaidren and his swords. "In da meantime, lad, ye start sharpenin' up those blades. T'is important for ye ta know ta take care of em, lest they serve ya well in battle." The two of them complied, with Aramant being somewhat reluctant. He felt they were being treated like children, and the thought did not bore well within him. He took a deep breath, calming down as he exhaled.

# CHAPTER XV

# ANSWERS

Wizera closed the door behind her before turning to Nez'rin. Her look seemed somewhat disturbed even from the lich's point of view. "Use whatever means necessary, Nez," she said with a regretful whisper. The lich bowed his head and nodded as he dismissed his human disguise. He caressed the chin of the unconscious acolyte. Necromantic energy began to pour out from the mage's empty eye sockets and nose, slowly making its way to his skeletal fingers. Their prisoner woke up, screaming as if waking from a nightmare.

"We need to have a talk," said Wizera from the back of the room.

The acolyte started to shiver, but his stare struggled to remain defiant. He noticed Nez'rin placing one hand over his head and chanting in a language that sounded different from any of the human race. The shiver intensified, and the acolyte felt something inhumanly painful. It was not physical in nature; rather, more like something spiritual. A black, smoking sludge began to drip from his eyes, mouth, ears, and nose, as he began choking on it.

"Can you feel it?" Wizera asked. "You know what's happening? Let me tell you. My friend here is squeezing the life essence in your body, compressing your soul as it's being crushed from the inside and forcing it outside." She became silent as she studied the acolyte's behavior. "Do you know what its color means? What a blackened soul means? It betrays your past. Your actions. And most of all, it betrays your affiliation with demonic forces." She signaled the lich to cease his chant for a moment, allowing the prisoner to catch his breath. The black sludge crawled its way back into each orifice from where it came, as if nothing had happened. The Silver Sorceress slowly approached him. "Whom do you serve? Why did you attack us? What were your orders? Tell me, and I promise you I will do everything in my power to cleanse your soul so that you may pass into the afterlife peacefully and untainted."

The acolyte spat on the ground before bursting into a state of uncontrollable laughter. "You... you want me to... to talk. And in... exchange for that, you promise me a... 'clean'... death? You strike a terrible bargain, Wizera of the Cerulean Order."

"How do you..." Wizera took a moment to regain her composure, after which her voice shook with fury. "How do you know that name?" she shouted.

"It was our job to be well-informed before coming here," answered the prisoner. "Although... we clearly underestimated your combat prowess. The master was right about you. Now I wonder if we were sent here as sacrificial lambs." He cleared his throat, then spat a second time after. "This is all you're going to get out of me, Sorceress: you lot meddled in affairs that did not concern you, and now punishment is in order. Before you realize it, you and all your family will burn."

Nez'rin held up his hand, signaling for Wizera to back off. A flicker of blue and dark energy spheres emerged within his empty eye sockets, almost resembling a pair of spectral eyeballs. His other hand started to emanate the smoking power that seeped within the mage, squeezing out his soul once again.

"You dare threaten Lady Wizera and her beloved ones? Foolish, pathetic puppet. After she offered to help your undeserving soul ascend to the world of the dead in a peaceful manner, you chose to spit in her face. Very well, since she showed your two options, and you seem reluctant to both, allow me to present a lesser known, option number three. Lady Wizera, forgive my audacity, but I believe it would be best for you if you do not witness this. What I am about to do to this man is not for the eyes of mortals. I humbly request for a moment of privacy with this cur."

The Silver Sorceress was taken by surprise. There had been few moments in history when she witnessed the lich being so expressive. To see him furious was even more of a rarity. A morbid curiosity wished her to stay and observe. Yet, she knew that if Nez insisted, it wouldn't be a wise decision. Wizera closed the door behind her, then heard the coughing and agonizing screams of the acolyte as she climbed the stairs back outside.

While Aramant and Thraik were busy at the forge, Haara, Elarin, and Thaidren began taking care of the bodies. The earth sorceress had instructed them to move their empty carcasses further away from the house and arrange them one next to each other. By the time Wizera had come out from Haara's underground chamber, their task was almost done. Thaidren figured the corpses would be incinerated. It would pose too much of a hassle to dig a grave for each of them.

"Why didn't we pile them up to burn them?" asked the young warrior.

"Because we're not going to," said Wizera, as she approached them.

Elarin tilted her head. "I take it that it is common practice in your world to incinerate the departed?"

"Sometimes," answered Haara, "but we're not doing that now. I'm going to send them back to the earth instead."

"Send them back to the earth?" asked both Thaidren and Elarin in unison.

"Yes. It is a ritual that many earth-users practice. We are born into this world, we live on this earth, and when our time comes, we ultimately become one with the earth. My magic can speed up the process of turning their bodies into nutrients for the soil."

The elf tilted her head once more. "Meaning you are making them rot faster?"

"In a sense, yet not quite. Decaying is more related to blood magic. I use my elemental affinity to bury them in such a manner that the earth will be able to absorb them faster. It won't turn them into bones and dust faster; rather, it will take less time for the soil to incorporate them, so to speak. I will channel them to strengthen the earth around them. To heal it and make it more hospitable for the growth of plants and trees. From there, it will invite the development of biological life as well. As part of the great life cycle of which we all are a part."

"I see."

"What about your kin?" asked Haara. "How do you honor the dead?"

Elarin took a moment of silence to find the right words to explain. "I come from a race that lives through worshipping the moon. We acknowledge it as our guardian, our goddess. In that spirit, when someone passes on, depending on their life accomplishments and how they were viewed by the people, we start with a prayer ritual during the first night after the person's departure. We dress the body in a unique, special garb made solely for these situations. It is a common belief that through these vestments, the moon goddess knows which of us need guidance toward the realm of the dead. With the remains being sealed after the ceremony, their coffins are never to be opened again. Their final resting place resides in giant mausoleums, built generations before ours, safe from the prying eyes of heretics who may dabble in death magic. It is through these traditions that we believe the soul finds its harmony in the afterlife."

The elf's tale mesmerized the atmosphere around while Haara performed the spell of earth-binding. Within the following moments, Elarin's voice subtly turned to a more saddened tone. Thaidren and the rest figured talking about her homeworld must be painful for her. With that in mind, none of them considered it appropriate to ask her more about it. After a few minutes passed, Haara's spell came to an end. Afterward, from within the underground chamber, Nez'rin emerged. Wizera was especially curious to find out what the lich learned from the acolyte.

"It is done," he said. "He has no more knowledge, useful to us, that I have not already extracted."

Aramant and Thraik were making their way toward them. The young paladin's armor looked as good as new, ready to taste the field of combat once more.

"Wha'cha all babblin' about here?" asked the dwarf.

"I was about to announce what I found out from our prisoner," answered the lich.

"Well, wha'cha waitin' for? A bloody drumroll? Spill da beans already, ye blasted sack of bones." The dwarf's eyes widened in an instant. He realized he may have denounced Nez'rin's identity to Elarin and Aramant. *Blast*. Apart from the two of them raising an eyebrow at his choice of words, they didn't seem to have taken them literally. By now, they had become accustomed to his way of speaking. With that concern out of the way, a second one emerged in the form of Wizera's gaze, which suggested he needed to be more cautious in the future. He remained silent for the time being, as her glare shifted back to the lich.

"Continue, Nez," said the Silver Sorceress.

"This attack was premeditated. From what I understand, it was not machinated too far in the past. The cultist mentioned this was a recently planned counterattack."

Wizera's eyes widened. "Wait, cultist? If we're dealing with a cult, then that's a completely different matter. Did he give you more information?"

"Yes," answered the lich, with a slight pause. "He was a member of what he called the cult of Kasm. Truly fanatic about his beliefs and their cause, with their ultimate goal reveling around reshaping the world. To put it in his words: make it a better place where the strong thrive, and the weak are cast off, ushering mankind toward a new stage of evolution. This will repair both our world and our kin, as he claimed."

"Those are troubling beliefs to operate on," said Wizera. "The Council of Mages has dealt with numerous cults in the past. Those that seek to save the world, or change it for the sake of a so-called better vision of the future were always the most dangerous. I will report this to them immediately, but I need you to detail it even more, Nez."

"Hold on a second," said Haara as she interrupted Wizera. "You said 'counterattack'. I don't recall any of us ever attacking them."

"Nevertheless, they seem to believe so. Their closest operations from here lay at an abandoned mine." Thaidren, Aramant, Thraik, and Elarin were shocked upon hearing these words. As the lich continued to talk, more and more of the situation began to make sense while also confirming the cultist's words. "They were extracting special minerals from there by using hired bandits, whom they provided with slaves as a workforce."

Aramant clenched his fist to the point where it felt he'd bent the plates on his gauntlet. *So, they attacked us here because we freed the slaves?*

Thaidren reached into his pocket and searched for the crystal samples he had retrieved from the mine. "We attacked them, mother. We freed the slaves at the mine." He paused and looked toward Elarin.

"They freed me and many others," added the elf.

Wizera ran her hand through her hair. "It makes more sense now." She saw Thaidren raising his hand, then placing the fragments in hers.

"This is what they were mining. Sorry I couldn't bring more samples."

Upon touching her skin, Wizera felt a small amount of her magical energy being drained off to the crystals. "Don't worry about it. These will do just fine." As she covered the shards with a piece of cloth, the sorceress had one more question in mind. "Nez, did he tell you who gave the orders? Who their leader is? Whom or what do they serve?"

Nez'rin did indeed get the information. However, the cultist was more determined to die than reveal his master's identity. Unfortunately for him, the lich had the means to interrogate him even after he decided his best course of action was to bite off his tongue. Death magic was particularly useful in that sense. "He said one of their higher-ups was known as Epakin. Whoever it is, he or she gave the order and mobilized the attack. I was able to extract a second name from him: Sera. I regrettably admit that I have no further knowledge than this."

*Epakin... Sera... The first one sounds human. The other one, I'm not certain yet,* Wizera thought. With all the information in mind, it was time for the Silver Sorceress to contact the Council of Mages and report her findings. *This is turning out to be progressively worse. After I notify the council, I'll take a better look at the shards. Maybe I can find out more.*

"What now?" asked Aramant.

"Now," answered Haara, "you let us take care of the important matters. You must heal your wounds, rest, and prepare for a possible second assault." She raised her hand, pointing at Thaidren and his group. "Whoever is injured, no matter how little, I want you to let me take a look and heal you." Her focus was more pronounced toward Elarin. "Especially you. A few days ago, from what I understand, you were malnourished and at death's door. You need to take care of yourself the most. I'll do my best to help you with my powers, but that alone won't be enough. Understood?"

The elf bowed her head in agreement. "Thank you. I will do as you say."

"There's plenty of spare beds in the house if needed," added Wizera. "We can continue this tomorrow. If you need me, I'll be in my study chamber."

"Is there any way I can be of further assistance, Lady Wizera?" asked Nez'rin.

"Take care of the body, then come see me, please."

"I will see to it at once," answered the lich.

"Thank you, Nez."

"You are most welcome."

"Enough with da pleasantries!" shouted the dwarf. "After repairin' two sets of armor and target practicin' with cultists, t'is time ta take a well-deserved nap. So, with dat said, I'm off ta me bed, right after I pour meself some sweet beer from one of da kegs in da basement. Yer welcome ta join me for a drink. If not, I'll see ya later." The dwarf ended up in a deep slumber over the table in the wine cellar for the remainder of the day and night. It was during the night that the others discovered how loud a drunken, tired dwarf can snore.

The following morning, Aramant found himself still sleepy after waking up several times during the night, wanting to go to the wine cellar and punch Thraik into silence. However, that was not the reason for his lack of sleep. Ever since their departure from the Cathedral of The Light, he had not been able to rest well. As far as the young paladin was concerned, he was in a stage of acceptance regarding everything that happened. Having found out that he still had family helped him substantially. Nevertheless, he was well aware that he would need more time to heal completely. He woke up with the dwarf standing next to his bed and shaking him.

"Rise and shine, blond princess," he said. "Beauty sleep's over. T'is almost noon."

Aramant slowly got out of bed, his eyes narrowed. He rubbed them and threw a distasteful look at Thraik. *Somehow, when we were on the roads, he wasn't so loud.*

"Quit lookin' at me like you're smellin' rotten eggs and get a move on. We're goin' on a journey."

"A journey?" asked Aramant.

"Aye, lad. Now get yer armor on and move. We'll be waitin' for ye downstairs."

The young paladin complied with little more than a mumble, while daydreaming of how he'd enjoy playing "whack a dwarf." After a long yawn and a healthy stretch, he put on his armor and went outside. Wizera and the rest were already there, waiting for him.

"So where are we heading?" asked Thaidren, knowing no more than Aramant.

"Grinal, the city of trades," answered Haara.

Thaidren and Elarin were unfamiliar with the name. However, Aramant had heard it being mentioned before, in his father's stories.

"It is a place for otherworldly trading," explained Nez'rin. "An inter-existential hub where creatures from other worlds gather and trade their merchandise between one another. Anything from smithing materials to magical scrolls and arcane knowledge can be found there if you know where to look."

"What does this have to do with us?" asked Thaidren.

Wizera sighed briefly as she rubbed her eyes. "After spending most of the night studying the crystals you brought from the mine, I've determined their purpose. They are naturally attuned to absorb elemental energy, but they can also act as catalysts for certain incantations if fueled up. An old acquaintance of mine informed me they can be found in Grinal, though they seem to be in short supply lately."

"Short supply?" replied Thaidren in a confused tone. "The bandit camp had at least two carts filled with them, on top of however more were still buried in the mine."

"They must've found a rich deposit. Either way, this is our only lead on finding the cult."

"All is good'n shiny, but what about the mansion?" asked the dwarf. "What happens if those bastards send another party ta attack?"

"We can't do anything about that," said Elarin. "Most probably they will. They know the location, and given that we repelled their first attempt, they will be better prepared a second time. When we return, it would be wise to teleport somewhere in the vicinity and scout ahead to be safe."

"Yes, I've already placed two different spatial anchors farther away from the house," replied Wizera. "But for now, let's focus on finding them while they'll be busy searching for us." She pointed at Thaidren and Aramant, then Haara. The earthen sorceress held out two hefty-shrouded mantles. "Wear these. Your paladin armors would draw too much attention."

As soon as they put them on, Wizera asked them to remove their right gauntlet as she drew a small bottle of blue dye from her bag. She then chanted, making the dye glow, and with a light brush, painted two runic symbols on their exposed arms. "It's going to be very hot where we're going. One rune will keep your body temperature normal." She then asked for everyone else to stand still as she painted another rune on each of their hands. "The second one is for communication. We're most probably going to separate into groups when we get there. If we are within a certain range of each other, we can reach out through thoughts. Now, with everything settled, is everyone ready?"

Everyone nodded. Soon after, the Silver Sorceress began conjuring words of power as she waved her hands. A circular breach, a portal, within the fabric of space opened, marking its way to the city of trades. One by one, each of them traversed on the other side, with Wizera being last. She was able to maintain the portal's integrity for a short time after ending her incantation.

Traveling through a portal felt different than teleporting. It was the first time for Thaidren and Aramant, making them feel nauseated as soon as they reached their destination. In the past, teleporting felt like they were fast-traveling within the same world. However, a portal felt like it was ripping their body apart piece by piece and reassembling it at the other end.

"Don't worry; it is normal when one is not accustomed to it," Elarin reassured them. "Your bodies get used to it over time."

After catching their breath, and a long session of coughing, the two of them stood, gazing at their destination. They realized they were in the middle of a vast, dried-up land. Before them lay a giant canyon filled with what seemed like a colony of ants, evermoving through endless floors that went from the top to the bottom of the pit. It marked a mesmerizing sight of surreal proportions to the eyes of those who had not got the chance to see the wonders of the world. Around the canyon's edges, several wooden elevators tied with stiff rope, dragged through pulleys, with two wardens guarding each elevator, stood at the edge of the canyon.

"Incredible," said the young paladin. "But why didn't we travel directly within the city?"

"It is warded against any form of spatial travel," answered the lich. "A means to maintain the security of the place, making sure that it will never be attacked the same way that we were at the mansion."

"Why wasn't the mansion warded the same way then?"

Wizera lowered her head. "The problem with warding a place against spatial travel is that it puts a great strain on the casting mage. Several mages can share this burden to ease it. The more participants in the ritual, the less pressure. Unfortunately, while I would've had the power to do so once, that is no longer the case. And I was also concerned that weakening myself even more would prove too great of a risk."

"That's of no relevance now," said Elarin. "Before we venture into this city, is there something else we should know about it?"

"Only to tread with care. Think of it as a bazaar filled with creatures from all around existence. There will be safe places to visit, as well as some more inhospitable ones. Considering our circumstances, it's more likely that we'll have to dabble into the more contentious parts."

Thaidren nodded. "Understood. So, how should we split up?"

"I'll go with Elarin," said Haara. "You go with your mother, while Nez'rin and Thraik go with Aramant. I trust the dwarf will do something stupid, so it's better if two people supervise him."

"I beg yer pardon? 'Somethin' stupid'? Me? Wha' gave you dat idea, missy? I be needin' supervisin' now? Who do ya think ye are? It is I who'll supervise em. Just ya wait and see," the dwarf replied in offense, tossing his head.

"Whatever lies help you sleep better at night."

The dwarf's face turned red. He turned around and mumbled as they filed into the elevator. As they passed by, the wardens remained still, initially. Upon the group's embark, they both thrust the end of their spears into the ground, inserting them into two keyhole-shaped spaces that activated the elevator. The group gazed at the numerous floors and tunnels dug within the canyon as they descended. The once-distant ants became fully fleshed-out denizens of the settlement, each of them like nothing they had ever seen before.

Aramant felt overwhelmed, in a curious way. *So many outer-worldly races*, he thought. *A shame we didn't come here to enjoy the place.*

# CHAPTER XVI

# OF HEAT AND DARK

Within the ginormous canyon in the dried lands that covered almost a quarter of the New Continent lay houses built within walls. Layers over layers of metal and wooden platforms, elevators, contraptions, caravans, and zip lines connecting different sections of a hub. Together they entangled in a chaotically beautiful mass that constituted the trade city of Grinal, home of the rarest items one could possibly seek in this world. A haven for traders of all kinds, brimming with infinite opportunity as much as a chance to find misfortune.

The elevator left them somewhere near the labyrinthian bazaar's middle floor. As they arrived, they nodded to each other and divided into their predetermined groups.

*Now remember*, Wizera spoke through her thoughts, *this link will break if we get too far from each other. Since I'm the one maintaining it, I am the focal point.*

*Extraordinary. Wait, all of our thoughts can be heard?* asked Elarin, her eyes widening.

*Since it's the first time you experience it, yes*, Wizera answered. *Most, if not the entirety of your inner voice, can be heard. However, in time you learn how to mask some of your thoughts. Skilled mages are taught how to communicate in this form from a young age, so they'll quickly learn to hide information in the event of this being used as an interrogation method.*

Upon hearing this, Elarin thoughts whirled out of control. She quickly unsheathed her dagger and made a swift cut on her hand, disrupting the runic symbol and her mental link.

Haara stammered. She stepped back, raised an eyebrow toward her companion, and glared at the elf.

"What the hell was that?" she eventually found her words.

Elarin made eye contact with the earthen sorceress. She calmly sheathed her dagger. "Apologies, but I cannot allow all of my thoughts to be heard."

"And why is that? You have something to hide from us?" In her mind, Haara continued to hear the confused voices of the others.

*Son of a…* wailed the dwarf in pain, as a whizzing sound pierced his skull.

*What just happened?* asked Aramant. *I felt as if one of the threads in my mind was ripped out.*

*That's what happens when someone cancels its link abruptly,* said Wizera. *Haara, what happened to Elarin? Are you all right?* With none of them answering, she began speculating the worst possible scenario. In the meantime, Haara was silent on both ends, still waiting for Elarin to answer her question.

"What I have are matters that do not concern you," she eventually replied. "There are aspects about me that I am not ready to share." She was aware of what could be the first logical thoughts that could pass through Haara's mind and reacted accordingly. "I am not a traitor. Not for this so-called cult, nor for anyone else. I serve no one, believe that."

Her eyes did not reflect mistrust, and her words seemed sincere enough, for now. Haara decided to keep an eye on her after this episode. It gave her the benefit of the doubt until proven otherwise. *Elarin has some personal reasons to not share all of her thoughts with us. I was the one who told her she could interrupt the link.*

Wizera was skeptical of Haara having done such a thing. *It is unwise, and I'm against it. We should be able to communicate with each other at all times.* She paused briefly. *Tell her that I won't enforce it on her, though. Just don't lose sight of one another. I trust you'll suffice for communication, Haara.* With the matter at hand having been settled, it was time for them to decide where each group would go.

*We should slowly head down to the bottom floors,* said Haara. *That's where the more questionable deals take place.*

*We will go there first,* answered Nez'rin. *For the moment, you investigate the middle levels. There is no point for all of us risking going there until we are confident we have to.*

*Fine, we'll continue our search on these floors, for now,* replied the earthen sorceress.

Wizera intervened with one last bit of information. *Nez, the crystals are commonly known as Quaar Crystals. Be careful whom you ask about them.*

*As you say, my lady.*

***

Thaidren and Wizera began heading to the city's top levels. Wizera led the way, with her son following behind. She seemed to know exactly where they were going. Eventually, the warrior gave in to his questioning, and spoke his mind out loud.

"Mother?"

"Yes?" she answered with a soft tone.

"Why are we going to the top floors? I thought Haara said we're most likely to find deals related to the crystals at the lower levels."

"The deals themselves, yes. But I'm hoping to find information regarding them up here. I have an old acquaintance who might help us."

Thaidren knew his mother to be a renowned sorceress with connections and notoriety all over the world. Still, the thought of her reputation reaching this place surprised him. "Have you been here in the past?" he asked.

"Once or twice, in what seems like a lifetime ago," she replied. "This place is not as bad as I have described initially. We may be looking for a secret organization now, but I also remember it as a wondrous place, filled with opportunities and a ton of different people to meet. As a young mage, there were plenty of times when I needed specific materials that could only be bought here."

"And are you sure this acquaintance of yours is still here? Can we trust him after all this time?"

She chuckled for a brief moment. "Don't worry about that. He's a good person. And I doubt he'll ever leave this place. He was born here, and has a knack for this way of life. You'll understand once you see him."

The people moving through the platforms were gazing in awe at Thaidren. Most of them were smaller than the Silver Sorceress, let alone him. To them, he was seen as an intimidating giant, perhaps serving as a bodyguard for the beautiful lady he accompanied. After several minutes of walking, they stopped in front of one of the crevice-built-in houses with several tables and shelves aligned near it. Each of them filled with miscellaneous items that were anything but familiar to the young warrior. From the back of the house, he heard a pair of loud footsteps approaching the door. A plump hand pulled aside the sheet hanging from the top of the door, and a joyous shout came from within.

"Wizera, my dear! It has been too long."

The Silver Sorceress smiled. "Indeed, it has been, Parab. How have you been?"

While the two of them were reminiscing about the past, Thaidren was studying Parab from farther away. A round person, definitely not a human, a bit taller than Wizera but smaller than him, with a chopped finger on his left hand and a prosthetic left leg made from rusty metal scraps. It seemed mechanized to some extent, puffing short bursts of steam every few minutes or so. One of his eyes also looked odd, resembling a black eye, making Thaidren think that he may have recently been involved in a fight.

"Great, great. Business is getting better by the day. The money is good. Well, as good as it can be for a guy like me. Oh, and I recently won an entire batch of artrinite[2] ores at a game of shlesh[3]."

---

[2] Artrinite: a precious ore that doesn't originate from Earth. Blacksmiths learned in time to use this otherworldly mineral to produce quality pieces of weaponry or armor that are lighter than steel, yet harder and more durable.

[3] Shlesh: a gambling card game that can be played by 2-8 players. The premise of the game is that whoever has the lowest value of cards in hand is the winner of the round, the reason behind it lies in the concept that every participant needs to gamble, but the lowest hand counts as being 'the one who lost the least', or 'the smartest bet', therefore, the winner.

"Glad to hear that," said Wizera. "Although, I thought you quit playing."

"Eh, what can I say, dear. It's my guilty pleasure. Keeps life interesting in a way."

Following their catch-up, Parab's attention shifted to Thaidren. He noticed the not-so-subtle way Thaidren studied his eye. He pointed at it with his good hand.

"It's not what it seems, good warrior. I know it looks like a black eye, as you humans call it, but trust me, I've been in no fights. This is just an illness that's been with me for some years. It impedes my vision a bit, but I've gotten used to it; it's nothing serious."

Thaidren's gaze turned to the ground. "Apologies, I didn't know."

The merchant chuckled at his apology. "Don't sweat it. I ain't one to take it to heart." His focus turned back to his old friend. "So, tell me, Wiz, who's this friend of yours?"

She looked at her son with pride, making her smile grow wider. "This is my son, Thaidren."

Upon hearing these words, Parab quickly moved next to the young warrior and gave him a big hug. Thaidren pulled back, although he didn't struggle to escape.

"Would you look at that. I've wanted to meet you for a long time. When I first heard Wiz was pregnant a couple of decades back, I was overwhelmed with happiness. And now, I finally get to meet you. Just look at how massive you are. Wiz, how in heavens name did you manage to give birth to someone his size?"

*He seems like a nice guy,* Thaidren thought.

The merchant raised his hand, and upon unclenching his fist, he revealed a small bottle with a purple liquid inside. "A gift from me, young one. Please accept it. It's a potion that helps you sleep well. Top of the market, free of charge."

Wizera intervened quickly. "Parab, you don't have to do this. I don't want any special treatment because we've known each other for a long time."

"I'm not treating you, Wiz. I'm treating your son. Allow me the pleasure of giving him this. Consider it a very late birthday present. Except for it, I promise you I'm going to treat you both as I would any other customer."

Thaidren and Wizera looked at each other. With a disagreeing exhale from the Silver Sorceress, she eventually accepted. "Fine, keep it."

"Much obliged, old friend," answered Parab. "Now, how can I be of help? Are you looking for something in particular?"

"Actually, yes. We're looking for some Quaar crystals. Do you know where we can get a hold of some?"

Parab removed his hat and ran his hand over his head, then rubbed it. "Hmm, they're not part of my usual trading stock, but I knew a few people who used to sell them. Problem is, I don't know why, but if what I heard is true, their value increased very much in the last year, with fewer and fewer merchants being able to acquire them in the first place."

"So, you're saying they're in short supply now?" asked Thaidren.

"Their demand was never that high to begin with, but they're certainly not as common as they were before, I can tell you that. There may still be some vendors on the bottom floors, but I don't have many friends there. To be honest, I try to keep myself and my business away from that place. 'Cause you know…"

"I understand," said Wizera. "Well, thank you for the information, Parab. As always, you've been of great help."

"It was good seeing you, Wiz. If you need anything else, no matter what time of the day, know that my shack is always open for you." He looked at Thaidren and raised his hand to shake it. "Your mother is a very kind person. Among all the humans I've encountered over the years, she counts within the very few who never judged me by my pretty face. Take good care of her and yourself." The young warrior nodded as he let go of his hand. "And what I told her also applies to you. Should you ever need anything, my door will be open."

"I appreciate it," he replied.

As they were heading back to one of the elevators to go down to the lower levels, Thaidren stared at the gift from Parab. He twisted it all around, looking at it for a few minutes before stuffing it into his bag. "He seemed like a nice guy."

"He truly is," replied the Silver Sorceress. "I wish you would've seen him back in the day when he was with Genra."

"Genra?"

Wizera sighed. "Genra was his wife," she eventually answered. "They were running the shop together. Unfortunately, she died right before I last visited this place."

"What happened to her?"

"I'm not sure. Parab was not exactly thrilled to talk about it, and I didn't push him either. The only thing I know is that she ventured down to the lower levels for a business matter and never came back. There were a series of abductions during that time, with the missing persons never to be seen again. He searched for her for months, calling in any favor he could in the process. I wanted to come and help him too, but I was already pregnant with you at the time and couldn't risk it."

"But he seems so joyous and happy," said Thaidren, frowning. "How can he smile like that after losing her?"

"It's a good question… Sometimes I wonder the same. I even feel envious of him at times. And guilty, because of that."

Thaidren figured this was not just about Parab anymore. "Sorry, I didn't mean to make you feel bad."

"You don't have to apologize. You didn't do anything wrong." She took in a deep breath and smiled at him. "Let's go down below. The rest are probably waiting for u — "

A sudden, thundering sound interrupted them, followed by a shockwave that disrupted most of the city-level platforms. On the opposite side of the canyon, a few decks beneath their level, several sections of the floor began to collapse, forming an avalanche of debris that swiped away the levels beneath them until reaching the bottom. Distant screams could be heard as people desperately tried to save themselves from falling or being swept away with the rubble. Eventually, the structures stopped collapsing, yet a significant portion of the area became inaccessible.

"What could've happened there?" Wizera and Thaidren wondered.

***

Elarin and Haara ventured further away from the other two groups, ending up on the side of the canyon opposite from where they initially entered. Since Nez'rin's group went to the lower levels, this seemed like the best option for them to cover more ground. The tension between the earthen sorceress and the elf had subsided, for now. However, after her recent gesture, Haara could not let her guard down entirely. She tried to dismiss any possible reason why Elarin would hide something from them, yet she could not help but wonder. The curiosity was eating at her.

"You have been quiet for some time," said the elf eventually. "Are the others saying anything?"

"Nothing important," answered Haara. "Apart from the dwarf constantly complaining about his feet hurting, they're silent."

"Is Aramant not thinking anything? Can humans clear their minds like that?"

Haara had not made herself clear. Aramant's thoughts could be heard. However, there was something odd about it. They were hard to hear, hushed as if he were at the edge of the link's maximum range. Yet, that was not the case, given that he, Nez'rin, and the dwarf were in the same place. "No, we can't. To be honest, his inner voice is simply... faint, I guess."

The elf sensed a subtle hint of concern in her words. "Does it bother you?"

"It intrigues me. Maybe he has some subconscious ability to tone down his thoughts without being able to hide them completely. Still, being able to do such a thing for the first time during a mind link is past rare."

"Well, 'past rare' does not make it unheard of. Perhaps he is a special case."

"Perhaps..."

"What about Thaidren?"

"Thaidren is... different, even by human standards. Wouldn't surprise me to know that not every thought of his can be heard."

Elarin's interest was piqued by Haara's statement. "What do you mean by that?"

She sighed. "It's complicated."

"Try me."

The earthen sorceress smiled. "I don't think I should be the one to tell you these things. Don't get me wrong, but I think that you should ask Wizera or Thaidren directly if you are curious." She turned back and stared into the open area. "Besides, we have other matters to focus on now."

"I understand," answered the elf. "So, where should we start? We walked past a dozen or more stores already. Were they of no interest to us?"

"These? No, they aren't. They specialize in selling contraptions of different kinds. They don't deal with magical items. We need to go to a specific part of the city where crystals are the main trading stock."

"I see. How do we get there?"

Haara pointed in front of her. "We're already here."

Within their visual prowess, tradesmen over tradesmen occupied the inner side of the floor. From merchants selling fake, decorative masterpieces to those who displayed precious magical stones, jewel crafters, and appraisal centers, all of them intertwining in an economic jigsaw puzzle in which only a few knew how to fully profit. Haara and Elarin blended in without difficulty, asking merchants about Quaar crystals and showing interest in other precious stones to avoid drawing unwanted attention. For a short time, they almost forgot about their mission objective, succumbing to the excitement and joy surrounding them and feeling hypnotized by the city's charm. After a while, they came across a tavern whose shopkeeper dealt with magical crystals of a more volatile nature. Upon asking him about Quaar crystals, his friendly attitude turned suspicious.

"And why would two beauties like you seek Quaar crystals?" he asked, raising an eyebrow.

"I require a few for a ritual that can't be done otherwise," answered Haara.

The merchant threw an intrigued look at her, remaining speechless for a few moments. "Hmm, are you sure you can't substitute something else for them? Look around; maybe you'll find something else."

"I've done my research, old man. There's nothing else I can use."

"Well, unfortunately, I haven't got a hold of any Quaar crystals in almost a year." He rubbed his long grey beard. "But perhaps I know someone in the lower districts who may still have some. Ask for a man named Jerib; tell him Ohzat sent you. His shop is right next to the Silver Pockets Inn, near the center of the bottom floor plaza."

Haara nodded at the man and thanked him. Before they had a chance to depart, the merchant interrupted them, his attention directed toward Elarin and her weapon.

"Pardon me, young elf, but I couldn't help but notice your exquisite-looking dagger. Lu'Derai artifacts are not a common thing in this world."

His words caught Elarin off guard. "You have knowledge about my kin?"

"But of course, my dear," said the old man. "I've even traded some moon elf artifacts back in the day when I dealt with more than crystals. I am well aware of their superb craftsmanship and quality. I simply could not let you walk past me without asking if you'd be willing to part with it. I know a few good merchants who'd be very interested in it, and you'd be generously compensated."

She smiled at the merchant. "Thank you for your cordial words, but I cannot part with it. It is a family heirloom, and it bears great sentimental value to me."

The merchant nodded in acceptance, yet had a hint of disappointment in his eyes. "I understand. As I said, I felt morally obliged as a man of the trades to ask you about it." He looked at both Haara and Elarin and saluted them politely. "Best of luck in finding the crystals."

"Thank you; we appreciate it," answered the earthen sorceress. As soon as they parted ways with the merchant, Haara reported their findings to the others. *Elarin and I found out some things about the crystals. Apparently, since last year they are in very short supply.*

*We've heard the same,* said Wizera.

*There doesn't seem to be any merchant at the mid-levels who still has them for sale,* added Haara. *Our only option is the lower levels. One tradesman pointed me to a local there, Jerib. Said his shop is next to the Silver Pockets Inn. His tongue should soften up upon hearing the name Ohzat. Nez'rin, your group should go and check out the place. We'll join you as soon as we can.*

*As you wish,* he replied.

*What if he's not willing to cooperate? Or worse, if he's in league with the cult?* asked Aramant.

*For the time being, act normal and don't insist if you sense him being hesitant. Once we regroup, we can question him a bit harsher if needed.*

As Elarin and Haara headed toward the lower levels, the elf noticed a suspicious-looking person watching them from afar. At first, she thought she was being paranoid. Yet, after a few minutes of walking and several turns, she subtly grabbed Haara by the arm and signaled her not to look back.

"Remain calm," she whispered. "Someone is shadowing us."

Haara gently nodded at the elf and continued to walk. "Are you absolutely sure?"

"I can spot a tail in my sleep. This one is not even subtle. Beware the hooded woman in the white mantle." They both remained silent, each thinking about what to do next. Haara was hesitant to stir up panic and alert the rest until there was no shred of doubt that Elarin's claim was valid. Before she had time to think this through, the stalker drew a rifle from her mantle and aimed at them.

"Look out," shouted Elarin as she tucked herself down to avoid the bullet.

Their pursuer aimed at the elf. The shot missed, but it did hit a barrel of crystals belonging to one of the district's shops. It proved to be loaded with volatile crystals, used as controlled explosives when mining. It detonated into a massive explosion, the shockwave knocking Elarin, Haara, and many others off their feet. The elf sprang up, and the culprit retreated by climbing down and jumping from one platform to another, deep into the lower levels.

"Elarin, wait," shouted Haara as she got back on her feet.

Unfortunately, the elf did not hear her. Her killer instincts kicked in, wanting to chase and enact revenge on whoever tried to kill them. Next to the earthen sorceress, several sections of the floor began to collapse, forming an avalanche of debris that swiped away the levels beneath them until reaching the bottom. Distant screams could be heard as people desperately tried to save themselves from falling or being swept away with the rubble. Eventually, the structures stopped collapsing, yet a significant portion of the area became inaccessible. Haara may have been fortunate enough not to count herself among the victims, but it was of little consolation to her.

*What have we done...?*

\*\*\*

Thraik was on the verge of exploding. He had had enough of people walking around the city who failed to see him. "I swear ta me own beard, if I get bumped into again, I'm shootin' whatever bastard does it in da foot." Ignoring him, Nez'rin and Aramant looked around in search of a shop that might sell Quaar crystals.

"Maybe that one?" Aramant asked Nez'rin, pointing.

The lich studied the shop. "That one seems to specialize in weaponry materials rather than conduit crystals."

The young paladin rubbed his head. Such terms and classifications were a bit off his usual spectrum of knowledge. Among the series of faces that surrounded him, a particular one caught his attention. A dark-haired woman, with one brown eye, the other one seemingly blind, dressed with an old red tattered mantle signaled him to come closer. Aramant noticed that her shop seemed devoid of any merchandise.

"Come closer, young one," he heard the woman. While skeptical about her intentions, Aramant felt compelled by curiosity to find out what she wanted. He complied with the request and took a seat at her round table, housed under a tent missing a side. It had all sorts of strange items on it, like artifacts, yet none seemed to be placed there as a means to trade. "I'm glad you decided to see past your skepticism."

"Do we know each other?" asked the young paladin.

"No, this is the first and last time we'll ever meet," answered the woman. "Allow me to introduce myself. I am Fivianora, once a renowned oracle. Now, I'm merely a relic of a bygone age, trying to earn her bread."

"I don't know anything about oracles, but you seem to me like a fortune teller."

The woman chuckled. "There is not much of a difference Aramant, only in name."

He stood silent for a moment, failing to remember when he'd mentioned his name. "How do you..."

"A proof that my words are not coated in lies, young one. I'm aware that your skepticism is present still. And yet, I figured that, having said that, perhaps you'll be more willing to listen now."

The young paladin jumped to his feet. "I don't have time for this." As he walked away, a gentle whisper came from behind.

"You're afraid that if I am a true fortune teller, I can tell you things about Samara."

Aramant's heart skipped a beat. His mission there, his companions present within the city's levels, the cult, all of it was suddenly put on hold upon hearing that name. "H... How do you know my mother's name?"

She looked down with a subtle smile. "I'm sorry for resorting to such a tactic. But it seems to have convinced you." She raised her open palm toward him. "Now, if you would..."

Aramant sat back at the table. Only this time, he was far more open-minded. The oracle stood speechless for a few moments before pointing at a handful of sage, burning in a clay bowl. "You should know that sage is meant to make this conversation private. Your friends won't be able to hear your thoughts as long as that burns. However, if you are against the idea, say the word, and I'll undo the ritual." He shook his head, signaling there was no need. "Good, now I'm guessing you have some questions for me?"

He was tempted to ask about his mother first. However, his priorities came back after the initial shock subsided. He decided to take a leap of faith and risk exposing them. "Can you tell me anything about a cult operating in this city?"

"You'll find them soon enough without my help." She frowned in concern. "There is something else I wish to tell you. Please heed my words with care." He nodded his head in acceptance. "Good. You have to understand that my ability works based on visual prowess. When I see someone, I sometimes see glimpses of their possible future. They're not set in stone, yet they will likely come to pass. My blind eye is a result of my desperation, at a stage in my life when I considered what I can do to be far more of a curse than a blessing." She took a deep breath. "When I saw you today, I gazed upon a lot of things. One of which is your sadness, and your scars from recent events that still haunt your soul. Trust an old hag when I say that in time it'll get better. However, you are about to meet someone soon. He was there when your father died, and they knew each other well. He will pose as a friend but do not let yourself be fooled, for it is he who will revel in your ill-being."

"What do you mean? Who are you talking about?" A chill ran down Aramant's spine, followed by a hand grasping his arm and pulling him up.

"What are you doing, master paladin?" asked Nez'rin as he threw a distasteful look at the smiling woman. "These women are nothing more than charlatans who'll say anything for a quick coin. Do not let yourself be persuaded by their seemingly benignant words."

"Wait, Nez, you don't understand," replied Aramant as he struggled from his grip. "She's already proved she's not an impostor. She said she's an oracle."

"I sincerely doubt that. I have not heard of oracles on Earth in over fifty years. The Council of Mages rounded them all up decades ago, either offering them the chance to join them or relieving them of their freedom."

The woman glanced at Nez'rin. "He is not wrong," she eventually replied. "Go with him; I've already told you all you needed to hear."

"Wait, what about Samara? What about my mother?"

"I'm afraid that's a story you're not ready to hear yet. Have faith; it is simply not the time."

From further away, the grunting voice of the dwarf joined in. "Ah, ye find our missin' lamb." He mockingly looked at Aramant. "Thought we'd lost ya, pretty face. Come on, we can go now. Stop starin' at ol' hags like her. Look for women that have around da same number o' years like ye at least."

Nez'rin let go of Aramant's arm as he accompanied them. He turned his head once more to the woman as she signaled him to let matters go. "Do not harbor ill manners for the old one. He means well."

*Old one…* Come to think of it, Aramant had never wondered about Nez'rin's age up until now. Whilst resuming their search, the young paladin seized the opportunity to try and find out more about him.

"So, how did you end up with Wizera and the rest?" he asked.

The lich was not too fond of distractions from their primary goal, yet he didn't mind answering. "I served them for as long as I can remember," he replied, knowing that he bent the truth a bit. "Back when Master Thaidren's father was still alive. And before that, I served his grandfather."

Aramant raised an eyebrow. "Grandfather? Thaidren's grandfather?" His focus shifted to the old man standing next to him. At first glance, he looked to be around fifty, maybe sixty years old. He felt overwhelmed with curiosity. "Forgive me for asking so bluntly but… how old are you?"

Nez'rin's face mimicked a faint smile, followed by a somewhat frightening chuckle, making the dwarf feel uncomfortable having known his true form.

*Damn sack o' bones knows how ta act',* he thought.

"Forgive my laughter, master paladin, I assumed you knew. Allow me to shed some light: we mages dabble into the primordial energies of existence in order to grow in power. That much, you know. However, there are elements other than primordial ones, into which some of us can tap to unlock even more of our potential. These elements are known as Arcane Elements and dabble into

manipulating aspects of reality such as temporal manipulation, spatial traveling…
as well as other forms of magic. As a result, for example, Lady Wizera and I are
able to prolong our lifespan."

"How?" asked Aramant. "And by how much?"

"Strictly theoretically speaking, by slowing down the effect of time on
ourselves. Although, it is a difficult and costly process. It demands a price of forever
weakening us, scarring our innate magical energy capacity once achieved. As for
how much, it is difficult to say. It depends solely on the subject's magical
capabilities at the moment of performing the ritual."

"Fair enough, I suppose. So, how old are you two?"

The lich hesitated for a moment, unsure if giving Aramant an answer would
prove beneficial. "I am eighty-nine years old. Lady Wizera is fifty-six."

*Fifty-six?! She's older than my father!* Aramant thought. Unfortunately for him,
everyone else heard him practically screaming his thoughts through the link,
including Wizera herself. She quickly figured out the context but did not mind
the subject being brought up. The Silver Sorceress remained silent, sparing
Aramant from more embarrassment, as did the others.

As they continued to search the lower levels, Haara's voice echoed through the
mind link.

*Elarin and I found out some things about the crystals. Apparently, since last year
they have been in very short supply.*

*We've heard the same,* said Wizera.

*There doesn't seem to be any merchant at the mid-levels who still has them for sale,*
continued Haara. *Our only option is the lower levels. One tradesman pointed me to a
local there, Jerib. Said his shop is next to the Silver Pockets Inn. His tongue should
soften up upon hearing the name Ohzat. Nez'rin, your group should go and check out
the place. We'll join you as soon as we can.*

*As you wish,* replied the lich.

*What if he's still not willing to cooperate? Or worse, if he's in league with the cult?*
asked Aramant.

*For the time being, just act normal and don't insist if you sense him being hesitant. Once we regroup, we can continue.*

With a well-defined objective at hand, the group pursued toward the center of the bottom floor. However, Nez'rin, Thraik, and Aramant had to pass through a narrow alleyway series to get there. *You'd think the bottom level would be less crowded and more open.* On their way there, the dwarf saw a crate of crystals similar in shape and color to the ones they were looking for.

"Hold on a minute," he said as he changed his course toward the shopkeeper. "Excuse me, sir, do these crystals happen ta be Quaar crystals?"

"Indeed, they are," replied the merchant. "You have a good eye, master dwarf."

Thraik didn't need any more words. He found what the entire group was looking for. There was no need to go to the Silver Pockets Inn anymore.

"And… for how much do ya sell 'em?"

The merchant burst into mocking laughter. "I am sorry, master dwarf, but these are not for sale. Perhaps I can interest you in something else?"

"Not for sale?!" he asked indignantly. "Then what da bloody hell are they on display for?!"

"Ah, you see, master dwarf, they serve for showcase purposes. Nowadays, these crystals are a rarity. Displaying them here could denote to someone that my goods are of the highest and rarest quality."

The dwarf calmed down, yet his frown didn't fade. "Oh, c'mon! I kno' da lot of ya. Ye have a price for anythin'. Stop babbling about this 'is not for sale' bull crap of yers and tell us what'll make ye part with em."

The merchant let loose a greedy smirk. The dwarf managed to pique his interest. Before he had a chance to say anything, Aramant intervened. He grabbed the dwarf by the hand and dragged him a few steps away from the shop.

"What are you doing?!" he whispered. "Wizera said to not push him if he's hesitant."

"She said about dat Jerib boy, who we no longer need, lad. She ain't said a word about this flunker." He struggled away from his grip. "Now, sit in da back and let me work me magic. Take some notes while ye're there." Aramant crossed his arms and rolled his eyes over. The lich remained unhinged by the dialogue.

"Now," said the dwarf as he was approaching the merchant, "we were talking about making a — "

A sudden, thundering sound interrupted them, followed by a shockwave that disrupted most of the city-level platforms. On the opposite side of the canyon, a few decks beneath their level, several sections of the floor began to collapse, forming an avalanche of debris that swiped away the levels beneath them until reaching the bottom. Distant screams could be heard as people desperately tried to save themselves from falling or being swept away with the rubble. Eventually, the structures stopped collapsing, but a significant portion of that area was affected, with Thraik, Aramant, and Nez'rin ending up buried in the rubble.

Aramant fell from the shockwave, along with the dwarf. They tried to reach out with their hands at anything that could be used to get back on their feet. After doing so and a second coughing session for Aramant since they got to this city, they realized what had happened. The upper levels collapsed on top of them, yet they were unharmed. From the little light rays coming from the debris' cracks, they saw Nez'rin standing with his hands raised. He managed to conjure a sphere of darkness right before they were to meet their end. However, the rubble's physical pressure placed over it took a tremendous toll on him to maintain it. The young paladin looked around the darkened room, trying to find a section that could be safely demolished.

"Here, lad," said the dwarf while looking through a small gap. "This wall leads outside."

"Make way!" shouted Aramant as he hurled Viz'Hock into the wall. It shattered as if it were made of thin glass, frightening the young paladin in the process. Once again, he became fully aware of the inhuman power the hammer was granting him. He froze for a moment, staring at his right hand as he seemingly began to hear whispers coming from his artifact. *Destroy... kill... burn...* It was the first time the young paladin was able to distinguish any of the words. He wished he hadn't.

"Hey, lad, quit yer daydreamin', and let's move." With Thraik getting out first and Nez'rin ending up last, once they got out from the rubble, it became clear that they still weren't outside. What the dwarf mistook for sunlight were a series of mirrors that reflected it, placed along the walls of whatever structure they ended up in. Above a wide, tall door, one such mirror hung near a small opening, seemingly leading outside.

"Do that again with this door, lad," said the dwarf.

Aramant tightened the grip on his hammer. He unleashed its power against the alleged exit with a relentless swing, only to end up bouncing from it as if hitting a rubber wall. A dark energy shroud rippled all across it, creating a ripple effect like that of a stone being tossed into a calm lake.

"What in the…"

For the first time since arriving here, Nez'rin's interest was piqued. "A darkness barrier," he said with an eerie voice. "It is designed specifically against physical attacks, but it should be weaker against magic. Allow me a few moments to undo it." He waved his hands and released the ancient words of power required. The barrier became fully visible, starting to wiggle chaotically as it slowly destabilized.

"Strike it again, master paladin!" shouted the lich.

Aramant let out a battle cry before unleashing his strength for a second time. The door cracked, creating several weak points ready to be exploited. Within a few more swings, its integrity eventually collapsed. With their way out being open, Nez'rin decided it was time to contact the rest.

*Lady Wizera, we have made a discovery. A secret passage leading to what seems like an underground level, sealed with darkness magic. We disrupted the barrier and opened the way through.*

*Good job, Nez,* answered the Silver Sorceress. *We're on our way.*

*An underground level? Does the city have this?* asked Thaidren.

*I doubt it's something official… but that seems to be the case,* replied Aramant.

*For the time being, just wait there. It's time for us to regroup.*

*You go on ahead,* said Haara. *I have to find Elarin first.*

*What? Where did she go?* asked Wizera with a concerned tone.

*We were attacked earlier on. The explosion happened because the assassin's bullet missed us. Elarin ended up chasing her. We got separated in the aftermath.*

Thraik silenced everyone for a moment. *Ye don' need ta search for da elf anymore,* he said. *She be here.* He pointed at Elarin with his arm as Nez'rin and Aramant shifted their attention to her. *And she brought a gift.* Walking in front of the elf, with her hands tied behind her back and Elarin's dagger pressing on it, was the woman behind the failed assassination attempt.

"Keep moving," Elarin said to the assailant.

*Wait, what's going on? What gift?* asked Haara. *I don't understand.* Wizera and Thaidren arrived shortly after Elarin's appearance.

*I think she captured the woman you mentioned,* said Aramant.

*Hmph, seems like I'm the only one separated from the group. I'll arrive as soon as I can.* In the meantime, everyone was curious to hear Elarin's story.

"Elarin," said the young paladin, "where have you been?"

"Haara must have told you we were attacked a while back. After this assassin tried to kill me, all I could think of was to catch her, so I pursued her to the lower levels. She proved quite the athlete." She paused briefly and smirked. "For a human."

"How'd ya find us, lass?"

"After capturing her, I paid a visit to the Silver Pockets Inn, hoping to find you there. She seemed quite nervous whenever I looked toward the collapsed part of the city, so I came here. After a few minutes of scouring around, I heard several loud bangs coming from the rubble. The next thing I saw was the three of you emerging from the wall a few meters away."

Wizera drew closer to the assassin. She pointed at the broken door and the passage leading underground. "What is that?" she asked with a threatening tone. "Where does it lead?"

She grinned mockingly. "What makes you think I know? Go see for yourself." She gasped as Elarin pushed her dagger against her back. "You're wasting your time on somebody who doesn't know anything," she grunted. "I'm just a hired hand. They gave me the robes and everything else. This door is as unknown to me as it is to you."

The Silver Sorceress reached into her bag, then raised a hand to the assassin's face. She unclenched her fist and blew a green powder into her eyes.

Elarin began to feel the prisoner losing her balance.

"I believe you," whispered Wizera as the culprit collapsed to the ground.

"What did you do?" asked Aramant.

"I took care of her," she replied.

The elf frowned. "She knows too much. We need to put an end to her before she gets the chance to awaken and alert those who hired her."

"Don't worry; that won't be the case," continued Wizera. "That powder will wipe out her short-term memory. She won't be able to recall anything from the last week or two." Her gaze focused on Elarin. "I'm not the type of person to solve all my inconveniences with murder."

"Well," replied the dwarf, "what are we waitin' for? Let's go and chop da bastards one fanatic at a time."

*We need to regroup first,* answered the Silver Sorceress. *This time, we're the ones on their territory. The last thing we'll need in there is to be separated.*

*You can go already. I'm not that far behind,* answered Haara.

"See? Da mud witch said she'll be here soon. Let's get a move on."

*A passage leading to a secret underground level that we know nothing of... previously sealed off with darkness and festering with who knows what other surprises. A lot of things could go wrong there,* Wizera thought without sharing with the group. Seeing the rest of them proceeding into the depths gave her no choice but to comply and follow along.

Not long after descending, the pathway widened, then branched out into two paths, then four, and so on, until the group realized they had entered a giant maze. *One city beneath another... This cult is far more of a threat than we imagined.*

*From now on, if anyone has something to say, do so through thoughts. We need to remain undetected for as long as we can,* said Nez'rin. In the meantime, Aramant signaled Elarin to stay silent. She nodded at him as they continued to roam through the eerie labyrinth.

Within a few moments, the group heard Haara's voice. *Something is wrong... The entrance... It's not where you said it would be.*

*Whad'ya mean, sister? T'is not like da door grew a pair o' legs and decided ta go for a stroll.*

*Your petty ridicule and scorn accent aside, there is no entrance here...*

*Are you sure you're in the right place?* asked Thaidren.

*Yes, I am sure, the only thing that's in front of me is a giant wall. Wiz, you think these cultists can conjure a regenerating barrier?*

Before the Silver Sorceress had a chance to answer, Nez'rin intervened. *Even if they were, that would not be the case there. I disabled the barrier entirely, removed it from its very core. Any traces of the magic used to create it were erased. You must be in the wrong place, as the master stated earlier.*

*Either that or... they were alerted when you removed it,* said Wizera. *They may have the means to reactivate it, or place another one, remotely.*

*If that's true, they must have at least a few master-level magic users.*

*Or someone on par with an archmage...*

Thaidren and Aramant had been taught the ranking system among mages since they were little. In the event they would ever have to deal with rogue, hostile magic practitioners, they were instructed on how to identify and accurately estimate their level of power. An archmage represented the pinnacle of the power chain. The title befitted an individual powerful and knowledgeable enough for one to expect anything from it. In terms of power, Wizera and Nez'rin were technically closer to archmages than master mages, the second highest rank. Yet, the title was never officially bestowed upon them.

*A-hem, so, what are we doing?* asked Aramant. *Do we wait for Haara? Should we go back for her?*

*It's too late to come back for me now*, answered the earthen sorceress. *Your best option is to go farther. I'll catch up with you as soon as I can; don't worry about me.* Aramant and the rest focused their gaze on Wizera, waiting for an answer. She showed a firm, affirmative nod and pointed forward. Haara would have to remain behind for now.

The underground city brimmed with lit torches, broad and narrow corridors alike, with multiple paths at every turn, yet it seemed dilapidated and devoid of people. It raised the group's concern to an alarming level, with Wizera seemingly being affected the most. *Either they are hiding from us, or not using these ruins' entirety*, she thought. *They must run underneath the entire canyon.*

*I don' like dis... T'is too quiet.*

*Don't jinx it,* said Thaidren as his breathing quickened.

Although each member was expressing their uneasiness in their own way, Elarin seemed surprisingly calm. While still on guard, she did not exude the same aura of paranoia that dwelled within the others. Her gaze was focused upward, wondering about the origins of the place and why the ceiling was so far off from the floor. There was enough space between them to fit three to four levels of Grinal.

After several minutes of aimless exploration, a sinister, harmonious humming began to echo through the halls. The group stopped for a few moments, trying to distinguish the words that came with it, but to no avail. As they pressed on, the corridor became wider with every step until it eventually led to an open space, similar to the plaza of the lower level of Grinal.

A giant temple occupied the center of the area, with a wide stairway leading up to the main entrance. Numerous cultists were standing on different steps, their backs turned at Wizera while the rest contributed to an ominous orchestra of incomprehensible words and hums. Soon after, the cultists ceased their ritual, and a single voice broke the momentary grave-like silence as it echoed through the underground halls.

"We've been expecting you," it said, followed by a laugh.

Elarin's eyes narrowed, focusing her gaze on the source of the voice. She then pointed at the temple's first step. "There."

"There's no need to point fingers, my dear," the voice continued. "I am not trying to hide from you."

Wizera intervened with a threatening tone. "Who are you? What do you want from us?"

A second laugh, more malevolent than the previous one, followed. The other cultists snickered before being silenced by a hand gesture from their alleged leader. "Want from you? We have no business with you. Or at least, that was the case until your son and his companions started to meddle in our operations. Now, we must remove you so that we may continue with our plans uninterrupted."

"Continue to do what exactly?" shouted Thaidren. "Enslave people and use them as tools until they break? To destroy families and kidnap innocent children's chances of a peaceful life?"

"All necessary evils, my dear boy. For you see, through them, we will ascend and reshape our broken world into a better place. Our master has shown us what needs to be done. We will serve to our very last breath if that proves necessary to accomplish our goal. Although I doubt you'd be able to understand."

"Your... last... breath?" murmured Wizera. She raised her hand and shot a spear of ice at the mysterious cultist. "Allow me to make sure you get yours."

Some of the cultists chanted in unison, raising a stone wall in front of their leader before the Silver Sorceress's spear had a chance to strike. "Is that what the famous Silver Sorceress is capable of? Your stories seem a bit exaggerated if so." He slowly walked around the wall, making himself seen once more. "Or perhaps age is finally getting its hold on you, my dear. Either way, I've always wanted to test my skills against a mage of your caliber. Do not fret. I won't let anyone interrupt our duel." He signaled to several of the cultists standing on top of the staircase, each of them holding a precious gem in their hand. With the other cultists chanting once more, they squeezed the gems, making themselves vanish into thin air.

At first, Wizera was confused. Whatever that ritual was supposed to be, it didn't seem to have done anything. That is until she started to hear the turmoiled thoughts of the others.

*Wha' in da…? Wha' happened?*

*Where are we?*

*What did he do?*

Upon turning around, Wizera suspected what the ritual had done. She had heard of such arcane applications in the past, yet this was the first time she saw one unfolding firsthand.

"What have you done?" she asked, her voice quivering.

"Ever since you arrived in Grinal, you were careless enough to presume we wouldn't be aware of your presence. Another costly mistake in your vulgar series of missteps that led you here. What your friends experienced, my dear sparring partner, was an involuntary spatial displacement. It was made possible by leaving a special powder made from the stones you saw my associates crush on their clothes. After all, in a city as crowded as Grinal, it's impossible to avoid bumping into people."

This was enough of a confirmation for Wizera to reassure her companions. *You were transported against your will. It's a specific and difficult to accomplish application of spatial magic. I never thought they'd manage to use it on us.*

*I didn't even know you could do that,* answered the young paladin.

*Under the right circumstances, it is possible,* answered Nez'rin. *At least we know that what they did was merely a means to separate us. All of you, be on your guard for what may come next. May we find each other safe.*

Wizera's thoughts were in a state of turmoil. *We can still communicate, meaning that none of them ended up too far away. But other than that, we're trapped and divided within enemy territory.* A giant, dark spear, similar to the Silver Sorceress's previous attack, flew at her, interrupting her thoughts as she dodged it.

"Now, now," said the cultist overseer, "you have no time to worry about others. I wouldn't want you to perish while daydreaming."

"Who the hell are you?" the Silver Sorceress asked a second time.

Her enemy smirked as he removed his shroud. Upon doing so, Wizera saw a display of small, purple-glowing cracks, starting from the corners of his eyes and going all along his face then reaching out to his neck. Next to where a pair of old scars that evoked an image of someone who had been at death's door once but avoided being dragged inside. "I am Epakin, and you, my dear friend, have meddled with the business of the cult of Kasm, for which I intend to enact punishment in the name of our mistress."

Wizera had no doubt now; this was a demon-worshipping cult. Whom do they serve, it did not matter for the moment. She could only think of her best options to defeat this master-puppet of Hell.

"Now," said Epakin as a sphere of darkness started to manifest near him, "shall we begin?"

# CHAPTER XVII
# FROM ONE MAGE TO ANOTHER

Aramant found himself in a small dome-like structure, all alone and with no apparent exit anywhere in his sight. His initial thought was to break one of the walls with Viz'Hock, yet not knowing what that might lead to, he was reluctant to do so. After a few moments of contemplation, a passageway opened. He did not rush toward it, though. Following a series of loud, heavy footsteps, a hulking figure emerged inside the dome from that same passageway. One that stirred a sentiment of familiarity and unease within the young paladin's soul. Giant in size, even by human standards, with a subtle red skin tone, glowing crimson veins on his arms and legs, and a pair of horns that started from above his eyes and rounded up to point with their tips upward. It was way too reminiscent of Baav's demonic form for Aramant's liking. *By all that is holy…* There was no doubt in his mind that this abomination was once a human being, perhaps even an innocent test subject. *What happened to him? How did he end up like this? Was he forcefully turned into this?* Those were some of the many questions that coursed through his mind.

*What do you mean, Aramant?* asked Thaidren through the mind link.

*It's just like back then. He looks like Baav.*

Thaidren suspected what Aramant meant by that, yet he had to ask to be sure. *What do you mean? The demonized Baav?* He did not get an answer in the form of a reply; rather, he experienced it with his own eyes, as he and Thraik, with whom he ended up paired, saw such a creature being released in their arena as well. *There's not just one of them…*

*One of what?* asked Wizera. *What are you two talking about?* Her attention focused back on her opponent.

"What have you done? What did you send to fight them?"

"Ah, you must be referring to my test subjects," answered Epakin, with a smug grin. "They are part of our evolution as humans, my dear. I'll admit, they're a bit absent in terms of consciousness or any form of intelligence whatsoever. But as our ancestors are to us, so will they be the stepping stones that lead into a new age of ascension."

"You're mad."

His smirk shifted into a disgusted frown. "Then try and put an end to my insanity. If you dare."

Multiple spikes started to form within the orb of darkness, ending up being launched from it toward the Silver Sorceress. She waved her hand and conjured a small wave of water in front of her that she turned into a frozen wall to defend herself.

*Lady Wizera,* she heard in her mind, *are you all right?*

*I'm fine, Nez. Though I can't really talk right now.*

*Try to resist. Me and Lady Elarin will reach you as soon as we can.* However, the probability that they'd be able to arrive in time seemed small, as an entire army of cultists welcomed them on the other side. They may not have been any stronger than the disposable lackeys that attacked them at the mansion, but they had a tremendous advantage when it came to numbers. With a quick look, the elf and Nez'rin estimated their number in the range of one hundred or so. *It appears that they have prepared all these giant chambers for us.*

On Wizera's side, magical energies surged through the battlefield like lightning bolts traveling through the dark clouds of an impending storm. Darkness and water, considered by many as being the most malleable primordial elements of them all, now locked into a clash for supremacy, with one herald representing purity and order, while the other chaos and uncertainty. Whenever the Silver Sorceress would attack, the grips of darkness would protect Epakin from harm. The equivalent in Wizera's case applied all the same. In theory, they were equals, like two sides of the same coin.

"Marvelous," said Epakin. "I take back what I said about your stories being overly exaggerated."

Wizera, on the other hand, had trouble speaking, as she panted from tiredness. Yet her face showed a mocking smile. "If… you have time to talk… then you have time to fight… better."

"Look at you, dear," the dark wizard replied with a peal of derisive laughter, "Undoubtedly I can hold this on for far longer than you'll be able to. Time is on my side in this fight."

With her pride taking a hit, Wizera grasped the harsh truth in her opponent's words. Judging by the glowing cracks near his eyes and all the scars that started from his neck and ended up God knows where, it was clear to her that Epakin's body had been altered — for lack of a better term — by the forces he served with such impudence. His limits far surpassed those of a normal human. She had to think of a plan to defeat him as quickly as possible, before the difference in their stamina levels would become the decisive factor. Unfortunately for her, he still had the advantage of territory. With no water sources nearby, and the absence of sunlight to diminish his powers, the Silver Sorceress had to deal with multiple hindrances when fighting against him.

There was not much time to get lost in her thoughts. She conjured multiple attacks at the same time, having invoked all three water phases in the process. With one hand, she summoned a cloaking mist, masking the water that surged through the ground, traveling toward Epakin's feet while several ice spears stood ready to be tossed at him from above her. On top of the sphere of darkness, the overseer enveloped his body in a dark-plated armor. Before he had a chance to complete his coating, Wizera sent her icy spears toward him, each of them aiming for his heart or his head. Upon seeing this, he immediately dodged her attacks, losing focus and dematerializing his armor. His gesture made the Silver Sorceress wonder.

*The sphere didn't protect him,* she thought. *Was it because of the armor? If that's the case, it means he can't concentrate on both of them at the same time.* Wizera paused briefly, taking advantage of the mist. She then took a deep breath and started to chant as her eyes began to glow a bright blue. With her hand raised in the air, she unclenched her fist as if she had released something into the air above. With the mist partially concealing her presence, Epakin could only see her in the form of a shadow, distinguishing only her posture. With an elegant move of his hands, he commanded the sphere to launch several spikes at her. At the same time, he took a page from her book and sent his shadow on the ground toward her.

"You think I didn't see the water on the ground? You're not the only one capable of sending multiple attacks at once." A flash of light enveloped the shadowy silhouette in the mist, nullifying the overseer's spells. In a temporary state of rage, he sent a second set of attacks, similar to the previous ones, at her. Their aim was true this time, yet Epakin was skeptical that it could've been that easy. As the mist around her cleared, he realized his skepticism was justified, for the only thing he managed to hit was a mass of water shaped like a human silhouette. A simple yet effective distraction that concealed his opponent's true intentions.

From his left side, he saw a spear of ice being hurled at him, too fast to be evaded. It struck him in his shoulder, making the dark sorcerer scream in agony.

"What's the matter?" he heard from his side. "Not talking anymore?"

Before he had a chance to react to her smug comment, the icy spear embedded in his shoulder started to melt, making its way to his nose and entering his lungs. Epakin began to cough uncontrollably as he struggled to breathe through his already half-water-filled lungs. Next to him, the Silver Sorceress was slowly coming at him, holding a staff in her hand that he didn't recollect she had when the fight started.

"I honestly hoped I wouldn't have to resort to using this," she said, as she glanced at it for a split second. "You were right to some extent. This thing puts a great strain on me nowadays. I can't summon it as recklessly as I once could. Though I have to say, I'll give you credit for forcing me to do so." An odd sentiment of pity enveloped her. "You and your cult meddled with the devils and let yourselves be seduced by their promises of power and ascendance. Yet, under your pride and conviction that the powers bestowed upon you were obsolete, you succumbed to arrogance and stumbled because of it."

"S… s… si… lence," growled Epakin as a gurgle escaped.

"I'm surprised you can still talk with your lungs full of water. But don't worry, I don't plan on killing you. You're going to come with me and receive a nice interrogation seat at the Council of Mages' headquarters." Suddenly, she felt compelled to move away from her enemy, as if a strange survival instinct had kicked in, warning her of an impending doom that awaited her.

Within the following moment, Wizera found herself paralyzed in shock as she saw Epakin getting back on his feet. He coughed uncontrollably, yet not like a man on the verge of drowning. Instead, he seemed to spew the water out of him. A few mouthfuls of blood were spilled as well, with the dark wizard wiping off his chin afterward.

"Congratulations," he whispered softly. "You've made me angry…"

"How did you…" With barely enough time to react, Wizera saw the blood spatters taking the shape of long needles, all of them aimed at her with the intent to kill. With a sudden wave of her staff, she washed away the attack."

*Blood magic*, she thought. *I can't believe he has both blood and dark magic.* With this new development in front of her, the Silver Sorceress began to understand why Epakin didn't drown as well. *He must've combined the water in his lungs with blood, overwriting my control over it, then spitting it out when he coughed.* A brilliant, and at the same time, frightening strategy. Seconds later, the blood assault resumed, with Wizera now having to guard against a second element. Not to mention, combining them would result in a dangerous element known to many as "black blood."

Epakin was now working on two fronts. On the one hand, by combining blood with water to diminish Wizera's control over it and, on the other, by constantly attacking her using darkness. Little by little, they both showed each other their cards. Now, with everything on the table, Wizera's hand did not seem to be the winning one. She focused her spells on defense to buy herself extra time to think of a strategy. Her problem was that with the discovery of Epakin's second element came the factor of accelerated healing. A feat that could be easily provided by the use of blood magic.

The shoulder she recently pierced with ice had already begun to heal, rendering her actions up to that point more or less useless. She held her staff with both hands, betraying a clear sign of her suffering from early to mid-stages of magical energy exhaustion. In a desperate state and with little else to lose, her mind came up with an idea. Nonetheless, a risky one, yet for the time being, it was the only one that seemed to give her a real chance at winning.

She waved her staff and chanted a few words of power, raising several water barriers and another cloud of mist, thinner than the previous one. With Epakin's vision blurred by the mist, she searched in her bag for the one thing she thought could turn the scales in her favor.

"Hiding behind barriers, sorceress?" asked Epakin with a pompous, mocking tone. "If I didn't know any better, I'd say you're beginning to succumb to fear." His voice changed to a more aggressive tone. "But I'm not so much of a fool as to underestimate you a second time." He started to chant, as his entire dark sphere morphed into a giant lance. The blood on the ground began to crawl its way up to the newly-formed weapon, coating and hardening it. It started to spin uncontrollably moments before it received the command to launch forward to its target. As the lance made contact with the silhouette shrouded by the mist, Epakin was well prepared that it was another decoy. He'd subtly placed some of the remaining blood around him, ready to answer his call at a moment's notice.

Be it for offense or defense, the dark wizard was covered from all sides. But, to his surprise, he'd realized soon after that Wizera had not created a water clone, as he watched the silhouette evade the dark lance. The lance turned back and tried to hit her a second time. Before reaching its target, the Silver Sorceress threw something undistinguishable at its master. He reflexively moved further away from the object. Within a couple of seconds, a giant oaken tree emerged from the ground, with its vines moving as if they aimed to entangle the overseer.

*This is it*, she thought. *Haara gave me this to use in an emergency. Now is as good of a time as any. Please, let it work!*

The vines kept stretching, attempting to capture the master puppet. *What is this abomination?* he thought. *Some sort of darkness or blood-suppressing relic?* His assumption was not far off. What Wizera had taken from her bag was a special seed created by Haara. Designed as an extreme measure of instant healing, the tree that grew from it would revitalize the user's target while also pursuing any forbidden forms of magic, such as blood or darkness, in order to cleanse or contain them. Be that as it may, it took Epakin a few waves of his hands to send his lance through the tree's roots, neutralizing the spell's pursuit. His anger almost turned into admiration for a short moment.

"Not good enough, dear," he shouted while letting out a manic laugh. His respite of mirth faded quickly as he found himself being washed away by a giant torrent in the shape of a snake. It ended up dragging him all the way down to the pit where the tree had had its roots. The hole quickly filled up with water, with Wizera not having to focus on maintaining its shape anymore. On top of that, this strategy rendered Epakin's blood-combining technique useless. She touched the water with her hand and froze its surface with a relatively thin layer of ice. Epakin's lance had faded into nothingness, with him summoning the element underwater to break the ice above him. Unfortunately, while he may have succeeded in emerging back to the surface, when he did so, the Silver Sorceress was waiting for him. She bashed him in the head with her staff as hard as she could. After dragging him out enough so that he wouldn't sink with his head under the water again, she waited to make sure he was unconscious, then let out a deep breath.

"The tree was not my last move," she said, panting. "Its roots were."

# CHAPTER XVIII
# 'A FRIEND WHOM YOU CAN TRUST'

Within the sinister halls of the cult of Kasm, somewhere beneath the underground ruins' central temple, Nez'rin and Elarin faced an army of cultists. Although they were not stronger than those they fought back at the mansion, they were in larger numbers this time. The lich was dealing with multiple enemies from a distance without putting in much of an effort. In contrast, his moon elf companion was taking the fight up close and personal. They both knew Elarin would not be able to assist Nez'rin in the event of him being overwhelmed, and at the same time, neither could he keep a constant eye on her. The conclusion was obvious: they would stay, as much as possible, out of each other's way. They may have ended up together, but they were mostly fighting alone.

The cultists seemed unled. Not a single one of them stood out from the lot. Even their powers didn't seem natural, a fact suspected by Nez'rin since his first encounter with them. *That would explain why their potential is so basic... so limited... If only their circumstances had differed, I would pity them for their frailty.*

While the lich had the luxury to contemplate over other aspects on the battlefield, it was a different story in Elarin's case. She was calm yet fully alert, evading spell after spell while studying the cultist's rhythmic symphony of projectiles to find the perfect moments to strike. Her mind slowly drifted away at some point, losing itself in memories of a distant past when she was but another Lu'Derai in training. She forced away these thoughts as the fresh blood from her dagger splattered and spread all around her, keeping her sharp and focused. She was dancing through her enemies, closing in on them one at a time as they fell to the ground. She aimed to remain the last person to fall, or better yet, be the last person standing when the melody of conflict was over.

In Nez'rin's case, he was not a dancer at all, but rather a maestro who formed and waved his spells to align and traverse the battlefield as he pleased, in a harmonious, deadly manner. Having been trapped with the elf in these halls, however, posed two problems for him. The first one consisted of having to desist from using his death magic, his most developed skillset. The other one was to maintain his humanly disguise. A feat that, ever since he put it on, had demanded a portion of his magical energy and stripped him of his full potential. Whatever what-if scenarios came to his mind, they were irrelevant. Even more so, they posed a distraction that needed to be dismissed. *Something is not right...* he thought after several minutes of constant fighting. *Their numbers are beginning to grow, even with us tearing them apart.* He figured they had already dispersed about fifty cultists so far. *If they have so many people here, they may pose a far greater threat than we initially suspected.* With the danger at hand ever-growing and Nez'rin's realization, the lich attempted to warn the Silver Sorceress and the rest about the situation but received no answer.

As the battle continued to rage on, several new pathways opened all around the arena. The elf and lich's resistance turned for the worst as they now had enemies pouring in from multiple directions. For Elarin, it meant little, as she was already in the center of their field. For Nez'rin, however, the dynamic had changed. When facing an enemy, be it larger in number than oneself, it was relatively easy for a magic practitioner to protect himself if all the attacks came from the same direction. Aside from that, he would now have to spread both his defense and attacks to cover more ground and not just from the front.

"You will not be able to last long, old man," he heard Elarin shouting at him from afar. In a way, he was impressed she had time to keep an eye on him.

"Worry about yourself, girl," he yelled back.

"That is not how this works. We may not have known each other for long, but at the very least, I need you alive to help me."

"And what do you propose?"

"For you to stop holding back."

Her words almost made the lich lose focus for a brief moment. "I beg your pardon?"

"Whatever it is that keeps you from using all your power, lose it."

*How is this possible?* he wondered with a sentiment of dread. *Does she indeed know, or is it a coincidence? Have I been careless?* His thoughts were interrupted by her shouts.

"Look, my kinship is of the Lu'Derai. I learned how to figure out when a person has something to hide since I was a child. No matter the reasons, if you continue to conceal your true power now, we may not survive."

"It is not that easy."

"Yes, it is. If you want to see your "lady," Thaidren, and the others after this, then you must unshackle whatever you've been hiding from me."

There was no more time to mull over the consequences. Nez'rin was well aware that she was right. But fortunately, in his case, he did not need to undo his camouflage. He only needed to unleash his true nature. *One secret at a time.* By raising barriers of ice and darkness around him, he formed a cocoon that offered him the protection needed to chant undisturbed. The lich waved his hands for a few moments before letting them down again. Upon slowly raising them upward, Elarin heard Nez'rin's true, sinister tone.

"Minions! Servants! Denizens of the cold dark! Rise from the endless abyss of the afterlife, and obey the command of your dark master!"

The piles of corpses left by the lich and the elf began to move, with each cadaver getting back on its feet and turning against their former allies. Elarin was shocked to see such a tremendous display of necromancy, yet she was the one who asked for it. Nez'rin's attention focused on the animated dead, steadily tipping the scales of the battle. The cultists' most significant advantage — their numbers — had been turned against them. Their defeat was now at hand. It was merely a matter of time.

***

The demonic experiment was staring right at Thaidren and the dwarf as it stood motionless before them. If it weren't for its menacing expression, he could've fooled them into believing he was a statue. He seemed… absent. An empty shell stripped of whatever poor soul had resided within it some time ago. Its humanity, its identity, all of it appeared washed away in place of something… primal.

For Thaidren, it felt even more disturbing, causing his mind to flood with dark thoughts and memories about Baav's betrayal. *It's not the same, but they do look alike,* he thought. From the back of his head, he heard Aramant's voice struggling to communicate through the mind link.

*It's not just the looks. Seems it fights the same way. Tread carefully!*

After a few moments of inactivity, the creature opened its mouth, letting loose a war cry that echoed throughout their entire battle area. Soon after, it charged toward Thaidren, guided by an instinct to take down the bigger target first.

"Buy me a few seconds, lad," shouted Thraik as he loaded his firearm. As the monster swung his giant axe at the young warrior, Thaidren unsheathed both of his swords and crossed them in order to block the attack. He immediately got a taste of the beast's physical strength, feeling that if it were a bit stronger, the blow might have shattered the blades. He scraped one of his swords against the other one as he bent down and slashed his opponent's abdomen before taking a few steps back. The cut proved to be superficial at best. This form of demonization seemingly hardened the skin of its subject. It started to make sense for Thaidren as to why it wasn't wearing much in the way of armor.

With his attack failing, it was Thraik's turn to give it a shot. He aimed at his chest and pressed the trigger, only to witness that the creature was also capable of incredible speed. It dodged the bullet with ease and shifted its focus toward the dwarf. Thaidren took the opportunity and froze the ground beneath him, making it slip and drop its weapon before it had a chance to reach his companion. *If I can make it unable to stand properly, we might have a chance,* he thought. The situation reminded him of his misunderstanding with Robnethen and how Thaidren held the advantage for most of that fight. He aimed to replicate that strategy and adapt it to this new threat.

The demonized subject groaned as it thrust its claws into the ground to shatter the ice. Its back slowly began to light up, eventually forming a line of fire along the creature's spine, then by lighting its hands afterward, crushing any hope for Thaidren's strategy.

The dwarf fired a second shot, this time hitting the abomination in the left shoulder. Unfortunately, that bullet didn't do much either. If anything, it angered the creature more. With Thaidren engaging in close combat once more, his fighting style adapted to a low pose and the idea of leaving multiple cuts, be they shallow or not. Eventually, they would damage the monster enough to put it down, or so Thaidren hoped. It was not a proven strategy, but for the time being, it was all he had. By imbuing his weapons with frost energy, Thaidren hoped to counteract his opponent's flames. However, the fiery touch of Hell was hard to extinguish and easy to reignite.

The demonic experiment charged at Thaidren a second time. The young warrior resorted to the same tactic by lowering himself and aiming for its abdomen and legs. Although his attack struck true, as soon as he passed by the creature, it grabbed him by his mantle, setting it aflame and knocking Thaidren to the ground. He rolled out and ripped the cloak from the shoulder pins holding it, with the added cost of losing his weapons. Before he could turn his focus back to his opponent, his enemy attempted to pummel him to the ground once more. Thaidren caught the creature by the hands with his own, letting his frost energy channel through them in a desperate endeavor to freeze them. As soon as the abomination felt the cold touch enveloping its palms, it released a burst of flaming energy, neutralizing Thaidren's powers, overwhelming them in the process. He screamed in agony as his gloves partially melted away, coating his palms. He let go of his enemy only to receive another punch, this time in the abdomen. For a soulless husk, this experiment seemed fond of irony. It threw the young warrior against a wall and tore through his armor as if it were made of tin. After several punches, his fists reached Thaidren's skin. He groaned as he heard the sound of his ribs cracking.

A round bullet hit the beast behind its left knee, making it lose balance and fall, Thaidren tripping over it.

"Lad, FINISH 'IM NOW," yelled Thraik as he threw Wrought, his prized axe, toward Thaidren. He caught the weapon and struck his opponent. The dwarf's weapon seemed more effective at tearing through the demon's tough skin, yet it was far from enough. In a burst of anger, the creature knocked Thaidren away and grabbed the axe from his hand, tossing it back at the dwarf and hitting him in the shoulder.

"Not dat spot again!" he screamed in pain as he shot his second round without aim. His left arm had been his bad one for over two decades, and now it ended up with a new, fresh wound that would only make it worse. He could not make use of it anymore, only watch the beast slowly limping toward him. For the first time in many years, the dwarf feared for his life. He turned to Thaidren, then looked back at his enemy with a fierce frown on his face.

"Y… Y'er not gettin' to me boy while dis… son of Kezerok[4] still has breath within 'im."

He reached the dwarf and thrashed him, throwing punch after punch and tossing him against a wall. The sound of breaking bones spurred the creature to continue, drowning him with a sentiment of mirth displayed by a seemingly sadistic grin that appeared on its face. However, the beast's bloodthirsty drunken state ended abruptly as a stinging pain seared through his back and came out from his front. It looked at itself and saw one of Thaidren's swords buried in its chest. The young warrior stood behind it, throwing punches at him as soon as he turned around. He imbued his fists with elemental power, creating sharp chunks of ice to cover them with each consecutive hit. He shook to the point where Thaidren himself did not know how he was able to stand, let alone fight.

Within a few more hits, the young warrior pushed the beast against one of the walls and continued to strike until his scorched hands bled through his ice gauntlets. Both he and the beast fell on their knees, with Thaidren rolling to the

---

[4] Kezerok: Also known as the "Dwarven Capital," this mighty settlement, named after a dwarven hero that contributed to its founding, stands as one of the most technologically advanced cities on Earth.

ground. To his horror, the creature stood back up after a moment of respite. Everything he threw at it proved insufficient. *No. How can he… After all the…* Believing he was now living on borrowed time, he took a deep breath and desperately tried to get back on his feet. Alas, his body would not respond anymore.

The creature began to limp toward the spot where the dwarf's axe had landed, only to return with it in its hand to finish the job. It raised its arm and let loose a triumphant war cry only to stop mid-air. Something caught its attention. At first, Thaidren did not understand why his opponent was hesitating. He looked at the beast and realized it was staring at its right side. There was nothing there except an empty wall. A moment later, Thaidren's attention shifted to it as well. From within it came a soft, beating sound, turning stronger and stronger with each beat.

***

Aramant drew the hammer from his back, holding a tight grip on it with both hands, standing still, waiting for his opponent to make a move. It was terrifying to observe such an abomination doing nothing but staring aimlessly, almost as if it was looking through him. It seemed confused yet somehow peaceful, gazing at the young paladin for a couple of seconds before showing a deep frown on its face. It picked itself up and raised its larger, more intimidating hammer from the ground and let loose a high-pitched shriek that pierced Aramant's ears like a needle.

The demonized subject rushed toward its target, jumping high into the air as it closed in on him and lifted its hammer above its head. As the weapon descended, Aramant dodged the attack with relative ease, although it was the emotional effect of the blow that he could not dismiss that easily. The impact shattered the ground as if it were made of glass, shrouding the young paladin's mind with dreadful thoughts of what might happen to him in the event of such a blow striking him. With these thoughts, he started to sense the hauntings of his artifact once more. His grip loosened and his hand shook for a split second. *I don't have time to deal with this.* The thought was soon interrupted by the sound of Thaidren's voice coming through their mental link.

*It's not the same, but they do look alike…*

Aramant couldn't agree more. These creatures bore a resemblance to Baav beyond their liking. And for him to hold the weapon responsible for his transformation in the first place, disturbed his state of mind even more. With each doubt, negative thought, or fearful scenario that he could imagine, the hammer was poisoning its host with a desire to let it be unshackled. It didn't matter upon whom; it only cared to be released.

The monster continued to swing its massive hammer at Aramant as if it weighed no more than a mere dagger. It forced the young paladin into a position where he could only focus on evading its blows without returning a single attack. This hesitation resulted in the creature grazing him a few times and managing to close in on him within the first moments of their fight. It threw him against a wall and tried to finish him off with a vertical swing. He dodged the attack and quickly regained his feet.

*It's not just the looks. Seems it fights the same way. Tread carefully!*

Aramant took a few steps further away and summoned the power of The Light to envelop his hammer, releasing a small beam of light energy to purge away the evil before him. The demon recognized the element, seemingly out of a primal instinct, and dodged it before making a swift turn and charging back at Aramant. The young paladin was starting to feel like he was facing a raging bull with him fully covered in red. However, a promising sign for him was that his state of mind was seemingly improving, with the intoxicating sensation from his artifact beginning to subside as a result of that.

Perhaps channeling The Light through it played a part in that. Perhaps it was related to him dismissing most of his negative thoughts. These assumptions would have to wait. For the moment, he had to direct his full attention to the creature. In and between the demon subject's relentless assaults, the young paladin gathered his thoughts in the hope of coming up with a plan to defeat his adversary. The most obvious answer had already been shown by the creature mere moments ago: it was afraid of The Light's power, the only known natural enemy of demonic energies. He would've preferred to have a more solidified course of action than resorting to the natural order, but considering the threat of him being overwhelmed increasing with each passing minute, that would have to suffice.

An underground base of operation with demonic subjects. A setup like this was entirely turned against the young paladin or any other paladin, for that matter. The Light had limited means to manifest below the surface, while the never-ending flames of Hell burned brighter underground. He did not know whether his allies were still alive or not. He did not know if they were still fighting or not. He did not even know how far away they were from each other. The last thing he had heard was Thaidren's voice, confirming he was fighting the same kind of monstrosity, before going silent.

*Kill...* he heard in the back of his head. Compelled by a fearful impulse, Aramant turned his back to the demon in search of the voice. There was no one there, and his gesture cost him. The next thing he saw when turning back was his opponent swinging its hammer at him, managing a direct hit to his side. The young paladin had barely found the time to react by putting his left arm between the hammer and his ribs, making it absorb most of the impact. He ended up on the floor, with Viz'Hock slipping from his grasp and ending up a few meters away. He groaned in pain as he desperately tried to get back on his feet using his good arm. After reaching back for the hammer, he quickly ducked another lateral swing from the beast before distancing himself from the creature. Half of his armor was compromised, becoming more of a burden that slowed him down rather than protected him. With that in mind, Aramant made a risky decision to strip himself of the armor parts rendered useless. Mainly the ones covering his entire left arm up to his shoulder and the cape, as a precaution. He wouldn't want the demon to grab him by it in an unexpected display of intelligence.

*Slay it!* he heard the same whisper again. This time he did not turn. Instead, he started to wonder who it was that he was hearing. It couldn't be coming from his opponent. The voice seemed to always come from behind him, even when facing the demon. What he had in front of him was an animal, driven only by instinct and common, basic logic at best. *It can't be it,* he thought before hearing another echo. *Come on!* After hearing that, the young paladin's curiosity turned to concern.

While distancing himself, he took his eyes off it and stared at Viz'Hock for a split second. *It can't be...* he thought while enshrouded in a strong sentiment of unease.

*Burn it with your rage!*

"Stop it," shouted Aramant, as he channeled the power of The Light through the hammer a second time and sent another burning ray at the creature. Having no means to dodge the attack this time, the creature used one of his arms to block the blast. It seared its skin, angering it as it let loose an agonizing screech. It started to charge furiously at the young paladin as he shot a continuous beam of light at it. The demon crossed its arms and pressed on through the pain, tackling Aramant and throwing him on the ground while trying to pound him with the hammer. He raised Viz'Hock, somehow blocking the blow. With a second attack imminent, the young paladin rolled out of the creature's range and made a quick charge at it, aiming to hit it in the chest. His strike was successful, yet the demon managed to strike Aramant's shoulder plate with his hammer's handle as well.

*End this inferior replica.* The demon ended up knocked on the ground, but slowly rose back on its feet while pressing its chest with one hand. Aramant began to scream. If there were any other intelligent beings on their battleground, they'd probably start questioning his sanity. He imbued himself and the hammer with light, not letting his opponent get the upper hand again. His fighting style became erratic, unrefined, and more primal. They were fighting on equal terms now. The fate of their battle could turn at each swing, with each blow that hit its mark turning the tide more and more in this chaotic scaling in which the upper hand of the combatants was constantly shifted. "Shut up," shouted the young paladin again. "Whoever or whatever you are, leave me alone."

The light in Aramant's hammer started to dim. He could feel the power slowly leaving him, like a constant flicker that would end in utter darkness eventually. Between the flashes of the forces that were to forsake him soon, the voice became more coherent, louder, enveloping, and silencing the mental link between him and the others without breaking it.

*What The Light gives you is but a glove...,* he heard it whispering. *I can offer you a gauntlet.* Aramant defiantly shook his head, almost as if he felt that whoever communicated with him could see his gesture. *Granting you so much more... You need only ask,* it continued. Aramant's hand shook all the while as he listened and fought for his life at the same time. *Why do you reject my beauty... my gift?*

"Who are you?"

*A friend whom you can trust... A wishful aiding hand, rooting for your survival.*

Its voice seemed seductive, yet it reeked of lies. Simply too suspicious and inhumane to stir any form of trust in the young paladin's heart. He finally understood what a burden the hammer was. It wasn't an ordinary corrupted artifact, repurposed for the use of the righteous cause. Something was inside it. Something evil, related to its original nature. Something demonic.

With his attention spread on two fronts, and his powers leaving him, Aramant received a full-on direct blow from the creature's hammer, tossing him against one of the arena's walls. This time he heard and felt some of his ribs cracking as he fell to the ground, unable to stand back up from the pain. His opponent roared and charged at him, preparing its weapon for a final, decisive blow.

*I remain your only option. Accept my help or die, young one,* the voice intervened once more. *Don't you want to reunite with your family?*

Whoever or whatever was speaking to Aramant, knew what buttons to press. In a quick flash of thoughts, the young paladin reminisced about all his family memories. The ones when he was a child, the ones with his father. The ones ever since he found out Wizera and Thaidren were family, as well as the realization that all the memories with his not-so-favorite, annoying ice-brain companion were a part of that.

Scenarios of whether his body would ever be found and receive a proper burial coursed through his mind. Perhaps his grave would one day lie next to his father's. Perhaps he would end up incinerated like the countless victims at the cathedral, his once beloved home. His sanctuary of good memories, now lying in ruins, just like he was standing now, broken and bleeding in front of an enemy that was not even aware of whom it was killing. A mindless creature that would end him just for the sake of bloodshed.

He refused to accept these thoughts. Aramant's inner flame refused to run out like this. *That day is not today.* He stretched his arm toward Viz'Hock and grabbed the hammer as tightly as he could.

"I accept your gift…" he whispered, "this time…"

A sudden surge of power emanated from the hammer, making the demon cease its charge and take a step back. Aramant's right arm felt hardened, stronger. With his eyes barely open, he saw his veins glowing in the same devilish nuance of red that reminded him of his father's murderer. They slowly began to expand from his fingertips to his entire arm and up to his neck until it stopped in his right eye.

The armor on Aramant's right hand was still untouched. He did not understand how he was able to see the veins where he could not see skin. He turned his head toward the creature and started to comprehend. With one eye, the one unaffected by the dark powers of the hammer, he could see as he always did. With the other, he saw the demon as a mere glowing silhouette. A luminescent red specter with no face, eyes, or expression, as if this newfound spectral sight allowed him to see beyond the capabilities of human eyes. While holding it, the hammer shattered on the outside, with a fiery glow, ever-growing from within. A molten core of rage and destruction reshaped itself over the handle of Viz'Hock until it took the form of a long saber.

*This is the most I can give you for now,* heard the young paladin. *Obliterate this ambulant insult.* He slowly got to his feet, realizing that he could now breathe painlessly, his eyes fixed on the demon. It did not advance, nor did it run. It screeched toward him as if trying to intimidate him. The sword ignited in a flame with embers of both red and black nuances, intertwined in a symmetric manner that allowed them to complement one another.

Aramant pointed at the creature with Viz'Hock. Within a split second, the weapon's flames grew, ending up being thrust in a frontal cone that covered the paladin's target with a blanket of darkness and heat. As the flames were reduced to embers, so did Aramant bask in the image of his enemy being reduced from an empty, soulless beast to a pile of black, charred bones. Soon after that, he breathed heavily, but the demonic powers did not subside.

*There is another,* whispered his alleged friend. He turned his gaze around, scouring for the target, spotting it within a moment's notice, behind one of the arena walls. Next to it, he saw two others. One gray, small silhouette, subtly flickering like a candle on the verge of being extinguished, and another, larger one, emanating a blue mist that inspired power, resilience. For a moment, it caught the curiosity of the young paladin more so than the other demon. With his last shred of consciousness, he realized that he probably saw Thaidren and Thraik, given the gray silhouette's size. He rushed at the wall, tackling it with his shoulder. The impact reminded him that even empowered, he was not immune to pain.

*There's no need for that,* said the voice in his mind. Aramant tightened his grip on Viz'Hock, concentrating on the shape of the weapon. The blade slowly began to reshape again, rearranging into the molten core that the hammer harbored. It then stretched out and solidified itself into the form of a fiery hammer, the antithesis of how its purified form looked. He hit the wall once with little result. Then a second time. Then a third. With each consecutive blow, he felt the wall slowly giving way, cracking more and more until its impending destruction drew near.

On the other side of the wall, something stirred the attention of the demonized subject that Thaidren and Thraik had relentlessly fought. At first, Thaidren did not understand why his opponent was hesitating. He looked at the beast and realized it was staring at its right side. There was nothing there except an empty wall. A moment later, Thaidren's attention shifted to it as well. From within it came a soft, beating sound, turning stronger and stronger with each beat until they both saw Aramant bursting in from the wall and rushing toward them. His molten hammer had reverted to its original flaming sword form as the corrupted paladin was charging his attack.

The creature roared and charged toward him as well. Unlike the other one, it seemed more confident, making Aramant smirk in exhilaration as they approached one another. In the blink of an eye, their fight was decided. The creature hit Aramant near his right shoulder with little effect. In contrast, the young paladin swung his sword through his opponent's skull, cutting through it until reaching almost to its jaw. The weapon ignited and burned away the insides of its head as the monster met its end and fell for the last time.

Thaidren found himself unable to move, speak, or even blink from the shock, unable to process what he was seeing. On the one hand, he and the dwarf were somehow saved from a fate they thought inescapable. On the other hand, their savior bore the mark of past corruption — a fate that befell someone they once thought to be the embodiment of benevolence and kindness. Eventually, he snapped out of his trance and shouted through the mind link.

*Mother! Something is very wrong with Aramant. I don't know how to explain, I — You have to see this.*

At the entrance of the central temple, Wizera had barely had time to catch her breath. *What do you mean?* she asked. *What's wrong with him? Are you all right?*

Thaidren looked at Aramant, with the young paladin's eyes fixated on him as well. Both of them did not utter a single word. They stood in complete silence, without even blinking.

*Aramant… He's…*

Before having a chance to explain what lay before his eyes, the young paladin collapsed on the floor, his flaming sword extinguished in tandem and turning black as coal.

Thaidren could not see whether his eye had turned back to normal or not, but the veins on his neck faded away. *He needs help,* he shouted internally.

# CHAPTER XIX

# THE SHIELD OF CONVICTION

Haara arrived in the nick of time to heal the injured. If it weren't for Wizera's quick thinking, she would have ended up lost within the labyrinthian city. Thanks to the magical runes left on each of them, the Silver Sorceress was able to pinpoint their approximate location. Unfortunately, she was in no condition to conjure up a portal anymore, forcing Haara to reach them on foot. With the underground city's geographic structure in mind, Wizera had created a tracking spell in the form of a small stream of water that branched from her location and reached out to the earthen sorceress, Nez'rin, and Elarin.

"It's going to be fine," whispered the Silver Sorceress to her son as she kept on casting restorative water magic on him, cleaning his wounds and helping him recover. "I'm here. It's all over now."

The young warrior looked at her as she held his head on her lap. With a shaking hand, he pointed at Thraik. His mother grabbed him by the arm and slowly eased it back down. "Shh," she said while moving her hand through his long silver hair, "don't move."

The simple act of breathing made Thaidren feel as if he were pierced by a hundred needles, even more so when trying to speak. "S... save h... him... first." The pain made him grunt and pant. Wizera was shocked that, even in his condition, his main concern was Thraik and not himself. She was proud to see this noble side of him, yet the circumstances that led to it were tearing her apart.

"I know," she said, her voice cracking. "Haara is taking care of him; you just rest and let me worry about him and Aramant."

He closed his eyes, and steadied his breathing.

While Thaidren's consciousness was slowly drifting into slumber, Haara signaled Wizera to check Aramant and his weapon.

"Last time I checked, the boy had a hammer," she said with a seemingly condescending tone.

"It's a long story."

She looked at the broken wall and what little scorched surface she could see inside the other dome, then her gaze focused back at the pitch-black sword. "I'm assuming it's not a joyous one."

Wizera looked at the same things that Haara did and sighed. "Believe it or not, in his case, I think we were lucky."

"You'll have to explain that to me because that boy over there is almost as bad at Thraik. I'm healing him first only because his life is in far greater danger."

For a split second, Wizera focused on Thraik more than her son. "But he'll survive, right?"

The earthen sorceress was hesitant to answer. She looked at the dwarf's injuries as she stripped him of his armor. "Help me with the blood."

The Silver Sorceress gently waved her hands, sending small water strips toward both Thraik and Aramant. A few moments later, the voices of Elarin and Nez'rin echoed from afar.

"Lady Wizera!" he shouted when he saw the Silver Sorceress on her knees with her son's eyes closed. "Is he…"

"No," she said. "He's alive."

Elarin slowly approached Aramant with dread and caution. She grabbed him by the shoulder plate and gently rolled him on his back. "Are they all going to be well?" she asked, her eyes fixated on Haara.

Wizera's tone turned bitter upon hearing no answer to Elarin's question. "You're avoiding the question, Haara."

She chanted ancient words of power that made roots come out from the ground, covering the open wounds of the dwarf. The earthen sorceress kept looking at him until she eventually whispered. "I don't know."

They fell speechless, with Elarin observing a strange, charred sword standing next to Aramant. It didn't take long for her to figure out that he had probably been holding it during the fight. Yet the weapon, if it could even be called that anymore, was in a deplorable state, way past being fit for battle. She slowly reached out for it to have a closer look. The cold hand of Nez'rin touched her wrist, preventing her from picking it up.

"I strongly suggest you refrain from touching that dreadful thing, my dear."

Elarin nodded. "Allow me to handle it." Within a moment's notice and a few words of power, the lich coated the scorched artifact with a thick layer of water that started to freeze. As soon as it covered it all, he wrapped the block with a piece of cloth decorated with magical symbols similar to the runes Wizera had put on Aramant and Thaidren. "It is done."

"What are we going to do with them?" asked the elf.

Haara pointed at the fallen paladin and the dwarf. "Given the injuries on these two, we can't risk moving them until they are stabilized." She sighed and looked around. "As much as any of us would like to leave this place, we need to stay here until they get better."

It was a terrifying thought to be forced to remain in enemy territory without knowing if the entire cult had been dealt with. Even with Wizera taking out their overseer and all the other accomplishments of her companions, there was no telling what else might await them. Should they be attacked a second time, it would mean a death sentence for them. The Silver Sorceress threw a concerned look toward Haara.

"How much time do they need?" asked Wizera.

"These roots will help close some of the wounds as well as send nutrients from the earth directly into their bodies to help them recover faster. It will have little effect on broken bones, so I can't say for sure. Could be an hour, could be four. It also depends on them. Their age, regenerative abilities, every aspect of their body will count. We'll have to hope for the best."

Wizera was unable to mask her concern at this point. She was put in a situation she would've never wanted to be in. The longer they waited, the higher the risk of them being attacked again by the remnants of the cult, if there were any left. Yet, if their desperation led to them leaving too early, it would result in the death of at least one of their party members. Within the chaotic maelstrom of thoughts that swirled inside her head, she heard Elarin taking the lead.

"Start with two hours. If the little one seems good enough by then, we leave; if not, we check again every hour." She looked at the Silver Sorceress. "Before any of this happened, when we were searching for them within this Grinal city, you visited an old acquaintance with your son."

Wizera nodded at her recollection, making Elarin continue.

"Are they trustworthy enough for you?"

Given how long Wizera had known Parab, her answer came in a heartbeat. "Of course."

"Then you go to them and see if there is anything they can provide us with to help. A healing potion perhaps." The elf turned to Haara. "Or an elixir to boost her elemental powers. Anything that can shorten the time we need to spend here, and does not put their lives in danger."

*She's right*, the Silver Sorceress thought as she regained her focus. She nodded a second time and waved her hands as she began to teleport herself.

"We will not let him out of our sight," said Elarin. "Nor the other two."

In a split second, Wizera found herself back at the upper levels of Grinal, next to Parab's shop, where she placed a spatial anchor a long time ago. Once outside, the Silver Sorceress realized that half a day had passed, coming up from her underground nightmare to a clear night's sky. There was no time to admire the stars. A few loud, chaotical bangs at Parab's door proved enough to wake up the merchant.

"What's with all this ruckus?" came from behind the door. "We're closed 'til the sun is up."

"Parab. It's me. Please open up."

The charismatic figure opened the door at the sound of her voice. "Wiz?" he asked with a concerned tone. "What are you doing here?" A closer look at her woke him up completely. "What happened to you?"

"I'm sorry for waking you; I really am, but I had nowhere else to go."

"Slow down, slow down, it's all right. Just tell me what happened."

"I need your help."

***

Inside the underground city's decrepit ruins, Elarin climbed up one of the columns to get a better view of their surroundings. With Nez'rin standing still, in a seemingly meditative state, Haara remained the sole person to keep an eye on the incapacitated trio.

"What is he doing?" asked the elf as she was almost tempted to study the lich to the detriment of scouting around.

"Leave him be," answered Haara. "He can't help them heal anyway."

After seeing there was no sight of any enemies, Elarin dropped off from the column and watched the earthen sorceress. The curiosity about her short-lived partner was eating at her. "Do you know he is versed in other forms of magic than water and darkness?"

Haara startled, almost losing her focus for a brief moment, looked back at Elarin without saying a word. For the elf, that silence was more than enough of an answer.

"But you knew that already," she continued while ambling around. "I suspected he was hiding something since before we arrived in the city. During our battle with the cultist army, he had no choice but to reveal his dark nature to me."

"Elarin, when this is all over, please give us a chance to expla — "

"We need to remain here for at least one hour or so. I would say explanations are a good way to pass the time." She had brief moments of silence between most of her sentences, showing she was carefully choosing her words. "Do not misinterpret my words for hostility; I am grateful to him that we did not end up as corpses for the sake of keeping his secret. However, in my homeworld, necromancy is a serious form of sacrilege toward the natural cycle of life and death. The sole reason why I did not jump down his throat after the battle was over was that I was inclined to give him the benefit of the doubt. Although I must say, it is against my very being to do so. With every inch of my body, and the very core of my soul, I am still resisting reaching for my weapon." From behind her, she heard the eerie voice of the one she was suspicious about.

"I appreciate your words, young elf. Yet, I believe that Lady Haara should focus her full attention on healing. If you wish to know about my story, allow me to shed some light on the matter."

Elarin's eyes carried a subtle hint of hostility in them. Yet, she chose to cast aside her thoughts until Nez'rin's tale would reach an end. She nodded at the old wizard and signaled him to continue. He returned the gesture with a bow.

"Thank you. Now, in order to understand how I became accustomed to the art of sacrilege upon the dead, I must start with the early years of my youth. I was gifted in the arts of manipulating the elemental energies of our world even back then. Furthermore, I was a rare case, having been born with an affinity toward two elements instead of one." He paused briefly, as if he was hesitant to dabble into the memory himself. "My younger brother's case was no different. He had an affinity toward fire and lightning."

"You had a brother?" asked Haara. Elarin seemed surprised by the information as well.

"Once. A dreadfully long time ago… yes. He was named Zin'raan. We both carried names of ancient humans, with each bearing a meaning behind them."

"What did his name mean?" Elarin asked.

The elderly figure let loose a nostalgic smile that even Haara believed to be genuine. "His name would roughly be translated as either "The Blade of Wisdom" or "Wisdom's Virtue." It befitted him like a glove, always eager to catch up to his older brother and surpass him. Always with a thirst for the arcane knowledge, the likes of which I have rarely seen."

"Given how you speak of him, I assume he is not part of the living anymore," said Elarin.

"No… he is not. He passed away in his twenty-first year, struck by an illness over which there was no known cure. It was not a fast process," he continued with a subtle mournful tone. "He fought the disease for almost two years before succumbing to it. It was painful to see him struggling with his own body."

There was hardly any need for Elarin to interrogate Nez'rin anymore. Both she and Haara became aware of the reason the lich underwent the path of death. Regardless of their understanding, he continued with his story.

"Eventually, the day of his burial came to pass. I remember holding my mother as tight as I could, trying to alleviate her suffering while Father dug the hole that was to become Zin'raan's resting place. He was doing his best to avoid bursting into tears as well. I, on the other hand, felt something more than mere regret and mournfulness." He took a deep breath and smiled. "Looking back, I have a clearer grasp of those sentiments. I experienced anger, turmoil, a state of denial toward my brother's death that I could not shake. With that in mind, I started to dabble in aspects of magic that toyed with the manipulation of souls. I studied for almost half a decade before attempting to bring back my sibling from the cold realm of the afterlife. It proved a naïve gesture on my part to do so."

"What happened to him?" asked Haara.

"He returned… unstable. His mind and soul were restored, yet his body had been beneath the earth for too long. It was decayed far too severely in spite of all the preserving techniques and spells I applied to it over time. It only managed to keep him alive, if you can call it that way, for a few hours' worth. Our parents were long gone by that time, having been spared the image of their eldest son defying the laws of nature on the body of their younger. Years continued to pass, with me refusing to abandon my pursuit and promise to Zin'raan that I would make it right the second time. I attempted to build an entirely new body for him, confident that it would turn the tides in my favor. In his favor. That attempt marked the final lesson I needed to understand: that there is no such thing as a flawless resurrection. No matter how versed one may be in the manipulation of necromantic magic.

Regardless of magical reserves or knowledge of the subject, nature is bound to retaliate upon the act of one defying it."

The elf stood silent for a couple of minutes, assimilating all the information from Nez'rin's story.

"You see, young elf," continued the lich, "there are innumerable cultures and worlds in existence that understandably so abhor necromancers. However, they often fail to accept that not all of us want to use these forbidden arts to conquer, kill, or destroy. Some have "strayed" on this path simply by being unable to accept their inability to alter fate."

Right on time, after Nez'rin's story came to an end, the Silver Sorceress reappeared next to them.

Haara hoped she brought the best assistance possible. "You're back."

"Yeah, sorry for taking this long," she replied. "I had to make a detour."

"Where?" asked the elf.

"I'll explain later. Have they gotten any better? She looked over at Thaidren, then at Thraik and Aramant.

"Thraik is better. Thaidren is still in the best condition among the three of them, and getting better. Aramant is stable from a physical perspective, but I can't say much about him being exposed to whatever corruption his weapon holds." She paused. "I think they are all stable enough for us to leave this forsaken place."

Wizera exhaled in relief. "Good. I've got us a few rooms at an inn located on the upper levels. Courtesy of a friend. Let's go." She started to chant to open a small portal beneath each of her fallen allies and Thaidren. Afterward, she conjured a larger one for her and the other members of the group to pass through. Haara traversed through the portal first, with Wizera having to pass through last. She saw Elarin staring at Nez'rin, almost in a threatening manner.

"Is everything all right?" asked the Silver Sorceress.

The lich remained silent, watching the young elf, then looking back at Wizera. Elarin's frown started to slowly fade, eventually being replaced by an expression of semi-acceptance.

"We are well," she said, giving a subtle nod.

They all entered the portal and traveled to the inn.

The following days were free of any incident. No one came searching for Wizera nor the rest to seek vengeance for their actions against the cult of Kasm. It eased the Silver Sorceress's concern, yet did not fully extinguish it. During this period, she showed a tendency to disappear for a couple of hours every two or so days, without revealing to anyone the reason or where she went. Haara did not care to ask, as she had been treating the wounds of Thraik, Aramant, and Thaidren.

During this time, Elarin served as Haara's assistant, helping her with small yet significant aspects, while Nez'rin focused his attention on placing protective spells around the inn, securing the place as best as he could. On top of that, he preferred to avoid interacting with the elf, for the time being, all while Elarin was distracting herself with assisting the earthen sorceress. Eventually, however, during their fifth day at the Bedstocks Inn, it was Elarin who reached out to Nez'rin.

"I had a few days to think about what you said. About your story."

The watching eyes of the old man followed her through the room. "I assume you are here because you reached a verdict." He did not reach for a weapon or anything of a sort, but sat on his bed and placed his hands on his knees.

"I am still unfamiliar with your kin's tolerance or lack of it toward necromancy. At first glance, I am to understand our people share the same beliefs when it comes to these practices." She picked up her dagger, still sheathed in its hilt, and placed it on the table. "Right after our battle with the cultists ended, I felt an almost uncontrollable urge to slit your throat and leave your bones with the other heretics. Yet I have chosen not to do so on the premise that in the short amount of time I have spent with you and your companions, none of you gave me any reason to harbor hostility toward you. On the contrary, you gave me reason to doubt my prejudices about the nature of the human race." She sat down on the bed next to him. "I have but two questions left for you if you are willing to answer them."

"Ask, and I will do my best to provide a satisfying answer."

"Did everyone know about your powers but me?"

He slowly shook his head. "The young paladin remains in the dark, the reason why I maintain my appearance. In time, perhaps I will consider revealing my secret to him as well, but for now, I believe he has been through enough. I doubt such information would prove beneficial to him."

"I see. For now, I will respect that decision, but I strongly suggest you do not keep it hidden for too long."

He nodded. "What is your second question?"

"In your story, you mentioned what the name of your brother meant in the ancient language of mankind. You never mentioned what yours means."

The lich chuckled. "My name's meaning? It has been a long time since I have given any thought to it. Its translation is quite ironic when I think about it. It means 'The Shield of Conviction' or 'Conviction's Bulwark.'"

Elarin rose from the bed, bowed before the old man, then closed the door behind her as she left.

The lich's thoughts took him back a few days. Right after they had defeated the cult of Kasm, to be exact. When Haara questioned Nez'rin's story. Their dialogue kept playing in his head in a strangely nostalgic way as he recalled it:

"That was quite a story. I must admit, you almost got me for a moment there. You're a dangerously good liar," Haara had said.

"The only aspect of my story that was dishonest was the manner in which my brother met his final death."

Haara had not continued the discussion.

# CHAPTER XX

# AFTERMATH

Dark images of destruction and mayhem clouded the mind of the young paladin as he slumbered. His right hand would occasionally stretch and clench its fist, trying to reach for something that wasn't there. A fever made him sweat, giving him the sense he was about to burst into flames. Undistinguishable whispers would haunt and accompany his every thought, refusing to give him rest. Nightmarish images of Baav's corruption and Attern's suffering flooded his head as well, making him experience a sentiment of helplessness and futility.

He rose into a sitting position, leaning his back against a wall, struggling for breath. With each one, the young paladin felt more stable, more anchored back to reality. It soothed his unrest, but it did not remove it entirely. He rolled his feet off the bed without getting up at first, then rubbed his face, wiping the sweat from his forehead and cheeks. *That was no ordinary nightmare...* His attention suddenly shifted to his right hand. It was normal, without the slightest hint of a shake nor demonic power coursing through its veins. With that relief in mind, he stood up, walked over to a mirror, and checked his right eye. It proved to be normal as well.

A chill traveled down Aramant's spine. Slowly but steadily, he started to put together the pieces of memory from the fight with the demonic experiments. *Plural.* He realized now that he had fought two of them. The flames, the cut-out skull, and the demolition of an entire stone wall... He slowly began to grasp that it had all been real. He found his armor lying next to his bed, cleaned of blood, and fully repaired. He left his room and walked down the stairs. On the ground floor, he saw a drunken Thraik, eyes narrowed, reeking of alcohol and barely keeping his balance in order to avoid tipping off his chair, arguing with the innkeeper at the bar. Upon hearing the creaking stairs and the young paladin's steps, he turned to him.

"Would ya look at dat," he said. "Da golden princess is finally awake. Enjoyed yer beauty sleep?"

Though the dwarf was the inebriated one, it was Aramant who experienced a strange sensation that mimicked a most dreadful hangover. He paid no mind to Thraik's rude comment as he took a seat near him. "How did we get here?"

"From wha' I understand, Wizera took care of us gettin' here. This place ain't much, but we have it all ta ourselves 'til we be ready ta go back home."

Aramant groaned as he rubbed his forehead. "Are we waiting for something?"

"Well, for starters, we were waitin' for ye. Ye're the last person ta wake up."

The young paladin sighed and waved a hand at the innkeeper.

"Can I offer you something, sir?" the innkeeper asked.

*Can't believe I'm going to ask this...* "Do you have anything for hangovers?"

The thin silhouette behind the bar glanced at him before smiling. "I might have something; give me a moment, please." His attention turned toward the dwarf as he took his empty ale mug away from him. "What about you, master dwarf? Can I get you anything else? Another round, perhaps?"

Thraik's eyes moved back and forth from the empty mug to the innkeeper, then back at his worse-for-wear companion, who somehow still had enough morality left to judge him. "Da earth witch said I shouldn't... hmm, bring me two more and a slice of apple pie." He then turned to Aramant. "Ye look like ye could benefit from somethin' ta eat yerself."

Aramant waved his hand in disagreement as his eyes narrowed and he gazed at the ground. *Maybe I should have stayed in bed,* he thought. A few moments later, the innkeeper returned with their drink orders. He gently pushed a large glass, which contained a bubbling eerie dark green substance, toward Aramant. Its smell alone proved enough to partially shake the paladin back to his senses.

"Forgive me if I sound rude, but what's this?" he asked.

"It's a family recipe," answered the innkeeper. "A concoction made from aromatic herbs that help against headaches, fine powder from energizing crystals, a few drops of orange juice, and a large spoon of honey — to sweeten the taste."

The young paladin was grateful for the intention, yet the more he looked at the concoction, the more he started to regret asking for it. As the dwarf laughed, Aramant eventually took a deep breath and drank the miracle remedy. The honey that was supposed to help with the taste clearly wasn't enough. It tasted horrible, reminding him of the time when he first tasted a batch of ale brewed by Issin at the cathedral, after which several paladins ended up with a serious case of food poisoning. Needless to say, his former superior was strongly encouraged to refrain from this short-lived hobby. It was viscous, warm, sour, and far beyond his taste. Aramant gagged and spluttered. As he continued to consume the rest of it, even the dwarf seemed to have sobered up and stopped laughing.

"Ye have some guts, lad."

"With remedies like these, it feels like I'm about to spill them all out," he answered, screwing up his face.

"Anyhow," said the dwarf, taking a sip from his mug, "I understand dat me and Thaidren have ye ta thank for savin' our arses."

"Don't worry about it. You would've done the same for me. Besides, I don't remember much of what happened." He looked at the empty glass, and pushed it away before turning back to Thraik. "How long was I unconscious?"

"T'as been almost three weeks, lad," answered the dwarf.

"Three weeks?" exclaimed the young paladin almost jumping out of his chair. "H… how could I have slept for that long? Why didn't you try to wake me? For how long have you and Thaidren been awake?"

"Relax, lad, t'is not like we're in a rush. Ya deserved ta rest, and we gave ya as long as ya needed. Besides, from what I've been told, ya've been through some nasty stuff."

"Yeah, tell me about it."

"Look, I only kno' what da rest told me and dat ever since I've met yer pa he's always been strugglin' with somethin' related to dat hammer. Don' take its corruption lightly. Ya've got away easy dis time, but who knows what could've happened."

"Don't worry about it. I won't let it happen again."

"Good, now let an old dwarf drink in peace. Go bother someone else."

The door opened and Haara walked in, adding to the dwarf's discontent. "Thraik!" she shouted. "I thought I made it very clear that you're not allowed to drink until fully healed. What were you thinking?"

"Was hopin' it would help with da pain caused by yer pesky voice," he murmured.

Seeing as she had no one to reason with, Haara's attention shifted to the young paladin. "Aramant, glad to finally see you awake."

"Glad to be back," he answered.

"Can we speak outside?"

He nodded and rose to his feet, then opened the door and let the earthen sorceress exit first. Lastly, Aramant closed the door behind him, leaving the dwarf to drink in peace, as he had put it.

"What's up with him? He seems… affected…" asked the young paladin.

Haara shrugged. "Who could say? Maybe Wizera has a better idea. I haven't known him long enough to tell if it's something new, or part of some aftermath effect." She fixed her eyes on him as if she were studying a lab rat, checking if anything was different. "Sorry for staring," she said after realizing it a few moments later. "I'm just worried about your recovery."

"It's all right, I don't feel any kind of pain right now. I must've healed already."

"I wasn't talking about that, and I think you know it, Aramant," said Haara with a mixture of concern and displeasure. "What you did was stupid and reckless, to say the least. Wizera has brought me up to speed about your hammer, but I never thought I'd be put in a position to try and cleanse you of its influence."

The young paladin remained silent for a moment. He took a few steps away from the earthen sorceress and sat down on a small wooden bench near the inn's entrance. "I know what I did," he eventually said. "But what else was I supposed to do? I had no chance against that beast, and neither did Thaidren and Thraik. I would've ended up dead if I hadn't done it. I had no choice."

"You infused your body with demonic energies, Aramant. I don't think you fully grasp what that means, as much as you claim you do." Her voice softened up as she explained to him the extent of his actions. "That kind of power, it's not meant for humans to control. It alters everything, from our bodies to our way of thinking. Often permanently. Somehow you seem to have gotten away with it pretty easily, but you must never use that power again. Even if it weren't for the corruption, you've imbued your body with a tremendous amount of energy, stressing it almost past its limit. Do you know what happens when a vessel is filled with more energy than it can handle?"

"I assume nothing good."

"The two most common scenarios are that the person either goes insane, or their body shuts down completely from being overwhelmed. You were on the verge of experiencing the latter, and there's no way for me as a healer to mend that."

"So, you didn't siphon the extra energy out of me?"

Haara shook her head. "Your body is young and seemingly stronger than an average human. It slowly removed the excess power on its own. But keep in mind your physical wounds took about two weeks to heal, whereas you eliminated the excess power just enough to wake up after three."

"'Just enough'? Does that mean I still have remnants of that power in me?"

"I can't tell you for sure. It is possible you still have some leftovers that'll be gone by the end of the week." She sat next to him and took one of his hands in hers. "What you must understand is that now your body has irreversibly changed in two ways: it will crave for the same power once more, at least for a while, and it will be far more susceptive toward it. Do NOT let yourself be swayed by temptation once more, or you could end up losing your life. That, or much worse."

"Did I... Did I have a part in Thaidren's and Thraik's injuries?" asked the young paladin as his voice trembled.

Once again, the earthen sorceress shook her head. "No. You actually saved their lives during your bloodlust act. But you should talk to Thaidren when he returns. He was still conscious when you barged in on his fight, and I think you gave him quite a scare."

Lastly, there was one more question that circled through Aramant's mind. "Where's my hammer now?"

"You mean the sword. Nez'rin sealed it off within an icicle and some magically imbued piece of cloth. I would advise you not to go and ask him for it, at least for a few days. If it were up to me, though, I'd consider giving up on ever wielding it again. Can't understand how the paladins ended up viewing that artifact as holy." She looked at Aramant like she was gazing at a naïve child, still unaware of the cruel aspects of the world he lived in. *And I can't understand why you cling to it as well,* she thought.

***

Thaidren, Wizera, and Elarin recently returned from the city, having shopped for some fruit as well as a few other food ingredients and miscellaneous items such as medicinal herbs that Haara requested. Once they arrived at the inn's entrance, the sight of Aramant, his fever broken, brought them joy. Thaidren, however, seemed to be more hesitant than the others. That was expected given he had witnessed the young paladin's corrupted state with his own eyes.

Aramant walked up to Thaidren. "Sorry for scaring you." His smile was weak, yet sincere.

Thaidren chuckled nervously. "For a moment, I thought you weren't able to tell the difference between friend and foe. I'm just glad that I was wrong, and you did what I could not."

Aramant smiled briefly as he exhaled. "Hmph, next time, learn to deal with such monstrosities yourself. I don't intend to wear the flames of Hell anymore." They both raised their hands and shook on it.

"Two things we can agree on," said Thaidren.

Wizera approached Aramant. "It's good to see you awake. How are you feeling?"

"Normal, all things considered," he answered.

"Good. We'll stay at the inn for another day or two for Haara to examine you and make sure you're fine."

"What are we going to do next?" Thaidren asked his mother.

"You won't be doing anything. I, however, have a task that requires my attention."

Her son raised an eyebrow. "Care to tell us what the said task is?"

"You don't need to worry about the details," answered Wizera.

"Mother, for good or bad, we're all adults here. How about you stop "protecting" us from the truth and keep us in the loop? Maybe we can end up being of help to you."

She remained silent for a moment, then sighed. "It would be easier to show you, but since we won't be going anywhere for another day or two, I'll explain." She paused, then continued. "When each of us fought the cultists, I was the one who ended up fighting their overseer, the man you all saw at the temple before we got separated. His name is Epakin, and his cult worships demonic beings with the hope of ascending to something more akin to them than humans."

"The demon-worshipping part was kind of self-deductible," replied Aramant.

"Anyway, our clash ended up with me managing to capture Epakin alive. He is now contained in a safe location where I intend to interrogate him about the cult. After that, I'll hand him over to the Council of Mages."

"Is it there that you kept disappearing during these last weeks?" asked Elarin.

"Yes. I was strengthening the magical bindings that prevent him from using his powers while also checking on him regularly. I partially deprived him of food and water as well. It'll make him more cooperative." She gave in to her thoughts briefly. "In fact, I was going to check on him today, one last time before we are to return to the mansion."

"Is it safe to return there, my lady?" asked Nez'rin. "If there are any remnants of the cult of Kasm, they might seek revenge on those responsible for their downfall. They know where the house is located."

"I wouldn't be concerned about them that much. Most of their forces have been dealt with as far as we know. Moreover, I've placed several more runic symbols at the mansion. To strengthen my magic there along with some spatial magic interference runes. They won't be able to teleport right to our doorstep a second time."

"I see. Then perhaps my talents would be put to good use if I go back right now and enhance the existing barriers while leaving some of my own. Two days will provide me enough time to secure the entire area."

"I'd appreciate that, Nez. We'll see you back there then."

With that matter settled and with Thaidren and the younger members of the group now informed, they spent the remaining two days resting and preparing for what was to come next.

***

The scorching heat of summer was at its peak over the last few days, making most of the potential customers of Grinal prefer the middle or lower levels, which were better shrouded against the heat, to make their acquisitions. It wasn't an unusual event for the tradesmen of the top levels, however. In time, they adapted and accepted the coming of this dried-up period in which money would be short. One such merchant was Parab, a charismatic character who owned a large shop on the city's third upper floor. He had installed a large blind over his shop that stretched over to his full tables. A device that he had procured many years ago from a traveler of another world was also helping him deal with the heat. Composed of a moving propeller attached to a metallic base, which held an energy crystal that would power it up and make it spin, creating a small yet effective air current. He wiped the sweat from his forehead with one hand before taking a seat near it while holding a cold drink in his other. From across the corridor of platforms and among the few silhouettes of people brave or loyal enough to still shop on this level, he recognized the blue and silvery robes of his dearest friend, Wizera. Her sight made his day a tad better and as she walked toward him, he jumped to his feet to greet her.

"Wiz!" he said, smiling. "How are you?"

"Hi, Parab. I'm fine, thank you."

"Tell me; what can lil' old me help you with today?"

"Nothing, old friend. I came by to tell you we're going to travel back to our home today. And to once again thank you for all the help you've given me. If it weren't for your potions, your connections to get the materials needed for healing bandages, and all the other things we used to heal Aramant, Thraik, and my son, I don't know what would've happened."

The merchant gently grabbed her by the chin and raised her head, showing her the same joyful smile that she had been accustomed to. "You have nothing to thank me for, dear. We've known each other for so many years, and our friendship means a lot to me. Both because of our loved ones' memory and because of us, individually. It was the least I could do."

She nodded at him, with a small smile. "Friends like yourself are hard to come by. I'm glad I had a chance to find one in this life."

Her words moved him. "I only return the same treatment I receive, my dear." They both remained silent for a brief moment, with Parab shifting his gaze behind him, then back at the Silver Sorceress. "How's your boy? Is he recovering well?"

"Yeah, he's fine now. Haara assured me there was no permanent physical damage. His youth certainly played a major role in that."

"He's a strong man, Wiz. I'm sure he's destined for great things."

"Some destiny… I sometimes wonder…" She looked at her friend, constantly sweating from his palms and forehead. He did his best to wipe it off and not look like a pig roasting in the sun's heat. She smiled and reached into her bag, taking out her vial of blue dye before signaling him to raise a hand. "Here, let me give you a parting gift. This runic mark will cool down your body temperature. Unfortunately, it will last for about three days at best, but I hope it'll still be of help."

"Three days of not caring about the heat? Are you kidding? Of course, it helps. Thank you very much. If I'd known sorcerers could do stuff like this, I would've thought of becoming one myself."

She laughed. "Believe me, it's better you didn't. I talk from personal experience when I say it's not always a joyous ride."

"Eh, probably. But I'd get to travel more."

She said her farewell to Parab and started to walk away. With each step, she felt a familiar urge to turn back and ask something that she had wanted to for a long time. This time, however, the sentiment felt much stronger. For so many years, every time she visited the city and Parab, she managed to keep it at bay. Yet, this time she decided to finally turn back and take a leap of faith.

"Parab?" she asked in a shy tone.

"Yes? Is there something else you wanted to talk about?"

"Forgive me if what I'm about to ask sounds bold, but…"

Parab's curiosity grew stronger. "But…?"

She eventually found the courage to utter the words she'd been dying to ask. "After everything that happened with… you know… how can you remain so… unchanged? I'm not saying that it hasn't affected you, but I see you as joyous as I've seen you since you were with Genra."

The merchant cast his eyes down, then looked to his right, to the bottom of the canyon where he had lost his beloved. His face lost his usual smile briefly before coming back, though altered with a trace of sadness. "Ah, so that is what this was about." He turned back from the Silver Sorceress. He brought her a chair and signaled for her to sit next to him. He maintained his seat next to the wind-blowing device. "Judging from the way you asked, I assume it has been bothering you for a while."

She nodded in shame, feeling that she had overstepped her bounds.

"Don't worry about it," continued Parab, placing a hand on her shoulder. "I understand where this is coming from. If the situation were reversed, I would've probably been haunted by the same question." He took a deep breath and stood silent, giving into his thoughts briefly, then carefully picked his words. "Look… I bet you'd love to hear me say that I found a secret recipe for happiness despite my losses. Truth is, old friend, there isn't one. You claim my smile hasn't changed at all, but it did. Although the idea of you not noticing makes me somewhat happy. You see… ever since I lost my dear Genra, I've had my fair share of not-so-happy days. There were nights when I woke up and wondered for a second why she wasn't in our bed, right next to me… before remembering the answer. There were some mornings in which I wished I'd never woken up at all. And some days, I wished to just leave all this behind me and go to wherever she ended up." He stood silent for a minute or two, slowly breathing in and out. "I never knew if she met her end down there or if somehow, she is still alive somewhere. I'm obviously rooting for the latter. Alas, I've felt it since a long time ago that that isn't the case. I feel that I know exactly where she ended up. Like I said, I want to go there as well sometimes."

"Parab…"

"But I won't. Not today, not tomorrow, not a second before my time comes." His gaze turned back to the Silver Sorceress's eyes. "I want to believe I will be reunited with her in the afterlife when my days will reach an end. And because of that, I also believe that if I succumb to despair and take my own life, I'd be facing her anger like never before, followed by my greatest fear: her disappointment." He looked around him, at all his items, at his house, then back at Wizera. "If I'd have listened to that impulse, I wouldn't have been able to help you when you needed it. Staying here proved to me that the living are not yet done with me. And neither am I with them. With that said, to get back to your question, I keep smiling because I know that she would've wanted me to do so. She would've wanted me to continue to live my life with joyfulness and excitement, the way that she remembered it, so that when we finally reunite, I won't have a depressing story to tell her. Instead, I'll have a wonderful tale about the rest of my life to share with her."

His words almost made Wizera shed tears of both guilt and mournfulness. "I'm sorry," she whispered, "for bringing these painful memories to the surface."

"You have nothing to apologize for, Wiz," he answered as he instinctively wiped an imaginary tear from his eye. "If she saw us right now, sobbing like two old farts, she'd probably bump our heads together."

The thought made them both feel a bit better while sharing a brief laugh. After spending a little more, happier time with each other, the Silver Sorceress said her farewells and traveled back to the Bedstocks Inn.

Parab wished her the best of luck and waved at her as she slowly drifted farther away from him.

# CHAPTER XXI

# NALYS

Thaidren and the others were packing their belongings, along with the supplies they acquired from Grinal for their return trip home.

"As soon as Mother gets back, we should be on our way, right?" asked Thaidren.

"Right," answered Haara. "You feeling homesick?"

"More like eager to have a chat with the cult's overseer, instead. Last time, I missed my chance to get acquainted."

"Easy now. Don't let the likes of him get to you."

"How can I not, knowing what he's done, knowing how many people have suffered because of him?"

"He is but a pawn. His master is who you should be interested in."

"Be that as it may, it doesn't excuse his actions," intervened Aramant.

Haara looked at both of them, remembering what it was like to be in the springtime of life with a bright fighting spirit burning at its fullest. "You two are still young. These kinds of things don't solve themselves overnight. Keeping your minds calm and your resolve true will hasten the process, but that shouldn't be your main concern."

They both nodded with Aramant's gaze turning toward his right hand.

"Without the whispers anymore, it should be easier," he said out loud without realizing it.

"What whispers?" Haara asked with an alarmed tone.

"Well, during my fight with the... monster, or whatever that thing was... I started to hear a voice in my head. I'm almost certain it was the hammer."

Haara's face turned white as snow. "Did it want to make a deal with you or anything of the sort?"

"It claimed to be a friend who could give me the power to defeat my enemy. I refused its offer up until the point when I was on the verge of dying."

"And that's when you accepted? That's when you turned?" With the earthen sorceress's voice turning angrier with each word, Thaidren and Elarin stepped back.

"That's when I told it that I'll allow it only this ti — " A hard slap over his face interrupted him. One that carried both an aura of a disappointed parent and that of an angry friend.

"You idiot. Wizera never told me this." She took a few steps back and briefly covered her face. "Good earth, it's far worse than I thought."

The Silver Sorceress's voice came from behind her. "Tell you what? What's going on?"

Haara lashed out at her. "You never told me the weapon harbors a demon." Her anger, however, lessened at the sight of Wizera's confusion.

"What do you mean? I never knew that was the case. Attern only told me it was originally a demonic weapon."

"Well, yours truly here revealed he heard whispers during his fight. Even more so, he was stupid enough to accept its power. But don't worry," she continued with a sarcastic tone, "he assured me it was just that once, right Aramant?" The young paladin stood silent while his aunt remained speechless. She sighed and rubbed her forehead. Amidst her thoughts, Haara's voice echoed. "This changes the entire dynamic. He should NEVER touch the artifact again. It poses too much of a risk." Her reaction was volatile, yet her words were not wrong.

*Why would he keep such a secret from me?* Wizera thought. *Still, he somehow seems well now. Is it because he hasn't made contact with the hammer since then or something else entirely? I can't believe the idea of Attern not knowing about this. But why keep it a secret?* After a few minutes of contemplation, she responded. "The hammer is sealed away and contained. For the time being, let's focus on getting back home and interrogating the cult's overseer." Her gaze shifted toward the young paladin. "After I'm done with him, I'll deal with this."

Aramant nodded while Elarin approached them.

"Now that we discussed this, are we ready to leave?" she asked.

"Yes," answered Wizera, "but we need to get back to the elevator at the edge of the canyon on the upper levels."

Haara frowned without adding anything else. She would not even look at Aramant.

On his side, the young paladin found himself confused. "Hold on a moment. When we entered the underground city, how did the overseer manage to teleport us? I thought we couldn't space travel inside the city."

"The city has an exterior barrier, similar to a giant invisible dome, if you will," answered Wizera. "We can't teleport from anywhere on the outside to its inside. Yet spatial travel is possible within the dome as long as we don't try to use it to get out. This is why we need to get back up, within a certain distance of the canyon's edge. From there, we'll be able to go home." With the answer provided, the group ventured back up to the city's exit. Upon distancing themselves several meters from the guarded elevator, Wizera started to conjure a portal.

With the series of unfortunate events coming to an end, there was still one remaining vestige that needed closure. It came in the form of the alleged human leader and overseer of the cult of Kasm, known as Epakin. A dark sorcerer with a past shrouded in mystery, even after Wizera mentioned his name to the Council of Mages. *Most probably a pseudonym*, she thought.

The Silver Sorceress had secured him in a remote location, far from prying eyes, yet her concern of him seeking escape was still unhinged. As soon as the group arrived back at Thaidren's mansion, her first instinct was to go back to where he was held to check on him. Nevertheless, she dismissed these thoughts in favor of helping Nez'rin establish more protective barriers, both to prevent spatial traveling and to give them an upper hand in the event of another attack.

"Right, now we can finally rest for a while, so I suggest you take advantage of the occasion," said Wizera. "I will go interrogate Epakin in an hour or two. If any of you want to join, feel free to do so." She turned to her son and patted him on the shoulder. "You should join me there."

Her words surprised him. "Really? How come the change of heart?"

"You were right; I've kept things from you long enough. You are a grown man now, and that means I have to include you in matters like this." She looked down. "Forgive me for taking this long to realize it. I guess the mother in me always wanted to shelter you from these aspects of the world."

From farther away, Aramant looked at them without hearing their conversation. Despite not living with each other for so long, their closeness made him somewhat envious and mournful with the reminder of his father's memory. He did not blame him for his parenting, although there was always a part of the young paladin's heart that wished they could've been closer. A piece of his soul residing right next to another that wished he'd realized all of this before his passing.

As soon as Thaidren and Wizera finished talking with each other, the Silver Sorceress turned her attention to him. "I don't know if you've heard our conversation or not." She took his hand in hers. "But in case you didn't, I'd like Thaidren to join me when I interrogate Epakin. And I think you should come as well."

Her words made Aramant smile. It was refreshing to be reminded that he still had a loving family beside him. However, his current plans differed from his aunt's offer. "I'd love to, but if it's all right with you, I'll stay at the mansion until you return."

"Is everything all right?" she asked.

"For what seems like a long time, yes, it truly is," said the young paladin, smiling. He reached into his bag and drew out a worn medium-sized book. "It's just that before Thaidren and I left the cathedral, I found Father's journal. I plan to use this free time to read through it. Maybe he wrote something about the hammer as well."

Wizera shook her head. "I see. Well, the demon in the hammer is yet another issue on our list, so if you find any useful information about it, all the better. Let me know if you do, once we get back."

"Will do." The Silver Sorceress started to walk away to prepare for the interrogation.

"Wizera?" Aramant asked.

"Yes?"

He took a few seconds to gather his words before speaking. "I understand the hammer became a far greater threat with the new information and all that, yet I can't help but wonder about Haara's reaction."

"What do you mean?" asked the Silver Sorceress in a confused tone. "Her reaction was justified. You should've told us sooner that you heard whispers coming from it."

"I know, but that's not what I meant. When she yelled at me, while justified, it also gave me the impression it was personal. It may be a stupid question to ask, but has she had previous experience with demons?"

"Yes... she has. But if you want to know more, I think it would be best to talk to Haara directly. That is if she wants to resurface those memories."

"I'll think about asking her after I've read a few pages of the journal and maybe when her anger cools down." He waved his aunt farewell, then went to his room.

All the while, Nez'rin was still occupied with raising more barriers with Elarin accompanying him. Perhaps she was fascinated by him after learning of his heretical powers. Perhaps she was merely suspicious, not wanting to let him out of her sight. It mattered not for the lich, as long as she did not disturb him.

Haara returned to her underground study chamber while Thraik walked inside the mansion and fell asleep, in his bed this time. With Thaidren probably spending some time with Wizera, Aramant had the entire upper floor of the mansion to himself. He lay on his bed, with his back against the wall, and opened the worn-out journal. The pages seemed from different eras, with some of them being on the verge of falling out. After carefully sorting through numerous pages and sorting out the information he deemed irrelevant at the moment, he concluded that the book was indeed what Attern claimed in his letter. Part bestiary, part journal, belonging to many users throughout time, serving as an index with personal logs regarding different aspects of existence. Eventually, the young paladin stumbled upon several passages written by his father. One of them, in particular, caught his attention.

*Assault on the Old Earth. Day 45. War of the Spider – entry 21.*

*The voice has subsided. I can no longer hear its maleficent whispers. It is finally silenced... For now... Unfortunately, I know this fiend all too well. As soon as Viz'Hock tastes blood again, so will its beast awaken once more. Since I took the hammer into my possession, I've heard it speaking to me so clearly only four times, this incident included.*

*Several weeks before we departed, I scoured every book, scroll, or other form of documentation concerning the weapon's origin, in hopes of understanding it better. I keep telling myself I will have a firmer grasp at controlling it then. Alas, I only remembered how limited our world is regarding information about the so-called superior beings. The only thing I managed to find was a text from an old scroll containing angelic symbols. Assuming their translation was accurate enough, I found out that the weapon's name, Viz'Hock, may be a clue to its origin. Although I'm not sure which translation is correct, assuming that any of them are in the first place, its name could mean either "Viz's Tail" or the "Tail of Hock," concluding that one word represents the name of the demon, and the other would transcript into "tail." As if the quantity of information wasn't frustrating enough, now its usefulness is as well... Useless... all of it...*

While shuffling through the pages some more, the young paladin found another possibly insightful passage.

*Assault on the Old Earth. Day 49. War of the Spider – entry 25.*

*Our total casualties revolve around one-fourth of the entire force. ~~I'm starting to think that Thieron's plan to have a small, compacted party may turn into a double-edged sword.~~ Haara would still not talk to me and... I don't blame her... but... I had to do it! Nalys was out of control; I couldn't save him. No one could've while on the battlefield. Between him and the queen's minions, I didn't have much time to act. Perhaps I was too hasty in my judgment... No, if I let myself think that way, Viz'Hock will sense it. After all of this is over... I'll have a lot to make up for toward Haara. If only my beloved Samara were here... She always knew how to quench the doubts in my foolish heart...*

"Mother," Aramant whispered as he gently placed a finger over his mother's name on the journal's faded page. A sudden knock interrupted his reading session. The door screeched as it slowly opened, revealing the earthen sorceress on the other side.

"May I come in?" she asked.

Aramant closed the book and hid it behind his back. "Of course."

She nodded at him and entered the room, taking a seat on the bed next to him. "Look," she said with her eyes looking at the floor, "my reaction from earlier may have been... exaggerated." She stopped briefly, her tone showing a subtle hint of residual anger, if only for a moment. "Don't get me wrong, you deserved the yelling, yet you didn't deserve the 'idiot' thing... and the slap. I came here to apologize for them."

Aramant looked at her, feeling both regret and a sense of fright. "You did hit me pretty hard, but I think I deserved it nonetheless." He exhaled deeply before continuing. "You wonder why I still cling to an artifact that is corrupt in nature. Even more so now that we know a demon resides within it. To be completely honest with you, I'm not sure myself. It should end up on the bottom of the ocean or someplace else where no man could ever retrieve it. I'm not going to make any excuses for accepting the demon's power back then, but at the same time, I'm not going to apologize for somehow saving Thaidren and Thraik's lives in the process. It was risky, it was stupid, I know. I also know it will never happen again."

Haara put her hand on the young paladin's shoulder. "As long as you wield it, there's always going to be a risk or a situation in which it might happen again. You have to let go of it. Permanently."

"I can't," he whispered.

"Why not?"

"Because for better or worse, that hammer is something my father left me. It's one of the few things of his I have left." He moved his hand to his back, revealing the journal to her. "He wrote about it too. He struggled with it, was burdened by it. The same creature that has now found a weaker link in the previous wielder's offspring. Unlike him, I wasn't able to resist its temptation." The young paladin passed the journal to Haara, opening it to the passages he had read. "He wrote about you too."

Haara looked at the lines of Attern's writing, murmuring indistinguishable words in the process. "That's why he was so vehement to change my mind about moving away." Soon after, the sound of Aramant's voice interrupted her line of thoughts.

"Nalys… who was he?" he asked.

She frowned angrily at the young paladin, then dismissed the impulse and took in a deep breath before answering him. "Nalys was… an exquisite sorcerer. A foolish one but exquisite nonetheless. A kind soul, a loyal friend, a husband the likes of which a young woman can only dream."

"I'm sorry, I didn't mean to…"

"No, no, it's all right," she told him, signaling that she still had more to say. "These entries, they're from the War of the Spider." The earthen sorceress ran her fingers across the name. "Hmph, I suppose your father has told you a story or two about that time. Those were… different times. More troubling, more… volatile. The world was on the brink of a global invasion. A life form remnant from the ancient conflict between the angels and the demons managed to evolve into something akin to its creators. It adapted to our world and seeped through the foundations of the earth itself, devouring and assimilating whatever it could while destroying anything it couldn't. Long story short, it was Thaidren's father who suggested we take the fight to their queen by forming a small, concentrated group of strong individuals that would infiltrate the nest and put an end to her. The fact that we are having this conversation, today, is a living testament to our victory."

She sighed, then paused for a moment. "However, Nalys and many others were part of the price we paid for such a triumph."

"How did it happen?" asked Aramant.

"He became reckless, in a manner similar to the way you did. Your act of allowing the demon to take control stirred a feeling of familiarity way more than I would've wanted. He was an earthen sorcerer, like me. Only his powers were far greater than my own, and his mastery over them even more so." She stopped momentarily, with her eyes fixed on Aramant's. "Do you know what's the darkest aspect of earth magic?"

Fearful of giving the wrong answer, the young paladin shook his head and shrugged.

She smiled briefly at his reaction before continuing. "Didn't expect you to. To make this as simple as I can, earth magic has the potential to do something that other primordial elements can't. As a paladin, you were always taught that angels reside within the sky. A notion that isn't exactly what you'd imagine, but I digress. Anyway, just as you were told that, so do we learn that demons reside beneath our feet. Earth magic can be used to invoke such a demon from the core of our world. A core that connects our world, as do the center of all others, with the Burning Hells." She paused yet again, wiping an imaginary tear away.

"In the heat of one of the battles that seemed to lead us to our peril back then, Nalys turned… desperate, I guess. He used his power to summon a demon from the depths of the Underworld and tried to bind it to his will. What followed was that the fiend possessed my husband instead of serving him, forcefully dividing our attention on two fronts instead of one. Somehow most of us managed to survive that day. Nalys, however, met his end there. Up until reading this, I didn't know if it was one of us or the Spider Queen's minions that ended him. In all that chaos, I couldn't focus on him without risking my own life. Fate must have a twisted sense of humor. Sending me on the same path with the son of the same old friend who happened to put my husband to rest."

"I'm sorry," whispered Aramant.

"For what? You're not responsible for anything that happened there. As for your father, don't worry about me blaming him either. I understand it had to be done. If we weren't on a raging battlefield, perhaps we could've contained him and attempted to exorcise the demon. But that wasn't the case. He made a tough decision that I clearly saw haunting him over the years. Now I am simply aware of what the reason was for his unrest."

"Do you think about him often?"

"There are days. I try to honor his memory through my actions, work, and research as a scholar of earthen sorcery. When Wizera first came to me, I agreed to join her on the premise that it would've been Nalys's decision. If it were up to my selfishness, I would still be at my home on the Old Earth." She put the journal back into the young paladin's hand. "But I don't regret listening to his will." The earthen sorceress got back up and started heading to the door. Before taking her leave, she stopped and turned, looking back at him. "I believe you and Thaidren are destined for great things, together and individually. But that atrocious sword, veiled by the guise of a holy hammer is not a part of your fate. It shouldn't be. I can't watch you make the same mistakes as Nalys did. I'll leave you to your business." She closed the door behind her, leaving Aramant alone with his thoughts, his journal, and hopefully with no other dark influence around him.

During the time in which Aramant and Haara had a heart-to-heart, Wizera had already transported herself, Thaidren, and Elarin to her prisoner's location. Using her arcane capabilities to bend the fabric of space, she and the rest ended up staring at a giant lake within a mountain area, tens, maybe hundreds of kilometers away from their home. The scenery was open, peaceful, with no human settlements, ruins, or buildings of any kind in sight. It stirred a sentiment of confusion in Thaidren's heart. To see a horizon entirely devoid of human touch made for a rare display of peace and serenity. All the while, Elarin was scouring for a hidden door or anything of the sort that could grant her a sense as to what was their purpose here, in the middle of nowhere.

"You won't find anything," said the Silver Sorceress with a broad, smirky smile on her face before stretching her hands and chanting. Within a few moments, the lake's serene, unmoving waters began to ripple as if a boulder was tossed directly into its center. A small whirlpool started to form a few steps away from them, growing exponentially as Wizera continued to manipulate the waters. After reaching a certain magnitude, it began to float above the lake, forming a giant sphere of crystal-clear water and leaving a gap inside the lake. Wizera then continued her display of power by creating a path of ice that connected the waterfront to the hole.

"Go on," she said in a casual manner. "I'll be right behind you."

With both Thaidren and Elarin being rendered speechless, they slowly proceeded along the path. As the Silver Sorceress followed in their footsteps, the bridge behind her started to melt, leaving no option for anyone else to follow them. Upon reaching the end of the path, near the gaping hole, the Silver Sorceress's two companions noticed a stairway that led to what seemed like a tunnel beneath the lake.

"I assure you it's safe," continued Wizera. "I created this place a long time ago, and I've been here plenty of times. Trust me."

Hesitantly, they both proceeded down the stairs, with Elarin taking the lead and Thaidren wishing he'd remain on the shore to stand guard. Seeing his view getting covered by the surrounding image of water while emerging into an underground tunnel that could flood in a matter of seconds made him think the cultist's base wasn't so bad after all. *At least we couldn't have drowned there,* he thought. Once they arrived at the bottom of the tunnel, they proceeded several meters in almost complete darkness, with the Silver Sorceress's staff being the only source of light, generated through its large blue gem on its end. Elarin's unease was subtle and under control. Thaidren, on the other hand, was emanating an aura of anxiety that could fill a quarter of the lake on its own. Among all the caves, dungeons, and temples he had been through over the years he had served as a paladin, this counted toward his most disturbing. After what seemed like too long of a time for his liking, the young warrior stumbled upon the steps of a wide staircase that climbed upward, leading to another, larger corridor, illuminated by torches spread around both sides.

Eventually, the group ended up in front of a metallic door, over which the Silver Sorceress slid out a key, before unlocking it. Upon entering, they found themselves inside a large circular chamber with a ring of torches near its center, surrounding a vertical plank on which the overseer of the cult of Kasm lay shackled. Several small streams of water from the ceiling ran across the room and disappeared into what seemed like a naturally formed sewage system, making both Epakin and Wizera's group realize they were still under the lake. It would certainly explain why they weren't able to see it from outside. It seemed a flawless dungeon chamber, especially considering the Silver Sorceress's powers. If she were to will it, she could flood the entire structure. The torches surrounding Epakin served a double purpose. In the event that the runic symbols painted on his body wouldn't suppress his powers entirely, the light provided by the flames would greatly weaken, if not completely invalidate any manifestation of darkness that he'd try to conjure. As for his blood magic, Wizera could only hope that the runes would be enough to hold it at bay.

"Exquisite," murmured Elarin as she gazed around her. "Considering your elemental affinity, this seems an impenetrable chamber." From behind her, the stuttering, hoarse voice of Epakin ruined her moment of appreciation.

"My, my. If I knew you were... to bring... visitors today, my dear... I... would've done some cleaning."

Wizera looked at her prisoner while speaking with Thaidren and Elarin. "Try to focus on the meaning behind his babblings. He's not as weak nor as senile as he pretends to be."

"Your words hurt me... my dear," he said before bursting into a few seconds of uncontrollable coughing. "You've been holding me here for quite some time, without any result. Have you ever... considered I may not know as much as you'd want me to?"

A stream of water changed shape and flew into the overseer's face, making him cough more.

"No, I haven't," answered the Silver Sorceress.

He spat on the ground. Despite his miserable state, Epakin grinned. "Ah, water... You know, I must acknowledge your interrogation cruelty. To make one thirst, then surround him with streams of water. A most unpleasant way to be reminded that roses have thorns."

"How about you leave the poetry for the Council of Mages and save your breath for something more productive? If I like what I hear, I may even throw in a less violent, refreshing stream."

Upon hearing her, the master puppet let out a peal of mocking laughter.

It angered Thaidren beyond the point where he could sit and observe their exchange of words. With a swift move, he unsheathed one of his swords and thrust it into Epakin's left leg.

He screamed in agony as he wrestled against his bindings. "Bastard! Cretins! All of you!"

The young warrior twisted the blade back and forth, carving out the prisoner's flesh. "Did I hit a nerve?" he scoffed. "Good. Now I suggest you start singing as best as you can while you still have both of your legs intact."

While he refrained from laughing a second time, the overseer did show a dismayed grin. "Insolent child, you know as little about interrogating as you know of — " He jumped and whimpered when Thaidren hit his heavy-armored fist onto the plank next to his head. The wood cracked near Epakin's face. A clear, unspoken statement that Thaidren was not in the mood to be toyed with.

"Talk. NOW!" screamed Thaidren, making even his mother flinch. Seeing him like this didn't disappoint her, yet it brought a somewhat eerie sentiment of familiarity to her. While lacking the usually required finesse, he posed as a terrifying interrogator. For their purpose, it was ideal, although her concern revolved around the overall implications of it. She had known all her life that she herself tended to have a temper, especially during scenarios similar to that. *Can't say I'm thrilled he got this from me,* she thought.

"Enough!" she eventually shouted as she backed Thaidren away from him.

"I must say, I'm impressed," replied the elf in the back.

Wizera briefly looked at her, frowning.

To add salt to the wound, Epakin's mocking replies did not cease. "You… can't even control your own child… my dear? Well, I'm not surprised."

"Why you…" said Thaidren, struggling from his mother's grasp, trying to reach the prisoner once more.

Considering the size difference between them, Elarin intervened by trying to hold him at bay as well. It didn't make much of a difference. After seeing their approach was mostly useless, the elf abruptly slapped the young warrior in the face, putting an end to his bloodlust.

"Why'd you do that?" he said, rubbing his cheek.

"Because you were boiling with anger," answered the elf. "Look at him. He is most certainly suffering, yet he begs you to give him more. Why do you think that is?"

From behind her, the overseer could hear their every word. "Wizera said he was using blood magic. What if by harming him, you give him the means to escape?"

"No," intervened the Silver Sorceress, "it doesn't work that way. It may have under normal circumstances, but I sealed off his control over the flow of blood. Unless he wipes out all the runes on his body, it will do him no good." She stopped for a brief period, murmuring something indistinguishable. "Unless…" She turned toward Epakin with an illuminated stare. "You want to die. That's it! You want to die! You don't fear it. You've embraced it already. If we were to end you now, you'd both preserve the information you have and, at the same time, believe you'll end up in whatever paradise your master promised." Wizera closed in on him and grabbed Epakin's chin and glared at him. "Demons do not offer safe havens," she whispered in his ear, "they defile them."

"I… wasn't promised a haven, my dear," replied the prisoner as he struggled to free his chin from her grasp. "I was promised power, ascension. Knowledge and prosperity the likes of which your feeble minds can't even begin to fathom. You meddled with our affairs, and I promised you… that there will be consequences. Don't celebrate and assume they're off the table simply because you took me off the board."

The elf sighed. "Ugh… this is going nowhere." She grabbed both Thaidren and Wizera and dragged them outside the chamber. "Allow me a few minutes in private with him. I will make him sing, as you would say."

Belatedly, the Silver Sorceress nodded, with a hint of confusion showing on her face. Elarin bowed and closed the door behind her. Within a few minutes of waiting and wondering, Wizera and Thaidren started to hear Epakin screaming. Concerned about what was transpiring inside, the young warrior forced the door open.

Upon entering, Epakin's eyes were flickering with darkness, yet it did not seem like he was in control. Wizera began preparing for an imminent disaster, channeling all the water that flowed inside the room to create icy spears and standing ready to flood the chamber if needed.

"Stay back! Stay BACK!" yelled Epakin. "You are NOTHING compared to my master. She will ascend us ALL. She will guide us to a new step in human evolution. We will no longer be insects in the face of the gods. We will be their EQUALS."

"I told you to stay outside!" yelled Elarin.

"What's happening?"

Before the elf had a chance to explain, the mad overseer started to shout once again. "Serathra! HELP ME." The runic symbols on his body began to glow red. The bindings that held his arms and legs rusted and crumbled. The wooden table dripped blood from its wood, cracked, and eventually snapped.

Epakin fell on his arms and knees, with a blood circle taking form around him as it coiled in a torrential swirl that slowly enveloped the overseer in a barrier of crimson torrent. Above him, fragments of distorted darkness formed, aiming to drop the torches to the ground and extinguish them. His screams started to sound different than those of a human, his voice gaining an eerie, echoing accent, as though a second one sought to speak simultaneously. The Silver Sorceress acted immediately. She aimed all the ice lances and launched them at the crazed overseer.

The darkness and swirling blood protected him, yet it did not seem like he was the one mastering them. Fortunately for Wizera, she had the upper hand, making one of her projectiles pass through his defenses and hitting him in the throat. Thaidren took up one of his swords and rushed at him, impaling the dark sorcerer in the chest and pinning him to the plank. With that much damage to his body, his eyes reverted back to normal, and all the manifestations of his magic subsided as he drew his last breath. After a moment of silence, the Silver Sorceress burst into an angry rage.

"God dammit!" she yelled.

From behind her, the words of Elarin managed to further increase her rage. "You scared him…"

"What the hell do you mean 'I scared him'? What did you do while we were outside?" Upon inspecting her, Wizera noticed Elarin had taken one of her leather gloves off. She had a small cut on her palm. "You gave him your blood?" she shouted.

"I'm confused," said Thaidren, trying to avoid getting between two women who seemed at the precipice of a potential conflict. "Can somebody please explain to me what you're talking about?"

The Silver Sorceress grunted in frustration. "Lu'Derai blood is one of the strongest biological hallucinogens known throughout existence. Ingesting it directly gives people nightmarish visions that end up turning them mad at best, with the alternative being that they can literally die out of fear."

"I did not picture you as adept in my kin's anatomy. I am impressed."

"I'm a sorceress. I know plenty of things regarding ingredients and other species. Not the point, though, as you don't seem to have had any idea how potent your blood is."

Elarin ran her hand through her hair, then covered one of her ears. "Truthfully speaking, I have not used it before."

"Tsk… figures," said the Silver Sorceress, still harboring her anger. "If I'd known, I could've warned you for crying out loud. Even more so, I could've used my magic to dilute your blood to control the dosage better."

"Well, having known all that, you could have proposed to give him my blood yourself."

"I was considerate. I didn't want to ask such a thing from you nor to strain his body more so than I did by depriving him of food and water."

"You think the idea of asking would have troubled me?"

"Well… yes… I thought that," answered Wizera as she calmed down. Amidst their apparent fight, Thaidren decided to step farther away and check Epakin's body. He somehow felt safer close to the dark sorcerer's corpse than them.

"It seems there was a misunderstanding between us then," continued Elarin.

The Silver Sorceress looked at the overseer's bloodied remains. "That's kind of an understatement, and I had already informed the Council of Mages I would deliver him safe and unharmed. Ugh!"

The elf took a few steps away, looking at the ground. "I apologize. I meant no harm. If it helps, I will accompany you to this council to take responsibility for my actions."

Wizera closed her eyes and rubbed her forehead, remaining silent for a few moments. "There won't be any need for that. I'll explain to them what happened. It will be a hassle to take the body with me as proof, however." Inside her mind, a swirl of negativity would not give her peace. *Dammit, another excuse for them to rub it in my face as if I wasn't despised enough as it is.*

"He did say something, however," said Elarin. "Before his bonds started to break, he mentioned a name: Serathra. I may not know much about humans, but the name does not seem to me as one of your kind."

"Most probably, it isn't," replied the Silver Sorceress as she moved closer to the body. Even from afar, it reeked of ash and sulfur. "If I had to guess, I'd say that was the name of the cult's true master. Most probably a demon. Well, we now know it is a "she" that pulled the strings in the order of Kasm."

Thaidren was still baffled. "But what of his attempt to break free?" he asked while examining the wounds on Epakin's wrists. "He broke the magical sealing runes and his chains. It isn't something a malnourished old man can do by merely uttering a name."

"He might have if he had a direct bond with the demon whose name he invoked."

"What do you mean?" asked Elarin.

"Demons are well known throughout history to be able to possess the bodies of people. For many of them, we are but mere vessels, similar to how we perceive our garments. Although, putting on a human is a bit harder than the mere act of getting dressed. The most notorious method is if the vessel itself decides to make a pact with the demon, case in which, upon uttering its name, it will transport itself inside the body and take control over it."

"If he could do that all along, why didn't he try to escape?"

"Because in most cases, when the demon decides to leave, he also takes the soul of the host with it to the pits of Hell."

"So, the process kills them," said Thaidren.

"Exactly. I doubt Epakin was eager to meet his end like this. Despite his big talk about 'evolution' and even after showing signs that he would welcome death, I think he was still clinging to life. Otherwise, as you said, I don't see any other reason for him not to have called out for the demon."

"You think she saw us?" asked the young warrior.

"Even if she didn't, the cult knows we took down their overseer. I just hope that they have been completely wiped out. I'd prefer not to discover that Epakin was merely replaced and their schemes press on. Most of which we still have no idea what they consist of."

While thinking it through, Wizera remembered one of her previous visits when she interrogated Epakin about the necromantic book she found in the abandoned mines. Judging by his reaction to seeing it, and assuming his words were true, the tome did not belong to the cult. Even more so, he would've wished it had. He seemed enthralled by it after the Silver Sorceress laid it before his eyes. *Was he telling the truth back then? Demon worshippers usually care more about bringing ruin to the living rather than tormenting the dead. Still... I'm not sure what to believe anymore.*

# CHAPTER XXII

# PRICE OF A LIFE

Within the divided continent of Iroga, where five kingdoms lie in semi-harmonious cohabitation with one another, a unified council was formed several centuries ago by the New Earth's mages to serve as a neutral faction with its primary purpose being to assure the preservation of peace. Additionally, the council served as a sanctuary for all aspiring scholars who wish to dabble in the arts of sorcery, to provide them with places to live, study, and even work for the organization, should they wish to do so.

The council's rulers were commonly known as The High Elements, a select group of arch-mages, each considered the most versed in their respective elemental affinity. Water, fire, earth, air, lightning, light, darkness, blood, and gravity, each embodied within the core of the council's rulers. Consequentially, there were a total of nine such members, each with its own title: Terras, Fury of the Tides; Vinral, the Hand of Flame; Connia, the World Pillar; Havara, Gust of the Heavens; Bantum, Thunder's Flash; Atolis, the Light of Dawn; Zarina, the Abyss Walker; Giteh, Red Droplet's Dye; and Oziria, the Unseen Drawn. They possessed equal authority and were in charge of different administrative aspects that covered all the council's duties.

The present-day marked one of the more peculiar occasions when all of them gathered in the same room to discuss and assess an important matter. They stood in a large amphitheater in the center of which the Silver Sorceress stood. Surrounded by them and other renounced mages who served as witnesses and a secondary, less influential opinion, Wizera remained speechless as she looked around her with both a sentiment of awe and inferiority toward them.

"Well now," said Atolis in a composed manner, "shall we begin?"

"Right…" continued Wizera. "So, as you know, over the last few months, I was tasked with investigating the potential rise of a new cult to determine if they possessed a threat to our political balance, or worse. Upon making direct contact with the cult, they identified themselves as the 'Cult of Kasm,' a heretical organization worshipping an alleged demonic master known as Serathra who promised to bring them and the human race to a new stage of evolution that would make us the siblings and equals of the devils of Hell."

"In other words, it was a demon's attempt to assimilate mankind through this religion," said Oziria.

"Disgusting," continued Terras, "I have heard that since the beginning of history, they have tried to do so several times. It is another thing to experience a takeover attempt during our lives compared to reading about it from ancient scrolls and manuscripts." After a few moments of chatter between the council's rulers and the other mages standing all around her, Wizera continued with her report.

"After we were attacked, we managed to capture and interrogate one of the assailants. He gave us the location of their central headquarters: the trading city of Grinal. After more research into the matter, we discovered that they were using mercenaries and bandits to mine Quaar crystals and sell them within the traders' capital. They may have been using them for purposes other than coin, but I cannot say for sure."

"Where is the prisoner you mentioned?" asked Oziria. Amongst the members, she was the most talkative. The other arch-mages preferred to listen and express themselves only when necessary.

"His injuries from the battle proved too severe. While Haara attempted to mend his wounds so that his life wouldn't be in danger, he eventually passed away."

"Hmph… so much for your healer, *Silver Failure*."

Wizera had been called that mocking name before. She and Oziria had more history together than the rest of the council, given that she was in charge of assigning high-class missions to sorcerers. On top of that, the Unseen Drawn was one of the youngest members of the high council, meaning there was also a significant age gap between them. In Wizera's eyes, she seemed like a talented yet disrespectful and narcissistic brat. In return, the Silver Sorceress seemed like an old hag whose reputation was overly exaggerated in the eyes of Oziria.

Wizera briefly frowned at her, then tried her best to maintain a formal tone. "I think it would be best to leave our personal tantrums for when we see each other in mission debriefs, Oziria." The thought of turning an insult back did cross her mind, yet she decided to focus on what was important. "As I was saying, we found out that their main source of funding came from various forms of trading in Grinal, so we went there to investigate. Unfortunately, our cover was short-lived, and through a series of events that involved an assassination attempt and other happenings, we ended up in a hidden underground ruined city."

"An underground city below Grinal? I've never heard of such a thing," said Zarina.

"If I'd have to take a guess, I'd say it's a forgotten remnant from the old days of the city's past. Before many of the levels were built, I understand it stood as a bottom-canyon capital only," answered Giteh, the oldest member of the high council.

"Perhaps. Either way, we ended up discovering this secret underground level. It was a decrepit, labyrinthian level that harbored a giant temple at its center. I'd say the temple itself was built by the cultists to serve their purposes. It didn't seem as old or in the same architectural style as the rest of the ruins."

"And you engaged in combat with the cult's master? The demon you mentioned earlier?" asked Vinral.

"We had no choice. Seeing as they became aware of our presence, a confrontation was inevitable. But no, we did not lay eyes upon nor engage Serathra. We ended up fighting the cult's human overseer, a dark sorcerer under the name of Epakin, the master puppet in the demon's schemes. We fought against him along with his followers and two experiments he created by means unknown to us… Demonized human soldiers, stripped of their personalities, intellect, and I suspect their souls as well."

"Assuming the experiments have been killed, did you manage to retrieve their bodies?" asked Oziria in a tone that betrayed her eagerness for a negative response.

At this point, Wizera had to resort to a lie to protect Aramant's involvement. "There was nothing to retrieve anymore. Their bodies were seemingly modified to disintegrate in the event of their downfall."

"Hmph. A fortunate convenience for your never-ending excuses," replied Oziria with a smirk. From her left, came the imposing voice of Terras.

"Enough, Oziria. Your childish feuds have no place here. Listen to what Wizera told you earlier." His words turned her grin into an irritated frown while making the Silver Sorceress gloat with a smirk of her own, aimed directly at the arch-sorceress. That changed, however, when his attention turned to her. "And the overseer? I understand you claimed to have captured him alive."

"I did… initially," she whispered.

"What do you mean by 'initially'?"

"Complications occurred… while interrogating him. He attempted to invoke the demon to possess his body. I had no other choice but to end him there."

The council members remained silent for a few moments, raising the Silver Sorceress's worry about what conclusion they might take out of this. Eventually, Terras's voice echoed throughout the chamber.

"Seeing as no one is inclined to speak first, I will. Wizera, your actions were derailed from those of an experienced sorceress such as yourself. It would be a lie to say that I am not disappointed in your results. However, I understand the circumstances forced you to act swiftly and without much time to prepare." He looked around at his fellow arch-mages, studying their reactions, and continued. "With that in mind, I propose that the Silver Sorceress be dismissed immediately, without any repercussions, or other judgments. I have no doubt she acted in both her and our best interests the entire time. Anyone else in favor of this verdict?"

Upon one of the council's high members announcing a potential decision to be made, the others had the opportunity to vote as to whether they agreed or not.

Wizera needed at least four other members to vote in her favor. Otherwise, an alternate conclusion would be sought.

"I agree," said Giteh, raising his hand. Havara and Zarina followed his gesture a moment afterward.

"I am against it!" shouted Oziria. "She should receive, at the very least, some form of punishment for her substandard results."

With only one more vote needed in Wizera's favor, the Silver Sorceress studied the members who had not expressed themselves yet. She knew enough to make an educated guess as to who might vote for her and who wouldn't. The person she was most uncertain about was Connia, the arch sorceress of earth. She was a few years younger than Wizera and had undergone the same arcane ritual to prolong her life, which made her look like she was in her thirties. She had never expressed her opinion on her over the years, mostly keeping herself on a neutral line.

While hoping for the last vote in her favor and thinking of what could happen with Thaidren and the rest if she were to receive the punishment Oziria itched for, she saw the raised hand of Connia and, to her surprise, Atolis, sealing the council's verdict.

"It is settled then," said Terras. "The Silver Sorceress will not be punished." Wizera's smile ended up short-lived, as the cold voice of Atolis pierced her moment of mirth.

"Do not mistake my vote for sympathy, Wizera. I merely considered the idea of punishing you for something we tasked you to do as being unfair. Besides, the frustrating grimace on Oziria's face is an added bonus for both of us."

*At least on this front, he and I can agree*, she thought.

"You are dismissed, for now, Wizera," said Terras. "We will inform you if there are any other developments on the cultist matter that require your involvement."

She bowed her head and thanked the council members for their understanding before leaving.

Over the next couple of weeks, the Silver Sorceress progressively spent less time at the mansion with her son and the others. Upon being asked by them why she simply implied she wanted to make sure no remnants of the cult were left to take their revenge on them, keeping her busy in the process. During her absence, Nez'rin and Haara were mostly in charge due to their maturity and because Thraik was too depressed over his frailty to manage such a role. Although his general state of mind seemed to improve, he still seemed far from his usual self.

Elarin took advantage of the opportunity to train herself in the woods from sunrise to past-sunset. Thaidren and Aramant chose to remain closer to the mansion's grounds, with the young paladin delving more into his father's writings in the journal and Thaidren spending half of his time trying to cheer up the dwarf and the other, training alone. He was aware that when they fought the demonic experiments, Aramant was heavily infused with a supernatural and volatile type of energy that boosted his abilities beyond that of a normal human. Yet, he was with one foot in the same boat as Thraik, frustrated with his limits and desperately wanting to surpass them. To prevent him from ever being rendered helpless again. To never depend on the hope that someone would miraculously pop up in the heat of battle and save him. *Hmph, next time, learn to deal with such monstrosities yourself.* A sentence that echoed with truth and a feeling of dread at the same time inside the mind of the young warrior. Before losing himself in thought further, Elarin appeared.

"Are you all right?" she asked while putting her hand on his shoulder. "You seem… distracted."

He simpered a bit at the idea of her showing concern for him. "A bit, yes. But I'm fine."

"Are you certain? Is there something I can do to help?"

"No, no, it's all right. Back from your training already?"

"I decided to take a break. One must know when to relax as well. Although, I was hoping I could speak with you for a few moments."

"Fine by me. Is something bothering you?"

"In a manner of speaking, yes. It is about your mother. I believe she is concerned about something."

"Well," answered Thaidren, "she is. About the cult of Kasm and if there are any members left."

"I meant something aside from that. She did not strike me as being concerned about the potential return of the cult. Rather, she gave me a feeling of having proof of that happening in the future. I have no basis to sustain my theory, but I think she may hide details from us. Perhaps she wants to take matters into her own hands alone this time."

Elarin had already proven herself to be a more paranoid companion than the ones Thaidren was used to when he and Aramant were serving under the guise of the Congregation of Paladins. Her assumptions, though, had proven true in the past, making them harder to dismiss than a mere feeling. "Even if that's the case, what do you propose?"

"For starters, let us share this prospect with the others. We can decide whether to act upon it or not, afterward."

"Fine, you go gather Haara, Aramant, and Thraik. I'll go search for Nez'rin."

The elf raised an eyebrow at the sound of the lich's name. "Come to think of it, I do not recall seeing him today."

"He is most probably in his chambers studying. He tends to do that a lot." In truth, Thaidren knew the reason behind Nez's absence. Not requiring sleep, water, or food, he'd locked himself in the underground chamber near the mansion to study and decipher the necromantic tome of unknown origin. Its secrets were right up his area of expertise, and the book was thick, intriguing him of the secrets it might hold. He had not left the chamber in days. *I guess it's about time someone went to check in on him*, he thought. He walked down the stairs to the tunnel that led to the chamber and knocked at the door. While there was no response, Thaidren realized the door was not locked. He slowly opened it, making it creak in a most displeasing way. In front of him, he saw the lich making a turn and saluting politely.

"Master Thaidren. What brings you here?"

"I came to check on what you've been doing over the past week, Nez."

His human mask raised an eyebrow in surprise. "Has it been that long? Forgive me; I have difficulties perceiving time as it is, let alone in this chamber."

"You have nothing to apologize for," answered Thaidren. "What have you been up to?"

"A most fascinating research, I must say. This tome provided me with a magnitude of insight I did not expect. The sheer knowledge the author gathered over time-knows how many years is astounding. It begs and taunts me at the same time to keep on delving through its secrets."

"What did you find so far?" asked the young warrior.

"An abundance of applications of new necromantic spells that I wish to put to the test soon, along with ancient history regarding the study of undeath and — " He paused for a moment, unsure if Wizera would agree to him revealing such information to her son.

"Something wrong, Nez?"

"Nothing, my liege. I got myself excited about the horizons that this tome offers me."

"Well, if it makes you happy..."

"What about you? Is there something on your mind?"

"You are the second person to ask me that today. Is it that obvious?"

The lich answered in a cold yet unsurprising tone. "No, I was merely returning the question as an act of common courtesy. But please, do not let my emotionally ignorant self affect you. State what is it that troubles you."

Thaidren sighed as he walked a few steps away from Nez and took a seat on a small chair near the exit. "Ever since we returned from Grinal, I felt haunted and displeased by the fact that Aramant had to save Thraik and me."

"If I may," Nez'rin replied, "I do not think it should, considering the fact that the young paladin had to resort to the horrendous act of embracing the powers of the Burning Hells to achieve such a feat."

"Be that as it may, he still managed to defeat his adversary and come save us. I know it shouldn't bother me because of the circumstances, but how can it not? I was powerless against such an enemy. I mean, at the end of the day, the result remains that we were saved because of him."

"And at what cost, you must wonder, young master. I understand your rationale, yet the fact remains that your friend almost killed himself in the process. He could have gone into a rampage back then, perhaps even ended up as the one that could have ended you. You three were all fortunate none of that happened, and he got away with it with minimal consequences."

"I just wish I'd been stronger," he whispered. "To prevent this kind of situation from ever happening."

Nez'rin's laugh almost gave in a subtle hint of mockery at the naivete of the words he'd heard. "You will learn in time, my liege, that there is no such thing as preventing certain situations from happening. You can prepare better for when they come knocking at your door. Perhaps even influence another scenery in which the result could have been better." He closed the necromantic tome and placed it on the study table before turning his undivided attention toward his master. "However, if it is more power that you seek, then there is something I can provide assistance with."

Thaidren suspected what the lich was referring to, making him boil with anger. "Nez, I hope you and I aren't thinking of the same thing," he said while grinding his teeth.

The lich frowned in confusion. "I merely reminded you of your best option to gain what you claim you desire."

"No!" he shouted. "That is not what I meant. Not THAT. I wish to become stronger on my own terms. On my own powers alone, not that of an accursed blade. We've been having enough of malignant artifacts lately, don't you think?"

"Very well," replied Nez'rin, seeing as the conversation was highly unpleasant for Thaidren. "I did not intend to anger you. Allow me to present one final aspect of the matter. Although I agree with you that the young paladin's case was more than enough, you cannot compare his weapon with that of your father's."

Thaidren closed in on Nez'rin for a split second, almost seeming as if he forgot he was speaking with a lifelong servant, teacher, and friend. His first instinct came in the form of grabbing him by the vestments and pinning the lich against the wall. As his fleeting moment of rage passed and his senses returned, he dismissed these thoughts. "There should be other ways."

"And there are, young master. Yet you must understand that there will come a day whe — "

The intimidating gaze of the young warrior focused on him, followed by his unyielding, deep voice. "That day is not today. This conversation is over, Nez!"

"I see. In that case, was there any other incentive as to why you wished to see me?"

Thaidren's anger toward the previous subject subsided upon remembering why he came in the first place. "Yes, there was. Has Mother contacted you in any way since you locked yourself up in here?"

"She has not contacted me at all. Has something happened?"

"It's more of a matter of nothing happening," answered the young warrior. "It's been almost a week, and we haven't heard anything from her. I'm starting to worry."

"Hmm, perhaps a locator spell will shed some light on her whereabouts and dampen your concern." He cleared the desk and opened a map of the continent. After putting weights on each corner of the parchment to prevent it from folding back, he conjured a dark sphere in which he stuck his hand, revealing a vial filled with what seemed like blood. "I will require a few moments."

"Is that Mother's blood? asked Thaidren.

"Indeed," answered Nez'rin. "When performing a locator spell, an element belonging to the person is usually required. Blood works best, but there can be a multitude of substitutes."

"Like what?"

"If not for the blood of the person, that of its relatives should suffice. Apart from that, personal belongings, usually with deep meaning or sentimental value might work as well."

"I don't want to know how you ended up having her blood."

"I can assure you, master Thaidren, Lady Wizera was the one who suggested and provided me with her blood for instances such as these. Considering she was correct to have such precautions made in advance, all the more reason to appreciate her intellect." The lich turned his attention back to the map and started to chant while dripping a few droplets of blood on it. Within a few moments, they gathered in a single mass that traversed the scroll until reaching its middle point. A point that showed nothing other than the middle of the ocean on it. The blood then started to boil violently, destabilizing its regular form and eventually ending up jumping to the roof of the chamber without falling back on the map. As Nez'rin ceased his channeling, his silent stare upward did not reflect a good omen.

"This may prove troubling," he stated in a baffled tone.

The young warrior was also puzzled. "What happened? Did the spell break or something?"

"No..." the lich answered with a whisper. "It behaved exactly as intended."

"I don't understand."

"Gather the others, young master," replied Nez'rin. "Your concern proved well placed."

"Hold on, Nez. What do you mean?"

"The blood jumped off the map, master. It tells us Lady Wizera is nowhere on it. She is no longer in this world."

Thaidren's heart skipped a beat as a chill coursed down his spine. "You mean she's...?"

"No. If she were dead, the blood would have turned black. Yet what I said still stands: she is no longer on Earth, and I highly doubt she left on her own volition."

Thaidren rushed out of the underground chamber and shouted the names of his companions. Upon gathering them, he and Nez'rin revealed what they had unveiled. Elarin looked at Thaidren with an expression of guilt on her face. She wished for her assumption to be wrong. Among the multitude of questions that rushed through everyone's mind, the young forced them away for the moment in favor of an idea.

"Send me to the Council of Mages," he said to Nez'rin.

While the lich was not fond of the idea, he understood the logic behind it. "Are you certain, my liege?"

"The longer we spend arguing over what we should do, the more there's a chance that we'll find her too — " He stopped himself from finishing his sentence. The prospect of being too late proved too real to be uttered out loud, too frightening.

"As you wish." Within a few moments, after conjuring the words of power he required to focus, the lich opened a portal leading to the capital in which the council had its headquarters. "You will have to traverse some distance on foot, master. The city is warded against spatial travel."

"I figured as much," he said while entering the portal. *I have no time to lose.* The portal closed behind him, silencing the atmosphere around those who remained behind.

"What should we do now?" asked Aramant.

Elarin looked over at Haara and Nez. "Is there any way to find out what world she ended up in?"

"Unless we have a cosmology map that includes the world itself in it, I'm afraid not," answered Haara. "And those are hard to come by." She ran her hand over her hair. "I honestly don't know what more we can do."

Aramant grabbed Thraik by the arm and dragged him a few steps away from the rest of the group. Alarmed and confused, the dwarf struggled and groaned at him, ready to even throw in a punch or two. "What'cha think yer doin', lad?"

"Make me a weapon," said the young paladin.

The dwarf frowned. "What in da blazes are ye mutterin' on about? Ye have a weapon; ye don' need one o' mine."

"Yes, I do. You were just too drunk and sad to notice when Haara told me to never use Viz'Hock again."

"'Drunken and sad'? Say dat one more time ta me face, lad."

"You heard me. Ever since we returned, you've done nothing but sleep half a day and soak yourself in alcohol the other. I understand that you're troubled, but snap out of it. If not for your sake, at least for Wizera's, for crying out loud."

The dwarf's grimace partially subsided, and his sense of reason started to kick in. He looked at the forge, then shifted his attention to the mansion. "I have some old spare weapons In da basement. Let me see if I can work somethin' up for ya."

# Chapter XXIII
## Brat of the Council

During Thaidren's visit to the Council of Mages, the young warrior ended up near the entrance to what was commonly known as Cologan, the Capital of Magic. Similar to Grinal in some aspects, it bore for a sanctuary to all scholars in the elemental and arcane arts alike. Unfortunately for him, he had no time to admire the city. The Council of Mages' headquarters lay in the city's center, surrounded by a tall stone wall and a multitude of potent magical barriers. Without a scheduled audience, it is close to impossible to gain access inside, under normal circumstances. The young warrior was well aware of that, yet he would not allow the circumstances to impede him. At each of the nine entrances scattered around the fortress's circular wall, a total of eighteen guards were constantly vigilant for potential intruders while serving as a prime check-in point for the scheduled appointments. Thaidren's mind calmed down little by little upon approaching them. Appearing tense before them would not benefit him.

"I request an audience with the Council of Mages," he stated to the guards.

Having recognized the craftsmanship and style of his armor, one of the wardens answered him. "Greetings, paladin. What brings you to the Capital of Magic?"

Having announced his request earlier, Thaidren refrained from an angry response. "I suppose you didn't hear me from afar. I came here to meet with the Council of Mages."

"I understand," answered the guard. "Please tell me the nature of your business and at what time your meeting is scheduled."

"The council doesn't know of my coming, but the matter is urgent. It concerns the Silver Sorceress. She has gone missing, and I believe they might possess some answers."

The warden raised his hand. "I am sorry to hear that. However, without a meeting planned, we cannot allow you to pass. You must understand we have orders from above to respect such procedures with the utmost strictness."

"Procedures be damned!" Thaidren kept his hands in sight and took a step back as the guards raised their weapons reflexively. "Please, she is my mother."

"I'm sorry, sir, but we simply cannot allow you to — " The warden stopped talking mid-sentence and bowed his head at Thaidren, as did the other one.

Confused by their reaction, the young warrior looked behind him. A short woman, with long light-brown hair, dressed in a dark gray and light-red robe in the style of what a mage would usually wear, decorated with the symbol of gravity, was studying him as she overheard his previous statement.

"You are the son of Wizera?" she asked as her eyes widened slightly.

The young warrior nodded. "Yes, my name is Thaidren, and my mother has gone missing. I know for a fact that she is no longer on Earth, but I don't think she left of her own will."

"And you believe she might be in danger?"

"My hopes are that she isn't... but..."

She waved her hand at the wardens, signaling them to open the gates, then pointed her finger at Thaidren. "Follow me. You can elaborate on it inside."

Thaidren nodded once more and entered the council's headquarters along with her. He was intrigued by his unexpected benefactor. It wasn't hard to figure out that the woman helping him was a member of the organization. However, something seemed strange in the way that the guards had reacted. *So strict, so formal. Must be hard for them to act like that in front of every member.* His attention shifted back to the woman.

"Can you grant me an audience with the high council?" he asked. "I'm sorry to ask even more of you after already doing me a huge favor, but — "

"Don't worry about that," she answered. "Although, sorry to disappoint you but the high council won't gather around merely for a missing sorceress. Even if it's about an exquisite one such as your mother. For now, you'll have to make do with me."

Her answer was far from what the young warrior was hoping for. Still, upon reflecting on her words, he realized she was right, despite his emotions. "I understand. I will tell you what happened. Thank you, miss…"

"You can call me Oz," she replied. "And please, stop thanking me so much. You are the total opposite of your mother." *Who would've thought someone like him came out of that witch?*

*Oz… Oz… Oz…* Thaidren's mind was starting to spin in a chaotic churl of thoughts. *I've heard that name before.* Within the following moments, it hit him. *Wait …* He stopped walking, and the sorceress turned back to him upon noticing.

"Something wrong?" she asked, frowning. "Forgot how to walk or something?"

*She's the arch-sorceress of gravity.* He looked at her once more, shocked at the thought of a small being such as her harboring so much power. On top of that, he never would've guessed a member of the high council could look so young. His initial impression placed her age around the same as that of his.

*That's why Mother called her a brat all these years!* With her look slowly turning to what seemed to be irritation, he ceased his silence. "You're… You're the br —" In a moment of carelessness, the young warrior almost called her by a name no one would be fond of being known.

Her answer almost made him faint from shame.

"Yes. I'm the 'brat' of the high council. Don't sweat it; your mother is not the only one who sees me like that. I try not to take it to heart." She sighed. "Calm down and tell me what happened to that wi — a-hem, your mother."

Considering there were not many details, it didn't take long for Thaidren to update her on the recent developments. After listening to him, Oziria patted Thaidren on the shoulder and signaled him to follow her. "I think you should see something," she whispered.

They arrived at a wide door, which she used her powers to open, revealing an old command center, rarely used due to the last few decades of relative peace and prosperity. It had everything from layouts of various lands of Iroga all the way to maps of elemental weaves — a sort of veins of the planet, commonly known as "World Strings" or "Leylines" — that flowed beneath the surface of the continent. Oziria infused one such layout, making it float, then turned to Thaidren as she closed the doors. "This conversation never happened; you understand?"

He nodded, then stared at the layout while Oziria continued talking.

"I don't know how much you and your mother tend to share, but I'll assume she told you that over the past months, she was tasked to investigate the uprising of a potentially dangerous cult."

"The cult of Kasm."

Oziria's briefing took an abrupt pause at the sound of that name. "Hmph, so you know a thing or two about them. Normally I'd question that, but it spares me some explanation, so I won't tell if you won't. Anyway, after your mother captured, failed to interrogate properly, and killed their overseer, the cult seemed to have dissolved. Or at least that's what we thought."

Thaidren's mind fabricated an endless number of horrible vengeful scenarios.

Oziria snapped her fingers in front of his eyes. "Leave the daydreaming for later. As I was saying, the cult is still active, albeit Wizera had dealt a serious blow to their resources. They became desperate and sloppy. We have been receiving dozens of reports of unusual activity that can be associated with demonic worshipping in the city of Ramdin. We suspect the remnants of the cult have moved there, and we were planning to notify the Congregation of Paladins to send a squadron there to investigate."

"Why not go there yourselves?"

"Mainly, because of two reasons: one, our job is to maintain peace, not organize manhunts for heretics; that is the paladin's territory. Second, having the power of The Light on their side makes your comrades more suited to fight against the forces the cultists worship."

"But you do have mages that use light."

"Indeed, we have. Still, it's not the same. Besides, as long as there haven't been any significant incidents there yet, no one from the high council will approve of a group of mages being sent on a wild goose chase based solely on potential false reports. You'd be surprised how many of these come up daily."

"So, you're telling me you'll sit idle, waiting for the cultists to make a move flashy enough for you to intervene?" The young warrior could not mask the rage in his voice.

"Watch your tone, boy. I've already given you sensitive information that shouldn't leave this building until tomorrow, after we've sent a request to the congregation. And I'm sure your mother told you that we aren't the best of friends."

"Then why go through all this trouble for her?"

"It's not for her. Call it a gift from our first meeting and leave it like that. Take what you will of the information and head to Ramdin if it's enough for you to go on, but be cautious."

She opened the door and walked with Thaidren along a large corridor, distancing themselves from the chamber. Upon reaching several patrolling guards, Oziria ordered them to escort the young warrior outside. He nodded at her in gratitude and left the building. As Oziria watched him leave, a shadowy silhouette manifested behind her. As it materialized, it shifted into a pitch-black-haired woman, seemingly older than Oziria, dressed in a dark blue robe.

"You are far kinder a person than you want to show," she said as she smirked.

"Zarina," answered Oziria with a deranged tone. "How long have you been watching us?"

"Does it matter, as long as I don't go to the other high members and tell them you've been spilling the beans?"

"It matters to me."

"Worry not. To be honest, I'm pleasantly surprised by your attitude. I thought you'd dismiss the boy instantly after hearing he's Wizera's son."

"A child should never have to suffer for their parents' sins. If you'd known me better, you wouldn't be surprised by me thinking that."

"If I were to guess, I'd say it goes deeper than that."

"Hmph, what can I say, I have a soft spot for pretty boys like him."

"No, no, no," said the dark sorceress while wiggling her finger. "I didn't mean that. You don't want to feel responsible for someone becoming an orphan."

Oziria's voice turned more and more hostile with each word. "Zarina… I strongly suggest you shut your mouth." All around them, every item, from candelabras to tables, chairs, and other pieces of furniture — anything that was not nailed to the ground or onto the walls — began to float. Zarina took a few steps back and complied with Oziria's menacing request.

"Before you succumb to your temper, try to remind yourself we are allies," said Zarina.

"Allies, not friends. Don't mistake the terms."

The dark sorceress smiled. "Maybe one day, when your heart will not be as filled with hatred and sorrow, as it is now."

"Keep dreaming," said Oziria.

"I don't have to," replied Zarina. "I just saw you showing care for another human being. A start in my favor, I'd say."

Oziria did not reply. She took one last menacing gaze at her and undid all the involuntary effects of her emotional state. With all the furniture back in place, she walked away, back to her duties, leaving Zarina behind.

She, however, was not done. In a split second, the dark sorceress covered the same ground Thaidren did, popping up right in front of him, startling him.

"I heard you were Wizera's son," she said to him as she sent shadowy tendrils to grab and help him get back up. "Need a portal home?"

"Now that you've mentioned it, yes," answered the young warrior. "I could use a portal."

His mysterious benefactor closed her eyes and started to chant. With a swift move of both her hands, she used the powers of darkness to tear through the fabric of space and shape it in a circular form. "Go on," she said with a warm tone. "Go and find your mother."

"Thank you…"

"Zarina. Don't mention it. And say hello to Wizera for me." A moment later, Thaidren found himself thrown inside the portal by his own shadow, influenced and altered by the Abyss-Walker's powers. While passing through, he realized her doorway felt different. *It's somewhat similar to Nez's portal*, he thought. Upon his arrival, the young warrior did not experience any side effects. No sensation of sickness, no vomiting. Nothing at all. The idea that he may have adjusted to spatial travel pleased him, although it posed little importance right now. What mattered was getting back to the mansion to inform everyone about what Oziria told him. *Mother may have exaggerated her depiction a bit. She seemed nice.*

# CHAPTER XXIV
# VISIONS OF RAMDIN

By sundown, Thaidren gathered the rest and explained to them what he found. "We need to go to Ramdin," he stated with the conviction that they would find some answers there. "Gather what you think will be necessary, and let's travel there as soon as possible."

While the others were sympathetic to Thaidren's eagerness, they were also aware he was not being objective.

Haara was the first to express her opinion. "Thaidren, we can't just rush into the city and search aimlessly for Wizera. We need a plan. Or, at the very least, the start of one."

"You have something in mind?" asked the young warrior.

"As a matter of fact, I do have an idea. I still have a magical potion from Grinal that will boost my connection with the earth. I can use it to channel the grounds surrounding and beneath the city to search for demonic energy signatures. If we're dealing with the remaining vestiges of the cult of Kasm, then I should sense something. If I do, I'll be able to pinpoint their location."

"How long will that take?"

"I'll need to be next to the city's border. I don't know exactly how much it'll take, but I'd say maybe about ten minutes or so."

"Will you be able to cover the entire area?" asked Aramant.

She sighed and shrugged. "That depends on the potency of the potion and how well I can concentrate on the spell, once I begin."

"Is it not going to look suspicious? To stand at the margins of the city chanting spells?" asked Elarin.

"It will not matter, we will merely require a higher degree of subtlety, and stealth," answered Nez'rin. "With that in mind, I suggest Lady Haara perform the ritual during nighttime. It will prove easier for us to infiltrate the city without raising the attention of prying eyes."

"Then it is settled. We will let Haara perform the ritual, then infiltrate this Ramdin settlement," continued Elarin. "This time, I recommend we do not resort to dividing into smaller groups. The cult may attempt to take us down one by one if we do."

"Agreed. Let us leave in a couple of hours, close to midnight," said the lich. "In the meantime, as the young master stated earlier, prepare yourselves with anything and everything you consider necessary."

The dwarf raised his hand at the young paladin. "Lad, gimme da sword I just gave ye. I'm gonna go sharpen it. It'll keep me from fallin' asleep as well."

Aramant smiled at the image of Thraik getting back to his regular self. He handed over his weapon and left to do his own preparation. The rest did the same, except for Thaidren, who grabbed the young paladin by the arm before he could enter the house.

"I'm feeling a bit tired," he whispered. "Do you mind waking me up in a couple of hours before we depart?"

He nodded at him. His response, however, bore a small hint of friendly mockery in it. "Getting old already? Fine, go get your nap. I'll wake you." *Let's say you deserve it this time*, he thought.

Thaidren walked upstairs and landed in his bed, falling asleep almost instantly. Within a few seconds, his loud snores echoed through the entire mansion. After the first hour into his sleep, his snoring stopped as he succumbed to a deeper slumber. He drifted into his memories, back when he was young and without many problems to deal with.

Among these happy memories, an old nightmare managed to slip through his thoughts, slowly overtaking them and growing like a cancerous, subconscious affliction. He recognized it. The same nightmare he had when he was little. The one with the silhouettes with blue and purple eyes. For years, he had had this nightmare, yet this time it seemed clearer, more vivid. It progressed further than he ever remembered, in a way stirring his curiosity to stay with it until the end. The images in his head started to move faster and faster, flashing forward and turning into sequences that seemed random and without much sense behind them.

Ultimately, the nightmare ended, yet Thaidren did not wake. The young warrior found himself at the border of an unknown city, alone. A few meters away from him, a shattered sword lay on the ground. He slowly closed in on the weapon, becoming more and more hesitant with each step, yet finding himself unable to stop. All around him, countless shattered metallic fragments were scattered, cracking as he stepped on them and letting loose spectral manifestations that resembled tormented souls. Some of them screamed upon being released, while others vanished silently into thin air. When he reached a short distance away, shadowy chains lashed out from the blade and wrapped around Thaidren, pulling him as if they had a mind of their own. His dominant hand, in particular, was chained up in such a manner to be pointed at the weapon's hilt, making the young warrior aware of its desire to be held. To be wielded. To serve. He struggled as hard as he could, freezing the chains and pulling himself back, yet to no avail. If anything, it tightened the artifact's grip. *No, no!* He yelled. He grunted. He continued to struggle in vain as he clenched his fist only to witness shadowy tendrils emerging from the weapon and forcing his palm to stay open.

Thaidren screamed as he jumped from his bed, with his forehead and hands sweating worse than after being struck by the harshest of fevers. Upon regaining his senses, the young warrior looked around in awe at the frozen room in which he stood. Even the bedsheets were frozen to such a degree that they crumbled upon the slightest touch. The next thing he knew, Elarin burst through the room's window, almost slipping and falling on the icy floor.

"What is the meaning of this?" she asked. "What has happened here?"

Before the young warrior had a chance to say anything, the door flew off its hinges. Aramant entered with the same alerting state as Elarin, slipping on the ice. He grunted as he got back on his feet and looked around the room. "By all that is holy…" he said.

Elarin's eyes were fixed on Thaidren's. She and Aramant witnessed them glowing while emanating an eerie light-blue nuanced mist. With the arrival of the others, they all reacted with shock.

"It has begun," whispered Nez'rin.

"What?" asked Thaidren. "What are you talking about?"

"Just like his father's," said Haara.

Thaidren stood up and walked to the nearest mirror to look at himself. Everything seemed normal to him. As the rest followed him cautiously, his confusion was increased by the minute. "I had a bad dream, that much I understand. I don't know how I ended up freezing the entire room, but you don't seem concerned about that. Why are you looking at me like this? Is there something I'm missing?"

"The Hiath, lad. You've awakened it," said Thraik.

"What? But I can't see anything."

"You will not be able to see it in a reflection, my liege," replied Nez'rin. "It is a natural precaution to avoid getting affected by its visual techniques." Before the lich or anyone else had a chance to dabble any more on the subject, the young warrior's eyes reverted to normal. "I suspect you have awakened them at a subconscious level."

Ever since he was a child, Thaidren was told of his eyes being uniquely special, what they meant, and that they would ultimately manifest one day. Although the details regarding the full potential of the Hiath remained a mystery, the only other person in history who possessed it and shed some light on what it could do, was Thieron. *Of all the times... of all days... it had to be today...* he thought.

"Hold on," said Elarin. "Can someone please explain what happened to his eyes?"

"It's a long story," replied Haara. "The short version of it is that he is evolving. The eyes are a sign of him getting stronger. Although, they seem dormant on a conscious level."

"Can ye control 'em?" asked Thraik. "Make 'em reappear."

"I... don't know how."

"It doesn't matter now," said Aramant. "Given that we're all awake and it's almost midnight, I'd say it's about time we head to Ramdin."

"Agreed," answered Elarin. "Nez'rin, please provide us with a portal."

"I am afraid I cannot grant you this request, master elf," answered the lich. "I have never been to Ramdin before."

"What does this have to do with getting there via a portal?" asked Aramant.

"Not having a clear image of the place you wish to travel to can lead to teleporting inside a wall or other structures," replied Haara. "Over the years, many reckless magic practitioners have lost their limbs or lives because of that. Nez'rin can teleport us there, but since he doesn't know exactly where, he'd be exposing us to these risks."

The earthen sorceress got on her knees and started to chant with her hands touching the ground. Within a few moments, two vines emerged from below the earth next to them, intertwining and forming a circle, inside which a portal opened. "I, however, have been there before. This'll get us close enough to the city. Hop in."

With Thaidren being the first to enter and Haara the last, the group ended up on a high hill near the outskirts of Ramdin. From a distance, they were able to see two entrances to the city. A promising sign for them, revealing that the outer walls might not have many men patrolling around. "The most suited point for me to use my magic will be right next to the wall," said Haara.

"Fine, let's get a move on," replied the dwarf. As he stood with his back to the city, he saw everyone else's faces change. Apart from the expected sickness on Aramant's face, they all expressed awe, shock, and dread. Upon turning his head, he understood why. A view the likes of which not many get to see; namely, a spatial rift. An unstable portal on a scale so large it could've swallowed the entire city and the surrounding lands, brimming and burning with the colors of fresh blood and molten lava. There was no doubt in anyone's mind that the cult had done something, yet this was on an unexpected scale altogether. It wasn't a mere demonic summoning or sacrificial ritual, but a gate from which an entire army could emerge.

# CHAPTER XXV

# ASHES OF RAMDIN

In the eastern hemisphere of Iroga, with a nearby opening to the shallow waters of the Sharis Sea, lies a mid-sized city with nothing in particular to differentiate from the others in the kingdom. A place inhabited mostly by common folk with no affiliation to magic or its applications. It is considered by many to be a secluded haven, shielded from most catastrophes that occurred throughout history, including the infamous War of the Spider. This is the reputation of the city of Ramdin. Plain, mundane, and peaceful. Many people prefer it that way. To live most of their lives in routine, without risk, even if it means losing the potential benefits that can be reaped from a more adventurous lifestyle.

All of that changed one night when Thaidren and his group arrived at its borders. The skies above the shore turned red as they found themselves eclipsed by the sudden opening of a spatial rift from which creatures from another world poured out like a swarm of death and destruction. A demonic invasion on a scale the likes of which Earth hasn't seen since the dawn of its early days. Mortified and in shock, the group stood silent and unmoving as they watched the flood of creatures invade the city. It was surreal. In a strange way, mesmerizing, if not for the common sense that marked it as an apocalyptic omen. Aside from the denizens of the Burning Hells, the rift spewed giant molten boulders, launched by devilish pieces of machinery created for the sole purpose of wreaking havoc and spreading ruin.

"Holy angels in Heaven," said Haara, a statement that would've been expected from Aramant rather than her. "We have to retreat! It's only a matter of time before they finish off the city and start expanding." She started to run, yet after looking back, she saw no one following. The rest stayed and continued to stare. "COME ON!" she shouted. The dwarf took a few steps, closing in on her, followed slowly by Elarin and eventually Aramant. Thaidren and Nez'rin remained frozen, unhinged.

"I can't, Haara," whispered Thaidren.

"Have you gone mad?" she yelled louder. "You have no idea what we're up against there. Those are REAL demons, not the failed, mindless shells you fought before. We need to warn the Council of Mages as soon as possible. Nez'rin, knock some sense into him!"

"She is not wrong, my liege," replied the lich with his usual cold tone. "However, Lady Haara," he stated as he briefly turned to her, "I will stay by the young master's side."

The earthen sorceress tried her best to hide her sense of terror. Her voice turned calmer after the initial shock subsided, sounding more rational. "Look, this is not the time to play hero. We're not in some fairytale in which you are unkillable. What do you plan to do exactly? Go in there and slay all the demons by yourselves? We need an entire army to deal with them; be rational!"

"I know," answered Thaidren.

Haara's tone turned agitated once again. "Then why are we still standing here? Why are you?" She started to chant and created a similar portal to the one made at the mansion. The other group members remained midway between the earthen sorceress and Thaidren, albeit closer to Haara.

"I think I know where Mother is, Haara. You go and warn the council," he said while clenching his fist, "but I can't turn back knowing she might be in there."

"You don't know a thing, Thaidren. There is nothing that proves Wizera is on the other side of that rift. NOTHING. I beg you, come with the rest of us. Don't make me tell your mother that you met your end like this."

Thaidren opened his mouth, yet no words came out. He closed his lips and slowly started to descend the hill. Nez'rin, Elarin, and Aramant followed him.

"Wait!" shouted Haara. "What are you doing? Have you all lost your minds?" She realized the futility in her words, but she couldn't follow them in their madness. The earthen sorceress rushed through the portal and ended up near the

Capital of Magic. As soon as her feet touched the ground, she darted toward the council's headquarters. *Fools! All of them!*

Back at the warzone, the dwarf watched for a few minutes as Thaidren and the rest were heading into the city. He could hear from afar the agonizing screams of the denizens of Ramdin, reminding him of other dire times he had experienced during his life. *Cities on the brink of destruction… a legion of demons… odds stackin' up against us, and a fool ta follow.* He contemplated the thoughts for a moment. *T'is almost like when I was fifty and not quite ripe. I think I'm startin' ta feel a bit better.* He rushed down the hill to catch up with his new-found group.

The cult of Kasm had been busy over the last few weeks. With the capture and removal of Epakin from their ranks, their demonic master, Serathra, had taken a more direct approach to overseeing the organization's agenda. By possessing a young female member of the cult, she managed to infiltrate Ramdin without effort. Along with her minions, she placed numerous Quaar crystals infused with her blood and magic throughout the city over time. Their purpose: to act as a multitude of spatial anchors that would allow her to sever the fabric of space with more ease, permitting her legion to invade and wipe out a major settlement of the human world. The next step consisted of progressively expanding in all directions as she received an endless supply of reinforcements over time. Like an infection, spreading throughout the lands of the world, turning every stone until all was either assimilated or destroyed. In return, she would reward her loyal subjects while exploiting the rest of humanity. Or so she claimed when she seduced Epakin and the rest of the cult with her tempting touch, kind words, and irresistible promises. Why or what could she want from Earth, it did not matter.

The sole concern for humanity lay in banishing the devil back to the burning pit it came from, preventing her plans from coming to fruition in the process.

Inside the sewer system of Ramdin, within the stone-carved tunnels of the city's underground, the cult had established a temporary base of operation. With Serathra waiting for her improvised, temporary-made throne to be completed, a report from one of her servants caught her attention. The cultist approached her with his head down, and his gaze on his feet. He kneeled and touched the ground with his hands as he spoke.

"Mistress," he addressed her with an obedient, respectful tone, "everything is going as you foretold."

The demoness remained indifferent in his statement. "What about resistance? Do we have any hostile forces?"

"There is no sign of any sorcerer squadron, nor that of the harbingers of light, mistress." These words managed to stir a subtle smile on Serathra's face. "However," continued the acolyte, "there is a small group of warriors that seem to have engaged with our forces. I am told they are being dealt with as we speak."

"A small group, you say?" she asked. "I doubt they'll be able to last more than a few minutes, yet it's better not to underestimate the potential of a concentrated force." She rose from her throne and started to amble over to one of the tunnels that led outside. "I will see to this myself. It'll help pass the time." As she walked across the corridor, her vessel's skin turned crimson before slowly melting away. Two bat-like wings emerged from her back, followed by a lengthy thin tail, reminiscent of a whip. Her eyes started to glow, shifting into something more akin to those of a lizard rather than a human being. After taking a few more steps, the back of her neck began to burn, inducing a slight sensation of pain and making her cover the spot with her hand, then gently rub it. *Seems like they'll have to wait,* she thought as she shed the last bits of her host's skin. *I am being summoned.*

***

Ramdin was being overrun by demons, which wasn't exactly what Thaidren and Aramant had expected when they first planned to visit the place. Most of them were lesser demons. Imps to be more precise. Devilish red and light-gray creatures able to do little more than throw a fireball or two at their adversary. In terms of size, they were not that impressive either, as it was difficult for them to reach proportions larger than a chicken. Apart from that, other demons seemed to resemble harpies, only with horns, sharper claws, and giant bat-like wings. While the two of them were glad they only had to deal with lesser demons, it was their numbers that possessed a threat that could not be taken in jest.

Around them, piles of corpses began to gather, with burning houses and other buildings collapsing over some of them. The imps were chaotic, disorganized, yet their numbers were sufficient as a prime, disposable wave in the grand assault on the city. Thaidren, Aramant, Thraik, and Elarin took care of the offense, as Nez'rin concentrated his efforts on defense, providing them with water and darkness barriers that rendered the imps' fireballs useless. With each hit, slash, and shot dealt to them, the group slowly advanced toward the center of the city. Their logic dictated that whoever was responsible for this atrocity might lie there, in the center of it all, basking in the fruits of its labor. Amidst their pursuit, Elarin decided to climb to the roofs of nearby buildings, jumping from one to another and avoiding most of the small demons. Furthermore, it provided her with a better view of her companions. Her blade thirsted for blood, and so did she. Killing demons proved particularly satisfying for her, given it was free of remorse. Amidst her elegant dance of death, she started to feel the absence of a second weapon in her other hand. It mattered not though; the prized dagger she carried was sufficient to deal with them.

Out of the four, Aramant was having the most difficulty. Despite being trained in the past to battle with any type of weapon, a sword did not grant him the same sentiment of comfort as a blunt weapon would. He needed time to adjust his fighting style to something more akin to that of Thaidren's. Still, he felt the blessing of The Light from within his body, this time free of any impurities caused by channeling it throughout his old cursed artifact. In the eyes of the demons, he posed for their greatest threat. The young paladin enjoyed the thought of being viewed by his enemies like that.

In the meantime, outside the walls of Ramdin, a small squadron of paladins had arrived at the Council of Mages' request to investigate the cult's activity. Seeing as it was already under siege, the appointed group leader sent one of their own to report back to headquarters, while the rest of the warriors engaged the enemy. However, their hopes of survival were slim in a best-case scenario, given they were a mere twenty men against a demonic army that counted in the hundreds, maybe thousands. They decided it would be best to attempt to hold their ground at the city exits. Their stand would be short-lived, unfortunately.

As Thaidren's group neared the city center, it became clearer to them that the rift on the horizon harbored far more demons on the other side, including some non-lesser demons that operated giant catapults along with other types of machinery of war. If they were to reach Earth's grounds, the situation would turn severely worse than they had expected.

During their advance, Nez'rin spotted one Quaar crystal, floating and spinning in place as it glowed in the crimson powers of Hell. With a quick swipe of his hand, he sent a bolt of darkness at it, shattering it. Consequently, he became aware of how the cult of Kasm managed to open a rift of such magnitude. The problem was that even if they were to destroy all the crystals in the vicinity, it wouldn't be enough to close the spatial anomaly anymore. *It is most likely to have Hellpriests channeling the rift to stabilize it, apart from the crystals,* he thought. *They merely served as a temporary means to weaken the fabric of space. Now, their relevance has diminished.*

In his moment of contemplating, one fiery projectile had almost managed to slip through his defenses and hit Thaidren. Luckily, the lich nullified the attack in time as he regained his full concentration on the battlefield ahead.

Eventually, the group managed to arrive in the central plaza of Ramdin. Without narrow streets to impede their vision, they now stood before the sight of a grim scene. All around them, they could see demons, human remains, and streets painted red with blood. The citizens tried to flee in hope of escaping, only to end up slaughtered like mere cattle. The winged demons and the innumerable imps set their eyes on the last remaining beings in the plaza, lashing out and flying toward Thaidren and the rest. In the heat of the moment, Thaidren came up with a plan. Untested, but a plan nonetheless.

"Nez! Conjure a barrier around you and everyone else as thick as you can!" he shouted.

The lich had no time to wonder or argue. The moment the young warrior gave the command, he complied and did as he was told. Thaidren closed his hands and bridged his dual swords together with his ice magic. He then got on one knee and thrust both of them into the ground, releasing an icy wave of frost energy that rippled all around him, creating a gust of cold wind that swiped away the flying demons. It extended for several meters, enough to put some distance between the group and the demons and make them hesitant to approach a second time.

A few minutes into the blast wave it seemed the demons would refrain from attacking them. As Nez'rin lowered the barrier, the fiends started to screech and howl at them, but they kept their distance. Soon after that, they stopped, all at the same time, turning the boisterous chaos of the battlefield into a deep silence, reminiscent of a long unattended grave. From the rift's direction, a mocking clap disturbed the short-lived moment of stillness.

# CHAPTER XXVI
# BEHIND EVERY DEMON

As the group turned to the beating sound, they saw a feminine demonic figure slowly walking toward them. She bore a bitter smile that betrayed a subtle hint of satisfaction.

"You," she said, "you are that group responsible for Epakin's death."

"You must be the demoness Serathra," replied Nez'rin. "Have you come to personally avenge his demise?"

"Avenge him?" she asked, while keeping herself from bursting into laughter. "I came here to thank you. You rid me of a nuisance." She paused for a brief moment to look at the frozen zone created by Thaidren. "He was a useful toy, I won't deny it, but he was too fanatical about his desire to ascend. And all that greed and lust for power… oh, how intoxicating. You humans can be such wonderful creatures at times. However, he still had a use for me when you snatched him, so I answered his summons back then. To try and save that incompetent fool when you and the Silver Sorceress showed the same cruelty my kin is capable of." Upon hearing his mother's nickname, Thaidren's gaze fixed on Serathra, like a predator who identified its prey. She looked back at him and caressed her forehead, covering her right eye in the process. "An ice lance through the right eye… a sword through the chest… Must've been painful," she said while smirking at the thought. "You… you're her son… I think I might've found something far more valuable on this rock than I could have imagined." A split second later, the demoness tilted her head to the right, avoiding a round bullet shot from Thraik's rifle.

"Y'eve talked too much already, filthy lizard."

She smiled seductively at him. "I suppose you're right, small one. The time for pleasantries is long overdue." As soon as her lips closed, Serathra lashed out toward them with incredible speed. By the time the group became aware she had moved, the demoness had already covered half the distance separating them. Aramant swung his two-handed sword horizontally toward her, forcing Serathra to jump into the air and over it. Her smile remained unhinged as she toyed with the group while the lesser demons surrounding them refrained from assisting her.

"Not bad, golden boy," she said to the young paladin. "I'll save you for last." She raised her hands into the air and summoned a giant flame in the form of a spike at the group's center. They quickly split up to avoid the attack, with the lich reacting the fastest among them as he sent tendrils of darkness to bind her. Instead of evading, she ignited her entire body, illuminating her surroundings and dissipating Nez's technique. The demoness then spread her wings and conjured several fireballs along their length before throwing them at the lich. He countered her attack with a water barrage.

With Thraik reloading his rifle, Thaidren and Aramant charged at her, engaging Serathra in close-range combat, but she evaded each of their blows with ease, angering them in the process. Farther from the arena, atop a battered rooftop, Elarin studied her movements, concealed by a cloud of smoke. She realized the demoness possessed no weapon, resorting mostly to her flaming power to deal with her opponents. In terms of combat style, she was more akin to an agile mage, rather than a fighter. Her evasiveness was also impressive, being on par with hers. Elarin concluded she had only one chance to surprise her, after which the elf could only engage Serathra in direct combat like Thaidren and Aramant were. *Not yet,* she thought as she sought an opportunity to strike. *Not yet.*

Another missed shot from the dwarf only contributed to his own sense of uselessness. Yet, he had no time to think about that now. Even if his projectiles were to distract the demoness for a brief moment, providing openings for the boys or the "sack of bones," it would be more than enough. Her combat expertise, however, seemed flawless, irritating them as she displayed her amusement at their trivial efforts. She might've had a couple of occasions to kill her opponents as well, yet she refrained from doing so in favor of toying with them a bit more. Eventually, after a few minutes into the battle, Serathra knocked down Aramant and Thaidren, after which, some of the imps at the border of the plaza began to throw projectiles at them. Aramant swung his sword at the demoness in a burst of anger, leaving him open to her attacks. She smiled at his recklessness and grabbed him by the right wrist, throwing the young paladin on his back, then signaling her minions to immobilize him once she got off of him.

"Patience, handsome," she whispered in his ear. "I told you I'm saving you for last." Had Serathra waited a second more, she would've ended up touched by Thaidren's blades. She knocked him away and summoned a circle of fire to impede his movements. While preparing another attack, she continued to avoid those of Nez'rin and the dwarf. Nothing seemed to make her flinch as she charged up a large fireball, then aimed it directly at Thaidren.

At this point, Elarin could no longer wait. Even though the timing was not right, if she were not to intervene, Thaidren might end up dead. She jumped over the roof of the highest building she could climb, gaining a vertical vantage point over her target. Within a sequence of swift moves with her hands, she threw several small knives that Thraik had given her. As the blades traveled through the air, hidden by the darkness of the night, a small flash of light reflected from one of them alerted Serathra of its imminent assault. She dodged every one of them, catching the last one between two of her fingers as a sign of mockery aimed at Elarin. The elf did not care for her gesture. She jumped straight at the demoness, unleashing the fury of her blade. Within a few swings, Serathra vaulted back several meters and conjured a wall of fire to prevent Elarin from closing in. The upper side of her left arm started to bleed from a wide cut from the elf's weapon that sliced her flesh. An act that wiped the smirk off the demoness's face, while Elarin gained one of her own.

"Arrogance," she said while looking at Serathra and shaking the blood off the dagger. "A demon's greatest enemy, and an opportunity for your last breath."

Her response came in the form of a charge, with the demoness shifting her style of fight. She was now using her spiked wings and her claw-like nails to try and cut Elarin the same way her weapon did her. Within a few moments, Serathra's claws started to glow red as they became imbued with enough heat to cause severe pain and burns, apart from the slash itself.

Thraik fired another shot, catching Serathra off guard and striking the membrane of one of her wings. However, Elarin noticed she did not flinch at all when the bullet pierced the wing, thus rendering her unable to fly. No screech, no screams of pain, not even a subtle hiss. *Either she did not feel pain, or there is something peculiar about her wings that eludes me.*

All the while, Nez'rin jumped to his feet and extinguished the ring of fire around Thaidren. They were now both able to assist the elf and dwarf. In Serathra's eyes, the biggest threat was Elarin, the only opponent who had legitimately managed to injure her. To her adversary's dismay, the demoness's wound had already begun to heal. When dealing with demons, the best option to end them is decapitation or to rip out their heart. If only she could achieve either one.

Before the young warrior and the lich had a chance to rejoin the fight, Thaidren got dragged by the imps and immobilized the same as Aramant. At the same time, Nez'rin found himself assaulted from all directions by fireballs. He conjured a barrier of darkness and water to protect himself, but he had little to no time to do anything with all the constant fire raining down on him. It did not take long before the dwarf shared the same fate as the two warriors. He grunted, struggled, spat, kicked, and even bit one of the imps before ending up unable to move. Elarin was now the only member of their group still standing. Serathra signaled her minions to stay back. She wanted to finish the elf without assistance.

Thaidren was desperately struggling to shake off the multitude of demonic monkeys that were all over him. Many of them even started to attempt to strip him of his heavy-plated armor. He was held by the arms and with his feet in the air, preventing him from rolling out or gaining a firm stand on the ground. His swords were taken from him and thrown as far as possible. Several imps removed his helmet, with one of them starting to punch and kick him in the face. It may have had the body strength of a child, but it was still unpleasant. In a burst of anger and desperation, he attempted to release a wave of frost energy once more. However, this time he reduced its radius, as he couldn't see clearly how far away he was from the others. He let loose a violent war cry and channeled his powers throughout his body. Then he focused on releasing his icy energy. Somehow, it worked, as an instant later, he found himself covered in frozen statues of dead imps, the unaffected ones reluctant to jump back at him.

In the meantime, the duel between Serathra and Elarin seemed to possess equal power for both combatants. Their agility was evenly matched. One had fire magic, the other one was skilled in wielding a dagger. One had wings that could be weaponized; the other was smaller than her adversary, thus harder to hit. As Thaidren burst out his elemental power to escape, Elarin turned to the young warrior in a moment of carelessness, driven by curiosity. In doing so, she allowed Serathra to seize an opening, impaling her in the abdomen with her hand. The elf began to shake uncontrollably as her mouth started to drip blood from its corners. She dropped her dagger and fell to the ground, closing her eyes at the sight of the demoness smiling at her defeat. Before she had a chance to gloat any further, she saw the young warrior standing and raising his hand in the air.

Thaidren yelled in anger as a giant ice lance started to form above him. In a matter of seconds, it turned so large it could block an entire city artery. His eyes started to glow the same way that they did before all of this began. The Hiath awakened once more, amplifying his powers to unknown strength, which allowed him to see where to throw his attack, regardless of where Serathra might go to try to evade it. Precognition, a forbidden and extremely rare ability among the creatures of existence, was now subconsciously in the hands of the Silver Sorceress's son.

Even in the prime of her days, Wizera could not manage to form a glacier of this size with ease. Serathra was now the target of the young warrior's fury, unable to fly away or run from a spell of such proportion. Thaidren shouted as he swung his hand in the direction of the demon, setting the course for his giant projectile and sending it at her. Within a moment, she ignited her body and closed her hands as she aimed at the ice, casting a whirlwind of fire in an attempt to nullify it.

Serathra's minions threw their pitiful fireballs as well, trying to add more literal firepower to subvert the attack. Despite managing to reduce Thaidren's attack to about half its power, it still landed a direct hit on the demoness, burying her in a mass of shattered ice fragments.

Her anger stirred a powerful flame that melted the frigid debris in a moment. Serathra jumped to her feet and screeched at Thaidren but he was already charging toward her with his hands imbued with frost. She grabbed him by the wrist as he attempted to pound her into the ground. As soon as she adapted to his physical strength, her palms ignited in flames, reminding the young warrior of a previous experience. He raised his leg and hit her in the stomach with his knee, making the demoness lose balance for a brief moment as she threw him, then distanced herself by a few steps.

They were both panting uncontrollably, with Serathra ultimately succumbing to desperation as she commanded her minions to wipe out her opponent. They remained unmoved, however, stopped from even throwing projectiles at him. The lesser demons were primal creatures, hardly harboring any cognitive capacity and knowing only to follow the orders of those they considered to be the strongest. Seeing their commander in such a condition made them hesitant, forcing Serathra to prove her merit to continue ruling over them. With her and Thaidren having used most of their energy, they could only stand in front of each other and hope that the other would fall first.

# CHAPTER XXVII

# LIES A RULER OF HELL

The young warrior was not even aware of the glow in his eyes. His vision was no different than on any other day. However, it took a turn for the worse as a few minutes into using them, he started to experience severe eye pain. He covered them with his hands and dropped to his knees. His vision should have gone dark, yet he could still see as clear as day. He was not in Ramdin anymore, but rather inside some sort of a sinister citadel. Decorated with metallic spikes, bones, and torches lit with the dark flames. Apart from that, strange contraptions were scattered all around the room, all of them resembling inhumane torture devices. Thaidren turned his head in an attempt to check his surroundings, yet, to his surprise, his line of sight remained unchanged. A split second later, it moved but not out of his own will. It made him conclude that he may be experiencing a predetermined point of view, perhaps that of somebody else. He started to see a slim silhouette approaching from a dark corridor. One that seemingly possessed a pair of giant feathered wings.

"Lad, lad!" Thaidren heard the voice of Thraik coming from near him. "Wha's happenin' ta ya?"

"Thraik, I can't see you!"

"Relax, lad," answered the dwarf in an attempt to calm down the young warrior. "Ye must be experiencin' some sort of vision. Tell me what are ye seein'."

The silhouette in Thaidren's view turned to its right while a maleficent, reptilian voice could be heard from behind the corridor wall.

"Mistress, there is still no word from Serathra. Should I send someone to fetch her?"

At that point, Thaidren realized there were higher-ranked demons than the monster he had fought moments ago. He expected the silhouette's voice to sound as heinous as the other one, yet ended up being shocked to hear the soothing voice of a woman. For a split second, he almost thought he was attending the serene display of a priestess's tone, perhaps even that of an angel. It inspired warmth, harmony, and affection, yet he knew that couldn't be the case.

"There is no need for that. Serathra is a big girl. She can take care of herself."

A sudden cough startled the young warrior. His sight turned toward the floor, still unresponsive to his will. Blood began dripping on the ground. Whoever Thaidren was spectating, he or she was injured. A prisoner of those horrendous beings. He didn't even want to begin imagining the atrocities it must've endured.

"My, my, my…" He heard the soothing voice of the winged silhouette again, "your eyes have never looked so beautiful, my dear." In the blink of an eye, the figure appeared right next to whoever he was spectating. At last, the young warrior could see the face of the cult of Kasm's true leader.

"Thaidren," shouted Thraik. "Answer me, lad."

*How can this be?* he thought. The young warrior felt as if hours had passed within the ominous citadel, yet in reality, time slipped by a mere minute or two. He shook off the sensation, took a deep breath, and described what lay before his vision.

"There's this woman," he said. "She doesn't strike me as a demon. On the contrary, she seems… almost angelic." The young warrior's description made the dwarf tremble. His lips parted, yet no words came out of them. Before he had a chance to snap himself out of it, Serathra had seemingly regained some of her strength back and started to rush at Thaidren. She ignited her claws and aimed for his head, only for her hand to be chopped away in an instant, before it could strike anywhere near him. An act that was not of his doing, nor that of any of his companions.

"Mistress… why…?" asked the demoness. The young warrior and the rest were shocked to discover that a denizen of Hell could shed tears.

"You've been a bad girl, Serathra," they heard. Upon turning to the rift, Thraik found himself paralyzed with fear, unable to utter a single word despite his desire to do so. On par with Thaidren's description, a slim feminine silhouette resembling a human emerged from the spatial anomaly. Her appearance struck as a being of impeccable beauty with fair pink skin. Bearing lustrous jet-black hair and the face of a goddess, her golden irises and vertically split pupils glowed with seductive radiance that distracted from the temples carrying two thick horns that protruded crookedly into reaching above the forehead, each ending with their tip close to the center, pointed at the sky. She wore a seemingly royal-looking white dress with light-blue and golden stripes intertwined in a web pattern over it, complimented by a flared bell sleeve over the left arm, all while its right counterpart stood with nothing more than a long, silky white glove that covered her slender hand. The same pure-looking attire was seemingly backless, from which a pair of wide, dark, raven-like wings stood in adornment, rooted on her shoulder blades. A split in her dress uncovered the left leg from the thigh down, raising bewilderment in Thaidren's mind as to why an alleged angelic being would adopt such a seductive clothing style. As she approached Thaidren, his eyes shifted back to normal, his pain turned into an afterthought. The mysterious figure stopped but a few steps away from him, remaining silent while folding her arms, giving an otherworldly allure of purity and innocence.

"Would you look at that," she said to him. "If I didn't know any better and you were missing an eye, I could swear I'm staring at the sight of Thieron's spirit." The woman studied Thaidren as if admiring a piece of art, subtly biting a part of her lower lip. "A bud, borne from the seed of a forbidden fruit thought to be extinct from the planes of existence. You seem to have inherited his charming aesthetics, young one... Tell me, what is your name?" With Thaidren unable to answer her, after a few moments of silence, the angelic figure's gaze turned from the young warrior toward Elarin, lying on the ground and bleeding out, then back at him. "How insensitive of me. You must be dying with concern over this poor girl's life." Her soothing voice continued to baffle Thaidren. It hinted toward an unrivaled level of benevolence, yet his very core was warning him of the pure evil before his eyes. The figure turned toward the elf and closed in on her. She reached toward picking Elarin up, holding her embraced within her now-stretched radiant black wings. Upon attempting to reach her head, Thraik fired a shot that pierced the woman's jaw, spreading blood and bone fragments all over the barely conscious elf. The mistress turned to him, and in a matter of seconds, her disfigured face reconstructed itself back to normal. As was the case with Serathra's wings, she showed no reaction that denoted physical pain.

"Toys like that can be dangerous. Don't you believe it's best to put it down?" she asked the dwarf. His hand started to tremble as he ground his teeth, then dropped his weapon on the ground a moment later. Thaidren and Aramant were shocked beyond words. *Why would he comply with her request?* they both wondered.

"Son of a…" whispered Thraik with his face showing undeniable resentment at the angelic figure.

"Now, now, there is no need for hostility," she stated while shifting her gaze from Thaidren to Aramant and the others. "If I wanted to hurt her, I wouldn't have been so delicate with her body." She caressed Elarin's hair and leaned toward her ear. "Hush, my dear. I promise you won't feel a thing."

As the elf closed her eyes, the next thing the others saw was the image of the yet-to-be-named woman covering Elarin's wound with her hand. She tenderly pressed on it as small torrents that resembled blood swept inside, repairing her damaged tissue and restoring her organs. Within a few moments, the elf woke up and took in a deep breath. The woman let her go and carefully pushed her back toward Thaidren.

"As you can see, there is nothing to worry about anymore," she said while positioning her hands in the same stature as before.

"Who… are you?" asked Thaidren.

"Lad!" shouted Thraik. "Listen ta me! Dis wench i — " Her look at the dwarf petrified his lips. After seeing him silenced, she turned back to the young warrior.

"Ordinarily, I'd take it to heart, not knowing who I am. Yet, the isolation on this rock and you being young make amends for your lack of knowledge. Allow me to introduce myself, darling: I am Kina, a daughter of the Burning Hells, a queen borne of faith's darkest aspects, made for these humble servants to serve."

She paused briefly as her face let loose a boastful simper. "Yet, I am most commonly known as the "Aspect of Heresy." Please, allow yourself to calm down, for there is no reason for you to believe you are in any danger. Don't you agree?"

Thaidren started to feel alleviated. Within a matter of seconds, he felt as if all the baffling and horrifying experiences he witnessed so far became irrelevant. Their impact on him had been entirely wiped out. It felt unnatural to shift to such a state so rapidly, and he was well aware of the fact. *What sorcery is this? Is it some sort of ability that she possesses?* he thought. *Could it be that that's the reason Thraik dropped his rifle?*

Aramant and Thraik remained speechless. After regaining her senses to their fullest, Elarin took a defensive stance toward Kina. "You are one of the seven rulers of Hell," she stated. "What could a being of your stature possibly want from this world? From us?"

Kina began to amble in a circular pattern, with everyone following her with their gaze. "I do not care for this world, my dear." She then pointed to Serathra. "It was all but part of a small festivity I've arranged for my dearest of daughters here. I provided her with an army and the freedom to choose any world in this cosmos to claim for her own. While I did not believe she would've chosen this one, I can't truly say that I blame her taste."

"This is all a game to you?" said Aramant. His tone came in a manner too furious for Kina's liking.

"Do yourself a favor and ease up that tone, little cub," she stated. "I doubt you'd want to see me in a bad mood. I believe that an apology is in order to come from your side, don't you think?"

"I… a… ap… I apologize." *What in the name of the Holy Heavens just happened?* Aramant shouted internally. With such a display serving as a final example, it became clear to him, Elarin, and Thaidren that this wicked demoness had the ability to influence minds. To what degree, they had no way of knowing, and it was preferable not to find out. *Such a frightening power… Stripping someone away from their free will,* they thought. There was no doubt she was in a league of her own, way above in the pyramid of power than they were. After barely managing to score a tie with her daughter, as she named her, confronting Kina would be an undeniable death wish.

"To answer your question," continued the Aspect of Heresy after putting the young paladin in his place, "yes, it was a frolic little game to spin within the never-ending hourglass of eternity we call time. It was also meant to be Serathra's send-away-from-home moment, to become independent and shine within the ranks of my army. When you have children, you'll understand how fast they grow. How fast you wake up one day and realize it's time for them to leave the nes — "

Her speech was interrupted by a handful of dark spikes that emerged from the ground, turning into flexible tendrils that began pursuing her through the air. A moment later, the mistress of heresy found herself shot at with a multitude of ice lances and bolts of darkness.

Nez'rin had had enough of her. "Step aside from them, fiend!" His barrage of attacks did not discard the smirk on Kina's face. On the contrary, she'd altered it to a more menacing state as she waved her hand once toward the lich, spreading a thin powder over him. He ceased with his assault in an instant and fell on his knees, with his hands touching the ground. A terrible scenario befell him as the necromancer began to feel his human appearance fading away and his true form being unfolded before Elarin and Aramant's eyes. With the elf and the young paladin gazing in shock at the lich's sight, their initial thought was the Aspect of Heresy's powder was responsible for his skeletal look. On Nez'rin's side, he began to feel overwhelmed by a sensation that had been long forgotten by him: physical pain. "How... how can this... be?" he grunted as he became aware he was doing yet another thing he hadn't for eons: breathing. After looking at his hand, he noticed the skeletal limb belonging to him had flesh attached to it, along with fully developed muscles and cartilages, but with no skin. Now he understood what Kina had done to him. She used blood magic to restore all of his organs and flesh, except for his skin. Eyes, brain, nerves, lungs, heart, blood vessels, muscles, cartilages, all of them restored to his skeletal body without truly resurrecting him. In contrast, he had been turned into a fully fleshed undead, still capable of experiencing pain. The sensation was too intense for him to bear. Even screaming made his throat throb with pain.

By observing her feat, Elarin, Thaidren, and Aramant could not help themselves but wonder how the Aspect of Heresy achieved such a complex endeavor without uttering a single word of power. All their previous displays of magic had manifested through the conjuring of words, be they in the ancient languages of mankind or that of otherworldly beings. She, however, required none. They could only guess that her spell was so trivial for her to cast that she didn't need to use words anymore. To say the thought was terrifying them to the bone would be an understatement.

"I had a feeling you looked familiar," said Kina whilst closing in on the tormented lich. "It has been a while, Nez'rin. I see time has had little effect on you, as always." Her gaze shifted back to Thaidren. "And now, with your current master resembling the previous one so much, I cannot blame you for being more hard-boiled than usual." The young warrior, while calm, remained unable to move away from the Aspect of Heresy as she approached him. She gently caressed a strand of his silver hair, uncovering the eye that it was partially shrouding. "Before your friends interrupted our conversation so rudely, I believe you were about to tell me your name, darling."

As expected, the young warrior felt an unprecedented sentiment of compulsion to obey her request. "Th... Th... aidren."

His response made her pupils dilate for a brief moment while she remained silent and unmoving. She then retreated her hand and slightly leaned her head to her right. She seemed lost in thought, unreadable as to what was going on inside her mind. "I see..." she eventually answered. "It suits you well..."

"What does that even mean? What do you want from us?" Aramant interrupted her yet again. However, this time he did not resort to a hostile tone. Having recently made her arm stop bleeding, Serathra asked herself the same question. Whenever her mistress focused on her, she would vehemently refuse to look into her eyes, gazing at the ground, similar to how a child does when it's scolded by its parent.

"Given everything that's happened here, darling, I am now aiming toward making the best out of a bad situation." She turned back to the demoness, with her tone turning more authoritarian. "Serathra!" she said while walking toward her. "I gave you my blessing to leave, my soldiers to accompany you, the freedom to pick whatever world your heart desired, and this is what you achieve? Over the course of five years, you barely established a cult on this planet while only making significant progress in the last months." She paused and frowned subtly. "That is if you can call what you did progress. In your last hour, when I was finally beginning to believe you'll prove yourself capable, what do I hear rumoring across the layers of Hell? That you barely managed to take over an unguarded town with only peasants living in it while a group of five people alone decimated your unorganized army and forced your hand to deal with them personally. And your ineptitude of even finishing them off brings even more shame to me."

After a momentary pause, Kina raised a hand abruptly toward her, like a wrathful mother ready to strike her child with force. Serathra reacted according to her metaphorical role by covering her face and neck with her arm and cowering toward the ground. After observing her pitiful reaction, Kina bowed down at her and raised her hand, granting her "daughter" the illusion she would be absolved of any consequence despite her failures. Serathra took her hand and let herself be lifted back to her feet. The Aspect of Heresy ran one hand through the demoness's fiery red hair, stopping at one of her four horns.

"Understand that you… have disappointed me, and it pains me beyond anything you could imagine, my dear…" Kina looked toward Thaidren and the others. "A child should be made aware when he does wrong," she said in a saddened manner. "Reason for which I propose a method of settling our misunderstanding." With her other hand, she pointed at the young warrior. "You, my dear prince of darkness, will fight my daughter, one on one, to the death. I promise you I will not intervene regardless of the outcome, so long as your companions restrain themselves as well. Either you'll win, and Serathra gets her well-deserved punishment, case in which I will let all of you walk away with your lives, or she ends up killing you and proves to me she deserves my lenience."

Strangely enough, the offer did not sound all that bad in Thaidren's mind. They surely could not fight Kina even if they were at their full strength. Should she keep her word, without her intervention, the enemy would lose a greater advantage than them. On the other hand, Thaidren was exhausted, unable to fight for the time being. Plus, it took all of the group's combined efforts to tire Serathra out before the young warrior had a chance to fight her on relatively equal terms. And that in itself was made possible by a subconscious power he didn't understand nor could control properly. *I doubt I have much of a choice right now*, he thought. *All things considered, this might prove to be the lesser evil.* He raised his fists to his chest, adopting a fighting stance, and nodded at the angelic-looking being. He then looked upon Nez'rin and right back at her. "Release him. And leave all of them alone."

Kina smirked at him. "Are you making demands on a ruler of the Burning Hells? Other mortals would not even dare to think of such." She flapped her wings in Nez'rin's direction. Within a moment's notice, the lich's flesh started to decay, and his agonizing screams increased for a moment. He was turning back to his normal self. "You are lucky I find authoritative men seductive. Make sure he behaves in the future," she whispered in his ear. "Now," the Aspect of Heresy continued as she took a few steps away from him and turned her gaze toward Serathra, "do we have an agreement?" Thaidren took a deep breath and nodded with a subtle hint of hesitancy. "Splendid." Kina then lifted her hand to her chest, drawing numerous blood splatters scattered across the battlefield, be it demonic or human, toward her. A sphere of blood the size of her head formed atop her palm. Within a split second, it burst into a circular pattern that created a bright red swirling portal next to her. "Go on, I promise it won't bite," she said. "It'll take you all home to the mansion."

"I… don't understand…," said Thaidren.

"You didn't think you'd be having your duel now, did you? My poor child needs to rest, and I'm certain you'll want to be at your full strength as well. Return in two days, at midnight. We'll find something to kill time while we wait." With a snap of her fingers, the Aspect of Heresy signaled the army of imps to release Thaidren's companions. Unlike Serathra, they seemed unquestionably obedient, without any need to seek if she was worthy of commanding them. They went as far as to retrieve their weapons as well, knowing they would not dare to spit in a ruler of Hell's merciful hand.

The group slowly walked past all the static demon minions and their leaders. Elarin and Thraik passed through the portal first, with Nez'rin following them. Before Aramant and Thaidren had a chance to traverse it, the young warrior realized there was still one more question that needed to be answered. Kina observed his hesitancy to proceed.

"Is there something wrong, Thaidren?" she asked with an emphasis on his name.

"Kina, who is the person in your citadel?"

"My citadel, what do you — " She paused for a few moments, followed by her hand covering her mouth as she gave in to a satisfied grin. "Don't worry, darling. No more harm will befall your mother. I promise."

The young warrior charged straight to her a split second after she'd finished uttering the words "your mother." Aramant quickly grabbed him with both arms and held him in a tight grip from behind, preventing Thaidren from doing something he would end up regretting. "Thaidren!" he shouted at him. "Get a hold of yourself. Don't you see she wants to antagonize you? If you charge at her now, the deal is off, and we are all as good as dead. Think, for the love of Heaven. You can't do anything against her even when you're at full power, let alone disarmed and wounded as you are now. Calm down, and let's go home."

"Let go of me, Aramant. I have to do something!" he shouted as he desperately struggled to escape his grip. "You heard her; she has Mother. How do you expect me to walk away knowing that?" Amidst their conflict, Kina was spectating with an aura of mirth. Despite every setback Serathra's cult had encountered by their hands, the development of the current situation still proved entertaining for the Aspect of Heresy. Yet, her smile suffered an abrupt end upon hearing the young warrior ask a question that managed to hit a sensible cord.

"She's a demon. We've been trained to fight them all our lives. How can we trust her?"

The next thing they saw was the maddened expression on Kina's face. Within a split second, the blue and yellow stripes on her dress turned black as coal combined with a nuance of red as bright as fresh blood, with the white on her attire turning gray. A second split in her dress was now revealing her right leg as well, shaping her attire into something more reminiscent of a tabard, slightly more ragged, yet in a somewhat organized fashion — if it could be called that way. It morphed into a vestment more fit for combat than its previous form. Thaidren and Aramant did not have much time to ponder about her attire, though, as from below their feet, several thin blood torrents emerged and entangled them, similar to the threads of a spider's web. They both struggled to escape, yet the more they did, the tighter the grip would become, making their ability to move progressively harder.

"See what you did?" shouted Aramant. "Now we're going to di — "

A puddle of blood jumped on the young paladin's mouth, coagulating and hardening within a moment's notice. Aramant was rendered unable to speak as Kina had only her right hand raised and pointed toward them. Her dress slowly turned back to its previous appearance as she approached them.

"Now, now, darlings, that is something highly rude of you to question…" Her tone was giving an allure of disappointment with a subtle hint of anger. "Perhaps your paladin academy hasn't taught you all the aspects about me and my kin. Allow me to let you in on a pervasive notion." She reached right next to the young warrior and placed her hand on the back of his neck, placing her chest on his. Following the next moment, Thaidren froze in place as the Aspect of Heresy stole a gentle, passionate kiss from his lips. She briefly bit her upper lip and fixed her eyes upon his. "A demon's word is a sacred bond. A demon's kiss is a promise. Questioning either of them is like asking a woman about her age. I understand it is considered a rude thing to do in your world as well."

Aramant felt sickened at the sight of what he witnessed. He tried his best to refrain from showing it, seeing as their situation did not need any more reasons to test Kina's temper. With their arrangement seemingly hanging by a thread, Serathra closed in on her master.

"Mistress," she addressed her fearfully. "Our scouts have reported a legion of warriors marching in toward us."

Kina ignored her. She looked at Thaidren and Aramant and released them from their bindings. "It is time for you to go. I have other guests to attend to. Don't forget, two days, at midnight. We will anxiously wait for your return." She flapped her wings toward the two of them, conjuring a pair of fleshy tentacles from the ground that grabbed and tossed them into the portal. After its closing, the Aspect of Heresy turned back to her subordinate.

"How many, my dear?"

"A couple thousand, my mistress."

"Good. Have your minions defend the city. They are to hold the ground inside regardless of the outcome."

"Mistress?"

"I feel like letting off some steam after the nuisances you've put me through."

# Chapter XXVIII
# Chains of the Lifereaper

Back at the mansion, Thaidren and Aramant had arrived after their prolonged meeting with one of the rulers of Hell. As soon as Thaidren rose to his feet and Aramant recovered from the spatial traveling sickness, the young paladin's gaze turned chaotically all around him until he found his target: Nez'rin. He pointed his hand at the lich and shot a small beam of radiant light at him, followed by another one with his other hand. The lich was fast enough to block his attacks, yet he did not counterattack. He could not blame Aramant for reacting in such a manner. To some degree, he became accustomed to him and vice-versa, only for the boy to find out that his human appearance had been a deceptive lie all along. He was too blinded by betrayal and driven by his teachings from The Light to see him as anything different than an enemy.

"Wait," shouted Thaidren as he tackled the young paladin on the ground, trying to immobilize him. "Aramant, calm down!"

At first, he did not even bother to answer. He grunted and struggled to escape his grip and get back on his feet with little to no results. After a few moments, he seemingly cooled off, making the young warrior let go of him as they both jumped up. A split second later, he fired a second beam of light toward the lich, yet he did not seem to intentionally aim at him. His gaze then turned toward Thaidren. "You... You KNEW about this?" Seeing as he was the only one reacting so surprised, his attention gradually shifted toward the rest of the group. "Hold on. You ALL knew?"

"I only found out recently that he is a necromancer," answered Elarin. "I would not have guessed he was an undead as well..." She remained calm yet alert. Her dagger was unsheathed, and she adopted a partially defensive stance. "Under normal circumstances, I would have reacted as he had," she addressed the lich.

"However, somehow, you did not strike me as a maleficent being during the time we spent together." Her gaze turned toward Thaidren and Thraik. "Seeing as you were aware of his condition, I expect a broad, detailed explanation from the two of you."

Nez'rin intervened. "If you'd allow me, master elf, I — " Yet another beam of light came on the verge of hitting him. In this instance, he was barely able to react in time.

"Silence!" shouted the young paladin. "I don't want to hear a word from you. I want to hear them," he stated whilst pointing at the dwarf and the young warrior.

"Agreed," replied the elf. "We deserve to know your reasoning for accepting him and why you deceived us." The latter was obvious, but Elarin wished to hear it said out loud.

"We hid da truth because of how ya'd react, lads," intervened the dwarf. "If we were ta present him as a lich firsthand, ye would've jumped on 'im without hesitation. We needed ya ta kno' him a bit before we could reveal dis ta ya. He's an annoin' sack o' bones, aye, but he ain't evil."

"But he is a lich!" shouted Aramant before fixing his gaze on Thaidren. "We were both raised, since childhood, to abhor and abolish any form of undead. They are a scourge in our world. Unnatural abominations that defy the laws of nature. How could you have stood by my side at the cathedral and learned from our superiors when your mother was harboring such a creature from the beginning?"

"Before I came to the cathedral, he was, for a short time, my teacher…" replied the young warrior. "Aramant, I know how this looks from your perspective, but — "

"You know NOTHING. I thought you might, but you don't. What if my father could see you now? After all his praising toward you, what do you think he would have said if he knew about… it?"

A distant voice came from the direction of the house. "He knew about Nez far before you were even born, Aramant. And so did I."

"Haara," answered the young paladin, "what are you doing here? And what do you mean by that?"

"After I went to the Council of Mages to inform them of the demonic army at Ramdin, they immediately contacted the Congregation of Paladins to mobilize a legion to intercept them before they could expand their territory. They will send some squadrons of sorcerers to assist them. Afterward, I came here to gather up some provisions before coming back to you, but I see I don't need to rush anymore."

"What about us being fools?" Thraik asked with a mocking tone.

"You still are, and it was the most idiotic choice you could've made," she replied as she cast her eye over their wounds. Nobody seemed critically injured, although Elarin's hole in her armor raised some questions. "Speaking of that, how did you end up here?"

"That can wait," Aramant interrupted her. "What did you mean when you said my father knew about Nez'rin?"

"Were you not able to understand the sentence? I meant exactly what I said, Aramant. Attern had known for a long time of Nez'rin's nature. He has been an unquestionably loyal servant in Thaidren's family for generations that far predate us. He met your father and revealed his identity while he served Thieron."

Aramant would have thought that after what transpired over the last few months, he wouldn't get shocked so easily anymore. "But... but... I don't understand."

"I may not be the one who should say this, master paladin, but not all undead are evil," said Nez'rin.

"You still shouldn't be allowed to exist...," he whispered while clenching his fist.

Elarin remained silent as she was assimilating the new information. She was still feeling unease at the fact that Nez'rin was both an undead and a necromancer. Yet, the dwarf's words carried logic. She understood the reasoning for hiding his identity. Her dagger dove back into its sheath, with her posture slowly shifting back to a less defensive one. The elf's gaze turned toward Haara. "You said he is a servant of Thaidren's family for generations…" She looked back toward the lich. "Tell me, lich, how old are you?"

"I stopped counting the years a long time ago, my dear," answered Nez'rin. "I can only tell you I have served them ever since the reign of the second Dark Prince."

Elarin leaned her head to her right. *Dark Prince…* The name seemed familiar to her, yet she couldn't put her finger on it. The elf briefly looked at Thaidren, then turned back toward the lich. "The story you told me… That of your younger self; was any part of it true?"

"All of it was true, my dear," answered Nez'rin. "I merely did not mention how long ago it took place."

"You became a lich to have more time to bring back your brother…," she said.

"Among other reasons, yes, that was primarily the one."

"What other reasons?" asked Aramant furiously as he attempted to charge toward him. Before he had a chance to do so, Haara entangled him with a multitude of thick vines that made him feel dizzy after a few moments of being touched by them.

"That'll calm you down for the time being… You just don't know when to give it a rest and listen." The earthen sorceress sighed and checked in on Elarin. Upon seeing she was unlikely to react as violently as Aramant had toward Nez, she conjured several wooden benches covered with a blanket of leaves on top of them. "Now, all of you, take a seat, let me examine your wounds, and most importantly, tell me everything that happened since we last saw each other."

After the dwarf finished the story, Haara was unsure of what to say or how to react. "After hearing all of you… I suppose you chose the best possible outcome, Thaidren. Even though it's still one that has a high chance for us to end up dead and for Earth to record another demonic invasion in its history."

"Haara, she has my mother… I just couldn't…"

The earthen sorceress raised her hand, signaling him to stop excusing himself. "I disagree, but that doesn't mean I don't understand. I've been in your shoes in the past, so let's cut to the part where you become stronger in order to kill the demonic bitch."

"The only attack that seemed to affect her was when I had the Hiath activated."

Thraik burst into laughter. "Ye should've seen dat, lass. He bumped a house-sized iceberg into her sorry arse. Don' kno' how she didn't end up squashed like a bug."

"What about him?" asked Elarin, pointing at a sleeping Aramant. "Is he going to be fine?"

"I sedated him, so he won't cause us any more trouble. Other than that, his wounds are mostly superficial." *And they heal up pretty fast even without my magic to assist his recovery*, she drifted into the thought briefly.

With everyone taken care of except for the lich, Nez'rin hesitantly approached Thaidren. "Master, if I may speak freely."

"I told you there's no need for you to ask permission for such things, Nez," answered the young warrior. "Speak your mind."

"Given our current state and Lady Wizera's, I do not believe you can ignore your best option of gaining power anymore." He figured Thaidren would react as furiously as he did the last time. Yet, his eyes showed sadness instead of the expected fury.

Thaidren took a deep breath without giving Nez an answer immediately.

"I've hated that weapon ever since my mother told me the story of how father died — " His speech was interrupted by the nearby elf who happened to hear his conversation with the lich.

"You have an artifact that can boost your power, yet you do not want to use it to save your mother?"

"It's not that simple."

"Yes, it is. There is an innumerable amount of people in your world or others who would give anything to have a chance to protect and save their loved ones.

Yet, they are bound by their powerlessness. You may resent it, but you do not need to enjoy using it while saving Wizera. If you dread the weapon so deeply, you can give it up as soon as you know her to be safe once more."

The young warrior remained silent. *No, I won't... But she has a point: I don't need to take pleasure in using it; I just need it to serve its purpose...*

"Done," said Haara. "All of your wounds are healed now. It is time you make a decision, Thaidren. Will you do whatever it takes to save Wizera, or do you want to risk it by fighting Serathra as you are now?"

Thaidren shifted his gaze from the earthen sorceress to Nez'rin. He was still hesitant to bring the subject into discussion, yet he was aware of it reaching its inevitable point. "Nez..."

"Yes, master."

"How much power will the blade grant me?"

"At first, you'll experience difficulties in adjusting to it, both in terms of the amount of power it will grant you as well as how challenging it will prove to maintain control over it. Yet, once you get through with the basics, it is bound to increase your power exponentially." The young warrior looked toward Elarin, then Haara, Thraik, and Nez'rin. "I can conjure a portal to the Forge of Souls in a moment's notice, my liege. You need but give the command."

Having taken a deep breath before opening his mouth, Thaidren eventually uttered the words he had hoped he would never have to. "Open it..." Upon hearing that, the necromancer raised his hands into the air and started to invoke the words of power he required. A small tremor marked the beginning of the portal's formation. Several bones emerged from the ground and aligned themselves into a circular pattern. Unlike the previous portals that Thaidren, Aramant, and Elarin have witnessed, it stood horizontally into the ground, picturing the image of a dark hole that spewed spectral essences from within.

"I will assist the master in retrieving the weapon," stated Nez'rin. "It is unwise for the rest of you to join us." Before he or Thaidren had a chance to delve into the gaping hole of this abyssal realm, Aramant's weakened voice interrupted them.

"Stop!" he said in a guttural attempt to shout.

Haara was surprised to see him awake. The potency of the spell she used on him should have knocked him senseless for half a day at least. Yet he awoke by himself within a few hours of it taking effect. "Your throat must be still affected by the spell. You shouldn't try to force yourself to talk."

The young paladin seemingly complied, having waved his hand at Nez'rin to signal him to come closer. He was still unable to stand on his feet, yet he got up from the bench and stood on it like he would on a chair. "I want it back," he murmured toward the lich. Everyone knew exactly what he was referring to, the reason for which Haara reacted in a most hostile manner.

"No," she raised her voice. "Is your brain still sedated? I told you to never use that foul weapon no matter the circumstances."

He turned his head toward her. "I don't care anymore; I've made my decision." His gaze shifted back to the lich. "It is my choice to make. If my father could bear that burden, so should I."

"Your father NEVER used the demonic power inside, for crying out loud," continued the earthen sorceress. Before she had the chance to keep on with her reasoning of this being a horrible idea, Nez'rin signaled her to stop talking.

"I will not retrieve it for you," said the lich in a cold tone. "Instead, I will grant you some time to think it through and tell you where it is hidden. The rest is up to you, master paladin." He closed in on Aramant and whispered something undistinguishable to the others in his ear. After that, he and Thaidren closed in on the portal.

"Decide on your terms, young one. I do hope I've made the right choice trusting you." The next thing that followed was the young warrior and the necromancer's passing into the ominous portal. It closed it as soon as they entered, leaving the area in a grave-like silence that was pierced only by the howling of the wind.

## CHAPTER XXIX
# PRAYER OF CRUSADER REINHOLD

A plain field, barren and devoid of any form of vegetation that stretched for as far as one could see. A harsh mountainside covered in snow and blasted with violent blizzards. The remains of a long-forgotten world, now reduced to nothing but dust and ash. No one is to tell which depiction is true in this secluded place within the realm of the dead, to which not even the denizens of the afterlife are granted access. Its location is ever-shifting, accessible only to those who have been here in the past or to the current wielder of the infamous blade forged here: Urostmarn, the Lifereaper. A weapon of great power left behind by the First Consciousness shortly before its unexplained disappearance from existence. A direct construction of the Creator that predates all species of existence, including angels and demons alike, known over the course of countless eons as the Forge of Souls.

Within this secluded place, Thaidren entered for the first time, standing as one of the extraordinarily few mortal beings to witness this construction with their own eyes while still anchored to life. Alongside him, Nez'rin remained unshaken by the sheer magnitude of the grand empty citadel that stands before them. The young warrior shivered uncontrollably, yet the sensation seemed dissimilar to that of simple coldness.

"Nez?" he spoke while his teeth chattered.

The lich slightly turned his skeletal head in his direction. "Yes, master Thaidren."

"It may sound redundant to ask, but… why is this place so freezing? And why am I feeling it? I've hardly felt any coldness in my entire life, even when atop mountains."

"What you are experiencing now isn't a matter of low temperature, my liege. Do not become alarmed by what I am about to say." Despite his preemptive warning, Thaidren had already imagined the worst. "This realm is within that of the dead. Your presence here is… unnatural to it, in a manner of speaking. As such, the very nature of this realm is trying to correct it."

"By killing me?"

"Fear not, master. Ever since you were an infant, Lady Wizera and I have placed numerous barriers on you to enhance your body for such conditions."

Thaidren raised an eyebrow. "Wait, you did what? You and Mother experimented on me?"

"You misunderstand. To experiment is to test what reaction certain spells, potions or rituals would provoke. We used only known and previously tested methods to help you develop into a more resilient version of yourself. It is not such an uncommon practice as you might think. I heard that even the paladins and some mages undergo such treatments."

"I still don't know what to think about that…"

"Had we not gone through with such methods, you would have hardly lasted over twenty minutes in this realm. Yet, it matters not for now," answered the lich. "We must make haste to the forge."

"Why are we in such a hurry?" asked the young warrior. "We still have around a day and a half until I have to face Serathra."

If Nez'rin had had a face, it would betray a doubtful expression on it. "There is one more aspect that you should be aware of, master Thaidren. In this world, time passes differently than on Earth. We have but an hour or two before you must confront Kina's disciple."

"You should've started with that. Let's pick up the pace." As they continued to march on, closing in toward the enormous structure made Thaidren feel smaller with each step.

***

Since Thaidren and Nez'rin's departure, Haara had desperately tried to convince Aramant to surrender his reckless thought of taking back Viz'Hock to no avail.

His stubbornness bred a chain reaction that enraged her all the more, making the earthen sorceress less rational and too emotional for her usual persona. Elarin was on par with her logic, yet she preferred to not express her opinion for the time being. For Thraik, Haara was annoying enough as she was, like an emotionally driven banshee as he would think. He chose to give it a go with the young 'lad' when or if the equally stubborn 'earthen nuisance' would give up to convince him herself. Until then, he'd enjoy his probably last two days of drinking.

About half an hour later into Haara's shouting, the earthen sorceress gave in to tiredness and headed inside the house. Aramant used this opportunity to clear his mind, temper his anger, and at the same time visit the place where Nez'rin had hidden the weapon. The lich was more cunning than he expected. After he and the other group members witnessed how Nez'rin sealed the demonic artifact, he figured he'd find it encased in the same block of ice shrouded within the runic-inscribed cloth. As it turned out, that was not the case. The lich had sealed Viz'Hock in one of the buried chambers of the ancient ruins that lay in the mansion's vicinity. He dug into the ground with his powers and created a room completely encased in darkness, giving the impression to an untrained eye that it was merely a burned-out stone wall. The young paladin reached out to the chamber, yet he did not retrieve his hammer immediately. He turned around and leaned his back against another dilapidated wall, reaching out to his bag from where he drew his father's book and shuffled the pages. His thoughts wandered away from the contents of the book. *What if she's right? She hasn't been crazy nor wrong about it, but... I still feel like I should somehow get past this obstacle, not avoid it. A part of me almost wishes that my father had struggled with its unleashed power once...* He felt guilty for harboring such thoughts. While continuing to shuffle through the book's dusty pages, Aramant found an earlier passage that stirred his curiosity.

*The hammer continues to plague my mind with whispers. Sometimes, I can hear it as clearly as I would a regular voice. Other times it is either cryptic or impossible to distinguish. In my most recent fight, I almost gave in and relinquished my will to it. The one thing that the foul creature inside it has is time. And patience. Yet when I utter the prayer of Reinhold, its violent nature seems to subside, albeit for a brief period. Even if it's a short-lived moment of peace and relief, it still helps...*

*The prayer of crusader Reinhold...* Aramant knew of this. A nostalgic flashback took him to a distant memory, back when he was a child. At that time, he was too young to start attending classes, yet his father would recite a different prayer at his bedside each night. However, the one of crusader Reinhold was the sole exception that he would repeat from time to time. To this day, the young paladin remembered its exact words.

*May The Light grant me the serenity to accept the aspects I cannot change*
*The courage to change the things I can,*
*And the wisdom to know the difference between them.*

Aramant stood still in front of the sealed chamber for several minutes. He thought over and over about what claiming back the hammer would bring back in his life. The young paladin was not as naïve as to believe that there wouldn't be occasions when the demon might pass its influence and intoxicating power back into him. He was even questioning his own judgment for having been influenced by the artifact's corrupt nature in the first place. He took a deep breath and cleared his thoughts, meditating on his motives as he calmed down the raging storm inside his heart. As far as he was concerned, some aspects remained certain: he did not want to retrieve the weapon, he merely considered it to be necessary; he did not crave its power; he aimed for either its containment or for it being used in the service of righteousness; lastly, he did not want to leave it unguarded, yet he was hesitant of carrying it himself as a burden. After taking all these aspects into consideration, Aramant reached a decision. *It is my legacy, my burden... my duty...* He channeled The Light's power within his body and launched a small beam toward the wall, piercing it and removing the dark seals that kept Viz'Hock hidden away. Its demonic form lay on an ancient pedestal, still bearing the same pitch-black color when he last wielded it. If he hadn't known any better, it could have been mistaken for a fragile historical artifact that would crumble at the slightest touch. Aramant raised his hand toward its hilt and unclenched his fist. Upon holding the sword, he heard an agonizing scream as he felt the demonic energies of Viz'Hock coursing through his body once more. With his right hand shaking from the power, combined with an urge to stop resisting it, Aramant closed his eyes, concentrating on controlling his breathing. "You will not sway me again!" he shouted before reciting the prayer of crusader Reinhold, at first in his mind, then with a whisper.

***

During that time, after taking a short nap, Haara went to the mansion's basement in search of the dwarf. Thraik was not drunk enough to be pleased by her presence, but he was aware of her troubled mind, so he allowed her to take a seat nearby. He looked at his half-empty mug of ale, then toward the earthen sorceress.

"Ye want one?" he asked.

She sighed and grabbed herself another jug before heading toward one of the large barrels. "At this point, sure… why not." As she took a seat near him, she chugged down her brew.

The dwarf smirked. "Ye got me fooled, lass. Didn't picture ye as a drinker."

"I'm not," replied the earthen sorceress. "Usually."

Thraik sighed, betraying the closest thing to a sentiment of compassion that he could express toward Haara. "He's not Nalys, Haara. Ye have ta accept dat."

"He may not be, but he's heading toward the same path as he did. I don't expect you to understand how this makes me feel. You weren't there."

Her bitter words somehow managed to sting the dwarf's heart. "Y're right, I wasn't," he murmured. After taking another sip from his jug, Thraik burped. He expected the earthen sorceress to comment on his uncivilized behavior, yet he received no such reaction. He pushed away the jug and turned toward her. "Look, I agree with ya. Da boy shouldn't take da hammer. But if I'm not mistakin' it, Wizera told me dat the same was told to his pa in the past, right? He may not hav' unleashed da power of da monster inside, but we both knew 'bout his lifelong struggle ta keep it at bay."

"That's exactly my point, Thraik," added Haara. "His best-case scenario consists of a life in which he can never let his guard down. Wiz and I aren't going to be here forever to cleanse him of the corruption when or if he goes berserk again." *I'm not even sure that I'd want that to begin with*, she thought.

"Well, da old sack o' bones already told him where ta find it. If he's goin' for it, there's not much we can do ta stop 'im."

"Hold on, where is Aramant now?" she asked.

"If we can't find 'im, ye know where he is…," replied the dwarf, pulling the jug toward him and taking another sip.

The earthen sorceress's tone turned angry. "Mark my words, Thraik: if he's getting the hammer back, after we get to save Wizera I won't be a part of the group anymore. I just can't." Amidst their discussion, the sound of Elarin's footsteps coming down the stairs interrupted them.

"I wanted to inform you that Aramant took the artifact back." Haara refrained from betraying her obvious disgust, with the dwarf remaining silent and chugging his brew.

*He's reckless, plain stupid, or both,* thought the earthen sorceress. *He doesn't even play a role in the duel. Thaidren does.* Despite her opinion and her previous emotional response toward the matter, however, she found herself reaching a point of unusual tranquility. Perhaps she had come to a stage of acceptance. Or perhaps she had reset her emotional state to that of indifference. Either way, her ultimatum toward Thraik was taking root in her mind with each passing moment. *Wizera, forgive me, old friend…*

# CHAPTER XXX
# SHARDS OF FATE

Everything around Thaidren and his loyal servant was eerily silent and stationary. Even the massive citadel that consisted of the Forge of Souls emanated a haunting aura of dread that the young warrior could not shake off. After walking for about half an hour since their arrival, the two of them had reached its wide, open gates. The sheer size of them would allow a giant to fit in with ease. Each side of the dual gate was illuminated by two large cauldrons in which an uncanny blue flame resided. There was no firewood or anything else on their bottom, meaning they were self-sustained. Nez'rin placed his hand on Thaidren's shoulder and warned the young warrior to avoid touching the flames at all costs. There was no need for him to elaborate on the subject.

Once inside, the halls progressively grew smaller as they traversed the corridor. It gave Thaidren both a sensation that the halls were shrinking and that he and Nez'rin were shifting their size to match that of the building.

"If this place serves only to reforge Urostmarn, why was it built as such a grandiose fortress?"

"No one is to understand the reasoning behind the Creator's logic, my liege," answered the lich. "There are two aspects that I am certain of about this place: how to travel here and its main purpose. Should there be more, of that I have no further knowledge of."

"How did you end up here in the first place?" asked the young warrior.

"The second Dark Prince brought me here. He did not require his blade to be restored back then. He merely believed it would prove useful for me to know how to transport myself and others here."

Thaidren's mind was brimming with questions. "You said that you served my family since the reign of the second Dark Prince. What about the first one?"

Nez'rin stopped advancing for a few moments, seemingly frozen in place. After several moments of silence, he managed to find his words. "The first Dark Prince... is a taboo subject, my liege. His life story is one of the most frightening and bloody in the entire history of existence. I strongly advise you not to mention him lightly. If possible, it would be best to refrain from mentioning the subject ever again."

"Won't you even tell me about him? I mean, it may prove useful to know about my family's past."

The lich's hesitance was evident, even without a face to betray his emotions. "I honestly doubt there will be any use of that sort of history. But if you insist, perhaps I will share what I know of him after all of this is over. For now, let us focus on the task at hand."

"Yeah... the blade...," said Thaidren in a displeased tone.

"Are you still reluctant to claim it?" asked Nez'rin.

"I would've preferred to never have to... But I have to dismiss my personal conceptions about the weapon and embrace my destiny, right?" The lich did not perceive it, yet there was a subtle sarcastic tone in Thaidren's question.

"In time, you will understand that embracing your nature is for the best, master Thaidren."

The young warrior fell silent.

The once humongous halls throughout, which they had been seemingly walking for hours, had finally reached a size matching theirs. In the distance, the light of an exit could be spotted. Upon reaching the end of the corridor, Thaidren remained speechless at the sight of the grandiose anvil that stood before him. Spewing light-blue flames from various valves and decorated with chains, translucent crystals, and skulls of beings he did not recognize, its imposing structure was indeed a testament to his unavoidable destiny and the Creator's unrivaled craftsmanship.

"I've never seen anything like this before in my life," whispered the Dark Prince.

"It would've been peculiar if you did, my liege," the lich replied.

Thaidren surveyed the corridor. The anvil lay surrounded by a multitude of exits, and its chamber seemed roofless. Yet, what he saw above him could not be described as the sky either. It felt as if he were standing in the eye of a storm in which a currently deserted fortress had been erected when time itself was but a young concept. After the overwhelming sentiment of awe started to subside, the young warrior turned his attention back to the lich.

"What about the sword?" he asked. "Where is it?"

"After your father's death, I gathered the shards of Urostmarn and brought them here. At this very moment, they lie inside the forge, awaiting its new master to grant it form once again." He pointed toward the forge's mouth. "I will make the necessary preparations for when you are ready."

Thaidren closed in on the forge's mouth. The fires within were yet to be lit. Upon bringing his head closer, he saw the hateful object that had ended his father's life, lying in pieces and carefully placed for its restoration. Within the young warrior's mind, only two sentences swirled in an endless loop. *I don't want this... But I have to...* He turned his head toward the lich and asked him how he would restore the blade.

"Patience, master," responded Nez'rin. "First, I need to oversee several safety precautions."

Thaidren felt perplexed by his statement. "Safety precautions? Against what?"

"Against those who would aim to prevent you from achieving your goal. Urostmarn has claimed many souls over the course of time in existence. People whose loved ones or allies ended up inside the blade may want to interfere out of hatefulness for you or your soon-to-become weapon."

"But I thought no soul has access inside here."

"Once we ignite the forge, its cloaking and protective barriers alike will shut down until the process is complete," answered Nez'rin. He pointed with his skeletal finger at a pedestal on which an empty hilt resided. "That, my liege, is what you'll be using when reconstructing the blade back to its original form, as well as when hardening it. You will have to focus your energy on the hilt, thus molding it into a hammer that will take the shape of one that you have seen in the past or are familiar with."

As he uttered these words, Thaidren's concerns grew. *That is if I can control its shape,* the young warrior wondered.

"You will ignite the forge and partially melt the shards before fusing them back together, with the hammer serving as a binding agent that draws power from your energy reserve." He paused for a brief moment. "Be warned, however. The process will be an exhausting one. You will be required to pour a great amount of energy into the blade in order to restore it, leaving you vulnerable and weakened as you do so."

"And how am I supposed to defend myself at the same time?" asked the Dark Prince.

"You are not. I will concentrate my efforts on shielding you from the spirits' ill intentions. You focus yours on Urostmarn."

The entirety of the details still seemed somewhat incomplete and unclear to Thaidren. He took one last gaze around his surroundings, then at Nez'rin as he threw him an encouraging nod.

"I take it you are ready, master?" he asked.

Thaidren nodded and moved toward the empty hilt. *Let's get this over with.* He reached the handle with his right hand and channeled his power through it. To his surprise, a hammer similar to Viz'Hock had taken shape in his hands. Once he saw him, Nez'rin raised his hands and began to chant. From the forge's floor, two pillars emerged below the position of his palms, reaching out to them until the lich placed his hands above and used them as conduits to channel his energy.

"Proceed, my liege," he said in a louder tone as a giant dome-shaped barrier enveloped the entire room, swirling with torrents of the ominous energy of death. "Whatever you hear or witness during the heating process, pay it no mind. I shall protect you, no matter the cost."

Thaidren closed back in on the anvil. He took one last look at the shards of his unwanted fate as the gaping fires inside the forge's mouth slowly enveloped them. The hammer was long enough so that the Dark Prince would be in no danger of standing too close to the flames. He placed one foot in front of the other and rotated his whole body as he swung his first hit upon Urostmarn. It felt reminiscent of ringing a giant church bell that echoed across the citadel's halls, deactivating all its natural barriers and allowing the dead to interfere with the young warrior's endeavor. The initial impact made Thaidren lose balance for a brief moment. He blasted a surge of power from his body through the hammer and into the blade, shocking his body into believing he had depleted his magical energy. This was what Nez'rin referred to, and there was still a long way down until he would be done. After taking a short moment to recover, the young warrior strengthened his grip on the hilt and proceeded to hit with the hammer a second time. This time, along with the previous effect, he heard distant screams closing in on him from all directions.

"Focus, my liege," shouted Nez'rin as he continued to channel with his hands placed on the rods. A split second later, several spectral apparitions gathered inside the chamber, within the remaining space outside the barrier, gently touching it at first before striking it violently. Their number had soon increased from a couple, to tens, then hundreds that came from the open roof above. Within the citadel's halls and outside its walls, all wrathful spirits toward the Dark Prince's bloodline gathered in a swirling vortex that encircled the ancient structure. Each hit by the young warrior stirred anger within them, causing a ripple effect that propagated not only within the far reaches of the realm of the dead but in all the other planes of existence as well. Nez'rin had warned Thaidren of this moment in the past. The process of restoring the blade acted as a beacon that would signal every soul, no matter its current state, that a new Dark Prince was on the verge of claiming the first vestige toward its predetermined path to ascension. Angels, demons, all living and unliving creatures alike would be made aware of his reveal as the next heir to the throne of the Creator.

With each strike on Urostmarn's broken pieces, the spirits would become more and more agitated, desperately attempting to breach the barrier Nez'rin was struggling to maintain. He would not admit it to his master, but the sooner he was done with the reforging, the better. Whenever he would make contact with the shards of the blade, the Dark Prince's Hiath would flicker for a split second, granting him visions of his recurrent nightmare. The broken weapon was seemingly sharing its last memory of being intact, of its previous master, and the looming shadow of the enemy who played a part in its shattering. Of the death energy that it had released when claiming Thaidren's father. These images provoked a sentiment of profound rage inside Thaidren's heart, making the young warrior struggle through his exhaustion with more conviction as he continued to hit along the rough edges of the blade until he reached up close to its hilt. The handle bore a skull sculpture belonging to a creature unknown to him, with two more miniatures of it on the lateral ends. Despite having horns, it did not resemble those of the demons he saw in the past. Perhaps it was another type of demonic creature. Perhaps it belonged to some other species entirely. With Thaidren continuously pummeling the blade in order to fuse back its shattered fragments, the sensation of coldness he experienced when he and Nez entered this realm had subsided. As he stood by the blue-fire-spewing forge, with the hammer draining off his power and surrounded by a barrier that kept an endless army of vengeful spirits away from tearing him apart, his body ended up covered in sweat. All around him, the undistinguishable shrieks of the denizens of the afterlife added to his sentiment of powerlessness against them. It gave the young warrior the impression that even if he were to restore the blade, it would be impossible for him and Nez'rin to fight their way through so many foes. He forced away these concerns and pressed on.

The skeletal hands of the lich began to subtly shake. It was not a mere matter of maintaining the barrier anymore. Nez'rin was on the verge of reaching his limits, unable to tell how much time he could buy for his young master anymore. On Thaidren's side, he was not far behind reaching his own limits either, as he struggled to breathe and not fall over from exhaustion. At this point, he began to imagine glimpses of possible future scenarios. He could not tell whether they were a result of his visual prowess or not. He pictured Kina slowly torturing the life out of Wizera's body, playing with her mind, flesh, and soul. The thought disgusted and enraged him, yet he found himself unable to lift the hammer anymore. He dropped the hilt on the ground and gazed for a second at the unfinished blade, with its carved runes flickering uncontrollably as the spirits basked at their seemingly imminent victory. Their war cries became louder with each passing moment, with the lich's barrier of death energy becoming thinner and slowly decreasing.

# EPILOGUE
# WAVES

Within the bowels of the burning domains of Hell, in one of its infinite molten circles that belong to the Aspect of Pride, lies a black, towering fortress. Having its main spire reaching out to the floor's ceiling, it forevermore stands as a testament to the demon race's mighty architecture. Decorated with spikes and sculptures of bones and monstrous figures, with some of them melted down over time, the structure known as Vardun has had many masters since its building. As for the present, with the approval of Hishig, the aforementioned Aspect of Pride, is one of the oldest devils in history that currently occupies this horrendous citadel. A demonic being, having been naturally born with a pair of tattered, bat-like wings, the rarest of genetical traits among its kin, that complimented his light gray skin and dark purple glowing magical tattoos placed on his chest, back, and arms, all of them forming and adding to his intimidating appearance. Presenting a pair of long twisted horns and an almost white-nuanced long hair, he is known throughout the demon realm's rankings as Ro'Noveran'Vo, or Ro'Nove by the other beings in the cosmos. A vicious intellectual hybrid that has earned his status due to his innumerable schemes plotted in service of his master. As a reward for such eons of servitude, he has received many favors and benefits, such as a small personal army under his command that occasionally helps him run his daily activities. His most trusted advisor, Hissver, one of the very few pure-blooded demons that roams the halls of Vardun, has served Ro'Nove since the days when time itself was a young concept and the raging civil war between the rulers of Hell was more a freshly lit up flame. His constitution resembled that of a large imp, except for an extra pair of horns, a more carnivorous-looking mouth complemented with a set of teeth that resembled those of a shark, and an intellectual stare within his eyes. He lies inside one of the apothecary chambers, studying the effects of various substances when an invisible wave of power sent a freezing chill down his spine, inducing an uncontrollable tremor throughout his body. It made the fiend drop an alchemical tube from his hand as he stood paralyzed for a moment.

A second reverberation made Hissver snap out of his trance, giving him the confirmation that an ominous existential event was taking place. And a familiar one, for that matter. He ceased his current activities and rushed outside the chamber, slamming the metallic door behind him before charging through the halls of the fortress. The demon's thoughts were chaotic, yet not illogical, with several of them echoing throughout his mind. *It's happening. The blade is being reforged. The master will surely have a plan of action prepared for this. The matter must be addressed at once.*

While passing through the corridors of Vardun, the advisor observed the reactions of the demons encountered on his way. All of them exuded a similar aura of unease in regard to the unsettling phenomenon. Some of the younger denizens of Hell even seemed confused as to what was happening. The tides of energy that captured their attention were irregular, with some of them occurring within seconds of each other, while others waited minutes before echoing throughout the fabric of the burning realm.

After traversing a hefty amount of the demonic fortress, Hissver's steps slowed down upon approaching a larger, double-sided metallic door. The inscribing of glowing runes and magical symbols painted on it pointed to it being shut not only by physical means but also by magical energies. An unwanted visitor could interpret that as either being the door of the fortress's commander's personal chamber, or a cage meant to hold back a potential threat even for the denizens of Hell. However, the latter was incorrect, with the demonic advisor waving his hands as his eyes began to glow while one of the symbols began to dim until fading away completely. The gargantuan gate opened, squeaking in a deranging manner as Hissver entered the chamber with caution. In front of him lay the devil master of the stronghold, having his back turned at the entrance and with his wings covering his silhouette from that angle.

"Lord Ro'Noveran, lord Ro'Noveran," said his faithful servant, breathing hard. "Forgive my intrusion, lord, but something urgent has — "

Ro'Nove partially turned his head toward him, spotting Hissver with the back of his eye. His slow, seemingly irritated gesture made the advisor refrain from continuing. Ro'Nove grunted as he made a complete turn and began to walk toward him. "And you think I didn't notice, Hissver? I am not in the mood for childish mockery."

"Pardon me, my lord," answered the advisor as he bowed before his master. "I did not mean for my words to be interpreted like that."

"Then state your business here! I am in the middle of making vital preparations."

Hissver's tone turned fearful. "W... With all due respect, lord Ro'Noveran, isn't this a matter that needs urgent addressing?"

"You misinterpret my words, advisor. When I said I'm in the middle of important preparations, I meant in regards to the matter at hand." He paused for a moment, throwing his gaze across his worktable, which was filled with tattered scrolls, crystals of numerous applications, and ancient artifacts, contraptions, and ominous tools fathomed in the demon realm. "So... the blade has a new master. The child of my old enemy has decided to finally reveal himself." A paradoxical mix of anger and mirth fizzed within him. His fist clenched so strong that his sharp claws pierced the inside of his palm. Ro'Nove took a moment and raised the hand to his sight, licking the blood from his open wound afterward. "A decision he will soon come to regret. Gather a squadron of azions and tell them to await my orders." The demon advisor bowed his head and walked back toward the double gate.

"As you command, my lord."

Ro'Nove opened up a small portal and stretched his arm toward it. He placed his hand inside it and dragged a giant fuming scythe from within as the weapon slowly ignited in a black-nuanced flame that swept all across the edge of the blade. "It's been too long since my last hunt."

# ACKNOWLEDGMENTS

"You should write it down." Five life-changing words from a life-changing soulmate. To my wife and "partner in crime" on this journey, Elena Sabina, thank you from the bottom of my heart. For all the times when you listened to my constant ramblings about this fantastical world I was so proud and happy to talk about. For being my first and most devoted fan. And for everything else that helped me gain the confidence to never stop marching forward with this endeavor. This may have all started in my head, but the credit for the story reaching the outside world is all thanks to you.

To my mother, Anca Silvia. Thank you for always letting me try new things and supporting me in pursuing each of them. It took a while to figure out what I really wanted to do, from learning to play the guitar to artistic drawing, and regardless of the outcome, you were there, encouraging me to keep going on as long as it made me happy. Thank you. I may not have ended up a renowned doctor, as you did, but I hope I can make you proud in my own way.

This one goes to my grandfather, Horia "Tai." Since I was little, you tried to make me enjoy reading by offering me access to a vast personal library, often offering to read them to me yourself. I'm sorry the child back then wasn't so responsive to it, but I've grown since then, and, despite having some catching up to do, it's all worth it thanks to the first incentive that you gave me many years ago.

To my brother-in-law, Mihai. Thank you for always answering the phone, or numerous messages I've sent you. Always eager to help me with an educated opinion and a hefty baggage of cultural insight, for which I sometimes still envy you. Without your help, this work of fiction wouldn't have ended up as good.

Bogdan, I've always known and appreciated you for never being the kind of person to sugarcoat things. Many a time brutally honest, yet trustworthy and reliable because of it. Having your support in writing this story down was a huge confidence boost that helped me believe that maybe, just maybe, the product of my imagination will prove worth sharing with the world. I hope I can make you proud with it, big bro.

Victor Alexandru, your passion for fantasy settings in general, combined with a vast insight into so many aspects related to them, have always been a well of knowledge, for which I am ever-grateful you've shared with me. Most of all, you've constantly challenged me with questions that stimulated my imagination and made me think above and beyond, in order to further develop my world. Thank you.

To Andreea and Radu, the godparents of my wife and me, I wish the best there is to be on your journey together in life, along with my deep appreciation for going through the unpolished draft of my first attempt at writing this story down, and, despite the state it was back then, still sincerely encouraging me to continue to keep doing it and pursue the dream of one day earning the honor of being called an "Author." Words aren't enough to reflect what major role you've played in making this possible.

Andrei "Petrica," there are too many things I wish to thank you for. From the endless support and help you've given me, to introducing me to the artist responsible for the book cover, (Adriana Dănilă, to whom I also owe, at the very least, a bucketful of gratitude), and all the way to that memorable talk about how you believe I have a sort of drive, as you've named it, that keeps me pushing forward and doesn't let me give up. I'll have to take your word for it on that one. You've always had my back, and I hope this story can make you proud, lil' bro. Thank you.

A special thank you to Bob Boze and Robyn Bennett, the editors who acted as both polishers for the story and invaluable teachers for me in the writing business. The numerous emails we've exchanged and all your insightful and professional notes on the manuscript helped me improve at a faster rate than I could've done on my own. Not to mention the quality of the said lessons. I will try my best to apply everything learned in the following volumes, and I hope to count on your help in the future as well.

Last but not least, to whoever is it you are, the person who went through the pages of this book, I want to say a sincere "Thank you." If by any means, this story proved to be to your liking, helped you make a flight or train trip pass with more ease, or even if you, at least, don't regret the decision of buying the book of this daydreaming unknown author, then the story has fulfilled its purpose, and I'm glad I could share this with you.

# ABOUT THE AUTHOR

This is Edward Loom's first, of many more to come, book. He was born in Romania, in the capital city of Bucharest, where he was raised and lives up to the present day. After numerous attempts to figure out what he enjoys and wants to do in his life, he found the answer in the form of writing down the world he imagined for more than a decade. In its twisted way, this dark fantasy setting served him as a means to escape the boundaries of our own world.

His wife, whom he met on the 24th of June 2017, listened to him talk about this story many a time, yet when she heard that his initial intention was to keep this universe hidden away from the world, she uttered five simple words that, somehow, changed everything.

At the moment of writing this, and after almost three years since Edward first started writing down his story, the book is finally done and ready to do what the author alone couldn't have imagined possible: to be sent out into the world.

*** 

In the event you end up liking the machinations of my mind, it may also please you to hear that the story, as a whole, is far from over. Thaidren's journey has just begun, and there will be numerous other volumes that will follow this one. I gladly invite anyone to read it until the end, when one day, I'll finally finish putting down the last world, of the last line, of the last paragraph, of the last volume. It's going to be a long, but hopefully, enjoyable for everyone ride.

Finally, if you feel like it, please leave a review of this book on Amazon.com and Goodreads when you have a moment. Regardless of whether it'll be good or bad, I will try to read them all. Most importantly, I'll try my best to make good use of them in order to improve my writing.

# HISTRIA
## BOOKS

Addison & Highsmith

**Other fine works of fiction available from Addison & Highsmith Publishers:**

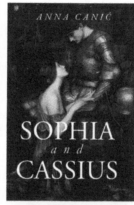

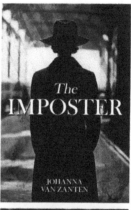

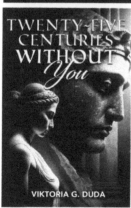

**For these and many other great books visit**

# HistriaBooks.com